Imbert de Saint-Amand

Napoleon III and his Court

Imbert de Saint-Amand

Napoleon III and his Court

ISBN/EAN: 9783337350161

Printed in Europe, USA, Canada, Australia, Japan

Cover: Foto ©Raphael Reischuk / pixelio.de

More available books at **www.hansebooks.com**

NAPOLEON III.

NAPOLEON III

AND HIS COURT

BY

IMBERT DE SAINT-AMAND

TRANSLATED BY

ELIZABETH GILBERT MARTIN

WITH PORTRAITS

NEW YORK
CHARLES SCRIBNER'S SONS
1898

Norwood Press
J. S. Cushing & Co. — Berwick & Smith
Norwood Mass. U.S.A.

CONTENTS

PORTRAITS

NAPOLEON III. AND HIS COURT

CHAPTER I

THE EMPEROR IN 1853

LA ROCHEFOUCAULD, author of the *Maxims*, says that it "requires greater virtues to endure good than evil fortune." In our previous volume we have described the exiles, misfortunes, illusions, and chagrins of Louis Napoleon. In this one we shall describe his joys and successes.

At the time of his marriage the second Emperor was happy. Everything smiled on him. He seemed to have made a pact with fortune. His only remaining regret was that his mother, Queen Hortense, who even in blaming his absurd Strasbourg expedition had never failed to console and encourage while every one else disowned and insulted him, was no longer there to behold his triumph.

In private, Napoleon III. had not the melancholy aspect attributed to him by Flandrin in a celebrated portrait. He loved life and was fond of power. Everything interested, nothing surfeited him. As much in love at forty-four as a young man of

1

twenty, he had a real passion for his wife. Looking at her, he would have been ready to repeat with
La Bruyère: "A beautiful face is the most beautiful
sight of all, and the sweetest harmony is the voice
of the woman we love."

The second Emperor, who had always been ambitious, found his new situation all the more enjoy-
able because he owed it to no one but himself and
had been its sole prophet at a time when all others
regarded his projects as the idle dreams of a vision-
ary. The flouted conscript, become a sovereign,
had a prestige at the beginning of his reign which
is not taken into account now that his figure is
more than overclouded by the final catastrophes.
The Napoleon of 1853 bears no resemblance to the
Napoleon of 1870.

One of the greatest geniuses of modern times,
M. de Lamartine, has thus expressed himself concerning the second Emperor (*Mémoires*, t. IV., livre
xxii., p. 56): "After a first conversation followed
by many others in grave circumstances, I recognized, in spite of my prejudices against his name,
the strongest and most serious statesman whom I
had met in all my long life. I said as much to all
of my colleagues, who, knowing my relations with
him, asked my opinion. 'My opinion,' I replied,
'is that Providence, who is wiser than we, has kept
a man in store for us who is superior to his rôle.
Don't imagine that you can trifle with a man like
that. By chance or inspiration the crowd has laid

its hand upon a great name for history.' Some of them believed me. I did not overrate him. His silence except when speech was necessary left ordinary men in doubt. For my own part, I did not long hesitate to rank him as much superior to his uncle, who was the foremost soldier but one of the most insignificant statesmen of his time."

If Napoleon III. was appreciated in this way by the founder of the second Republic, it is easy to divine what flatteries were heaped upon him by his courtiers and attendants. It was surely praiseworthy in him not to become intoxicated by their incense, but to maintain in prosperity the absolute calm from which he had never departed in adversity. He did not abuse his victory, and tried to speak and act, not as the chief of the imperialists, but of all Frenchmen. Napoleon I. had said: "To govern with a party is to become dependent on it soon or late. Nobody will catch me in that snare. I am national. I will make use of all who have the ability and inclination to follow me." Napoleon III. said: "I wish to inaugurate an era of peace and conciliation, and I summon all without distinction who will act with me for the public welfare." He would have preferred to gain the republicans, for his personal tendencies were progressive rather than conservative, his seat was on the left benches rather than the right.

The founder of an absolute empire, in 1853 he gave men room to hope for a liberal one. In the

speech he delivered from the throne on February 14
occurs this curious passage: "To those who may
regret that greater liberty has not been accorded, I
will reply that liberty has never helped to found a
durable political edifice; it crowns it after it has
been consolidated by time." He closed his discourse as follows: "Let us thank Providence for
the visible protection it has granted to our efforts.
We shall persevere in this path of firmness and
moderation, which reassures without irritating,
which leads to prosperity without violence, and
thus prevents reaction." Napoleon III. was not a
party man. He sincerely desired prosperity, progress, and peace. The confiscation of a portion of
the property of the Orleans family was probably his
sole derogation from that policy of pacification
which became the foundation of his system after the
violent measures of the Coup d'Etat and the unjust
deportations which followed it.

Studying the second Emperor at the beginning
of his reign, we shall propound the following
questions: Was Napoleon III. good? Was he generous? Did he love the people? Was he industrious? Was he religious? Was he inclined to
peace?

Was Napoleon III. kind and good? Even his
adversaries have recognized his kindness. It was
his leading characteristic, that which dominated
all the others. M. Emile Zola sums up as follows
the portrait he has drawn of him: "At bottom a

kind man haunted by generous dreams, incapable
of a bad action, most sincere in the unshakable
conviction which carried him through the events of
his life, and which was that of a man predestined
to a part." M. Emile Ollivier lays stress in these
words on the influence exerted over himself by the
affectionate nature of the sovereign: "He was capable of friendship. No one has ever heard him
speak well of himself and ill of others. . . . His
eye, dull or severe to indifferent persons, to his
friends was keen, charming, lighted up by an affectionate gleam which captivated. . . . Kindness
was the chief trait of his moral character, a constant, untiring, inexhaustible kindness which made
no difference between great and small, between
friends and enemies, an affecting kindness which,
alas! was perhaps irreconcilable with the inflexi-
bility essential to the leaders of men. Spiritually
he was akin to Marcus Aurelius and Saint Vincent
de Paul. Walking out once in his youth, a beggar
extended his hand for alms; having no money, he
gave him his gloves, his handkerchief, and his
watch-chain." His affability was perfect and his
equanimity unalterable. As polite to the least of
his servants as to a great lord or a sovereign, he
wished to see all around him happy. Those who
lived with him throughout his entire reign cannot
remember to have seen him exhibit a sign of anger
or impatience.

M. Ernest Pinard says: "The Emperor was

grateful. He never forgot a service rendered; he
sought to repay it a hundred-fold. It surprised him
that the Bourbons should have done so little for
Brittany, the heroic Vendée, and the descendants
of the victims of Quiberon. He was an absolutely
faithful friend by nature far more than by calculation. Hence he overwhelmed with favors those
who had surrounded him in his days of peril and
misfortune." He abundantly rewarded his accom-
plices of Strasbourg and Boulogne, but he also
rewarded those who had done their duty by aiding
to arrest him. As M. Fernand Giraudeau has
reminded us in his remarkable work, *Napoléon III
intime:* "To M. Chopin d'Arnouville, prefect of the
Lower Rhine at the time of the Strasbourg affair,
he intrusted several missions, and made his son an
advocate-general at Paris. The son of the sub-
prefect whose energy brought his second attempt
to such a speedy close, became in 1852 one of his
strongest prefects. He made the mayor of Boulogne, who had actively assisted in his arrest, an
officer, and the gendarme who first laid a hand upon
him a chevalier of the Legion of Honor." To sum
up, the Emperor was humane, compassionate, for-
getful of injuries received. He had meditated on
that beautiful saying of Bossuet: "When God
formed the heart and the entrails of man, He placed
goodness there as the peculiar character of the
divine nature, and to be as it were the sign manual
of that beneficent hand from which we come forth.

Goodness, then, should be the very foundation of our heart, and at the same time the chief attraction we possess for gaining the good will of other men."

Was Napoleon III. generous? One may say that he was so even to prodigality. The day of the Coup d'Etat he distributed fifty thousand francs, all that was left of his private fortune, among the troops. The idea of hoarding up never occurred to him when he became Emperor. He gave to friends and enemies, to those who were indifferent to him, to everybody. He considered himself as the usufructuary of the imperial palaces and bound to make France the chief gainer by them. He dwelt in them like a traveller who, installed in a furnished house for an indefinite time, spends as much money there as possible. For him the only charm that money possessed was that of giving it away. He took especial pleasure in putting his opponents under pecuniary obligations, and as he did not count on the gratitude of those whom he benefited, he sought no other reward for almsgiving than the gift itself. Every month he spent his civil list to the last sou, and it was twenty-five millions a year. He had asked that it should be but twelve. But without his knowledge, and through a stratagem of M. de Persigny, who induced the Senate to believe, untruly, that the sovereign desired a civil list of twenty-five millions, a decree of that body fixed it at that sum. The only use the Emperor made of it was to favor trade, encourage literature, science, and the arts, and to succor the unfortunate.

Did Napoleon III. love the common people? "Above all," writes M. de La Gorce, in his masterly *Histoire du Second Empire*, "he loved the people, not especially his own (for he was more humanitarian than patriotic), but all peoples, that is to say, the poor, the feeble, those without place or position." The great aim of his home policy was to increase as much as possible the moral and material well-being of the majority. He made inquiries on all sides in order to find out what could be done in favor of the unfortunate classes. Any one who came to propose a social reform which seemed practicable was received, listened to, and encouraged. The publication of the accounts of his civil list shows that it was literally that of the poor. At the end of every quarter, he secured at his own cost, by the intermediation of the prefect of police, a shelter for small tenants who had been evicted, or prevented their eviction by paying the arrears of their rent. We read in M. Ernest Pinard's *Journal:* "The Emperor often summoned to the council, or after the council, the prefect of the Seine and the prefect of police, in order that, in company with his ministers, they might study a series of measures in favor of the classes in straitened circumstances. There was question of taking goods out of pawn at certain dates, of diminishing the tolls on articles of prime necessity, of lowering the tax on personal property for small tenants."

Finally, let us cite these lines from M. A. Granier de Cassagnac: —

"The first and chief preoccupation of Napoleon III. was the question of poverty. He did not hope to abolish, but he persistently longed to ameliorate it. 'Every man whom I make comfortable,' he said to me, 'is a recruit whom I abduct from the theories of socialism.' But he saw only three fertile sources whence comfort could proceed: labor, family life, and desires ruled and limited by religion. . . . He wanted at any cost to give an impulse to agricultural labor. . . . With equal passion he desired to better the condition of the working population of cities. . . . All Europe knows now that the Emperor died poor; but the cause of his poverty is not sufficiently well known. Now the cause is this: The Emperor had despoiled himself through generosity. In the seventeen and a half years of his reign he had given away ninety millions."

To sum up, Napoleon loved the people and was always very indulgent toward their errors. Twice in 1849 he asked amnesty from the ministerial council for the insurgents of June, 1848, who had been transported *en bloc* and without trial, in accordance with a law passed by the National Assembly. His then ministers twice refused this amnesty, which was nevertheless so just. As to love for the people, many republicans, alas! might

havc taken lessons from the second Emperor. He
was the friend of the working classes, of the
peasants, and of the poor. His greatest honor in
history will be to have devoted himself to the cause
of the proletariat.

Was Napoleon III. industrious? Excepting meal-
times and a short excursion on horseback or in a
carriage, he worked all day and frequently all the
evening. He read all letters and petitions addressed
to him. He never failed to preside at the ministerial council, which met either at the Tuileries or
Saint-Cloud on Tuesday and Saturday of every week
at nine o'clock in the morning. Following all
affairs, whether home or foreign, with the utmost
attention, he read a great many journals and a daily
analysis of the diplomatic despatches sent to the
Minister of Foreign Affairs. His messages and
speeches from the throne were written with a rare
elegance of thought and diction, and he always
revised them himself. He was in personal relations
with many journalists, whom he inspired and in
reality collaborated with. Whatever may have been
said to the contrary, pleasure took only a secondary
place in his life. At the Tuileries and Saint-Cloud
he worked as diligently as he had done at what he
called the university of Ham, the prison where he
finished his political education. A writer of distinction, he was deeply interested in literature,
especially in historical works. Versed in the sciences, he followed their progress and discoveries

with the utmost attention. During his reign authors received 2,200,000 francs, and scientists and inventors 2,500,000 francs from him. Few men have possessed such varied attainments or set in motion so considerable a mass of ideas. In fine, the Emperor was very laborious, very active, and not many sovereigns have fulfilled their tasks with so much zeal and conscientiousness.

Was Napoleon III. religious? M. Ernest Pinard writes in his interesting journal: "I have often heard it asked whether he were a religious man or a fatalist, and I think I may reply that he was both. Such is the opinion of those who knew him best. The two verdicts are not contradictory, and this dual tendency has existed in many superior men." In 1852 a leader of the Catholic party addressed a report to him on liberty of instruction, to which he replied: "My mother brought me up a Catholic, and I shall remain loyal to my faith."

The imperial government, even while favoring the clergy and the monastic orders, was never accused of clericalism. The popular origin of the dynasty saved it from such recriminations as were aimed at the theoretical alliance between the throne and the altar during the reign of Charles X. The candidate elected by plébiscites could do what a monarch by divine right would have found very difficult. As M. Fernand Giraudeau has judiciously remarked: "Had one of the princes said, 'Religion is the basis of every government which

comprehends its mission'; had he affirmed 'the
great principles of Christianity, which teach us
virtue in order to insure a good life, and immor-
tality that we may die well'; had he restored the
Panthéon to Catholic worship, introduced cardinals
into the Senate, facilitated the development of
religious congregations, restored the almoners of the
army and navy and created almoners of the last
prayers, caused Mass to be said in camps, recommended abstention from work on Sundays by a
ministerial circular, had Lent preached at the
Tuileries by foreign monks like Ventura and
Jesuits like de Ravignan; had permitted prelates to
communicate freely with the Holy See and between
themselves, to restore the long-suppressed provincial
councils, to forbid teaching the doctrine of 1682 and
to adopt the Roman liturgy; had he never visited a
city without paying his first visit to its cathedral
and addressing his first word to God, — would not
the censorious public speedily have denounced his
'clerical tendencies,' and sought to produce a reaction? Coming from a Bonaparte, such words and
acts provoked neither grimaces nor raillery; on the
contrary, they obtained general approbation."

Later on, the Roman question somewhat disturbed
the concord between the Emperor and the clergy.
But in 1853 there was complete mutual understanding. At that period Monseigneur Salinis, Bishop
of Amiens, declared that the Emperor had given the
Church "the greatest freedom it had enjoyed since

Saint Louis." When laying the first stone of the
cathedral of Marseilles, the chief of the State said:
"My government is the only one that has supported
religion for its own sake. It supports it not as a
political instrument and to please a party, but solely
through conviction, through love for the good that
it inspires and the truths which it teaches." Let us
add that in 1853 the Emperor, far from giving scandal in the fashion of Louis XIV. and Louis XV.,
led an irreproachable private life and was the most
affectionate and faithful of husbands.

Was Napoleon III. inclined to peace? Alas! not
enough so. But in 1853, the happiest and most
prosperous year of his reign, he seemed to be sincerely so. On opening the session, February 14,
the Emperor said in the speech from the throne:
"The government means before all things to ad-
minister France wisely and to reassure Europe. . . .
When France expresses the formal intention of
remaining at peace, she must be believed, for she
is strong enough to fear nothing, and consequently
to deceive nobody." As a pledge of his intentions,
he simultaneously announced a new reduction of
twenty thousand men from the effective force of
the army, which had already been reduced by thirty
thousand men in 1852.

And yet, by 1853, perspicacious observers might
have foreseen that the sovereign would not always
remain pacific. On September 20, after a review
at Satory, he addressed this significant language to

the troops: "In difficult times what has upheld
empires if not these assemblages of armed men
drawn from the people, fashioned by discipline,
animated by the sentiment of duty, and, in the midst
of peace, when egotism and self-interest usually end
by enervating all, retaining that devotion to the
fatherland which is founded on self-abnegation, and
that love of glory which is based on contempt for
riches?"   To regain its natural frontiers for France,
to give nations the right to dispose of their own
destinies, to divide the powers that had united
against Napoleon I., — such were the dreams that
already haunted the mind of the second Emperor,
but which he still had sufficient prudence to conceal.   Accustomed under the reign of Louis Philippe to hear the opposition declaim against what
it called "peace at any price," and rise in revolt
against the Holy Alliance, which, after all, had
harmed France less since the close of the first
Empire than has been pretended, he was, alas!
fated to aggravate the treaties of 1815 by dint of
seeking to destroy them.   Let us add that the present condition of minds in France bears no resemblance to what it was at the beginning of the second
Empire.   At present, bitter experience has taught
us the cost of a disastrous war.   In 1853, France,
cradled in the imperial legend, thought herself
invincible.   The officers, eager for advancement,
dreamed of nothing but dangers and glory.   Napoleon III. was about to allow himself to be carried

away by a military current which he should have
had the sagacity and strength to stem. We persist
in believing that the Bordeaux speech would have
been the best and most fertile of programmes, and
not for France alone but for all Europe. The first
Emperor had been the Napoleon of war. The second
should have been the Napoleon of peace.

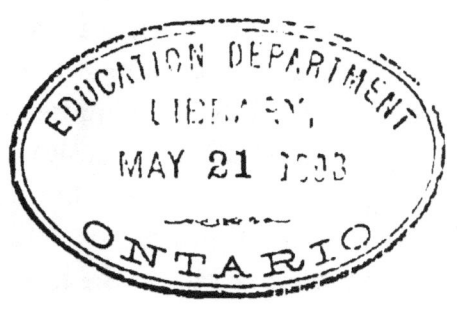

CHAPTER II

THE EMPRESS

OUR work entitled, *Louis Napoleon and Mademoiselle de Montijo*, terminates on January 30, 1853, at the moment when the Emperor and Empress, returning from Notre-Dame, re-enter the palace of the Tuileries. Napoleon III., appearing by turns on the two grand balconies of the hall of the Marshals, one of which gave on the court and the other on the garden, presented to the people and the army the new sovereign, whose greeting, full of elegance and affability, of majesty and supreme grace, drew from the crowd a long murmur of admiration. A few minutes later the married pair set off for the château of Saint-Cloud, where they had chosen to spend their honeymoon, in a coupé drawn by four horses, preceded by two outriders and followed by a travelling-carriage for the service and two baggage wagons. The hats of the postilions were adorned with ribbons.

The Empress was happy. Yet the radiant sky of her happiness was flecked by some faint clouds of sadness and melancholy. Just as she was finishing her toilette before going to the ceremony at Notre-

16

Dame, an old Spanish servant had said to her : " I entreat you, madame, do not wear that necklace of pearls ; I am afraid of it. Remember what they say in our country: ' The more pearls one wears on the day of her marriage, the more tears she sheds the rest of her life.' " Nevertheless the Empress had worn the necklace. But the remark of the servant had left a painful impression, and, thinking of the sufferings endured by the Women of the Tuileries, she reflected that perhaps her eyes would soon be reddened and scorched by tears like theirs.

On February 1, a fine winter day, the Emperor, driving his own phaeton, took the Empress from Saint-Cloud to the palace of Versailles. She was very simply dressed and had neither an escort nor a lady to accompany her. M. Eudore Soulié, the regretted curator of the museum of Versailles (father-in-law of M. Victorien Sardou), has told us that on alighting from her carriage the Empress asked him to show her all the portraits of Marie Antoinette. She meditated long before those five portraits, two of which were painted by the Swedish artist Roslin, and two by Madame Vigée-Lebrun. The Empress, who had always had a cult for the memory of the martyr-queen, also wished to make a sort of pilgrimage to the Little Trianon.

Some days later, — the 10th of February, — she went with the Emperor to visit the museum of sovereigns at the Louvre, the creation of which had been determined on by Napoleon III., and which was

soon to be thrown open to the public. This interesting museum, whose dispersion has been a misfortune
from the point of view of respect for history, occupied five large halls adjoining the Louvre colon-
nade. The most precious relics of both the royal
and imperial monarchies had been collected there.
The Emperor had said to Comte de Nieuwerkerke,
superintendent of the Beaux-Arts : " Remember that
I wish to bring together in the museum of sovereigns
all that can revive the memory of the kings or
emperors of France, all that bears the impress of
their individuality. Cover the walls of the hall of
the Valois or the Bourbons with lilies, just as you
will sprinkle with bees the great purple mantle of
the hall of the Emperor." The aspect of this last
hall, filled with souvenirs of the victor of Austerlitz,
and dimly lighted, produced a striking impression.
One might say with the *Moniteur*, that Napoleon
had thenceforward two great funeral monuments on
the banks of the Seine, one at the Invalides, where
his body lay, the other at the Louvre, where his
spirit hovered.

What affected the Empress Eugénie most at the
museum of sovereigns was the collection of souvenirs of Marie Antoinette. A spectator of this visit,
Comte Horace de Viel-Castel, shall describe it:

" The Empress," he says, " wished to have the
beautiful testamentary letter of Marie Antoinette to
Madame Elisabeth read to her ; the Emperor seemed
profoundly thoughtful and affected. The souvenirs

of Louis XVI. and Marie Antoinette always moved him deeply. There was something sad and striking in being present at this reading, made before a young and beautiful empress at the beginning of her reign and still in the first bewilderments of an un-hoped-for happiness. There was in it a lesson from misfortune, a sob from bygone times. . . . The Empress listened in silence and with tearful eyes to those last words of a mother ready to ascend the scaffold, of a mother who at that terrible moment could not even embrace the children whom she left in the hands of her executioners."

February 14, at the Tuileries, in the hall of the Marshals, the Empress was present at the opening of the legislative session. She sat in a tribune facing the Emperor's throne, with the Princesse Mathilde on her right and the Comtesse de Montijo on her left. At the close of the ceremony, the great bodies of the State saluted her in the name of France, and her face showed keen emotion. "People admired her," M. A. Granier de Cas-sagnac has said, "because they saw that she was beautiful; they honored her because they knew that she was good; and if the six hundred thou-sand francs' worth of diamonds offered by the city of Paris, and reserved by her wish for the bringing up of poor girls, did not glitter on her person, the splendor of the absent necklace was far surpassed by the halo of affectionate respect which rose from the hearts of grateful mothers.

. . . She had entered Notre-Dame chosen by the
Emperor; she left it adopted by France."

March 12, the Empress went with the Emperor
to visit the educational institute of the Legion of
Honor at Saint-Denis. According to custom, a
velvet dais had been prepared to receive Their
Majesties. They would not accept it, but went
directly to the chapel occupied by the pupils. The
Emperor thanked the chaplain who had just invoked the blessing of Heaven upon him. "I am
happier," said he, "than on my previous visit, since
I am this time accompanied by the Empress, who
is henceforward the protectress of this house and
who knows so well how to acquit herself of the
task." On leaving the chapel, they went to the
refectory and the playground. The sick pupils in
the infirmary could not be forgotten. The Emperor and Empress went to them with encouraging
and kindly words. Then, after visiting the basilica
of Saint-Denis, they walked to the further end of
the town.

Less than two months after the marriage of her
daughter, Madame de Montijo went back to Spain.
M. Prosper Merimée escorted her as far as Poitiers.
On returning to Paris, he wrote a letter, not to
compliment but to console her. "It is a terrible
thing," said he, "to have daughters and to marry
them off. But what would you have? The Script-
ures say that the woman must quit her parents to
follow her husband. Now that your duties as a

mother are accomplished (and, in truth, nobody can deny that you have married your daughters very well), you must think of living for yourself."

In the fine work which he has devoted to the author of the *Chronique du règne de Charles IX*, M. Auguste Filon writes : " While Mérimée assisted at the beginnings of the young Empress, it was like a fairy scene in a theatre whose splendors are about to be renewed. . . . More than once, during the early months of 1853, he must have wondered if he were dreaming, or if he were still playing comedy at Carabanchel. This little girl, whom he had taken about, scolded, amused, whose slim fingers, nervous and timid, had clung fast to his in passing through Parisian crowds, people now addressed — and he like the others — as 'Your Majesty.' On that brow, where he had watched the birth of the first languors and the first reveries, sparkled the famous jewels which told the story of four centuries of monarchy and empire, — the history of France in diamonds. He had aided in teaching her the language of this people over whom she was going to reign ; the words which he had been the first to implant in her memory she was about to lavish as so many favors, and they would overwhelm their recipients."

Mérimée was made a senator June 23, 1853, and the Empress embraced her husband heartily when he told the good news. To these details M. Auguste Filon adds : " What charmed Mérimée, now

that he saw things at short range, — what he was
truly delighted to repeat to Madame de Montijo,
— was the way in which the Empress played her
part, or, as he expressed it, worked at her trade.
She was not merely the central figure in an admirable living picture, but a veritable sovereign.
She knew how to speak and how to keep silence,
she saw clearly and correctly, because she sought
what was good and studied the duties of her state
in order to devote herself to them. He was struck
with her good sense when it was proposed, with
a view to please her, to introduce bull fights in
France. She comprehended that a bull fight in
Paris would be a scandal or a fiasco, perhaps both,
and the project fell through."

It may be said in all sincerity that the Empress,
at the beginning of the Empire, had gained all
suffrages. What was particularly pleasing in her
was, as has been said by the Comtesse Stéphanie
de Tascher, "a kind of timidity and doubt of herself combined with triumphant beauty and her
new and lofty situation." At this time, she and
the Emperor set the example of a most united
and affectionate family. Napoleon III. said: "No
woman could suit me better; she is devoted, cheerful, good, intelligent." In every circumstance he
displayed a thoughtful affection for this beloved
companion with whom he was sincerely in love;
he always thee'd and thou'd her and called her by
her pet name; when he looked at or spoke to her,
he seemed a lover rather than a husband.

The Empress Eugénie had neither male nor female favorites; nor was she surrounded by any of those coteries for which Marie Antoinette was so cruelly blamed. In 1853, the women of the court of Versailles, whatever any one may say, behaved excellently, and it was the Empress Eugénie who set them the good example.

At this period, no one would have dreamed of reproaching the Empress on account of the splendor of her jewels or the richness of her toilettes. On the contrary, people would have taken it ill if she had not been the most elegant woman in the Empire. They thought well of her for encouraging the industries of luxury and promoting Parisian trade. France, which loves pomp, desired that no court in the world should surpass that of Napoleon III. in magnificence. It was the Empress who had the most beautiful toilettes in Europe. It was the Emperor who had the handsomest horses and the finest carriages. Republican simplicity was abandoned. People delighted in uniforms, court dresses, ornaments, trained gowns, full-dress performances, grand balls. "The distinctive trait of the Empress Eugénie," writes M. A. Granier de Cassagnac, "was elegance in all things, — in mind, in tastes, in her manner of receiving, in her person. It was through this quality, which seems essentially French, and of which Paris is the supreme judge, that, during seventeen years, she exerted an unexampled prestige around her, — not simply in the sphere of the throne, but in all the social circles which she entered on her journeys. She was beautiful and gracious everywhere and to all, — among patricians and among peasants, at Paris as at Biarritz. . . . Although many women especially favored by nature and by fortune have attracted admiration and received homage at the court, never has any one heard it said that a single one of them had equalled, much less effaced, the brilliancy of the Empress."

People were grateful to the new sovereign for reviving the most brilliant traditions of the ancient monarchy. She was sympathetic even to the adversaries of the Napoleonic dynasty. Before her marriage she had frequented legitimist and Orleanist salons, where she had left behind her the pleasantest memories. None of those who saw her in 1853, either at the Bois de Boulogne in a carriage *à la daumont*, preceded by an outrider and escorted by a mounted equerry, or at the palace of the Tuileries, where at grand balls she wore the crown diamonds with so much majesty, can ever forget her dazzling image. People were happy to be able to salute her on the promenade, or to watch her at the theatre, where her entry into the imperial box was always greeted by applause.

In 1853 the Empress Eugénie did not occupy herself with politics. She had no need to exert a special influence, because there existed an absolute conformity between her sentiments and those of the Emperor. The policy of Napoleon III. was at that time essentially conservative and religious. Foreboding that he might soon have to war against Russia, he would have taken good care not to offend Austria, of whom he had need.

Protector of the Papacy, he appeared like a modern Charlemagne, and in no manner announced the intention of relinquishing a part which gained him the ardent sympathies of the clergy and those of the Catholics of France and of the entire world. Hence the Empress had the great joy of being in perfect community of ideas with her husband.

Intelligent, active, well educated, the Empress led a very busy life. Good works occupied a portion of her days. The rest she employed in fitting herself for her rôle as sovereign, in giving audiences, in serious reading, in making acquaintance with new books, and keeping up with the movement in literature and the arts.

To sum up, everything smiled on the Empress Eugénie at the beginning of her reign. She was really popular, because she had three qualities the blending of which formed the most harmonious whole: beauty, goodness, and charity. Since the calamities which have overwhelmed her, the august widow of Napoleon III. loves to recall this epoch in which she shone with such a vivid splendor. She does not say, like Dante, that there is no greater pang than a reminiscence of happiness in days of misfortune.

CHAPTER III

THE TUILERIES

THE aspect of palaces depends very greatly on their occupants. At the periods when it was profaned by the crowd, the château of the Tuileries wore a morose and sinister appearance. On becoming the abode of a powerful emperor and of a dazzlingly beautiful empress, and the centre of a young and powerful government, it resumed its former prestige. The lugubrious souvenirs attached to its history seemed to be effaced. The hour was at hand when, completed by the finishing of the Louvre, with which it would form one and the same palace, it would constitute the most grandiose and majestic residence of the world. Never had Rome, even in the times of the Cæsars, a similar edifice.

During the first months that followed the Emperor's marriage, the château of the Tuileries was as brilliant as it was animated. No one dreamed as yet of such a contingency as a speedy war, and worldly pleasures were undisturbed by any disquietude or preoccupation. During the carnival several balls were given at the Tuileries, and during Lent concerts by the best male and female singers. Every Thursday evening Their Majesties received the high functionaries and their wives.

The Duc de Bassano, the Emperor's grand chamberlain, and the duchess, lady of honor to the Empress, General Comte de Tascher de la Pagerie, grand master of the household of the Empress, his son and his daughter-in-law the Comte and Comtesse Charles, his daughter the Comtesse Stéphanie, canoness, lodged in the Tuileries in the apartments situated behind the pavilion of Marsan, and giving on the Rue de Rivoli. The weekly Friday evenings of the Duc de Bassano and the Wednesdays of the Comte Tascher de la Pagerie were very elegant. "People really amused themselves at that epoch," writes the Comtesse Stéphanie. "I recollect that one evening my brother conceived the notion of giving a ball where all the guests should be dressed as mummers. The festivity was at its height when a band of dominos suddenly invaded the salons. My brother received them with the utmost courtesy, and everybody respected their incognito ; but this did not hinder us from suspecting our illustrious neighbors of having invaded our frontier, followed by several of their intimate friends. The fact is that these amiable dominos seemed greatly amused by our gaiety, and to take part in it."

This fête gave the idea of fancy-dress balls. The grand master of the Empress's household offered one

to the sovereign, and his daughter the Comtesse
Stéphanie has given the details of it in the pretty
book entitled *Mon Séjour aux Tuileries :* " Our
apartment," she says, " had become a fairy garden,
a parterre of flowers over which passed and repassed
marchionesses and shepherdesses, fools, devils, peasants, Turks, Greeks, people of all times and of
every country. And amidst this gaiety and animation, where we amused ourselves with uncovered
faces, dominos went up and down like shadows, in-
triguing and contriving every means to avoid being
recognized. This mystery gave piquancy to the
fête, and all the more because we knew that the two
highest personages of France were hidden beneath
the domino."

Towards eleven o'clock a first quadrille, led by
Comtesse Charles Tascher de la Pagerie, and composed of male and female dancers, all of whom were
powdered, entered the salons. The quadrille was
continued by a minuet and followed by a slow and
cadenced waltz. A second quadrille came next, led
by Comtesse Stéphanie de la Pagerie. Disguised as
Neapolitan peasants, the dancers carried distaffs of
flowers with which they formed an arbor. The
ballet terminated by a tarantella which was loudly
encored.

Then, slowly and with measured advance, came
gigantic bottles of champagne. Their corks suddenly popped out, and splitting from top to bottom
they gave egress to sailors who began to dance. The

fête ended with a supper to which the guests sat down. The young Empress took great pleasure in these balls, so picturesque and animated, and yet carefully restrained within the limits of propriety.

To sum up, the court of the second Emperor, notwithstanding its magnificence, its luxury, and its brilliancy, gave little offence to the innate sentiment of equality in France, because this court, splendid though it was, had no privileges, either from the political or the social point of view. No entailed estates, no birthrights, no hereditary seats in the Senate, no tabourets for duchesses, no prerogatives for titled personages. A plebeian, a self-made man, a writer, a scientist, was on the same footing at the Tuileries as a man belonging to the most ancient nobility. The Emperor selected his orderly officers on their record; he concerned himself about their merit and in nowise with their origin. In spite of its etiquette and its high functions the court of Napoleon was not in any way a court of the old régime. The aristocracy which figured in it was merely a superficial one which was not at all incompatible with modern society and the principles of 1789. This is why the majority of Parisians, ordinarily of so carping a temper, beheld without offence the splendors of a court which afforded them a brilliant spectacle without attacking their rights or constituting a scornful coterie to their detriment. At bottom, the second Empire was merely a sort of compromise between opposed régimes, a transition

between royalty and the Republic.   One wonders
why Napoleon III. did not imitate the example given
by Napoleon I. in the first years of his reign, and put
the name of the Emperor on the coins beside the
name of the French Republic.   He might thus have
reminded himself that France had just saluted in
him the glorious parvenu, the crowned democracy.

In his prison at Ham he had written to George
Sand, January 24, 1845 : "If before the public eye
I keep to my title of prince, it is because this title
has always been disputed by men and governments
who regard the French Revolution as an accident
and all that the people have established from 1789
to 1812 as illegitimate.   So long as France shall
have princes I will not tear up my certificate of
baptism ; but as soon as she recognizes none but
citizens, I will cheerfully pass the sponge over my
past."   This did not prevent Louis Napoleon from
transforming himself into Napoleon III.

But it was not without long hesitation that he
resolved to put an end to the Republic.   In his
character, his ideas, his policy, and even in the organization of his court at the Tuileries, he retained
certain aspects of republicanism.

CHAPTER IV

THE PALAIS-ROYAL

THE Palais-Royal was assigned as residence to the last of the brothers of Napoleon I., Prince Jerome Bonaparte, and his son, Prince Napoleon. On the right, in the court of the Horloge, is the entrance of the grand stairway, one of the finest that exist in Europe. This admirably proportioned staircase, with its marvellously carved baluster, leads to the apartments of the first story of the right wing of the palace,—the Valois wing,—which were those of the Ducs de Valois, and in which King Jerome installed himself in 1853. His bedroom was that of King Louis Philippe and Queen Marie Amélie. It is the room situated between what is now the cabinet of the director of the Beaux-Arts and that of the director of Civil Buildings; it is used at present as a waiting-room. Next to it is a small room where Marie Amélie wrote her letters, and which she called the *écrivanie*, in Italian, *scrivania*. Part of the Valois wing is now occupied by the Finance section of the Council of State. The hall of the Tribunal of Conflicts is the former dining-room of the Ducs d'Orléans, King Jerome,

31

and Prince Napoleon. It was there that the Regent
gave his famous suppers.

Prince Napoleon installed himself in the Nemours
wing, on the right side of the palace and looking
out on the Horloge court. The Palais-Royal had
just been very well restored, and the luxuriously
furnished apartments were magnificent.

Until Napoleon III. should have a son the
imperial heredity had been established in favor of
King Jerome and his descendants. The Emperor
had announced this decision by the organic statute
of December 26, 1853, prefacing it, however, by
this sentence: "We hope that it may be granted
to us under the divine protection to contract an
alliance which will permit us to leave direct
heirs."

In 1853 harmony existed between the Tuileries
and the Palais-Royal. It was not easy, at this
period, to make any sort of opposition to the
Emperor, the absolute master of France, who dis-
pensed all favors according to his own good pleasure.
King Jerome and Prince Napoleon knew very well
that if he had chosen he might, without arousing
the slightest ill feeling, have preferred to them the
descendants of Lucien Bonaparte, if not in accordance with the imperial constitution of the first
Empire, at least according to the rights of primo-
geniture. By a senatorial decree of November 6,
1852, Napoleon III. had been left at liberty to
regulate the descent of the crown as he pleased, and

it was to the sovereign's good-will that Jerome and his son owed the favors heaped upon them.

Born November 15, 1784, the former King of Westphalia had just passed his sixty-eighth birthday when the second Empire was proclaimed. He knew very well that this restoration was due solely to the initiative and the audacity of his nephew, whom he had sharply blamed for his participation in the insurrection of the Romagna and the ill-concerted enterprises of Strasbourg and Boulogne. Authorized to return to France toward the close of Louis Philippe's reign, he had maintained excellent relations with the King. At the moment when the Revolution of February broke out he was on the point of obtaining not simply the official cessation of his exile, but a seat in the Chamber of Peers and an annual endowment of one hundred thousand francs. One may say that at this epoch he was an Orleanist, like the majority of his former companions in arms.

Under the second Republic King Jerome refused to be nominated for deputy; nor, in spite of the advice said to have been given him by his friend, M. Thiers, would he be a candidate for the presidency of the Republic, but effaced himself completely in presence of his nephew, whose candidacy he supported. Louis Napoleon was grateful to him for it. Resuming possession of the rank of general of division, to which he had been appointed forty-two years before, Jerome became, December 27,

1848, governor-general of the Invalides and guardian
of his brother's tomb. Not long after, he received
the baton of a marshal of France. December 2,
1851, at the very moment when his son was expressing himself violently against the Coup d'Etat, he
went on horseback and in uniform to the Elysée
and formed a part of the escort of Louis Napoleon.
When the Senate was constituted, he became its
president, but retained the post but a short time.
Since the re-establishment of the Empire he had
enjoyed all the honors and prerogatives of the first
prince of the blood.

Having contracted a morganatic marriage with a
noble Florentine, the Marchioness Bartholini, with
whom he installed himself at the Palais-Royal, he
found himself to have had three wives, two of whom
were still living. The first one was an American,
Miss Elizabeth Patterson of Baltimore, whom he
married December 27, 1803, when an officer of the
navy. But the First Consul, whose consent had
not been asked, based upon his brother's minority
the right to declare the nullity of this marriage in
spite of the latter's entreaties. Separated from his
young wife, Jerome continued to feel great affection
for her. She took refuge in England, where her
son was born, July 7, 1805. This son established
himself in the United States, where he married an
American, and lived under the name of Patterson-
Bonaparte, surrounded by general esteem. Shortly
after the restoration of the Empire Jerome received

his son and grandson, MM. Patterson-Bonaparte, at Paris, and displayed real affection for them. His grandson, a handsome and brilliant young man, was authorized to take service in the French army. He distinguished himself and merited the cross of the Legion of Honor in the Crimea.

Since November 29, 1835, the former King of Westphalia had been the widower of the noble and virtuous Catherine of Wurtemberg, whom he had married August 23, 1837, and who had shown him such devotion in both good and evil fortune. The Marchioness Bartholini, with whom he contracted a morganatic union, had been lady of honor to this princess.

King Jerome led a more than princely existence at the Palais-Royal. Officially he had only the title of Imperial Highness, but he was always addressed as Sire and Majesty. His manners were those of a man of the old régime. His resemblance to the great Emperor, the part he had played in the Napoleonic epic, his valiant conduct in times of victory as well as on the day of Waterloo, his long experience and his exquisite courtesy, gave him a real prestige. One could not look at this veteran of the imperial legend without emotion. Napoleon III. displayed towards him an affection blended with deference, and the former King of Westphalia had equal reason to be pleased with the Empress.

In Prince Napoleon the republican quickly ceded his place to the prince of the blood. His opposi-

tion to the Coup d'Etat was not of long duration.
Honors, luxury, endowment, a princely household,
— nothing was lacking to him. Prince, Imperial
Highness, senator, he was appointed general of division and grand cross of the Legion of Honor without
opposition. Splendidly lodged at the Palais-Royal,
everybody addressed him as Monseigneur. In 1853
he had two aides-de-camp, Captains Ferri-Pisani
and Roux; an orderly officer, Jerome David; and a
private secretary, M. Emmanuel Matthieu. Fond
of letters, the arts, and pleasure, he possessed,
thanks to his novel situation, all the means to
gratify his tastes, and after having undergone so
many trials he led at last a life as agreeable as it
was brilliant. In the Montpensier wing of the
Palais-Royal, very close to his apartments, was a
door which communicated directly with the Théâtre-
Français, on a level with the first tier of boxes. It
was the Prince's favorite theatre. He professed a
special admiration for several of its great actresses.
For a long time he had led a very simple existence.
At the time of the Coup d'Etat he occupied a modest
lodging in the Rue d'Alger, and his then manner of
living was in singular contrast with the splendors
of the Palais-Royal. The comfort of his new life
did not divert him from his taste for study. Well
educated, very learned, greatly interested in the arts
and sciences, diplomacy and politics, he managed to
combine work and pleasure. Arsène Houssaye has
said of him: "Like Napoleon I., he talked of every-

thing in picturesque language and with a knowing and unpremeditated ease. . . . At the Théâtre-Français, where he often came, we met each other at all extraordinary representations, especially on Rachel's great days. When he came to the final rehearsal of a new piece, he never made any mistake as to its success or failure, even when every one else did so. . . . It was always Prince Napoleon who suggested the topic of conversation; I never heard him say a word which was an offence to morals or the French language, although he used that freedom of speech for which he was well known. And with what eloquence, at once natural and princely, he said everything. . . . He loved ancient and modern art with equal passion. Not a painter, not a sculptor among those who go to the Villa Medici, knows as he did the marvels of the Greeks and Romans."

Of all the Prince's gifts eloquence was the chief. Few words were so vibrant and full of color as his. He talked on all subjects with remarkable freedom and vigor. M. Ernest Pinard has written in his journal: "I said one day to Prince Napoleon: 'Monseigneur, what an admirable lawyer you would have made if you were not a Highness.' Both a talker and an orator, he commenced calmly, then his voice would rise; his language was measured and metaphorical. He would rise, stride about, as if physical movement aided the gestation of the idea. He would take a chair to lean upon it as a deputy does with the tribune. Again he would stride up and

down the room, and, after a lively sally, look at his
interlocutor with a triumphant smile. He was a
dilettante of controversy." He was not merely not
afraid of discussion, but he sought for it, he loved
it. Rather than be uncontradicted, he would con-
tradict himself.

This prince, whose faults were incontestable, but
who has often been judged too severely, had real
qualities, among others a probity equal to every
proof. He was averse to speculations of every
kind, even those that were correct and irreproachable. He never dreamed of making use of his lofty
situation in order to increase his fortune. He
managed it economically without seeking to enlarge
it. Money-dealers inspired him with invincible
repugnance. The humble style of living which he
was obliged to adopt after the fall of the second
Empire does honor to his memory.

Prince Napoleon has been styled a Cæsar in the
wrong place. This description is not exact. He
had not the manners of a Cæsar either during his
cousin's reign nor at the epoch, after the death of
the Prince Imperial, when he became the head of
the Napoleonic dynasty. Unlike the Cæsars, he
did not pay court to the masses. He solicited
neither the support of the press nor the favors of
the populace. He despised and sometimes even
braved public opinion.

On more than one occasion the differences of
opinion between Napoleon III. and his cousin were

more apparent than real. At bottom they had a real affection for each other. Born April 20, 1808, Napoleon III. was fourteen years older than the Prince, who was born September 9, 1822. The Emperor's sentiment toward his cousin was not unlike that of an elder brother for a younger one. They had known the trials of exile and adversity together. Louis Napoleon had occupied himself with his cousin's education, and in Switzerland had given him lessons in mathematics. Having been elected a deputy in 1848, before the future Emperor, Prince Napoleon opened the way for him and aided in inducing the Assembly to validate his election. If he sometimes opposed him when Louis Napoleon had become Napoleon III., it was an opposition which never ceased to be dynastic, as they used to say under the parliamentary régime, for he never entertained for a moment the notion of establishing a competition between the reigning and the younger branch of the Bonapartes. The few republicans whom he admitted to the Palais-Royal were not of the sort that was dangerous to the Empire. In foreign politics they both held very advanced ideas. Both were partisans of Italian independence and the principle of nationalities. They were at one in uniting their cult for Napoleon I. to respect for democracy. Even at the very times when they were supposed to be least in harmony, they were often pursuing the same end. One may say that there was a right side and a left at the court of Napo-

leon III.   The right was represented by the Empress
and the left by Prince Napoleon.   The Emperor, one
of whose principal political rules was the maxim:
Divide to reign, did not complain of this state of
things.   Possibly it did not displease him to remain
the supreme arbiter between divisions which it depended on a single word from him to continue in
existence or to cause to disappear.   In fine, the
Prince Napoleon, a character as complex as his
destiny, wavering and diverse as the vicissitudes
of his troublous and harassed existence, was a man
full of contrasts, autocratic and liberal, half great
noble, half democrat, clinging by his origin to the
past and to the future by his ideas, appearing by
turns on the extreme left of the Palais-Bourbon in
the character of a tribune, and at the Palais-Royal
under the Napoleonic aspect of a prince surrounded
by all the honors and prerogatives of his rank.

CHAPTER V

IN 1853 the foremost woman in France, next to the Empress, was the Princesse Mathilde. All historians and chroniclers who may study the court of Napoleon III. will give a place in their narratives to this beautiful and witty princess, who has retained all her feminine prestige even after the fall of the second Empire, and who will always be remembered as a superior woman and a generous and intelligent protectress of letters and the arts.

Mathilde-Lætitia-Wilhelmine, daughter of Jerome Bonaparte, former King of Westphalia, was born in exile, at Trieste, May 27, 1820. Her mother, Catherine, born February 21, 1783, married August 23, 1807, died November 28, 1835, was the daughter of the first King of Wurtemberg. She it was who showed such virtue and such courage in adversity that Napoleon, on the rock of Saint-Helena, rendered solemn homage to her by saying that she had written her name in history with her own hands.

Louis Napoleon was in love with his young and charming cousin and had ardently desired to marry her. On this subject we read in the memoirs of

41

Comte Horace de Viel-Castel: "I have just heard
from Ferdinand Barrot, an eye-witness, an anecdote
which is not known and perhaps never will be.
When Prince Louis Napoleon learned at Ham,
where he was a prisoner, the marriage of his cousin
with Anatole Demidoff, all the affection, or better,
the love, which he had for this princess awoke in
him; he began to weep bitterly and said to Barrot:
'This is the last and heaviest blow that fortune had
in store for me.'"

November 1, 1840, the Princesse Mathilde married in Florence a Russian, Comte Anatole Demidoff, Prince of San Donato. This marriage was not
happy. When the Princess separated from her
husband, the Emperor Nicholas justified her in
doing so. On this occasion he showed a benevolent
interest in her for which she was always grateful.
She came to France in the last years of the reign
of Louis Philippe, who gave her an excellent reception. In his *Souvenirs*, Prince de Joinville cites in
the front rank of those who frequented Queen Marie
Amélie's evenings "the Princesse Mathilde in all
the splendor of her beauty."

The Princess lived in Paris during the entire
period of Louis Napoleon's presidency, and her
salon was the first in which the Prince-President
met Mademoiselle de Montijo.

At the beginning of the second Empire the Princesse Mathilde was thirty-two years old. She was
dazzling. This is the portrait which Arsène Hous-

saye has drawn of her in his *Confessions:* "She looked the princess to perfection, with her heraldic and Olympian head which carried the crown so well. Style, intelligence, and goodness shone on that countenance worthy of marble. Hence she has inspired more than one beautiful bust like that of Carpeau. Hers was the sovereign beauty of force and sweetness, line and expression, style and charm, kindness for everybody and raillery for fools. . . . She has received the homage of all foreign courts, as well as of that of Napoleon III. But she was not fond of applause. A simple compliment from a contemporary master for one of the charming pastels she draws so cleverly touches her far more nearly."

The Emperor, who had a lively affection for his cousin, did not treat her as Madame Demidoff, but as the daughter of the former King of Westphalia and the grandchild of the King of Wurtemberg. He conferred on her the title of Imperial Highness, and she was always spoken of as the Princesse Mathilde. In 1853 she had three ladies to accompany her: the Baronne de Serlay, born Rovigo, the Comtesse de Gouy d'Arcy, Madame Ratomska, and a private secretary, M. Ratomski. Her retinue was absolutely princely. Although she cared little for display, she was present at all official ceremonies and the fêtes given at the Tuileries, Saint-Cloud, Compiègne, and Fontainebleau.

The house occupied by the Princesse Mathilde exists no longer. It was situated on the corner of the

Rue de Courcelles and the Boulevard Haussmann.
Madame Octave Feuillet, widow of the celebrated
dramatic author, writes in the pleasant volume
entitled *Quelques années de ma vie:* "The salon of
the Princesse Mathilde was that of an artist princess
and a very great lady. All intelligent Paris was to
be seen there, renowned authors and painters, princes
and ambassadors from every country. The reception rooms, and even the winter garden, were filled
with exquisitely grouped objects of art. Pictures
by great masters, statues of bronze and marble,
Chinese vases out of which rose gigantic palms, old
tapestries of great magnificence, adorned the palace
of the Rue de Courcelles. . . . When I went up
the beautiful staircase, over which Chinese draperies
fell in silken cascades, where peacocks ranged at
intervals along the balusters trained their iridescent
fans like half-opened jewel boxes, it seemed as if I
were ascending the stairs of one of the sultanas
whose stories have been told us by Scheherazade."

Again Madame Octave Feuillet shows us the
Princess entering the banqueting hall, with her
statuesque arms, her long train, the triple row of
pearls on her magnificent neck. "I see her," she
adds, "seating herself as on a throne in front of the
gilded eagle which spread its wings above the fruits
and flowers of the table. And especially I remember her diffusing her charming smiles and glancing
at each guest to see if all were at their ease."

M. Ernest Pinard, former Minister of the Interior,

has also described, and not without admiration, this justly famous salon: "The Princesse Mathilde," says he, "received every Tuesday and Sunday. She was in the incomparable splendor of her Roman beauty, and in her the artist enhanced the woman. All foreigners of distinction who passed through Paris had themselves presented by their ambassadors at these reunions of the Rue de Courcelles; they did not forget the way there, and now they come without the ambassador. It was a sort of neutral ground on which assembled academicians, painters, composers, novelists, magistrates, diplomats, financiers, politicians, and men of the world."

Comparing the salon of to-day with that of the second Empire, M. Pinard adds: "At the present time, the receptions of the Rue de Berry recall those of the Rue de Courcelles. Death has made many gaps in the salon, the dark heads have become white; but the tact and intelligence of a superior woman still win devotion. It is not merely faithful imperialists, but those who are loyal to art, to letters, and to science, who go there; even the old who have disappeared have found successors."

The salon of the Princesse Mathilde has remained what it was of old, a salon whose habitués occupy themselves mainly with art and literature. Under the Empire the cousin of the Emperor took no part in politics. She confined herself to using her tact and amiability in such a manner as to contribute to the maintenance of harmonious relations between the Tuileries and the Palais-Royal. Nevertheless, we shall observe that, although accustomed not to intervene in diplomatic questions, she did not disguise her sympathies for Russia and the Czar, to whom she was nearly related, her own mother and the mother of the Emperor Nicholas having been princesses of the house of Wurtemberg. There were two women, the Princesse Mathilde in Paris, and in Saint Petersburg the Grand Duchess Marie, daughter of the Czar, married to a son of Prince Eugène de Beauharnais, who ardently desired an agreement between Napoleon III. and the Emperor Nicholas. If these women had been authorized to counsel the two sovereigns, many woes might have been spared both France and Russia. The two princesses judged things more correctly than the most skilful statesmen and the most consummate diplomatists.

Up to the birth of the son of Napoleon III. only three persons bore the title of Imperial Highness at the Emperor's court: Prince Jerome, Prince Napoleon, and the Princesse Mathilde. The other princes and princesses belonged to what was called the Emperor's civil family, and merely bore the title of Highness. Their position was thus regulated by the imperial almanac of 1856: "The sons of the brothers and sisters of the Emperor Napoleon I., who do not form part of the imperial family, bear the title of Prince and Highness with their family name. In the second generation only the eldest sons will bear the title of Prince and Highness; the others will have only the title of Prince. The daughters of the princes who are related to the Emperor will have the title of Princess until their marriage; but when they are married they will have merely the name and titles of their husbands unless by virtue of a special decision to the contrary. Princesses of the Emperor's family married to private individuals, French or foreign, will have no other rank at court than that of their husbands."

The imperial almanac of 1856 mentioned as having rank at court, among the princes and princesses of the Emperor's family, Their Highnesses Prince Louis Lucien Bonaparte, Prince Lucien Murat, Prince Joseph Bonaparte, Prince Joachim Murat, Princesses Bacciochi, Princess Lucien Murat, Princess Joachim Murat. The imperial almanac of 1853 had mentioned as princes of the civil family of the Emperor only His Highness Prince Louis Lucien Bonaparte and His Highness Prince Louis Lucien Murat.

We have just examined the court in 1853. Now let us give a rapid glance at the city.

CHAPTER VI

PARIS IN 1853

PARIS, on the morrow of the Emperor's marriage, had an animation, ardor, and gaiety that were extraordinary. No one took any further interest in politics. To amuse themselves and make money was the double aim of its population. With the exception of a few superior men little thought was given to lost liberties. The press by its excesses and the tribune by its violence had so wearied the public that it did not seem to regret that the one was muzzled and the other destroyed. A régime far more rigorous than that of the ordinances which had caused the downfall of Charles X. seemed a perfectly natural thing.

People had been so satiated with parliamentary discussions and emotions that no one wore mourning for defunct parliamentarism. The Corps législatif, elected by universal suffrage for six years and composed of about two hundred and sixty members, possessed only very restricted powers. It contented itself with discussing and passing the laws prepared by the Council of State. The deputies could not be ministers, and the ministers never made their appearance at the Corps Législatif. The sessions were public, but there was no tribune, and the reports of the daily press consisted merely of the publication of the minutes drawn up by the President. No discussion of the address, no interpellations, no possibility of causing the fall of ministries. The Senate was composed of five hundred and fifty members appointed for life by the sovereign. Its sessions were not reported. It did not participate directly in any legislative or judicial powers. Laws were submitted to it, but solely that they might be examined as to their conformity with the Constitution and be opposed by it should they prove to be contrary. The cardinals, marshals, and admirals of France were senators by virtue of their office.

At the beginning of 1853 the Senate and the Corps Législatif occupied attention, not by their parliamentary labors, but by two magnificent fêtes which they offered to the Emperor and Empress, one at the Luxembourg palace, and the other at the Palais-Bourbon. Comte de Montalembert, then a member of the Corps Législatif, refused his subscription to the ball, but sent the amount to the mayor of Besançon, begging him to apply it to some work of charity. The mayor refused the somewhat factious offering. In Paris the friends of parliamentarism said, " To overthrow the tribune may pass for a while ; but to replace it by a ball is really too much."

Never had the whirl of fashion been more animated than in 1853. At that period balls and great entertainments were not given in spring, as they are at present, but in winter. All the salons were open by the beginning of January. In the fashionable quarters, Faubourg Saint-Germain, Champs-Elysées, Chaussée d'Antin, there was scarcely a street where one could not see windows sparkling with lights and hear the echo of joyous orchestras. The official circles set the example of the greatest luxury. Fêtes of rare magnificence were given at the Tuileries, at the ministries, the embassies, and at the houses of the great officers of the crown. People amused themselves greatly, likewise, in the Faubourg Saint-Germain and in financial circles. The fashionables of all parties went on Mondays, Wednesdays, and Fridays to the Opéra, and on Thursdays and Saturdays to the Théâtre Italien before going to the ball. People stayed up later than they do at present. The balls kept up until morning. The great restaurants, such as the Café Anglais and the Maison d'Or, remained open all night. On the boulevard the animation never ceased at all. The balls ended with the carnival. But during Lent, up to Holy Week, there were concerts at the Tuileries by the principal singers of the Opéra, the Théâtre Italien, and the Opéra-Comique ; brilliant receptions in the ministries and the embassies ; in legitimist society continuous aristocratic routs.

Even the adversaries of the government rejoiced at seeing the red spectre vanish, and thoughtlessly gave themselves to pleasure. In the *Revue des*

Deux-Mondes (Chronicle of the Fortnight, February 28, 1853), M. de Mazade wrote : " We are no longer in those gloomy periods of late years when we could not meet each other in the mornings without asking about the catastrophes of the previous day, the triumphant revolutions, the thrones that had been upset, the crowns dragged through the mire of riots. It is like a torrent that has returned to its bed." At this moment no one was disturbed about foreign affairs. The Eastern Question scarcely interested anybody but the diplomatists. The public at large perceived no dark spot on the horizon. No one believed that Napoleon would so quickly abandon the programme of his speech at Bordeaux : "'The Empire is peace." Business men, merchants, manufacturers, had never been in such good humor, because they had never made so much money. The speculators of the Bourse were in high feather. The middle class rejoiced at being freed from patrol duty and removing barricades, and from hearing the drums beat the call to arms or the general. The service of the National Guard, so dangerous and tiresome a few months before, had now been transformed into a diversion. The citizen soldiery, formerly so turbulent and active, had become both well disciplined and quiet.

Paris was about to be transfigured, and to become the capital of capitals. The Emperor had decided already on the completion of the Louvre, the prolongation of the Rue de Rivoli, the construction of

the Palais de l'Industrie, the creation of vast means
of communication between the railway stations and
the central quarters of the city, the opening of large
empty spaces and squares which would make light,
air, and verdure accessible to all, the transformation
of the Bois de Boulogne into an immense pleasure
park destined to become the finest promenade in the
whole world.   July 1, 1853, Baron Haussmann installed himself at the Hôtel de Ville as prefect of
the Seine, where his administration was to last sixteen years, and to work great prodigies.   He was
about to appropriate to himself what Louis XIV.
said to Mansard : " Build, keep on building ; we will
advance the money, and foreigners will pay it back."

M. de la Gorce has said in his remarkable *Histoire
du second Empire :* " Such was the condition of the
country in 1853 : in the spring, fêtes so innumerable that they became as fatiguing as labor itself ;
important transformations on the point of being
accomplished ; a notable increase of public wealth ;
a future so assured as to permit of long designs ; a
society which was frivolous but not devoid of benevolent aspirations, lacking liberty but not feeling
the want of it ; many men of great intelligence left
in the shade or voluntarily withdrawing thither, but
no one as yet estimating the void created by so
many unemployed forces ; . . . many germs of corruption and error, but thus far so deeply buried that
no one foreboded the evolution which would cause
them to bud forth."

Much has been said of imperial corruption. Was the second Empire more immoral than the third Republic? We do not believe it. The men of 1897 are not so gay as those of 1853, but they are not more moral. The lessons of misfortune have not changed the French character. There is the same thirst for pleasure, the same need of luxury, the same inclination for comfort and material enjoyments. And yet on one point there is an improvement : obligatory military service for all has inured the young men to fatigue and disciplined them better than of old. By suppressing the right to buy a release from it, the new laws have not merely strengthened the principle of equality which is the foundation of our political and social system, but they have given, not as formerly to some, but to all, those martial aptitudes of which France has a right to be proud. Apart from this progress, which is real, we do not believe in any perceptible difference between the morals of the Paris of 1853 and those of the Paris of to-day. The republicans are not more austere than the imperialists. Virtue is not more highly honored now than then. Human passions do not alter much. Simply there are epochs when vices are more elegant than at others, and when pleasure, like luxury, is more in evidence. The surface of things changes, the bottom does not. The setting is more or less brilliant, but the play is always pretty much the same. Neither under the Empire nor the Republic will France ever be Sparta.

CHAPTER VII

THE REPUBLICAN PARTY

NOW let us give a rapid glance at parties in 1853. The one which seemed the feeblest of all was that which had the greatest force and future: the republican party. To judge from appearances one would have said that it was annihilated forever. Universal suffrage seemed absolutely opposed to it. It would have been useless to search for a partisan of the Republic in the Corps Législatif. At Brussels where they gave lectures, like MM. Bancel, Challemel-Lacour, Deschanel, and occupied themselves with literature, like Colonel Charras and Edgard Quinet, the fugitive republicans exerted no sort of influence. In London they were more militant, but they were aware that they never assembled without the presence of traitors and spies in the pay of the French police.

A sort of fatality weighed on the republicans in 1853. The most honest among them were bitterly calumniated, represented as the enemies of God and social order, and held responsible for the anarchic passions and excesses of the demagogues. On the other hand, the June days had dug an abyss between the moderate and the advanced republicans. The latter bore a deeper grudge against General Cavaignac than against Napoleon III. In fact, it was the general who had given the signal for excessive repression and the wholesale deportations. In his fine work, *1739 et 1889*, M. Emile Ollivier has written: "The most revolting thing about the Coup d'Etat, the transportations without trial, having been inaugurated by the Republic after the June days, people did not experience the same indignation against this abominable proceeding as they would have done had they not been accustomed to it already." The radicals and socialists were possibly more hostile to General Changarnier than to Napoleon's heir, and a royalist restoration would have been more hateful to them than the re-establishment of the Empire. Workingmen made doleful reflections on the iniquity of human judgments. Four months ago they had been treated as heroes, now as scoundrels. And yet, from the legal point of view there was no difference between the revolution of February and the insurrection of June. In presence of a strong government and a well-disciplined army, no one dreamed of making barricades. The Emperor, driving his own phaeton, went unescorted through the populous quarters where riots had formerly been organized.

Still, there were at this epoch several attempts against the life of Napoleon III. Members of secret societies had resolved to fire upon him as soon as a suitable occasion should present itself. Having

learned that he intended to go to the Hippodrome
from the château of Saint-Cloud on June 6, 1853, the
conspirators grouped themselves along his route.
But the police received timely warning and arrested
them. On the third of the following July another
plot was arranged by some Frenchmen and a Belgian
named Meren. On that day the sovereign was to
go to the Opéra-Comique. The conspirators had decided that when his carriage was passing they would
come up shouting " Long live the Emperor ! " that
Meren would then give the signal by firing two pistol
shots, when the conspirators, flinging themselves
upon the carriage, should poniard Napoleon III.
They were arrested at the very moment when they
were about to carry out this scheme, and on his exit
from the theatre the sovereign was greeted by the
acclamations of the crowd.

At the same time, there was nothing in common
between the attempts of certain fanatics and the
sentiments of the majority of the republicans. Napoleon III. had no personal aversion to this party.
It would have gratified his most ardent desire to be
able to rally them to the support of his government.
These republicans, whose sincere convictions and
indomitable convictions he knew, were the adversaries whom he respected and feared. His first
thought, on taking possession of the presidency of
the Republic in December, 1848, had been to offer
the presidency of the Council of Ministers to M. de
Lamartine. All notable republicans who should have

come to the Elysée, or later to the Tuileries, would have met there a courteous and hearty welcome. In 1849 the Prince had thought of Victor Hugo for the portfolio of Public Instruction and the embassy to Madrid. As Emperor he bore no ill will to the poet for having written the *Châtiments*. Concerning this we cite a passage from M. A. Granier de Cassagnac (*Souvenirs du second Empire*): "I was one day in the cabinet of the Emperor at Saint-Cloud. As he was rummaging among some papers, chance put under his hand a fine and memorable circular addressed by Victor Hugo to the electors of Paris in 1858, and in which, divining the schemes of the demagogues, he predicted that one day they would tear down the Vendôme column to convert it into copper sous.

"Still holding the paper, the Emperor remained thoughtful for a moment, and with a sad smile: 'Do you know that?' said he to me, holding out the paper. 'Is it not fine and haughty? Well! I have to accuse myself of and to regret a very great fault. Victor Hugo showed me personal affection and rallied to my cause. One day I was too exacting, and I wounded him. A man of his worth would have been a power in my government and shed lustre on my reign.'"

One may say that if Napoleon III. had not been emperor, he would not have been a monarchist but a republican. By his youthful antecedents and his personal tendencies he belonged far more to the party

of the left than to that of the right. In Italy he had
shared the opinions of the most advanced liberals
and fought in the ranks of the carbonari. In Switzerland and the United States he had made his appearance as a true democrat. In France he had attained
to power only by means of the Republic and republicans. In his captivity at Ham he had neglected no
means of winning the sympathies of such persons
as Louis Blanc, Ledru-Rollin, and George Sand.
After the revolution of February, it was men of the
extreme left, such as Crémieux, Louis Blanc, Jules
Favre, who had flung open to him the doors of the
country and restored his rights as a citizen. As a
deputy he had sat on the left benches. As President
of the Republic he would perhaps have remained
faithful to his oath if he could have been re-elected
by legal means. After the Coup d'Etat which gave
him absolute power, he had hesitated for a whole
year before re-establishing the imperial régime.
Even after liberty of the press had vanished he allowed *Le Siècle* if not to preach the Republic, at
least to use language which charmed the republicans.
Remaining alone after the disappearance of its contemporaries, this journal enriched itself by an enormous circulation and became a power which was not
displeasing to the sovereign, He said that *Le Siècle*
was the *ministry of the opposition.*

Possibly Napoleon III. had a presentiment that
his reign would be the transition between royalty
and the Republic. Recognizing the exigencies of

modern society, he felt that it is the chief duty of a government to better the condition of the majority, that the time of the *pays légal*[1] was over, that the middle class oligarchy was no longer able to rule France, that the revolution of 1848 had inaugurated a new era, and that universal suffrage, like the abolition of slavery, was a conquest that nothing could wrest from the democracy. Preferring the workingmen, the peasants, the proletarians, to the middle classes, he labored at the formation of what one might call the *Fourth Estate*. In his foreign policy he was not a conservative but a revolutionist. In the depths of his conscience he could not avoid recognizing that he had wronged the Republic to which he owed so much, and perhaps he regretted it more than once, for he was not ignorant of the prestige exerted over the democracy by the mere word Republic. But, in 1853, the country if not the sovereign seemed to forget all that, and the republican party appeared to cause no anxiety to the Empire.

[1] The body of citizens enjoying restricted franchise.

CHAPTER VIII

THE LEGITIMIST PARTY

THE legitimist party bore still less umbrage to the Empire than the republican party. After the revolution of 1848 the partisans of the Comte de Chambord had played a not unimportant political and parliamentary rôle. In the Constituent Assembly, and afterwards in the Legislative Assembly, they formed a homogeneous group of which M. Berryer was the eloquent leader, and which had sometimes a decisive influence in the ballotings. A fervent legitimist, the Comte de Falloux, Minister of Public Instruction under the presidency of Louis Napoleon, had powerfully contributed to the success of the law on liberty of instruction which was so dear to Catholics. The legitimist party had then rendered signal services to the heir of the Empire. Its principal leaders, headed by M. Berryer, had voted for him at the time of the presidential election and supported him energetically in his struggle with the elements of disorder. Several prominent personages of the society of the Faubourg Saint-Germain had shown themselves in the salons of the Elysée and received the warmest welcome. Very

60

few legitimists were pursued at the time of the Coup d'Etat, and those who were arrested were immediately released.

The affair of December 2, which excited such wrath among republicans and Orleanists, left the adherents of the elder branch of the Bourbons rather indifferent. "I think that at this date," writes M. de Falloux in his *Mémoires d'un royaliste*, "a grave error crept into the mind of the Comte de Chambord, and that it had a fatal influence over the rest of his career. The facile success of the Coup d'Etat, the applause which followed it, the public suffrage by which it was sanctioned, persuaded the Prince that, apart from the violence of the proceedings and the choice of men, there was in it a useful lesson, possibly a good example. He failed to consider that France would concede to the descendants of Bonaparte, the organizers of modern society, what it would refuse to the house of Bourbon, inevitably linked to the souvenirs of the old régime. To expect from the masses of the people the same attraction and confidence towards the head of the traditional royalty as for a scion of the race which, by the civil code, had implanted equality in public methods, would be the most deceptive of illusions. Yet by what other motive can one explain the sudden change which took place in the mind, or at all events in the attitude, of M. le Comte de Chambord?"

One would have said that the head of the house

of Bourbon, sharing the sentiment of France, was
tired and disgusted with parliamentary agitation.
"I do not think," says M. de Falloux again, "that
the Prince was a very advanced liberal before the
2d of December, but in his relations with his own
party he had availed himself sufficiently of parliamentary methods to give reason for thinking that
he would practise them on the throne without great
repugnance. After the 2d of December, he also
seemed to unmask a certain concealed absolutism,
and thenceforward aimed at consulting no one,
which is worse than to ask advice at times from
evil counsellors."

Under the government of Louis Philippe, the
legitimists had been authorized by the Comte de
Chambord to swear allegiance to the King of the
French and to sit in the Chamber of Deputies. In
1852, the Prince changed his mind and prescribed
to his adherents a complete abstention from all
elective functions involving an oath to support the
new Constitution. Hence the legitimists found
themselves at once thrust out from all political
life; through obedience to the Prince, innumerable
resignations were handed in from every side, and
the legitimist party passed from active life to the
immobility of death. M. de Falloux was not slow
to comprehend the blow thus given to royalty by
the Comte de Chambord. "France," he wrote at
the time, "has escaped from the *pays légal*[1] of M.

---

[1] The body of citizens possessing the franchise under restricted
suffrage.

Guizot; it will escape more completely still from every *pays artificiel*, still narrower and more special, which shall refuse to associate itself fully with its destinies, conflicts, and dangers. . . . A great social battle has begun. Whoever systematically fails France nowadays, in virtue of a command, will be a deserter in the eyes of the country. Its affections and rewards will be gained by worthier combatants."

When the Empire was proclaimed, the Comte de Chambord thought it his duty to make a public protest. But this document, written in a masterly style, was academic rather than practical, and the Emperor's government dreaded its effect so little that it was reprinted on the first page of the *Moniteur*. Notwithstanding this protest, made as a tribute to conscience, the head of the house of Bourbon offered only a platonic opposition to the Empire. We have frequently had occasion to chat with the men who, for several months in every year, had the honor of sitting at the Prince's table and of living near him. They have told us that until the war of Italy, which he had severely condemned, he had approved the conduct of Napoleon III. If he had attained to power, a Constitution analogous to that of 1852 would not have displeased him, and he would not have destroyed universal suffrage. He was pleased with the Emperor for repressing the excesses of the press, and thus succeeding in accomplishing what the ordinances of Charles X. had vainly attempted. Doubtless it was not agree-

able for the heir of Saint Louis to see a Bonaparte
renewing to his own profit the alliance between the
throne and the altar; and the mystic dithyrambs
of the bishops in honor of Napoleon III. could not
fail to shock the susceptibilities of the man of
divine right. But the Comte de Chambord none
the less approved the Emperor for keeping guard
at the Vatican and maintaining the temporal power
of the Pope by force of arms. He must have been
as favorable to the French policy of 1853 as he
was inimical to that of 1859.

Moreover, the Prince endured his position as a
sovereign in exile with a resignation full of noble-
ness and serenity. None of those who surrounded
him forgot that he was the head of the most ancient and illustrious family in the world. Louis
XIV. had not been treated more respectfully at
Versailles than was his descendant at Frohsdorf.
All who went there to pay him homage were
charmed by the elevation of his sentiments, the
affability of his greeting, the grace of his amiable
and cheerful disposition. Born September 29, 1820,
he was thirty-two years old when Napoleon III.
ascended the throne. Married since November 16,
1846, to the daughter of the Duke of Modena, —
the most reactionary sovereign of Europe, — he had
no children, but did not despair of having some.
Robust and enjoying perfect health, there was a
fund of joviality in his character which made him
almost happy. If he became ambitious, it was

through a sense of duty. ' His mother, the Duchesse
de Berry, had no influence over him. Never would
he have undertaken so audacious a venture as the
resort to arms in 1832, nor did any idea of renewing or essaying any attempt similar to the fiascos
of Strasbourg and Boulogne ever occur to him.
Having imposed on his adherents what some of
them have rather spitefully called the "policy of
folded arms," he awaited the decrees of Providence
with a sort of mysticism. His greatness riveted
him to the shore, and from afar he contemplated
the course of events with imperturbable dignity.
Napoleon III. esteemed such an adversary, but he
did not dread him.

CHAPTER IX

THE ORLEANIST PARTY

NAPOLEON III. feared the Orleanists far more than the legitimists. The partisans of the July monarchy were more active and militant than those of the Comte de Chambord. The Orleans princes who had fought so brilliantly and left so many sympathizers in the army could not accustom themselves to repose. Their partisans were more attached to liberty of the press and parliamentary government than the legitimists and could not reconcile themselves to the disappearance of institutions which had been the programme and the apology for the reign of Louis Philippe. At Claremont and Twickenham there were angry recriminations which did not exist at Frohsdorf.

In the Legislative Assembly the Orleanist deputies had made a bitterer fight against Louis Napoleon than had the legitimists. On the 2d of December the first had been imprisoned and exiled, while the second had only been under arrest for a few hours. Still, in spite of the Coup d'Etat, a number of the friends of the Orleans princes thought of rallying to the new government,

but the decrees of January 22, 1852, by which a part
of the fortune of the princes was unjustly confis-
cated, made a breach between them and the victor
of December 2.

A brother-in-law of Queen Isabella, and established in Spain, the Duc de Montpensier chiefly
occupied himself with the affairs of that country.
The Duc de Nemours, who was more of a legitimist
than an Orleanist, and who would greatly have
desired a fusion between the two branches of the
house of Bourbon, endured his exile with truly
Christian resignation. But the Duc d'Aumale
and the Prince de Joinville, the one so popular in
the army and the other in the navy, could not
habituate themselves to living so far away from
their companions in arms.

"Of all the princes," M. de La Gorce has written,
"the one most in evidence was already the Duc
d'Aumale, at once soldier, scholar, and artist. To
alleviate his exile he took pleasure in ornamenting
his residence at Twickenham, and he chiefly adorned
it with souvenirs of his country and his military life.
Beside his hearth, stricken since by so many deaths,
were then growing up two sons, to whom he had
given the beautiful names of Guise and Condé.
That great name of Condé dazzled him, and as he
could have no share in history, he already dreamed
of writing it. All this natural activity made exile
still more insupportable, unsuited as it was to his
age, his temper, and his generous eagerness; and

his face, like those of his brothers, never lighted
up except on days when some beloved guest arriving from France restored for a moment the illusion
of his lost fatherland."

As to the Duchesse d'Orléans, who lived sometimes in Germany and sometimes in England, where
she gave her two sons, the Comte de Paris and the
Duc de Chartres, a thoroughly French education,
she was obliged to give up the struggle but not her
hopes, and she declined the fusion because, as guardian and mother, she felt unauthorized to dispose
of the sole political possession of her children: the
independence of their future.

In Paris the Orleanist party was reduced to
powerlessness, but the Orleanist spirit survived.
It was personified in the partisans of freedom of the
press and parliamentary institutions. It had representatives among the most illustrious members of
the French Academy and the best writers on the
Journal des Débats and the *Revue des Deux-Mondes.*
The politicians described as doctrinaires had denied
none of their principles or ideas. M. Guizot and
his friends could say: *Impavidum ferient ruinæ.*
In spite of the restrictions imposed upon it, the
press could make an opposition which, however
veiled, however measured, still had its importance,
and the readers of journalists so able as Cuvillier-
Fleury, John Lemoine, Jules Janin, and Laboulaye,
read between the lines things which could not be
openly expressed. To perspicacious observers it

was evident that the apparently dead Orleanist party would come to life on the day when France should return to its fondness for parliamentarism.

If Napoleon III. had listened only to himself, perhaps he would have been less hostile to the Orleans family. But such men as M. de Persigny, who was vexed at seeing him choose his ministers among former Orleanists, succeeded in making him afraid of the princes and in suggesting measures little in harmony with his character and his policy of pacification. Yet the Emperor should not have forgotten what he owed to the July government. If a Bourbon had made two such attempts as those of Strasbourg and Boulogne against Napoleon I., he would probably not have met with such patience as Louis Philippe had shown to the imperial pretender. Louis Napoleon had been amnestied after the Strasbourg conspiracy without even asking pardon. After that of Boulogne he had been imprisoned, but he had been well treated in the fortress of Ham. He had been authorized to retain there, as companions in captivity, General de Montholon and Doctor Conneau. He had received numerous visits, he had collaborated with several journals, and the proof that his detention was not too rigorous is that he escaped.

Nor should Napoleon III. have forgotten all that the July monarchy had done for the glory of his uncle. After restoring the tricolor, Louis Philippe had covered the marshals of Napoleon with favors.

He had replaced the great man's statue on the summit of the Vendôme column. He had sent one of his sons, the Prince de Joinville, to Saint-Helena for the remains of the Emperor, and brought them into Paris amidst a triumph and an apotheosis unexampled in history. It is curious to observe that the fame of the victor of Austerlitz was far more celebrated under the reign of Louis Philippe than under that of Napoleon III.

Would not the second Emperor have acted wisely if, instead of yielding to idle fears and pusillanimous counsels, he had said to the Orleanists: "You have done a great deal for the memory of my uncle. For my part, I will do a great deal for you. I will reopen to your princes the doors of the country. I will restore their commissions. I am not afraid of their presence under the flags. I have known the bitterness of exile. I do not wish to have any exiles under my reign."

It may be maintained that laws of exile are injurious to those who pass them, and that pretenders are less dangerous at home than abroad. At home they are more easily watched, and the fear of being banished dictates prudence on their part. Abroad, the saying of Tacitus may be applied to them: *Major e longinquo reverentia.* Distance increases respect. If Louis XVIII. had remained in Paris throughout the period of the Empire, in a house of the Faubourg Saint-Germain, under the name of the Comte de Lille, the Restoration would probably have been impossible. If Louis Napoleon had lived in France, under the reign of Louis Philippe, such an existence as he could have led, without fortune and with many debts, might perhaps have destroyed his prestige. Has the presence on French soil of the Comte de Paris, pretending to the royal crown, and of Prince Napoleon, pretending to the imperial one, compromised the safety of the third Republic?

Supposing that Napoleon III. had abrogated the law of exile which weighed upon the members of both branches of the Bourbon family, what would have happened? The Comte de Chambord would not have accepted the grace offered him, but his exile, by becoming voluntary, would have been less interesting. As to the Orleans princes, they would have returned to France, and we are convinced that if they had been restored to their rank and to active service in the army and navy, they would loyally have performed their military duties. General Trochu has related in his *Mémoires* that when he took possession of the government of Paris, the Empress asked him if it did not seem that the time had come to call for the patriotic assistance of the Orleans princes. The general thought the question ironical, a snare. We incline to think he was mistaken. The Empress was doubtless sincere. She thought that if the sons of King Louis Philippe had been summoned to the army, — as, for that matter, they had asked to be, — they would not have betrayed the Emperor.

Unfortunately for them, all the dynasties have
exiled each other. The first Empire proscribed the
Bourbons. The Restoration proscribed the Bonapartes. The July monarchy proscribed both the
Bonapartes and the Bourbons of the elder branch.
The second Empire proscribed the Bourbons of both
branches. Each dynasty has paid the penalty of
retaliation. To each of them might have been said:
"Suffer the law thou hast enacted." *Patere legem
quam tulisti.* In his programme as a candidate for
the presidency of the Republic, Louis Napoleon had
inserted this wise sentence: "I who have known
exile and captivity long ardently for the day when
the country may without danger put an end to all
proscriptions and efface the last traces of civil
discords." Why did not Napoleon III., who had
nobody to fear at the beginning of his reign, recall
the words of Louis Bonaparte?

CHAPTER X

A T the moment when France thought it had inaugurated a period of absolute prosperity, a storm was gathering at the other extremity of Europe. Agreement between two men would have been enough to maintain the peace of the world. Their amity would have advanced the cause of civilization by giant strides. The misunderstanding which divided them was to drag after it incalculable disasters. We are persuaded that a few minutes' talk between them would have spared humanity the slaughters which stained the middle of the nineteenth century with blood.

Born July 6, 1796, the Emperor Nicholas was fifty-six years old when Napoleon III. ascended the throne. The sovereign of Russia was then at the height of his prestige and his power. His gigantic height, his fiery eyes, his martial and imposing air, pointed him out as the subduer of peoples. He considered himself the delegate of God upon earth, the champion of legitimacy, the supporter of thrones, the vanquisher of the revolution, the Agamemnon of sovereigns. Brought up with severity in his child-

73

hood by General Lambodorff, he was harsh to others
but rigorous to himself.　He had given Saint Petersburg the aspect of a camp.　Cadets of but seven
years old wore uniforms and helmets there, and
gravely saluted officers passing in the streets.

The Emperor Nicholas had displayed extraordinary energy from the time of his advent to the
throne.　December 26, 1825, he came out alone
from the Winter Palace, and in order to reach his
horse, which it had been impossible to bring to him,
he passed through the crowd of insurgents as far as
the spot where the Alexander column now stands.
"During this passage," he said afterwards, "I
scarcely foresaw the issue of this wretched day; but
no sooner did I find myself on horseback, and that
I had mastered the crowd, than I no longer doubted
of success."　In fact, the Czar went straight up to
the insurgent soldiers, and, addressing the regiment
which was uttering seditious cries, he said: "This
is not your place; this is where my faithful soldiers
belong; go over yonder, among the rebels, and take
your arms with you."　And he subdued the military
sedition by this act of decision and courage.

Nor did the intrepid sovereign display less firmness when the cholera broke out in Saint Petersburg
in 1832.　The people had risen and massacred in
the hay-market several physicians, thinking that
they were poisoning the sick by order of the government.　The Czar went instanter into the midst
of this furious crowd, accompanied by Count Orloff:

" Off with your hats and kneel down," shouted he, "and begin by making the sign of the cross with me, and praying God to abate the scourge, instead of drawing down His wrath upon us by your crimes." Then, when the people had obeyed him, he made them understand their injustice and their mistake, and recalled them to reason.

During the European crisis of 1848 and 1849, the Emperor Nicholas had posed as the defender of social order, as the governor and the Providence of sovereigns. After suppressing the insurrection of Hungary against the Emperor Francis Joseph by the armed intervention of Russia, he asked of Austria a sum so moderate that it did not even cover the cost of the campaign, intending thus to show that money had no value in his eyes, and that Russia was rich enough to fight solely for the glory of its arms and the triumph of its principles. The young Emperor Francis Joseph said to him at Warsaw, in front of the statue of Sobieski: "There is the first saviour of Austria. You are the second." And the two sovereigns fell into each other's arms. When the Czar appeared in Germany, it was less as a traveller than as a suzerain. In the Germanic Confederation he had formed for himself a submissive and respectful clientèle.

At Saint Petersburg the Emperor appeared to the people, of whom he was the idol, at times under a familiar aspect, and again in majestic pomp. On the same day, one might see him walking alone in

the streets and returning to the Winter Palace in
the first passing droschky; then presiding over a
grand ceremony regulated by him according to the
most exact and pompous etiquette. An autocrat
even in the smallest things, he occasionally performed police duty on his promenades. One day he
brought back to his barracks a soldier who had left
it in the night without permission. Another time,
meeting a foreigner who was tranquilly smoking in
the street before him, he said to him politely: "Sir,
you seem not to know the law of this country. Permit me to tell you that if a police officer should find
you smoking in the street in this way, you would
get into trouble with him. That is why I recom-
mend you to throw away your cigar immediately."
It is added that the foreigner was much astonished
on afterwards finding out that the obliging person
who had given him this warning was no other than
the Emperor.

There was in the life of the Czar a mixture of
Asiatic ostentation and thoroughly military simplicity. His reception rooms in the Winter Palace
were as magnificent as his bedchamber, which we
have visited, was modest. He slept on a narrow
iron bedstead, at the side of which was a soldier's
musket and a pair of old slippers which the Empress
had embroidered for him soon after their marriage.
He was not only the handsomest man in his Empire,
but the most robust. It was said in 1853 that he
had never been ill but once in his life, and that dur-

ing this sickness, which lasted a fortnight, he had insisted on lying on a sofa, wrapped in a military cloak. Unacquainted with fatigue himself, he could not comprehend it in others; he kept his court constantly on the alert. Kindly and affable as a rule, but inexorable and terrible when he had to punish a functionary guilty of peculation or prevarication; capable of generosity, but disposed to extreme severity when he thought duty required him to be implacable; considering himself as a great judge appointed by Providence, he drew from religion itself the conviction that his mission as a defender of divine right and the orthodox faith had a sacred character.

Was there an impassable gulf between the Czar and Napoleon III.? We do not believe it. Russia and France had sympathies in common, and the two sovereigns might have come to an understanding. Napoleon III. was not intentionally the ally of the Turks. In his youth he had longed to fight against them under the standard of the Emperor Nicholas. Hence a policy tending toward the emancipation of the Christians of the Orient would not have been contrary to his antecedents. Nor could he forget that the Emperor Alexander, the brother and predecessor of Nicholas, had been in 1814 the friend and protector of the Empress Josephine, Queen Hortense, and Prince Eugène de Beauharnais; nor that in 1839 the Emperor Nicholas had given his cherished daughter, the Grand Duchess Marie, in marriage

to the son of Prince Eugène, Duc Maximilien de
Leuchtenberg, and that this princess was using all
her influence at her father's court to maintain
friendly relations between Russia and France.

As President of the Republic Louis Napoleon had
had every reason to be satisfied with the Emperor
Nicholas. He was represented at Saint Petersburg
by a minister plenipotentiary, General de Castelbajac,
a distinguished soldier and member of an old Gascon
family, who received there a much more cordial
reception than had been given to the representatives
of Louis Philippe.

The Coup d'Etat had produced a good impression
at Saint Petersburg. General de Castelbajac wrote
to the Minister of Foreign Affairs, Marquis Turgot,
December 15, 1851: "The Emperor and the Chancellor of the Empire have received the news of
December 2 very favorably; they both consider the
expectation of what might happen in 1852 as detri-
mental to the tranquillity of Europe. The proclamations of the President of the Republic have confirmed
the Emperor Nicholas in the high idea he entertained of the loyalty and courage of the Prince."
And on January 1, 1852: "The Emperor does not
conceal the fact that he is heartily in favor of Prince
Louis Napoleon, who seems to him to have rendered
a vast service to France and Europe, which on an
appointed day were menaced by the united attempts
of the party of disorder. His Majesty has praised
the conduct of our army in the highest terms."

January 29 General de Castelbajac sent to Marquis Turgot the following account of an audience granted him by the Czar the day before: "The Emperor expressed the most sympathetic sentiments toward Prince Napoleon, and the political satisfaction he had experienced from the latest governmental measures, the promulgation of the Constitution, and more particularly his preamble. He manifested his admiration (this is his own word) several times for the frankness, the precision, the virile eloquence of this important document. 'By all that he has just done,' said the Emperor to me, 'the President of the Republic merits the gratitude of France and of all Europe. He has recognized the position better than all the statesmen of the last two reigns, better than any of us, and if he follows his political programme exactly, without allowing himself to be influenced by vulgar ambitions, he will have established himself in politics and history at one stroke above us all.' "

Naturally, Louis Napoleon had been affected by such flattering words. We believe that at this period nothing would have pleased him better than a Franco-Russian alliance. He had said before the Chamber of Peers, September 28, 1840: "I represent a principle, a cause, and a defeat. The principle is the sovereignty of the people; the cause is that of the Empire; the defeat is Waterloo." He knew very well that he could never avenge this defeat unless he were in accord with Russia. Hence we

incline to think that he would have preferred the
Russian to the English alliance.   But we shall see
hereafter that he had no room for choice.   In 1852
he neglected no means of gaining the good will of
the Emperor Nicholas.   He sent to Saint Petersburg
on an exclusively personal mission a Frenchman who
had belonged to the horse-guards in Russia, and of
whom the Emperor Nicholas had retained a favorable impression.   This was the Baron de Heeckeren,
who said to the Czar: "Sire, the Emperor Alexander, your brother, frequently wrote to Queen
Hortense.   If Prince Louis Napoleon supposed that
it would be agreeable to you to have these letters,
I am convinced that he would send them to you
with pleasure."   "Certainly," replied the Emperor,
"I would like to have Alexander's letters, and I
would thank the Prince for his courteous action.   I
know the Prince already; I held him on my knees
at Malmaison when I went there with my brother
Alexander to pay my court to the Empress Josephine
and Queen Hortense.   Make him understand that I
shall never be one of his adversaries."   The letters
of Queen Hortense were sent, and from that time
a very courteous correspondence was established
between Louis Napoleon and the Emperor Nicholas.

CHAPTER XI

ALTHOUGH the Czar showed his sympathy with the President of the French Republic, he did not desire that Louis Napoleon should become Napoleon III. September 3, 1852, General de Castelbajac wrote to M. Drouyn de Lhuys, Minister of Foreign Affairs: "I know that the Emperor always employs the most amiable expressions in speaking of the Prince; but he invariably follows them by others which, in spite of himself, display anxiety. 'The Prince must not spoil his position,' he will say; 'he must continue to govern with prudence,' and other phrases the real meaning of which is that, in his opinion, the Prince ought not to change the form of government." In the same letter the general adds: "The Northern courts have little sympathy for us. What they feel about us is a mixture of fear and distrust."

It is curious to observe that the Emperor Nicholas was unfavorable to both the Comte de Chambord and the Orleans princes. What he would have desired for France was the maintenance of the Republic. General de Castelbajac wrote in No-

vember, 1852 : " If the Emperor does not disavow
his legitimist principles, he none the less holds the
Comte de Chambord and the Orleans princes very
cheap. He considers the latter as the revolution
incarnate ; and as to the former, though he likes
and pities him, he tells me that he regards him not
simply as impossible, but as dangerous, and that if
it depended on him to replace him on the throne,
he would take good care not to do it in the existing
state of Europe."

At the same period the general thus expressed
himself to M. Thouvenel, then political director in
the office of the Ministry of Foreign Affairs: " The
Emperor admires Prince Louis Napoleon; he considers him as the saviour of France. But absolute
sovereign though he be, he believes that with us
the Republic is, and will long continue to be, the
strongest obstacle in the way of an outburst of
mobocracy. It will seem strange to men who do
not know him, and even to those who do, that he
advises the continuation of our Republic. But
when he says : Keep the Republic strong and conservative, and beware of the Empire, it is the loyal
counsel of a friend who points out the danger and
wishes to keep us away from it."

At bottom, what chiefly displeased the Czar in
the restoration of the French Empire was that he
saw in it a violation of the treaties of 1815, which
had stricken the family of Napoleon with perpetual
deposition; he also thought it an attack on the

traditions of the Holy Alliance, of which he considered himself the champion. A monarchy based upon election and popular sovereignty appeared to him a negation of divine right, which he regarded as a dogma of faith. He had besides a presentiment that if Louis Napoleon became emperor, he would dispute with him the rôle of arbiter of Europe, and that the second French Empire would not resist the temptation to follow the warlike paths of the first.

Badly informed by his minister plenipotentiary at Paris, M. de Kisseleff, and by several Russian ladies, the Princesse de Liéven, Madame de Kalerghi, Madame de Seebach, and the Princesse Menchikoff, who were then in France, the Emperor Nicholas had supposed that Napoleon III. could have only an ephemeral authority, and that to contract a serious alliance with him was impossible. The Czar had formed his opinion of imperial France from what was said about in the salons of the opposition. He had been led astray by both his secret and his official diplomatists.

Still, when he found all governments recognizing the new empire, the Russian sovereign concluded to recognize it also, but with a reservation of detail which wounded Napoleon III. Instead of styling the Emperor of the French "*my good brother,*" he addressed him as "*my good friend.*"

Napoleon III. was offended. But, always master of himself, he took the thing wittily. On this subjoct we read, in M. Rothan's work, *L'Europe et le Second Empire:* "January 5, 1853, the Emperor received the Russian envoy with great ceremony. He took the Czar's letter from his hands, but instead of passing it unopened to his Minister of Foreign Affairs, as is customary, — for he knew its contents from the copy in cipher, — he broke the seal. He leisurely unfolded it, and, after reading it attentively, he begged M. de Kisseleff, in his most caressing tones, to thank the Emperor Nicholas warmly for his kindness, and especially for the expression, *my good friend,* which he had employed ; for, said he, 'if one puts up with his brothers, he chooses his friends.'" M. Rothan goes on to say : "An attaché of the imperial legation, M. de Meyendorff, who was present at the audience, told me one day that M. de Kisseleff stopped short as he was going down the staircase of the Tuileries, and giving him a troubled look, like a man who regrets having been made the instrument of a mistake, said, 'Decidedly, he is somebody.'"

Now let us see by a despatch addressed to M. Drouyn de Lhuys by General de Castelbajac, January 16, 1853, how he was received by the Emperor Nicholas when he presented the letters accrediting him to the Russian court as the minister plenipotentiary of the Emperor of the French.

As soon as the general was introduced into the Czar's cabinet, His Majesty came to meet and embrace him, saying : "I am glad that our affairs are at last terminated; I thank the Emperor Napoleon for it, and also for having confirmed you in your position near me, my dear general. It pleases me to see in this a proof of his friendship."

The Czar received his credentials, and then, having dismissed the master of ceremonies and his assistant, who had introduced General de Castelbajac, and, as is customary, having made him sit down opposite him at his writing-table, a conversation which lasted nearly an hour spontaneously took place between them.

General de Castelbajac: "Sire, I rejoice with Your Imperial Majesty on the moderation and extreme good sense of the Emperor Napoleon, since they prevent the repose of Europe from being endangered, and I am especially grateful for his continuing my confidential functions near you. I wish I could respond to this confidence by assisting to renew the natural and useful alliance which ought to exist between our two nations, and which the late negotiations must have chilled."

The Emperor Nicholas. "The Emperor has too much elevation of mind, heart, and character not to make a sane estimate of my position as well as his own, and I hope that our frankness and mutual esteem, I may add my affection for him personally, will perpetuate our agreement. I have always told you, and I repeat, my dear general, that no one approved more than I, or did more toward inducing the sovereigns my allies to approve the bold and

skilful deed of December 2, and all the patriotic
conduct of Prince Louis Napoleon. If he has the
confidence in me which I deserve, no one is more
disposed to support his governmental measures,
which I admit to be useful to all Europe, and all
that may be to his personal advantage. But with
all the political changes which I have seen in France
since coming to the throne, how can I as a sovereign
prudently bind myself to a future which will not be
his, or depend directly upon him, with any chance of
its continuance? Be assured, my dear general, that,
as I have told you before, there is no question in my
mind of the Comte de Chambord, whom I regard as
impossible and even as dangerous in France ; but I
am loyal, and I will promise only what I can perform, and God only can guarantee the future."

G. de C. "True, Sire, God only can guarantee
the future, but sovereigns can settle or unsettle it
by acts which inspire either confidence or distrust.
Fortunately the Emperor Napoleon is strong enough
to be moderate ; he is wise in thinking that a good
friend is better than a doubtful brother, and I am
sure he may rely on the well-known loyalty of
Your Majesty as well as upon your concurrence in
all that may be useful to both countries, and the
general interests of Europe."

The Emperor. "The Emperor Napoleon has long
been assured of my confidence, and I hope he will
treat me as a real friend by giving me his, because
with me words are not mere sounds, but have a real

meaning. I am expecting his reply to my letter, and you may assure him of my wish that we should be on intimate terms, since between men capable of mutual esteem they may often be more useful than purely official relations. If he will address me in writing, or confidentially through you, I will reply with equal frankness; we may not always hold the same opinions, but candid and direct communications may result in mutual understanding and agreement."

General de Castelbajac concludes as follows the despatch in which he describes this interview with the Czar: "I must not forget to remark that the first words of the Emperor Nicholas were addressed to me in the presence of the master of ceremonies and his aid; consequently were meant to be heard and repeated, and I have no doubt they will bring me a throng of visits from the well-drilled Russian courtiers."

We have just proved that at the beginning of 1853 the terms in which the Russian and the French emperors spoke of each other were by no means those of irreconcilable adversaries. At this period there were no signs either in the official world, the press, or the salons which could indicate that war between the two empires was imminent. If the Russian sovereign had sent an envoy to the Tuileries whose sentiments towards France resembled those entertained by General de Castelbajac towards Russia, we think that an understanding would have been established between two great nations which, instead of suspecting and trying to thwart each other, might amicably have divided the supremacy of Europe, France in the West and Russia in the East. With a few mutual concessions the *two good friends* might have ended as *two good brothers*.

Unfortunately it was otherwise, and the Emperor Nicholas instead of confiding in France turned to England, a fact which he must afterwards have regretted bitterly. At a soirée given at the palace of the Grande Duchesse Hélène on the 9th of January, 1853, he said to the ambassador of Queen Victoria, Sir Hamilton Seymour : "It is essential that our two governments should be on better terms. When we are on good terms I have no anxiety about the West of Europe; what others think is really of small importance. . . . You see, we have a sick man on our hands, a very sick man; it would be a great misfortune if he should slip out of them some day before all necessary arrangements are made."

January 14, the Czar went so far as to formulate a scheme of division with the ambassador : " The Danubian principalities," said he, " are in fact an independent State under my protection; that solution may continue. Servia may receive a similar form of government, and Bulgaria likewise ; there is no reason that I know of why we should not make an independent State of that country. As to Egypt, I perfectly comprehend its importance to England. All I can say is that in case of a partition after the

downfall of the Ottoman Empire, if you take possession of Egypt, I shall have no objections to make.
I will say the same of Candia; that island may suit
you, and I do not know why it should not belong to
England."

The English government not merely repulsed the
offers of the tempter, but, notwithstanding their confidential character, it made them public by including
the account in the official documents communicated
to Parliament. The intention of the Emperor
Nicholas had been to entice England into a partition
of Turkey to the exclusion of France, and he had
failed.

It must be owned that in spite of the liking
showed by the Czar to General de Castelbajac, he
never at any time made overtures to him resembling
those he made to Sir Hamilton Seymour. At bottom he had never been pleased that Louis Napoleon
should have transformed himself into Napoleon III.,
and notwithstanding his advances he never made
any attempt to establish serious relations with him.
It may be affirmed that France would have accepted
the Russian alliance which England contemned. If
Nicholas had said to General de Castelbajac what he
said to the British ambassador, there would have
been no Crimean War, the days of Tilsit would have
been repeated, and the face of the world would
have been changed.

CHAPTER XII

A T the beginning of 1853 the long and laborious negotiations going on at Constantinople on the subject of the Holy Places interested but a very few persons, and the public, knowing little about a question relegated to the cautious precincts of chancellors' offices or the silence of cloisters, did not imagine that a litigation whose character seemed more theological than political could ever disturb the peace of Europe. Any one who would like to know the details of this question, which was the primary cause of the Crimean War, may find them in M. Louis Thouvenel's remarkable work: *Nicolas Ier et Napoléon III.* In the papers of his illustrious father, the author has found papers which are a complete summary of the affair of the Holy Places.

The capitulations concluded between France and Turkey at various times since Francis I., and notably in 1740, provided that the Latin monks should retain in Jerusalem the sanctuaries which they had possessed from time immemorial. However, in consequence of the encroachments of the Greeks and Armenians, supported by Russia, they had lost their hold of several sanctuaries. When, in 1850, Prince Louis Napoleon ordered General Aupick, French minister at Constantinople, to remind Sultan Abdul Medjid of the imprescriptibility of the ancient privileges of the Latins in Jerusalem, he suspected neither the consequences which such a claim was likely to entail, nor the inveteracy with which the Emperor Nicholas would defend the Greeks against the Latins. It was forgotten that public opinion counts for nothing in politics in Russia but that it is all-powerful in religious matters; that the Czar, considering himself as a sort of hieratic personage, a crowned pontiff, regarded all the orthodox of the Ottoman empire as his protégés, his "faithful"; and that to maintain his prestige in their eyes was the chief object of his ambition. Hence the question of the Holy Places had extraordinary importance for him. He saw in it the touchstone of his influence in the Orient. The monks were but supernumeraries in this religious drama. The principal actor was the Czar himself.

February 8, 1852, the Sultan had issued a firman which was a sort of compromise between the claims of France and those of Russia. It stated that as the great cupola of the church of the Holy Sepulchre belonged to the entire temple, the exclusive claims of the Latins both for this and the smaller cupola, as well as for the place of the descent of the Cross from Golgotha, the arcades of the Virgin, the great church of Bethlehem, and the grotto where Christ

was born, were not just, and that things must remain in their existing condition. But the Sultan
had granted three privileges to the Latins which
French diplomacy endeavored to represent as important successes. Firstly, he had consented to restore
to the Latin patriarch of Jerusalem, the delegate of
the Holy See, the key of the great door of the church
of Bethlehem; secondly, he had given orders that a
star with a Latin inscription which had disappeared
in 1847 should be replaced in the grotto of the
Nativity; thirdly, he had granted to the Catholic
commission the right to celebrate its own worship
concurrently with the other rites in the church called
the Virgin's Tomb.

In reality these concessions amounted to very
little. Yet the Emperor Nicholas would not consent to them, and when it became a question of
carrying them into execution, France encountered
in Jerusalem a crowd of difficulties. At the end of
February, 1853, Napoleon III. said to M. Thouvenel:
"I do not know the details of the affair of the Holy
Places; I regret the fuss that has been made about
them, and still more the exaggerated importance the
matter has assumed, but we cannot yield the little
we have obtained."

Meanwhile the question of the Holy Places had
not diminished the friendliness of the Czar toward
the representative of the Emperor of the French.
General de Castelbajac wrote to M. Thouvenel
February 15, 1853: "I have given a great fête, ball,

and supper on the occasion of our Emperor's marriage. Chancellor de Nesselrode, all the ministers, the entire court, and all the diplomatic corps came to it with alacrity, and also the hereditary Grand Duke and his three brothers in the most friendly way. The effect of this has been all the better because these princes had never set foot in the French legation, neither under King Louis Philippe nor the Republic. Nor had they been for a long time at any reception at the foreign legations, which in general are held very cheap in Russia. As to the Emperor and the Empress, since their family troubles and the loss of their youth, they go nowhere, and I was unwilling to expose myself to a refusal which they give to everybody, but which under existing circumstances might be misinterpreted by the public. I beg you to let me know precisely to what extent I may intervene in the question of the Holy Places, which *must* be terminated."

A fortnight later General de Castelbajac sent a despatch to M. Drouyn de Lhuys, in which he said: "I have received the congratulations of the Emperor Nicholas on the marriage of the Emperor Napoleon. He told me that he had three portraits of the Empress Eugénie, one in Andalusian costume, and that he had just received a bust of Her Majesty by M. de Nieuwerkerke, which he thought very good. As to portraits, I regret having no better ones to offer to the Russian court, where they are so greatly interested in our Empress."

Finally, we cite this curious passage from a letter of M. Thouvenel to General de Castelbajac (March 1, 1853): "I will tell you that the Russians are perfectly well treated at our court, and that the salon of the Princesse de Liéven is again frequented by our statesmen. People are beginning to talk, too soon perhaps, of the advantages of an alliance with Russia. If in the contingent future at Saint Petersburg such an alliance is actually possible, it would be a bad time to choose for quarrelling with us about a key! The presence of the grand dukes at your ball has produced the best effect here, and everybody credits you with the change for the better in our relations."

At Paris as well as at Saint Petersburg the maintenance of the peace so necessary to both emperors and to their peoples was sincerely desired. It seemed incredible that for matters like a key, a lamp, a passage, a dormer window, two nations such as Russia and France, with so many common interests and mutual sympathies, could come to blows and shed torrents of blood. To sensible men such an hypothesis seemed a criminal absurdity. The two capitals abandoned themselves gayly to the pleasures of the season. The definite settlement of the question of the Holy Places seemed close at hand, and in Paris it was believed that the matters of detail which delayed this solution would be easily overcome. Things suddenly changed their aspect. Unexpected tidings came like thunder out of a clear

NICHOLAS I.

sarabia, and has visited the Black Sea fleet in the roadstead of Sebastopol. Hardly has he arrived in the Turkish capital when he openly sends to Athens one of the heroes of Navarino, Vice-Admiral Khorniloff, to confer with Otho I., King of Greece; and the wife of this prince, Queen Amélie, believing herself destined to become Empress of the East, tells her courtiers that she will install herself on the shores of the Bosphorus in the palace of Bechik-Tasch as soon as Constantinople becomes the seat of the new Greek Empire.

The Porte is anxiously awaiting what the redoubtable and mysterious ambassador may have to say. March 10, he is received by Sultan Abdul Medjid. To the general stupefaction he presents himself before the Commander of the Faithful in citizen's dress, in a frock coat, instead of in uniform, as is the custom. Everybody is wondering whether this arrogant diplomat carries peace or war in the creases of this garment. The offence seems to have been carried as far as possible, and yet it is only just begun. After the audience with the Sultan, the Czar's ambassador is obliged by etiquette to call at once at the Ministry of Foreign Affairs. The minister, Fuad Effendi, is waiting for him at the door of a salon brilliantly decorated for the occasion. The Prince passes this salon, and, instead of entering, goes disdainfully on his way. The next day he makes the Grand Vizier understand that in refusing to enter the house of the Minister of Foreign

Affairs he had not intended to insult the Turkish
government, but had thought it impossible to treat
with a *deceitful minister.* Never have the rules of
etiquette and the diplomatic proprieties received so
rude a shock. Fuad sends in his resignation. The
alarmed Abdul Medjid accepts it, and in the place
of Fuad appoints Refaat Pasha, *recommended* to His
Highness by the Emperor Nicholas.

Is the Czar about to urge matters to a crisis, and
will the mission of Prince Menchikoff result in war?
General de Castelbajac does not think so. He writes
from Saint Petersburg to M. Drouyn de Lhuys,
March 14, 1853: "I think the chief object of the
Emperor Nicholas is to resume ascendancy in
Turkey, so as to gratify his religious and political
tendencies, and more particularly the religious
fanaticism of his people, with which he is obliged
to reckon. It is a purely moral influence which
Prince Menchikoff is to exercise. The armaments
are formed simply to aid this moral action, and also
to respond to those of Austria, and not leave to her
in the eyes of the orthodox Greeks the sole honor of
an energetic act of protection." Not long before,
Count de Leiningen, ambassador extraordinary of
Austria, had obtained from the Sultan by means of
a menacing ultimatum the recall of the troops who
were blocking Montenegro.

In spite of his optimism General de Castelbajac
was very sensible that the peace of Europe was by
no means certain. "However," he adds, in the

same despatch, "the Emperor Nicholas is ready for war, and we must avoid pushing him into it in spite of himself, which would be only too easy on account of his fear of the fragility of the Turkish Empire, the ambition of his young officers with his son Constantine at their head, and the patriotic and religious fanaticism of his people and his army."

The general concluded by these wise and noble words: "I am far from adhering to the system of peace at any price; but I prefer a peace that may honorably and usefully be maintained to a war which, under existing political and social conditions in Europe, would in any case be a frightful moral and material disturbance, even if it did not lead to the triumph of the modern barbarians. My fears I express to my country in an undertone, and my opinion concerning the danger of a war to all Europe in a very loud one at Saint Petersburg. As to peace at any price, the national dignity, the firmness of character, the energetic and prompt decision which the Emperor Napoleon displays in every important emergency, are so well known to France and Europe that pacific measures would not win him the blame, but the general gratitude and approbation both of France and foreign nations."

Meanwhile the vague and indeterminate character of Prince Menchikoff's mission was beginning to cause the diplomatists some apprehension. March 16, he had sent to the Porte his first official communication. In it he recalled the fact, apropos of

the affair of the Holy Places, that for a year Turkey
had done nothing to satisfy the claims of Russia
against the firman of February 8, 1852, and the
advantages it conferred on the Latins. By a second
communication of March 22, he claimed not a mere
rectification of the firman, but a diplomatic arrange-
ment in virtue of which Russia should be treated at
Jerusalem on the same footing as France. He
demanded that the key of the church of Bethlehem
should be taken from the Latins, that they should
be excluded from the Tomb of the Virgin, that the
Greeks should be authorized to undertake alone and
at their own cost the reconstruction of the great
cupola of the church of the Holy Sepulchre, and
finally that Turkey should bind herself to make no
changes at Jerusalem without a previous understanding with Russia.

In Paris the tranquillity of the people concerning
the Eastern question was already somewhat disturbed. The journals were expressing certain fears.
In the *Revue des Deux-Mondes* (Chronicle of the
Fortnight, March 31, 1853) M. de Mazade wrote:
"It is in every way essential that at certain moments
public attention should be concentrated on a single
point and absorbed in the expectation of one of those
events which take precedence of all others and sum-
marize a situation. When this is not one of those
revolutionary convulsions which imperil the general
order of societies, it is one of the incidents which
serve to measure the fragility of peace and the

balance of power in the West. A courier who arrives with an unexpected message causes a fluctuation on the Bourse, that thermometer of the emotions, hopes, perplexities, and often the superstitions of public opinion. What is the unique preoccupation under which everybody has been living for several days in Europe? One perceives at once that it is the Eastern question, and the new aspect it has suddenly put on in consequence of Prince Menchikoff's mission to Constantinople. This dark spot which has been rising lately on the horizon has unexpectedly been transformed into an almost threatening cloud. News is anxiously awaited every morning. What was the secret of this extraordinary mission? Under one form or another does not Prince Menchikoff carry with him the sentence of the downfall of the Ottoman Empire?"

The situation was still further aggravated by the return of the English ambassador, Lord Stratford de Redcliffe, to Constantinople, April 4, 1853. Accustomed for a dozen years to rule on the shores of the Bosphorus, where he appointed and deposed grand viziers and ministers at his pleasure, this haughty and vindictive diplomat, who assumed the manners of the proconsuls of old Rome, had never forgiven the Emperor Nicholas for having refused to accept him, in 1833, as minister of England at Saint Petersburg. This old grudge helped to excite him against Russia, and made him one of the principal authors of the war in the East.

The dispositions of France were still most conciliatory. Instead of sending back to Constantinople the Marquis de La Valette, who had obtained the firman of February 8, 1852, the cause of such wrath and recrimination, a new ambassador, M. de Lacour, was appointed. He had had no hand in the previous negotiations, and on April 5, 1853, he arrived in Constantinople as the bearer of the most moderate and sincerely pacific instructions.

The question of the Holy Places presently took a secondary rank. The Porte having consented to the restoration of the church of the Holy Sepulchre in its present form, and to the erection of a Russian church and hospital in Jerusalem, Prince Menchikoff offered no further objection to the other privileges which France had obtained for the Latins by the firman of February 8, 1852. But the Prince put forward another claim of widely different importance. He demanded the conclusion of a treaty by which the rights and immunities of the Church and of the Greek rites should be placed under the protection of Russia. What the Czar really wanted was the *official protection* of Russia over all its coreligionists in the Ottoman Empire, carrying with it civil and administrative jurisdiction, which, according to the Russian interpretation of former concessions by the Sultans, formed the appanage of the power exerted by the Greek patriarchs over the faithful of their communion. May 17, the former grand viziers, pashas, and ulemas, assembled in full conclave at Constantinople, unanimously repelled this claim.

Since May 4 Prince Menchikoff had left Pera and withdrawn to the Russian frigate *Bessarabia*, anchored opposite Budjukdéré, in the upper Bosphorus, near the Black Sea. The following day he had presented himself without asking permission at the palace of the Sultan, who had just lost his mother, and said to him: "I entreat Your Majesty to weigh thoroughly the possible consequences of prolonged resistance to the wishes of the Emperor Nicholas." Finding that he could obtain nothing, in spite of his energy, the impetuous ambassador left Budjukdéré on the frigate *Foudroyant*, in the night of May 21–22, 1853, and re-entered the Black Sea, his heart filled with rancor. His attitude had been menacing, but no one as yet believed that war would be the result, and Napoleon III. had by no means abandoned the hope of preserving peace in the East when he went to establish himself at the palace of Saint-Cloud on the 25th of May.

CHAPTER XIV

SAINT-CLOUD, DIEPPE, AND COMPIÈGNE

THE Emperor and Empress left the Tuileries, May 25, 1853, for the palace of Saint-Cloud, where they intended to spend the summer. What pleased the Empress Eugénie best at Saint-Cloud was not the splendor of the château, but the leafy twilight of the park. She loved to stroll beneath its trees, that had stood for centuries, and across its verdant sward, to climb its picturesque hillocks, to look at the great fountain, the arcades framed by symmetrical architecture, the two cascades whose waters fall from one height to another and from which flashes a white foam sparkling with a thousand reflections under the sunlight, or at night beneath the lustre of colored lamps. She liked to go up into the observatory of Demosthenes, that little Greek monument situated on a platform whence the Seine can be seen flowing at the foot of the park, and on the horizon the principal public buildings of Paris: the Arch of Triumph, the dome of the Invalides, the Tuileries, the Louvre, the towers of Saint Sulpice, the Panthéon. In 1853 the second Emperor and Empress Eugénie tranquilly enjoyed the pleasure of reigning at the château of Saint-Cloud. They found it a delightful place.

During the invasion of 1815 Blücher, who had installed himself and his pack in the chamber of Henrietta of England, and made a veritable kennel of it, admired none the less the splendors of the castle and the park. Dining with Metternich, he said to him : " A man must have been a fool to run off to Moscow when he had all these fine things at home ! " It was, in fact, from Saint-Cloud that on May 9, 1812, Napoleon I., surrounded by a splendid court, made his ceremonious departure for that Russian campaign which was to be so fatal to him. Alas ! it was also from Saint-Cloud that Napoleon III., destined never to return, departed for a still more lamentable expedition. But in 1853 no thought was given to either past or future woes. The new Empire, full of youth, enthusiasm, and self-confidence, fancied that the thunderbolt would never strike it.

The Emperor and Empress left Saint-Cloud for Dieppe, August 20, 1853. The journey occupied four hours and a half. All along the road houses were draped, and the imperial train was greeted by the people with hearty acclamations. At Dieppe the approaches to the railway station had been taken possession of by an immense concourse of spectators who, with incessant shouting, accompanied the Emperor and Empress to the Hôtel de Ville, which had been made ready for their reception. In

the evening the whole town was illuminated. The
sovereign and his charming companion went on foot
and unattended to the terrace of the bathing establishment.   The next morning they went to hear
Mass in the church of Saint Jacques, which contains
specimens of every variety of the pointed arch. The
transepts date from the twelfth century, the nave
from the thirteenth, the porch and the bell-tower
from the fourteenth, the chapels from the fifteenth,
the choir, the porch tower, the treasury, and the
Virgin's chapel from the sixteenth and the Renais-
sance.

The quarters of Their Majesties at the City Hall
were very simple. They had been furnished in Per-
sian linen and carpeted with matting. This simplicity contrasted agreeably with the splendors of the
Tuileries, Saint-Cloud, Fontainebleau, and Compiègne. August 27, 1853, the Emperor and Empress visited the lace establishment founded in 1826
at her own cost by the Duchesse de Berry, where a
large number of young girls simultaneously find the
means of livelihood and the benefits of a Christian
life. In the evening they went to a play in the
theatre which the same princess had opened August 8, 1826, and which had been built in six
months. August 29, Their Majesties received the
visit of King Jerome and Prince Napoleon, who
came from Havre on the imperial yacht, *La Reine
Hortense*, and in the evening were present at a concert given in the City Hall. The beach had never

been more elegant. From morning to night the long street which borders it was thronged with superb equipages, some of which were drawn by four horses. At the casino the animation was extreme. The days of the Restoration seemed to have returned. The Emperor, more than ever in love with the Empress, was transported with the few days of seaside life which he snatched from politics. At that time, hoping that the clouds gathering in the East would soon be dispelled, he peacefully enjoyed the happiness granted him by Providence. September 10 Their Majesties left Dieppe and returned to Saint-Cloud.

Napoleon III., after studying for himself the various schemes which for nearly a century had been elaborated in vain, had just determined on the execution of a series of works which were to afford the port of Dieppe every possible improvement. The beach was a sorry-looking place. Immense earthworks cut off the sea view without availing for the defence of the town. Old and mutilated towers were in the way of embellishments. All these obstacles were to disappear at the will of the Emperor. Covered with grass plats and flowers, the beach was to be transformed into a superb promenade more than twelve hundred metres in length, beginning at the cliff of the château and covering the whole space between the town and the sea.

Napoleon III. and the Empress went from palace to palace, from ovation to ovation: after the château

of the Tuileries that of Saint-Cloud ; after the acclamations of the people of Dieppe those of the de-
partments of the North. Starting from Saint-Cloud,
they reached Arras the same day, where they found
deputations from nine hundred communes of the
Pas-de-Calais. Each commune had its banner, each
banner its device. The Sisters of Charity had
placed the little orphans in front of the asylum, as
if to put them under the patronage of the Empress. From the top of a triumphal arch representing the ancient gateway of Arras, young girls rained
flowers on the imperial carriage.

September 23, after having visited Valenciennes,
where companies of miners in their working dress,
carrying their implements and with their mining
lamps in their caps, defiled before them, the Emperor and Empress made a ceremonious entry into
Lille. The mayor offered to Napoleon III. the keys
of the city, the same which had been offered to
Louis XIV. and Napoleon I. The Emperor went
out on foot the next day to visit the hospitals. In
the evening he and the Empress attended a superb
ball in the Hôtel de Ville.

September 25, Their Majesties visited the camp of
Saint Omer, the 26th Dunkirk, the 27th Calais and
Boulogne. Everywhere the same huzzas and the
same ovations met them. At Boulogne, the city
where Napoleon I. had equipped a fleet and formed a
camp for the invasion of England, the English resi-
dents sent to Napoleon III. an address expressed in

enthusiastic terms : " We pray God to spare Your Majesty to France in order to cement its friendship with Great Britain and make the two countries the guardians of European liberty. . . . If the world has admired the prowess displayed by Napoleon I. on battle-fields, it admires no less the magnanimity of his successor whose Empire is peace. . . . We pray Heaven to shed its sweetest blessings on Her Majesty the Empress, whose merits and virtues adorn the throne and whose happiness is the constant care of the most chivalrous affection."

After the official reception, the Emperor admitted a deputation from the fishermen from Boulogne, who offered the Empress a silver fish enclosed in a net of the same metal, and addressed to Their Majesties a compliment in verse recited by one of those women who, as she remembered, had formerly had the honor of complimenting Napoleon I.

Their Majesties then entered an open calash to go and see the column dedicated by the Grand Army to the glory of the founder of their dynasty. The tent of Napoleon had been set up a few paces in front of this column when for the first time he distributed to his companions in arms the cross of the Legion of Honor. His successor stopped there for a few minutes and described to the Empress this national ceremony. He might have reminded her that it was in front of the same column he had himself made such a wretched failure, August 6, 1840, in his attempt against Louis Philippe;

that here had been assembled the garrison, the
National Guard, and the populace, shouting "Long
live the King!" while he, throwing himself into
the sea, in hopes of swimming to the packet boat
by which he had come, had been arrested in the
midst of the waves by boatmen and gendarmes.
And now he beheld a triumphal arch erected above
the harbor in his honor. The vessels were draped
with flags. Marines, soldiers, the people, made the
air ring with enthusiastic huzzas. What a difference between those two days: August 6, 1840,
September 27, 1853!

On the 28th Their Majesties arrived at Amiens.
Here the reception was remarkable on account of
the discourse delivered in the cathedral by the
bishop of the diocese, Monseigneur de Salinis.
Never, probably, had Napoleon III. and the Empress Eugénie been made the subject of such wildly
enthusiastic praises. Never had the alliance between the Church and the Emperor been celebrated in such lyric strains.

The Emperor and the Empress left Saint-Cloud,
October 12, 1853, to go to the palace of Compiègne,
where they remained until the 27th. Compiègne
might be called the imperial country seat. There
Napoleon III. led for several days the life of a
great English nobleman. He had made a formal
entry there in December, 1852. This time he returned more simply. The Empress found herself
with pleasure once more in this château, where.

the year before, she had not been a sovereign, and where the Emperor had experienced so true and deep a passion for her. As in the preceding year, they breakfasted and dined in the gallery of fêtes. After dinner they assembled in the salon of the maps, so called because, under the guise of hangings, it contained three immense maps of the forest of Compiègne. Here the guests chatted and danced without an orchestra, but to the music of a mechanical piano which possessed only three airs: a waltz, a quadrille, and a polka.

October 26, at one o'clock in the afternoon, the guests took leave of the Emperor and Empress to return to Paris. A few minutes later Their Majesties and the Grande Duchesse Stéphanie of Baden repaired to the station, where a special train was in readiness to take them to Chauny, in the department of the Aisne. From there they went in a carriage to the fortress of Ham, where they arrived at half-past three. In the time of his splendors, Napoleon III. loved to recall his unhappy days. When he was a prisoner at Ham, he had conceived an affection for the Abbé Tirmache, curé of the town. On becoming Emperor, he had appointed him chaplain of the Tuileries with the title of Bishop of Andras. October 26, 1853, the former curé was once more in the fortress of Ham to receive the quondam prisoner. Napoleon III. spent an hour in showing the Empress and the Grande Duchesse Stéphanie the fortress of Ham and the

sorry lodgings in which he had been incarcerated
during six years. He made them take a collation
under the linden-tree where he had so often
offered lunches to the school children. Their Majesties, leaving marks of their munificence behind
them, returned from Ham to Chauny just at night-
fall. The town and the manufactories outside of
it were illuminated, and the people shouting energetically. In the evening the Emperor and the
Empress were back at Compiègne, whence they
departed for Saint-Cloud the following day, Octo- .
ber 27.

CHAPTER XV

AFFAIRS in the East had become singularly complicated during the sojourns of Napoleon III. at Saint-Cloud, Dieppe, and Compiègne. We left them May 21, 1853, — the day when Prince Menchikoff, exasperated by the ill success of his mission, took his departure from Constantinople. It was not England in the first place that thought of defending the integrity of the Ottoman Empire; it was France. On this subject one should read the chapter entitled, *Origine de la guerre de Crimée*, in the memoirs of the Duc de Persigny. It is the history of the council of ministers which was held at Saint-Cloud at the close of Prince Menchikoff's mission. The question was raised whether it would not be opportune to send the French fleet to some point in the neighborhood of Turkey, — to Salamis, for instance, — to be within reach in case anything should happen. The Minister of Foreign Affairs, M. Drouyn de Lhuys, was in favor of temporizing. M. de Persigny, Minister of the Interior, was energetically opposed to this.

The Emperor ended by saying: "Decidedly, Persigny is right. If we send our fleet to Salamis, England will do the same; and the union of the two fleets will bring about the union of the two peoples against Russia." Then, to the consternation of the council, he turned to the Minister of the Navy and said : "M. Ducos, draw up at once a telegram ordering the fleet of Toulon to sail for Salamis."

At this time the alliance of England with France was far from being decided on. The Tory ministry, with Lord Aberdeen at its head, did not appear favorable to it. In the first place the reestablishment of the Empire had raised the most lively apprehensions in all classes of English society, and everybody in England imagined that the hidden purpose of Napoleon III. must be to revenge Waterloo. Queen Victoria did not at first desire a war against Russia any more than did Napoleon III. England, like France, was to be drawn on by a fatality stronger than the will of sovereigns or their peoples.

M. de Persigny's prediction was realized immediately. Public opinion in England forced the ministry to follow the example of France. June 14, 1853, the English fleet of Malta, commanded by Vice-Admiral Dundas, rejoined the French squadron in the roadstead of Besika, between Tenedos and the coast of Asia, at the entry of the Dardanelles.

And yet the Czar and Napoleon III. sincerely

desired peace. Neither would recoil from his position; but both would have been glad had any unforeseen circumstance prevented them from going further. Alas! it was not so. Events marched on with deplorable rapidity. June 17, M. Balabine quitted Constantinople with the entire Russian legation. This was the first open rupture. On the 26th, in a solemn manifesto addressed to his people, the Emperor Nicholas declared that, "relying on the glorious treaty of Kainardji," he demanded from the Supreme Porte a promise to maintain faithfully the privileges of the Orthodox Church; and that "if obstinacy or blindness wilfully prevented this, he would call God to his assistance and march to the defence of the faith."

July 3, the Russian troops stationed in Bessarabia crossed the Pruth and invaded the Danubian principalities.

September 25, a grand council convoked at Constantinople by the Sultan declared for war by a vote of one hundred and sixty against three.

October 8, the Turkish generalissimo, Omar Pasha, summoned Prince Gortchakoff, commander-in-chief of the Russian army, to evacuate the Danubian principalities within a fortnight.

October 18, on the refusal of Prince Gortchakoff, war was declared between Russia and Turkey.

The English and French fleets crossed the Dardanelles and occupied the roadstead of Béïcos in the Bosphorus. But this was only a simple demon-

stration, and peace between Russia and the two
great Western powers was to remain intact for
several months to come. The man who was at the
time the most convinced and eloquent defender of
this attitude was a military diplomatist, the minister of France at Saint Petersburg, General de
Castelbajac. His despatches to the Minister of
Foreign Affairs, M. Drouyn de Lhuys, and his
private letters to the director of political affairs,
M. Thouvenel, are documents which represent him as
the adversary of the prejudices of his time, and as
the precursor of the existing Franco-Russian understanding. We cite some extracts from this curious
and prophetic correspondence : —

General de Castelbajac to M. Thouvenel. — October 19, 1853. "It is useless for me to recon-
sider the situation on all sides. I cannot see the
necessity, and still less the advantage, of a war for
France, while on the other hand the most serious
inconveniences and most fatal consequences may
result to her from it. England is protected from
these consequences, at any rate from revolutionary
consequences, which are beyond all doubt the most
important to avoid. Besides, she has two interests
that we have not : the destruction of the fleets of
all nations, and the prevention of Russia's march
towards India. It seems to me, therefore, that
everything should induce us not to follow England
too far, for her commercial interests will always be
different from those of the continental powers."

General de Castelbajac to M. Drouyn de Lhuys.
— October 18, 1853. "So long as the revolutionary principle is not completely extinct in the Western states, Russia is to be considered, and union between governments, as I think, is the first thing to make sure of; and peace is the only means by which can be obtained that indispensable condition to the stability of social order. War would rekindle all the suspicions between governments, all the revolutionary hopes of the rabble, and very soon bring about the enfeebling of the principle of authority so skilfully and energetically restored with the Empire by the worthy successor of the great man who founded it upon the ruins of revolutionary France."

General de Castelbajac to M. Thouvenel. — November 16, 1853. "However it may be, whether peace or war, it is not my business to settle the question, but it is my business to watch things carefully and in an unpretending manner. If force alone is to decide, that is the most convenient. There is nothing to do but take sword in hand and march forward. That is my old trade, and I shall not be the last to remember it if it is necessary to the honor or the interests of my country. Meanwhile, however, I am living with my *enemies* as if they might once more become my *friends*, and this system makes our relations less painful and investigations easier. I must even render this justice to Russian society, that it avoids saying in my hearing anything which could wound me, even indirectly."

In reality, there was not the least personal animosity between the two sovereigns, while between the two nations there was not merely no hatred, but an invincible sympathy. The relations between the two courts remained correct and even courteous. In August the Czar personally thanked General de Castelbajac for the reception the Russian general Ogareff had met from Napoleon III. and Marshal de Saint-Arnaud, and for all the facilities afforded him for visiting the French military establishments. At the same time General de Castelbajac was present at the manœuvres of Krasno-Selo, where the Czar treated him with kindness, and expressed in the most gracious manner his regret at not seeing French officers in the camp.

The Russian sovereign displayed his affability not simply towards the representative of Napoleon III., but towards Frenchmen of the humblest condition. September 16, the general wrote to M. Thouvenel: "The Emperor Nicholas came alone to the Jardin Mabille of the country, situated about half a league from Saint Petersburg, and during an hour and a half strolled through salons filled with women who were more than light, with cigar smokers whom he detests, and in gardens made brilliant by a grand illumination and fireworks set off earlier than usual in his honor. He came in a drosky, with nobody but his coachman, as, for that matter, is his daily habit. He chatted with one and another, particularly with the milliners and petty French shopkeepers, whose free and easy ways and gossip amuse him."

A few days afterwards the Czar went to the Emperor Francis Joseph in Moravia, to witness the military manœuvres of Olmutz. There he met a French military mission, under the direction of General Comte de Goyon, aide-de-camp to Napoleon III. The Czar gave the French officers a particularly amiable reception, and publicly invited them to follow him to Warsaw. But they were not authorized by their government to accept this unexpected invitation.

October 15 General de Castelbajac wrote to M. Drouyn de Lhuys: "The chancellor tells me that in inviting General de Goyon the Emperor Nicholas had no intention but that of testifying his sympathies for the Emperor Napoleon and the officers of the French army; that before giving him this invitation he had asked him whether his time and his actions were free. The chancellor adds that his sovereign had directed Comte de Stackelberg to accompany General de Goyon and the other officers, whom he had invited, as far as V.`rsaw, where he had had lodgings made ready for the. at the palace; that the news of their departure fc · Paris, which was telegraphed to Warsaw, had e idently displeased His Majesty, and that he had written about it to M. de Kisseleff, forbidding him to make any recriminations on the subject."

On the other hand, M. Drouyn de Lhuys, in a despatch to General de Castelbajac, used these words concerning the incident: "The Emperor has keenly appreciated the kindly attentions on the part of the Emperor Nicholas of which the officers of his army present at the camp of Olmutz were the objects; but the orders given to General de Goyon assigned a purpose and a term to his journey. It was neither conformable to rule nor worthy of the two sovereigns that the aide-de-camp of one of them should find himself accidentally, and as if by chance, beside the other. At any time when the Emperor Nicholas may wish to send Russian officers to witness the manœuvres of the French army, they will be received among us with distinction which they merit, and on his side the Emperor Napoleon does not doubt that the same welcome would await French officers in Russia. But, in order to maintain their character, these demonstrations should be announced beforehand and accomplished with the usual forms."

General de Castelbajac had still such a hope of continued peace that he sent for his wife to come from Paris to Saint Petersburg. M. Thouvenel wrote to the general, October 14, 1853: "Madame la Marquise de Castelbajac has done me the honor to call on me. She came for news, and I told her all that I knew. Nevertheless she is going to rejoin you. I ardently desire that the Latin proverb, *Audaces fortuna juvat*, may be applicable to her, and that things may turn in such a way that you may remain at your post and M. de Kisseleff at his. We certainly shall not take the initiative of a rupture of diplomatic relations."

The Marquise de Castelbajac, born La Rochefoucauld, bravely undertook her journey in spite of the alarming news. Her husband wrote to M. Thouvenel November 11 : " The courier has arrived with my wife, whom some one had frightened at Berlin. Still she was unwilling to beat a compromising retreat, and, like a true diplomat, she disappeared from Berlin to await an answer from me at the house of the Duchesse de Sagan, as if her intention had always been to stop there. Her return to Saint Petersburg produces a very good effect."

Still, the horizon was becoming darker. The diplomatic attempts essayed at Vienna by the representatives of the great powers to obtain an agreement between Russia and Turkey had failed. Hostilities continued in western Wallachia between the Czar's troops and those of the Sultan. The Empe or Nicholas heard with a mixture of surprise and anger of the success of the Turkish army, under the command of a Croatian renegade, Michael Lattas, who had become a pervert under the name of Omar Pasha. November 30, the Russian fleet of the Black Sea, commanded by Admiral Nakhimoff, sailed from

Sebastopol and surprised in the open roadstead of
Sinope a Turkish squadron which was taking reinforcements to Batoum.   This it destroyed completely, ruining at the same time a part of the
city. "The blow struck at Sinope," wrote M.
Drouyn de Lhuys at the time, "has not affected
Turkey alone." It was evident that the English
and French fleets were about to enter the Black Sea.
Chancellor de Nesselrode no longer expected peace.
"My dear general," said he, in a melancholy tone
to the minister of France, "it is sad to end my
career at such a point, when I have always been
the apostle of peace!   This is what Lord Stratford
de Redcliffe's pride will result in.   Probably a general European conflagration, in which none of us
can avoid losing, and by which only the revolution-
aries can profit."   After having begun in so brilliant and joyous a manner, the first year of the
reign of Napoleon III. was ending amid the most
serious complications.   In spite of the promises of
the Bordeaux speech, one could already say that
the Empire would not be Peace.

CHAPTER XVI

LOOKING at Paris in the beginning of 1854, no one could have suspected an approaching storm. It is the height of the fashionable season. Dancing is going on in the official world, in the salons of the Faubourg Saint-Germain, and in banking circles. The theatres are filled. Never have there been greater luxury and animation. No one dreams of depriving himself of a diversion or a pleasure. The Turks and Russians are fighting in the valley of the Danube, it is true, but that is a long way off. Wealthy Parisians still fancy that France will be wise enough not to meddle in their quarrels except diplomatically.

Such is also the impression of General de Castelbajac. January 2, 1854, he writes from Saint Petersburg to M. Drouyn de Lhuys : "Notwithstanding the irritation which the news that our fleets are in the Black Sea has occasioned in the Emperor Nicholas, I have reason to believe that his conciliatory disposition remains unaltered, that he still desires to avoid at any cost a conflict with our ships, and that his own will not budge from Con-

123

stantinople unless those of the Sultan attack or insult them under the protection of ours, for henceforward it is the national Russian pride and the wounded self-respect of the sovereign which are the chief elements in the question, and not his ambition or the material interests of his empire."

January 9, the general writes to M. Thouvenel: "I do not think we shall receive our passports. If Muscovite pride revolts, it will be with reflection. Therefore I think we shall have time to breathe and take precautions for our retreat from Russia. Whatever may happen, I am ready to execute resolutely and conscientiously the orders of the minister. I shall find this easier than to differ in opinion with the whole West concerning the facts relating to Russia. But in that I must always act according to my conscience, before, at the time, and afterwards, not having, God be thanked, the silly pretension to direct in any manner the policy of the Emperor Napoleon, although I am a fervent disciple of his work."

In Saint Petersburg, as in Paris, people continue to give parties and frequent theatres. Russian society is irritated against England, but not against the French. General de Castelbajac adds: "Day before yesterday, during a dinner given at Chancellor Nesselrode's, his niece, Madame Kalergis, sided warmly with the French, but especially with the Emperor Napoleon and the Empress Eugénie. Addressing M. Seniavine, Muscovite and orthodox to the full, she said : 'You do not seem to be of my opinion?'—'Not altogether, I admit.' —'Well, then, you are wrong,' retorted Madame Kalergis, 'for all I have just said of the Emperor Napoleon and the Empress Eugénie as man and woman and as sovereigns is the most exact truth, and I have nothing to retract on the subject.' — Monsieur de Nesselrode put an end to the discussion by bantering his niece on her *animation* against Seniavine, but without the least ill-humor and with approval of all the good things she had said of the Emperor and Empress."

At the same time the great Russian ladies who are in Paris are always most cordially received. January 13, Colonel Fleury, first equerry to the Emperor, and commander of the regiment of Guides, gives an entertainment which is all the more elegant because the invitations to it are so few. The next day, General Bosquet, one of the heroes of the coming war, writes to his friend, M. Rivet: "Life in Paris is what you know and can imagine, excepting some amusing incidents like the little ball given yesterday to thirty or forty persons at the house of the colonel of Guides, which assembled the *pretty* women of Paris in a charming little company. I amused myself there until the lights were put out, about three o'clock in the morning. There were a good many Russians, and among others the niece of Prince Menchikoff. It was very easy and charming."

General Bosquet does not yet regard war as prob-
able. In this same letter he adds : —

"M. Pietri, prefect of police, beside whom I
sat at dinner yesterday, thinks that some news
indicating that Nicholas has listened to propositions
of peace has arrived, which has caused a rise of two
francs on the Bourse. Take into consideration that
no preparations have yet been made in France; the
cavalry has neither men nor horses; neither has the
artillery; no order has yet repaired the lack of ac-
coutrements for both arms, or provided for the necessary increase of new material. To judge from the
faces of people in our society, one surmises that they
dread a war, even while desiring its possible advantages for a new dynasty and the clearer and more
precise renewal of public opinion. But as there are
chances that the game would turn out badly should
the Emperor absent himself, since there is more than
one risk depending on the life of a single man, and
finally because a great deal of money would have
to be spent without hope of gaining much except
glory, they begin to think that it would be better
to wait, and they parley with all the precaution of
men who would like to obtain a result without
fighting."   \

Meanwhile the political horizon was growing
darker. The next day after General Bosquet wrote
the letter we have been quoting, General de Castelbajac, usually so optimistic, thus expressed himself
in a despatch addressed to M. Drouyn de Lhuys:

JANUARY, 1854 127

"I had been informed in the most positive manner that the Emperor Nicholas was determined not to take the initiative of a rupture. This morning he changed his mind in consequence of the arrival of a courier from Prince Menchikoff. The news of the entry of an English frigate at Sebastopol, to give the notification of the maritime powers, has driven the Emperor Nicholas beside himself with rage. He exclaimed : 'This is too much. I will not endure this English arrogance ; the honor of Russia is compromised ; England forces us into war. Let the responsibility of it rest on her before Europe and before God, who knows that I desire peace !'—I think I ought to inform you that, for some time past especially, the Emperor Nicholas blames nobody but England ; still, he cannot be thinking of declaring war against England alone."

With the exception of military men, dazzled by hopes of advancement and glory, the French were almost unanimous in their desire to maintain peace. Even the Emperor Nicholas would not allow any one to mention the word *war* in his presence. January 14 General de Castelbajac wrote to M. Drouyn de Lhuys : "Some days ago the Empress of Russia asked the Emperor how a declaration of war was made. 'Why do you ask me that question?' he replied in a severe tone. 'You ought to know that I wish for peace, and that I have never declared war on anybody.'—It is reported from all quarters, even from the Empress and the Grande Duchesse

Marie, who is very well disposed towards France and the Emperor Napoleon, that in his family the Emperor Nicholas has always expressed the wish to end the war with Turkey as quickly as possible, to avoid any conflict with France and England, and to be allied with France, for whose sovereign he openly declares his esteem and personal liking. But he is irritated against England, and perhaps still more perplexed how to retrace his steps without humbling his own pride and the honor of his nation, whose patriotism and religious fanaticism have reached their highest point."

The Czar had just sent his most intimate confidant, Count Orloff, to the Austrian capital, and it was hoped that his mission was pacific. Such was the ardent desire of General de Castelbajac, who wrote to M. Thouvenel, January 24 : " I hope that there will at last be a solution in one way or another, and seeing that the scene is nearer, that you will know it directly and even sooner than we. I believe that Count Orloff has full powers, and that he is in a position and has the energy to use them, unless new incidents should arise on the part of Austria and from the conference. God grant that all may end well, and above all by peace ! In short, may it end in one way or another ! It would be rather humiliating to human nature, to the moral character of man made in the image of God, if all the sovereigns, the statesmen, the great and petty diplomatists, should be fatally led into the wrong road, into a path contrary to their wishes as well as to the interests of nations and of entire humanity. For once one would have to turn Turk and say like them, with resignation and patience : ' God wills it ! ' But I am a Christian and not a fatalist, and until the last minute I will labor and advise : ' Do what you ought, come what may.' "

There was a grand ball at the Tuileries, attended by the Russian minister and all the members of his legation, on the very day on which the general was writing this pacific letter to Paris from Saint Petersburg. The fête was apparently not disturbed by any gloomy thoughts. Under the light of chandeliers, and to the sound of orchestras, the château presented a joyous and magnificent aspect. The Emperor wore the uniform of a general of division, with white knee-breeches, silk stockings, and buckled shoes. The Empress, wearing the principal crown diamonds with supreme grace, was resplendent in beauty. All the military men, all the functionaries, even the magistrates, were in uniform, with knee-breeches and silk stockings. All other guests wore court dress and swords. All faces were unclouded. The Emperor danced the opening quadrille with the Princesse Mathilde, and the Empress with the English ambassador, Lord Cowley. No alarming conversation was carried on. No one believed that war was imminent, if only because all the generals agreed in saying that no preparations for it were being made.

January 29, Napoleon III. wrote in person to the
Czar in the most friendly and conciliatory terms.
He said to him : "Let us declare that an armistice
will be signed ; the Russian troops will abandon
the Principalities, our squadrons the Black Sea.   If
Your Majesty would prefer to treat directly with
Turkey, you might appoint an ambassador who
would negotiate with a plenipotentiary of the Sultan,
and the agreement resulting from these deliberations
would be submitted to a conference of the four powers (England, Austria, France, and Prussia)." Napoleon III. concluded by disavowing all sentiment of
animosity, and of all the assurances contained in his
long letter, this was certainly the sincerest and most
true.

While awaiting the reply, which would be either
peace or war, Paris continued to enjoy itself.   January 28, there was a ball at the Hôtel de Ville, where
five thousand guests found plenty of room for dancing in the splendid salons, newly frescoed by Leh-
mann and Eugène Delacroix.   The next day King
Jerome gave a little ball in honor of the Empress.
The former sovereign thought that war was imminent.   Drawing General Bosquet aside, he said to
him: "You will have splendid things to do in this war
in the East.   I am confident that you will do better
than your elders, because you know more than they.
I wish you the best kind of luck."   But in spite of
King Jerome, General Bosquet still believed in the
maintenance of peace.   On the 30th he wrote to

M. Rivet : " Dear friend, this is what I really think:
the Emperor dreads war too much not to keep a
tight hold on the reins, and make every possible
effort to preserve peace ; all Germany is as anxious
for it as we are ; it is only England who wants war,
so as to destroy the Russian fleet and defend the
passage to India, which would soon belong to Russia
if she were allowed to gain peaceable access to Constantinople."

To the general the proof that peace is desired is
the absence of all preparations for war. In the same
letter he adds: " In France there are no preparations
for war, or almost none. The artillery could supply
only fourteen fully-equipped batteries, keeping only
one battery of instruction in the depots for each
regiment. The cavalry has from forty to fifty horses
per squadron, and no more men than horses. You
see that the economy practised has put the army
in a very backward condition, even on the serious
peace footing which precedes that of war. The infantry companies contain each thirty or forty men,
and the magazines are empty. Nothing, or almost
nothing, is being done to supply the deficiency, and
spring is coming on. You see, they will draw back
and there will be no war as yet. There are plenty
of reasons for that, drawn from the condition of
minds in Europe, and too little to gain from war.
Then, too, there is Orloff's mission, which everybody
interprets as peaceful."

How did the month of January terminate at Paris?

By an article in the *Moniteur* of the 31st, which was
an invitation to luxury and increased expense. " In
fêtes like those of the Hôtel de Ville and the Tuileries," it said, "something more than a vast display of
magnificence must be noted. Their real object is to
favor the laboring classes. Following the example
of the Emperor and the Empress, the municipal
council of Paris has thought that the cost of a
grand ball would fall back in a shower of gold on
all the industries of the city. The most efficacious
charity is that which, while giving work, manages
to sell the products of it. If it is good to succor
indigence, it is still better to prevent it. In societies like ours, even the industries of luxury form a
considerable part of the public wealth."

This call for luxurious expenditures received ready
response. A period opened in which war and pleasure marched abreast. Never were combats more
bloody, and never fêtes more brilliant.

CHAPTER XVII

THE DECLARATION OF WAR

THE month of February begins. It is that in which the rupture will be consummated. The official world of Paris now entertains very slight hopes of peace. On the first of the month the Minister of Foreign Affairs, M. Drouyn de Lhuys, sends a courier to Saint Petersburg, reflecting as he does so that he will doubtless be the last. Having been officially notified that the commanders of the English and French fleets in the Black Sea have been ordered to protect the territory and the flag of Turkey from the attacks of the Russian fleet, the Russian minister at Paris, M. de Kisseleff, has just made known that he is about to ask for his passports.

M. Thouvenel, director of political affairs, writes to General de Castelbajac, February 1 : " From the day when we begin to act, we have decided to move quickly and with firmness. France and England united ought to strike none but terrible blows. I deplore with you the extremity to which the obstinacy of the Emperor Nicholas reduces us, but we can do ourselves the justice of saying that we have done all in our power to dissipate it. . . . I pre-

sume we shall not have to write to you much longer
at Saint Petersburg, and it is possibly our swan-song
that we are sending you to-day.   It is less rude
than that which Sir Hamilton Seymour is ordered to
sing in the ears of Count Nesselrode.   I doubt if he
will be allowed to finish it.   It will be no disadvan-
tage for the future that the difference between the
two characters should be maintained to the very
end.   So good-by, general, doubtless only for the
moment."

But at this time the intended recipient of this
letter was still unwilling to despair of peace.   Here
are two extracts from his despatches to M. Drouyn
de Lhuys : "February 2, 1854.   All thoroughly considered, I am for peace, if we can have it with honor
and security, and we can, I think, without really ced-
ing what we wish to assure, namely, the integrity
and independence of Turkey.   As to its duration as
a Mussulman empire, the future will settle that, I
hope, under circumstances more favorable, politi-
cally and morally, than now exist in Europe, and
without increasing the power of Russia, which is
important."   "February 10.   I begin to hope that
though there may be a diplomatic rupture, there will
be no war.   To me this result appears certain if
Austria and Prussia hold firm.   The Emperor
Nicholas is waiting for news from Count Orloff and
the latest despatches from M. de Kisseleff and M. de
Brunow before replying to the Emperor Napoleon.
There is something extraordinary about the delay of

all these couriers, which, in the general desire for peace, is favorably interpreted."

Diplomatic relations have been broken off, but there is still no declaration of war. M. de Brunow and M. de Kisseleff departed, February 6, the one from London, and the other from Paris, leaving consuls behind them to attend to current commercial affairs. They have withdrawn, but they remain near the frontiers.

To the great surprise of the diplomatists accredited to Saint Petersburg, this is the moment chosen by the Emperor Nicholas for conferring the broad ribbon of the order of Saint Alexander Newski on the minister of France. General de Castelbajac accepts this decoration, providing that he receives his sovereign's authorization to do so. "I have thought," he writes to M. Drouyn de Lhuys, " that it might be useful to my country's interests to preserve my good relations with M. de Nesselrode, and above all the kindly sentiments of the Emperor of Russia. I have also thought that a favor accorded to the minister of the Emperor Napoleon, while none had ever been granted to a minister of King Louis Philippe, might have a political signification of some importance. And lastly, where I am personally concerned, I have thought that a proof of esteem and affection from a political adversary could not be other than honorable, especially from a great sovereign and a man of such worth and character as the Emperor Nicholas."

Chancellor Nesselrode had joined in the sentiments

of the Czar. He wrote to the minister of France :
" His Majesty the Emperor, desiring to give you a
proof of his personal esteem and the sentiments you
have inspired in him by your invariably frank and
loyal language, has charged me to transmit to you
the insignia of his order of Saint Alexander Newski.
Happy to be on this occasion the interpreter of the
kindly intentions of my august master, permit me to
offer you my most sincere congratulations, as well as
the assurance of those feelings of attachment and
high esteem which I have invariably cherished
towards you."

Not only had the English minister, Sir Hamilton
Seymour, received no decoration, but the ill will of
the Emperor Nicholas towards him was as manifest
as his friendliness towards the French minister.
General de Castelbajac really entertained a sincere
attachment to the Czar. He wrote to M. Thouvenel,
February 11 : " In his painful indecision, his religious scruples on one side and his humanitarian
scruples on the other, in his wounded pride, confronted by the national sentiment and the dangers
incurred by his empire, in his violent struggle between all these different sentiments, the Emperor
Nicholas has grown ten years older. He is really
unwell, morally and physically. The change in him
distresses me, and I cannot avoid deploring the moral
contest of this noble intelligence against the rooted
habit of domination and what he considers religious
duties and political necessities.

" The sovereign, born with the finest qualities, has been spoiled by the adulation, the successes, and the religious prejudices of the Muscovite nation, which are just now being carried to the extreme. To get an exact notion of this, you would have to go back in thought for several centuries. Take an example : it is rumored here among the people and in society that a supernatural being, wearing a monastic habit, suddenly appeared to the Emperor Nicholas as he sat at his writing table in his cabinet, and said to him : ' Nicholas, son of Paul, is it a motive of human ambition or a religious motive which is deciding you to attack Turkey ? ' — ' A purely religious motive,' replied the Emperor. — ' Then you can go on, and God will crown your holy arms with the most brilliant success.'

" It is of no use for the Emperor to say that nothing of the kind has happened. Everybody believes in his vision. This is surely the fanaticism of the ancient crusaders."

All is over. The last hopes of the military diplomatist have vanished. He is about to leave this capital, where up to the last moment he has received from the sovereign and Russian society expressions of such real sympathy. " My dear colleague," he writes to M. Thouvenel, February 15, " Oriental fatalism carries the day against reason and even against self-interest. You were quite right in supposing that your last letter was the 'swan-song.' My answer is still more sad, and may well be a

death-song for a great many people. . . . I leave
on good terms with everybody, hoping that some
unforeseen circumstance, some good inspiration of
the Emperor Nicholas, or an ingenious formula of
some diplomatic sphinx, may suddenly arrive to
pacify hearts and arrest arms that are ready to
strike."

On the same day the general thus expresses himself in his official correspondence with M. Drouyn
de Lhuys : " When your despatch of February 6
reached me last evening, the English minister had
received his passports twenty-four hours earlier, and
consequently I had asked for mine the morning
after. Before departing, I will take leave of the
Emperor Nicholas in a private audience, which, for
that matter, His Majesty has already had the kindness to request himself. To the very end he has
shown by his acts and words to the representatives
of the two countries his sympathy for France and
his irritation against England ; and this difference,
although less marked, has nevertheless been very
evident in the attitude of Saint Petersburg society.
On the part of the sovereign it has been at once the
expression of political calculation and the enthusiasm of a self-willed and passionate character ; on
that of Russian society it is flattery in the first
place, but it is also real patriotism and preference
for France, whose language and social habits it
adopted a century ago."

In addition to this, the despatch of February 15

describes General de Castelbajac's final appeal in behalf of peace : " In my last interview with the Emperor Nicholas," he writes, " I once more represented to him the dangers of his position, the responsibility already weighing on him for having invaded the Danubian Principalities in time of peace, and the still greater one he was about to assume by a war which he himself feared would become general and revolutionary. On this head I reminded him that he was acting in fatal contradiction with the moral and political ideas of his whole life, and against his opinions and the services he had rendered to the conservative cause. At last, after circumventing him on all sides, I added: ' But, Sire, it is impossible that some formula cannot be found (for, as a matter of fact, nothing but a felicitous formula is needed) which shall spare Europe an alarming future, and secure a peace which will be in the interest of all sovereigns and all humane and reasonable men.'

" The Emperor said to me, ' Orloff has made known my replies to the propositions of the conference, and I will tell Nesselrode to send them to you.' Then, pressing my hand affectionately : ' We shall see each other soon, I hope. I do not wish to give you your passports; but if you absolutely will leave me, do not go without bidding me good-by, or my very friendship will forbid me to forgive you.' "

It is curious, but at the very moment when war

was about to be declared between Russia and
France, there was given at the Opéra-Comique of
Paris the first representation of a piece which is a
sort of apotheosis of Peter the Great. It was *L'Etoile
du Nord*, the music by Meyerbeer and the words by
Scribe. It had been intended to delay the produc-
tion of this opera on account of the political situation, but Napoleon III. had just given orders to
bring it out without delay. With the Empress he
was present at the first representation, which took
place with extraordinary brilliancy, February 16.
Had the hall been ten times larger, it could not
have contained the crowd that for two months had
been trying to secure seats. All the illustrious
persons that Paris contained, whether in government, science, literature, and art, met at the Opéra-
Comique. The ladies, all in ball dress, vied with
each other in beauty, luxury, and elegance. Many
distinguished foreigners came for this express occasion to Paris. England, Belgium, Germany, had
sent their most competent critics. The piece and its
interpreters, Mademoiselle Caroline Duprez, daughter of the famous tenor, Mademoiselle Lefebvre,
Bataille, Hermann-Léon, Mocker, had a great success. The close of the second scene is well adapted
to enrapture *Holy Russia*. Peter the Great goes
into the midst of the revolted soldiery, and, uncov-
ering his breast, says: "Here I am. It is I,
strike!" At these words all prostrate themselves.
The Czar pardons, and the conspirators rise up to

march against the Swedes. Does not this scene recall the military insurrection so magnificently repressed by the Emperor Nicholas on the day he came to the throne? At bottom, there is not the least hatred, not the slightest antipathy, between the French and the Russians who are about to slay each other. The Parisians applaud the triumph of Peter the Great as much as if they were subjects of the Emperor Nicholas.

Three days later the *Moniteur* published this note : " Paris, February 18. The reply expected from Saint Petersburg arrived this evening. The Emperor Nicholas announces that he will not accept the conciliatory propositions made to him."

In this response to Napoleon's friendly letter of January 29, the Czar wrote : " Whatever Your Majesty may decide, no one will ever see me recoil before a threat. My confidence is in God and my right, and I can vouch that Russia will be able to show in 1854 what she was in 1812."

February 20, General de Castelbajac addressed his last despatch to M. Drouyn de Lhuys : " Yesterday I saw the Emperor Nicholas, M. de Nesselrode, and Count Orloff. My conclusion from their long conversation is that there is no change in the political situation as it appears in the letter of the Emperor Nicholas to His Majesty. On the contrary, it seems to be aggravated by the daily increasing enthusiasm of the Russian people for war. The final preparations, momentarily suspended, have been resumed with new ardor since the latest declarations of France and England on the mode of occupying the Black Sea. The English and French legations leave to-morrow evening and day after to-morrow morning, with an interval of a few hours, so as not to lack horses. If the wretched state of the roads does not prevent, I shall be in Paris March 2."

General de Castelbajac fulfilled his task nobly to the end. History will do justice to this man of honor who, wiser and more far-sighted than his contemporaries, had the penetration to think, and the courage to say, that a struggle between such nations as France and Russia was a calamity not merely for them but for the entire human race.

February 21, the Czar addressed a proclamation to his people in which he said : " Are we not still the same Russian people whose valor is attested by the memorable annals of 1812? May the Most High enable us to prove it ! In this hope, fighting for our oppressed brethren) who confess the faith of Christ, Russia will have but one heart and one voice wherewith to cry : God ! Our Saviour ! what have we to fear? Let Christ arise and let His enemies be scattered ! "

March 2, 1854, at the opening of the session, Napoleon III. thus expressed himself in his speech from the throne : " The business depression is hardly over when war begins. Last year I promised to do all in my power to maintain peace and reassure Europe. I have kept my word. I have gone as far as honor permitted in order to avert a struggle. Europe knows now, beyond all peradventure, that if France draws the sword, it is because she has been compelled to. It knows that France has no idea of aggrandizement; that she merely wishes to resist dangerous encroachments. Besides, and I love to proclaim it loudly, the time of conquests is past, never to return; for it is not by extending the boundaries of its territory that a nation can henceforward be honored and powerful, but by placing itself at the head of generous ideas, by spreading everywhere the empire of right and justice."

After examining the causes of the dispute, the sovereign added : "Let no one ask us hereafter : What are you going to do at Constantinople? We are going there with England to defend the cause of the Sultan, and nevertheless to protect the rights of Christians; we are going there to defend the liberty of the seas and our rightful influence in the Mediterranean. We are going there with Germany to help her maintain the rank from which it seems to be the intention to make her descend, to safeguard her frontiers against a too powerful neighbor. We are going there, in fine, with all those who desire the triumph of right, justice, and civilization."

Like Nicholas, Napoleon III. invoked the Most High, ending his speech with the following words : "Confiding especially in the protection of God, I hope soon to arrive at a peace which no one shall hereafter be able to disturb with impunity."

March 27, the Secretary of State went to the Senate and the Legislative Assembly to read there the following declaration : " The Emperor's government and that of Her Britannic Majesty had declared to the Cabinet of Saint Petersburg that if the quarrel with the Sublime Porte were not replaced within purely diplomatic limits, and also that if the evacuation of the Principalities of Moldavia and Wallachia were not commenced immediately and concluded by a fixed date, they would find themselves obliged to consider a negative reply or silence as a declaration of war. The Cabinet of Saint Petersburg having decided that it would not reply to the preceding communication, the Emperor charges me to make you acquainted with this resolution which places Russia and ourselves in a state of war, the responsibility for which rests solely upon that power."

Alas! nothing is more contagious than war. After a long and fruitful peace Europe enters upon a fatal period. The wars of the East and of Italy, of 1866 and 1870, will flow from each other, and after all these struggles will come in conclusion an armed peace as dolorous as war itself and possibly more burdensome. Torrents of blood are going to be shed, and what for?

CHAPTER XVIII

THE WAR OF THE ORIENT

THE war, until the landing of the English and French troops in the Crimea, was called the war of the Orient. We do not pretend to write its history. That has been done in the masterly works of M. Camille Rousset and General Fay. We shall merely recall the impression produced in Paris by the different phases of the struggle, and bring to light from the correspondence of the heroes themselves and the testimony of eye-witnesses the French and Christian sentiments of the men who covered themselves with glory during this period so filled with dangers and sufferings.

The army, though taken unawares, and not even knowing what was to be the scene of its operations, showed itself full of ardor and confidence. Its commander-in-chief was Marshal de Saint-Arnaud, who, although already stricken by a mortal disease, wished his memory to be made illustrious by something different from the Coup d'Etat. At first but three divisions were sent to the Orient, one of which was confided to General Canrobert, another to General Bosquet, and the third to Prince Napoleon.

By the 25th of February the Prince had written to
the Emperor: "Sire, at the moment when war is
about to break out, I come to beg Your Majesty to
allow me to join the expedition in preparation. I
do not ask for an important command or a distinguished title; the post which would seem to me
most honorable would be that which would bring me
nearest the enemy. The uniform I am so proud to
wear imposes duties which I shall be happy to fulfil,
and I wish to deserve the high rank given me by
your affection and my position."

General Bosquet, who, from the political point of
view, had not been in favor of the war, nevertheless
trembled with joy at the thought that he was about
to take arms. "My heart is joyful," he writes,
March 7, 1854; "my twelve thousand men are
nearly all old soldiers of Africa, and the majority
of the officers friends and brothers in arms. I have
sixteen hundred Arabs in my division — native
sharpshooters; twenty-two hundred zouaves of the
3d regiment, — those with whom I have fought so
often in Kabylia, — it is a family; Canrobert is a
brother to me. Verily, this is not a rude war, but
a real pleasure party."

General Bosquet was only forty-three years old.
He was born November 8, 1810. He was the fin-
ished model of a soldier. March 12, he wrote from
Paris to his mother, whom he fairly worshipped:
"My good mother, I start this evening for Mar-
seilles with Canrobert; we should be there by the

morning of the 15th and go on board the *Christophe Colomb* as soon as we have ascertained that our little flotilla is thoroughly ready. . . . It is a great honor for me to be one of the two generals of division who go in the van to carry the flag of France in the Orient. Last evening the Emperor bade us adieu after dinner, wishing us good luck as he embraced us and shook our hands. A few minutes before, the Empress had given us a medal of the Virgin and a very good likeness of herself in bronze. My friends in Paris would not let me go without amulets either, and the good Madame Thayer, whom you so rightly call an angel, has sent me a cross, the copy of that which Charlemagne wore, and which is still seen at Aix-la-Chapelle. With that and the good prayers from Pau, I start with a very easy and confident heart, disposed to bear haughtily against Russia the sword of France, which is that of justice and civilization."

Marshal de Saint-Arnaud, who had grown very religious as he grew old, departed in similar sentiments. "Marshal de Saint-Arnaud has been unknown," writes M. A. Granier de Cassagnac in his *Souvenirs du Second Empire*, "for that lofty and noble nature did not expand completely until within the last six months of his existence, under the sky ⸫ the Orient, in the atmosphere of glory, and already beneath the hand of death. The wake of his vessel is tinted with a reflection from the crusades; and he has a lofty fashion of combating

and of wrapping himself in the shroud of his victory,
which reminds one of Saint Louis and of Bayard."

Before embarking at Marseilles the future victor
of the Alma stopped at Lyons. Marshal de Castellane, who was in command at that city, wrote in
his journal, April 17: "Marshal de Saint-Arnaud,
commander of the army of the Orient, arrived at
Lyons the 16th, at six in the evening, in a mail
coach, with the Maréchale de Saint-Arnaud; he had
notified me that he would come to my house on his
arrival; I wished to spare him this trouble and went
to see him; he said he was very well; he said that
leaving the ministry had benefited him. The fact
is that he is out of bed, but he is very thin, his eyes
are glassy, he is bent; I imagine that he will find it
difficult to endure the fatigues of the campaign."

From Marseilles the marshal wrote to his brother,
M. Leroy de Saint-Arnaud, Counsellor of State, this
noble and affecting letter: "With courageous men,
with good men, God always ends by speaking, because His voice is the only truth, the only consolation. Once this holy voice is heard, one does not
lend the ear to other things. I have been quite
naturally led to God by the ordinary road taken by
human frailty: sorrow, meditation, prayer. God
has not repulsed me, and you may be sure that I
shall never take another backward step. To the
vehemence, the irritation which ruled me, have succeeded calmness and a possibly too serious gravity,
but it is connected with my malady. I have suf-

fered so much! I hope I shall soon recover a gentle
gaiety, but I cannot conceal from myself that all my
ideas are grave and serious. I read the *Imitation of
Jesus Christ* a great deal, and this admirable book,
which penetrates me with admiration, also inspires
me with a painful distrust of my strength."

April 26, the marshal wrote to his sister, Madame
de Forcade: "We embark to-morrow, and the next
time we write you it will be from Constantinople.
Constantinople! How our projects take wings, how
fate makes sport of man, how the will of God is
sovereign over ours! . . . I saw the good curé of
Hyères, and we had a long talk."

March 31, Generals Bosquet, Canrobert, and de
Martinprey arrived with the vanguard at Gallipoli,
a town situated at the northern extremity of the
Strait of Dardanelles, almost at the entrance of the
Sea of Marmora. It was there that headquarters
were established.

May 9, after merely touching at Gallipoli, Marshal
de Saint-Arnaud arrived at Constantinople. During
four months he lived alternately in the Turkish
capital, Gallipoli, and Varna. All the uncertainties, all the agonies, of the situation reappear in his
correspondence of this period. He states how badly
calculated the enterprise has been, what sacrifices
will be necessary, what slaughter awaits the army.
He had started so joyfully, and already he is so sad!
May 27, in a letter addressed to the Emperor from
Gallipoli, he complains that his troops lack the most

necessary things, and adds: "One does not make
war without bread, without shoes, without soup pots
and canteens." His health constantly became worse.
He suffered inexpressible tortures with admirable
patience.   Listen to Dr. Cabrol, his physician,
confidant, and friend: "In the middle of his cruel
nights, after long hours of violent sufferings, the
Marshal would say: 'Yes, I offer my pains to God,
He alone can allay them.   If He sends them to me
in expiation of my faults, my faults should be all
atoned for, for these pains are so great and poignant
that they might expiate even the greatest crimes.'
After this kind of prayer he would take his wife's
picture and cover it with kisses, saying: 'Yes, thou
alone canst console me.' His life had become a
struggle, a perpetual conflict between soul and
body."

There are the most curious alternations of feverish
exaltation and overwhelming sadness in the correspondence of this intrepid soldier.   May 30, he wrote
from Gallipoli to his brother: "Since I came here
everything has changed its face, everything goes.
I have held reviews, talked with the leaders and the
soldiers; every one is confident and holds up his
head.   I wept with joy and pride in passing through
the ranks of thirty-eight thousand Frenchmen.   I
admired the soldiers whom I am charged to lead to
victory.   How many victims we shall deplore!
That devouring activity which you know in me,
brother, animates and prevents me from being ill.

They say that I was never better. The crises are leaving me; I am regaining my strength and my youthful appearance. God will have pity on this fine army in having pity on its leader."

"Yéni Kalé, June 20, 1854. — On the 17th the Sultan reviewed the 3d division. His Highness did two things which will make an epoch in Turkey. He galloped twice, and came to salute the Maréchale, who watched the review from a carriage. He said very gracious things to the Maréchale and offered her his kiosque at Therapia. . . . The Sultan talking in public to a Christian woman is a revolution!"

We find the same martial ardor, the same French and Christian pride, in General Bosquet. June 12, he wrote the following letter to his mother, from Adrianople: "Last Sunday I went to the Catholic chapel, followed by all my officers on horseback and in full uniform. We were preceded by a fine picket of infantry and a brilliant escort of cavalry. The few Catholics of the country almost hide themselves so that it may be possible for them to practise their worship. Well! we went to chapel with our heads up, through a population who saluted us and who said to each other: 'There is the French chief going to say his prayers'; they will no longer dare not to respect the Christians. . . . Thy son, who is always the same honest fellow, trying to do right before God and men, is preparing as well as he can the march of a portion of this army which, I sincerely hope, will inscribe one more beautiful page in the military annals of France, and another in the history of the deeds and exploits of our country in honor of the civilization of the world."

It is the old national adage, the *Gesta Dei per Francos*, the *Acts of God by the French*. Curious contrast, — these warriors who are going to the help of Mussulmans talk and act like knights of the Middle Ages, like crusaders. The moment has come for them to display all their heroism, for the hour of great sufferings, of terrible trials, is about to strike. Marshal de Saint-Arnaud writes from Constantinople, June 24: "In a few hours I embark, leaving the Maréchale in good health, but very sad. This is the real separation, this is the beginning of the war."

On arriving at Varna, June 25, the Marshal learns the most surprising news. During the night of June 22–23 the Russians had raised the siege of Silistria. The army had expected to come up with them on the banks of the Danube, and, behold, they had recrossed the stream, they had evacuated the Danubian Principalities, fearing to see Austria enter the lists. Made a few months earlier, this evacuation would have prevented war. But now it is too late. Carnage is inevitable.

Totally disconcerted, Marshal de Saint-Arnaud wondered what he was to do. The most cruel perplexities tortured his soul, the most atrocious sufferings his body. Read his heart-rending letters to his wife: "Varna, June 28. I need complete repose, moral and physical, and all repose of mind and body is interdicted to me. May God have pity on me, I pray to Him a great deal, but without success. I am daily more disgusted with grandeurs and high positions. I no longer dream of anything but resting very tranquilly with thee at Montalais. Unfortunately, I cannot; I ought not to retire at present. I belong to my country and the Emperor. I will stay until the end, but I am making a great sacrifice. . . . Everything tires me, — talking, writing, marching, mounting a horse, — everything causes me pain. My God, what a life! And yet I have suffered enough."

To his daughter: "Varna, July 7. I have a large magnifying glass through which I look at thy portrait, and which, by doubling its size, gives it a striking expression which is certainly thine. I spend my time in looking at thee, in opening my heart and telling thee my griefs and my hopes; but who knows what God has in store for us."

The cholera broke out, and made terrible ravages in the army. The Marshal hoped that movement and change of air might overcome the epidemic, and he ordered an expedition into the Dobrudja, where there was no encounter with the enemy, who had withdrawn. But the scourge increased in the most frightful manner, and the decimated troops beat a retreat. The expedition, lasting only a few days, had been nothing but a lamentable and dismal promenade. Even this was not enough. At seven o'clock in the evening of August 10, just as the Marshal was getting off his horse after visiting the cholera patients, a violent fire broke out at Varna. Five hours were spent in struggling against an almost certain loss. The fire whirled around three powder magazines, — the English, French, and Turkish. Ten times the marshal despaired and was on the point of giving the signal of retreat. At three o'clock in the morning the danger was somewhat less. Two hours later the fire had been mastered.

The Marshal wrote to Madame Forcade: " Varna, August 18, 1854. My dear sister, while you are sweetly reposing in the shades of Malramé, I am struggling painfully against all the calamities imaginable. They have all struck at me, yet without beating me down, — cholera, conflagration, plague, fire, and water. While my heart has been torn by anguish, I have always shown a calm and smiling face. I have seen my friends, my companions in arms, my soldiers, who are my children, mowed down by cannon, and I remain standing above this charnel-house. One might think that in my body, broken by sufferings, worn by labor and thought, strength is increased by the decrease of it in those by whom I am surrounded. What an experience at the end of my life! I shall come out of it, my sister, because I have faith and a heart which nothing weakens. If I succumb, I shall fall with honor; that is the only sentiment of pride that I permit myself."

In the same letter the Marshal adds: "What a century! What a year! The world is tossed like an angry sea under a darkened sky. Here at the end of the year we shall see many things. For me, I would like a grand stroke, a splendid victory, and then a complete, an absolute repose." The splendid victory the Marshal will have. But the absolute repose, alas! will be that of death. Then, in thinking of Montalais, his country-seat at Meudon, and of Malramé, he exclaims at the end of his letter: "Ah! Montalais! ah! Malramé! when shall I wrap myself completely in your gentle quietude, far from affairs, from anxieties, and from men. But not from women, dear sister; I am too gallant to think of that. If ever again I find myself in the midst of my reunited family, he would be very mad who should try to separate me from them."

After so many perplexities and cruel uncertainties a ray of light was to illuminate the Marshal's mind. His dream was to find himself at last confronting a clear and definite goal, to see the enemy face to face, and this dream was to be realized. The announcement of a near and energetic campaign raised the soldiers' spirits. The epidemic had ceased. Nothing was now thought of but victory. General Bosquet had written in an order of the day, June 19: "Every one must remember that for French troops the difficulty is not to fight the enemy when they are within reach, but rather in the fatigues of the long marches which precede the combat. The model of the soldier is he who knows how to accommodate himself to and gayly endure privation while awaiting the festival, the long-desired day of battle." This day is approaching. The war of the Orient is about to be called the Crimean War.

CHAPTER XIX

BIARRITZ

LET us see what Napoleon III. and the Empress Eugénie were doing between the outbreak of the war of the Orient and the landing of the allies in the Crimea. Thus far no one dreamed in France of the frightful proportions the war was to assume. Counting on the support of England, people were expecting a speedy and glorious peace. The situation appeared so favorable that the Emperor thought he might absent himself from the capital without inconvenience, and quietly spend a few weeks of country life at the extremity of his empire, in the department of the Lower Pyrenees.

The health of the Empress required sea baths. For this purpose she selected a bathing station which was particularly agreeable to her on account of its proximity to Spain, and which she was to make a fashionable resort, as the Duchesse de Berry had done for Dieppe. This was Biarritz. Napoleon III. resolved to go there with the Empress, for whom his passion was still as lively as at the time of their marriage. But first he went for several days to Boulogne, in order to review the expedition-

157

ary troops about to sail for the Baltic under the command of General Baraguey d'Hilliers. He arrived there on July 11. The next day he reviewed the troops and addressed them in the following proclamation: "Soldiers! Russia having constrained us to war, France has armed five hundred thousand of her children. England has set considerable forces on foot. To-day, our fleets and armies, united by the same cause, are going to take the lead in the Baltic as well as in the Black Sea. English vessels are going to transport you thither, a fact unique in history, which proves the close alliance of two great peoples, and the firm resolution of the two governments not to recoil before any obstacle in order to protect the right of the weakest, the liberty of Europe, and the national honor."

The imperial proclamation ended by words full of confidence and enthusiasm: "Go, my children! Attentive Europe offers openly and secretly its prayers for your triumph. The country, proud of a conflict in which she threatens only the aggressor, accompanies you with her ardent desires, and I, whom imperial duties retain far from the scene of action, will have my eyes on you, and presently, in seeing you return, I shall be able to say: They were the worthy sons of the victors of Austerlitz, Egypt, Friedland, and the Moskowa. Go! God protect you!"

A copy of this proclamation was distributed to each of the soldiers of the army of the Baltic immediately after the review.

July 13, Napoleon arrived at Calais. The English squadron, composed of a large number of men-of-war, frigates, and steam corvettes, was lying in the roadstead ready to take the troops of the French expedition aboard. The officers of the fleet and a great number of sailors were mingled with the population of the city, as well as a crowd of English people who had come there for the occasion and loudly applauded the Emperor. The 14th he reviewed the troops camped on the glacis of Calais. Then he went aboard the frigate *La Reine Hortense*, and visited the English fleet, which saluted him with all its cannon. The vessels were hung with flags and the sailors in the yards. Napoleon III. boarded the flagship, where Commodore Grey received him at the head of all his officers. Thence the Emperor returned to Calais, which he immediately left for Saint-Cloud.

The *Moniteur* of July 19 contained the following: — "Their Majesties departed to-day for Biarritz. The Emperor accompanies the Empress to the sea baths which have been prescribed for Her Majesty. The Emperor will return in August to take command of the camp of Boulogne.

"Biarritz, July 21. Their Majesties have just arrived in good health. The people thronged about them on their journey, and saluted them with the liveliest enthusiasm.

"July 22. Last evening the Emperor and Empress took a walk in the midst of an animated crowd, who

manifested by hearty cheers their pleasure in beholding Their Majesties.

"Paris, August 12. The Emperor, desiring to
visit the department of the Lower Pyrenees, will
not return to Paris until the end of the month.
The Empress, however, on account of the state of
her health, is obliged to prolong her stay at
Biarritz."

August 14, Napoleon received at Biarritz the congratulations of the Empress on his feast day. At a
grand banquet given in Paris at the Hôtel de Ville,
the same evening, the prefect, M. Haussmann, expressed himself as follows: "Gentlemen, in the name
of the city of Paris I have the honor to propose the
health of His Majesty the Emperor Napoleon III.

"Under the ægis of His Majesty the city of Paris,
in the midst of events which keep the whole world
in suspense, quietly and perseveringly pursues the
accomplishment of works of public utility which
must also contribute to the éclat of the imperial
throne. She is proud and happy to prove by this
notable example the profound and unshakable confidence of the country in the wisdom not less than
the firmness of the sovereign who has restored her
legitimate and decisive influence in the councils of
Europe, and who causes the noble sword of France,
the foe of all iniquitous violence, the protectress of
rightful causes, the avenger of the sacred law of
nations, to glitter once more in the Orient, that
classic land of the great battles of humanity."

THE EMPRESS EUGÉNIE

adds: "Those who have the happiness to perceive the Emperor in his promenades, who witness the seemingly quiet life which His Majesty leads at Biarritz, cannot resist a profound sentiment of admiration and respect when thinking that it is to this imperial abode, remarkable only for its elegant simplicity, that the great affairs of France and Europe have just converged, quietly and without outward disturbance, and that from there go forth those resolutions which daily make France greater in the eyes of both her friends and her enemies."

The letter terminates with this vindication of the second Empire: "Eighteen months have elapsed since the re-establishment of the Empire; and already in France, so long disturbed, quiet is so thoroughly established, authority is restored to such a point, that the Emperor, at two hundred leagues from his capital, can direct all the affairs of the country by his superior and powerful will without retarding them in the least, without permitting any interest to suffer, without delaying any explanation.

"And at what moment do we see this realization of a strong and national power? At the time when in the North and in the South, at Rome, at Athens, on the Black Sea and on the Baltic Sea, the French flag is waving, and our diplomacy is speaking so nobly and playing so glorious a part! The will which directs these fleets, these armies, these negotiations, the power which sets all these springs in motion, is at one of the extremities of France! And under the impulsion of this will, under the action of this puissant force, everything moves, everything marches towards the end so gloriously pursued. What finer eulogy could be made of him who in so short a time has created so strong an organization, and whose firm hand regulates all its movements?"

The Russians having evacuated the Danubian Principalities, had been replaced there by the Turks. The Ottoman vanguard had entered Bucharest, August 5. August 19, a telegram from Dantzic brought favorable news. The French expeditionary corps had taken possession of the archipelago of Aland in the Baltic Sea. The fortress of Bomarsund had been taken. August 20, the Emperor addressed this proclamation from Biarritz to his troops in the Orient: "Soldiers and sailors of the army of the Orient! you have not fought as yet, and already you have obtained a brilliant success. Your presence and that of the English troops have sufficed to constrain the Russians to recross the Danube. . . . The First Consul said in 1799: 'The first quality of the soldier is constancy in enduring fatigues and privations; valor is only the second.' The first you have shown to-day; who will dispute the second with you? Hence your enemies, who are scattered from Finland to the Caucasus, are anxiously seeking the point at which France and England will aim their blows, foreseeing that they

will be decisive; for right, justice, and warlike
inspiration are on our side.

"Already Bomarsund and twelve hundred prisoners have fallen into our power. Soldiers, you
will follow the example of the army of Egypt; like
you, the victors of the Pyramids and Mount Tabor
had to contend against sickness and soldiers inured
to war, but in spite of the plague and the efforts
of three armies, they returned in honor to their
country.

"Soldiers, have confidence in your commander-in-
chief and in me. I watch over everything, and I
hope, with the help of God, soon to see your sufferings diminish and your glory increase." August
27, after visiting Pau, the Emperor left the Empress
at Biarritz and returned to Paris.

CHAPTER XX

LEAVING Paris August 31, 1854, Napoleon III. arrived at Boulogne-sur-Mer at eight o'clock in the evening and installed himself in the Brighton hotel. The houses were hung with French and English flags. The sailors' wives and daughters wore their traditional costume.

September 2, Leopold I., King of the Belgians, and his eldest son, the Duc de Brabant, came from Ostend to Calais, whither the Emperor went to receive them. The packet boats were incessantly bringing crowds of tourists from England who wished to see the meeting between the two sovereigns. After a few moments of repose, Napoleon III., King Leopold, and the Duc de Brabant went aboard the imperial yacht, *La Reine Hortense.* The Emperor wished to do the honors of this vessel in person to his guests. After carrying the general-in-chief of the expeditionary army to the Baltic Sea, it had just returned, bearing the report of the taking of Bomarsund. The sailors were on the yards, and the flags of France and Belgium floated from the top of the masts.

In the morning of September 3 the two monarchs went from Calais to Boulogne in an open carriage drawn by four horses. The sovereigns, both in the uniform of generals, and wearing, one the broad ribbon of the Legion of Honor, and the other that of the order of Leopold, were in the back of the carriage ; the Duc de Brabant, wearing the uniform of a colonel of grenadiers, was in front. The Emperor spent the whole day with his guests, who departed at six in the evening, escorted by him to the Belgian vessel on which they embarked. The interview had been most cordial.

September 4, Napoleon III. received the visit of two young and gifted princes, one of whom, already King of Portugal, was to die prematurely in 1861 and be succeeded by the other on the throne. These were King Pedro V. and his brother Louis, Duke of Oporto. Very well received by the Emperor, they visited the camp of Honvault with him and went away the same evening.

The next day, September 5, Prince Albert, husband of Queen Victoria, arrived at Boulogne. The most precise and circumstantial details of this visit may be found in the English work published by Sir Theodore Martin under the title : *The Life of His Royal Highness the Prince Consort*. Nothing more modern, nothing more in conformity with the new tendency of history to linger over the intimate and familiar details of contemporary events, can be found than this book, the principal documents of which were communicated to the author by Her Britannic Majesty in person. In former times they would not have been given to the public. Besides extracts from the Queen's journal, they include the letters addressed to her by Prince Albert, in which he described with as much candor as unreserve his current impressions of men and things. The notes he sent to the Queen during the four days he spent in company with Napoleon III. all find place in the narrative. They are followed by an account drawn up by the Prince himself and entitled : *Memorandum of my Visit to Boulogne.*

The weather was magnificent on the 5th of September, 1854, the sky empty of a cloud. From early morning the whole population had deserted the city for the jetty. A crowd of sightseers had operaglasses or telescopes bent on the sea. At half-past ten the Queen's yacht, the *Victoria and Albert*, with the French tricolor at her stem and the royal British standard at her stern, doubled the cape of Capécure. Conveying the Prince Consort and the Duke of Newcastle, Minister of War, this vessel was followed by two steamships, the *Black Eagle* and the *Vivid*, both carrying the same flags as the royal yacht. The excitement of the immense crowd assembled on the shore reached its height when it saw the Emperor, preceded and followed by a detachment of a hundred guards, arrive on the quay to receive the Prince there. This mark of cordiality impressed the crowd, because it was exceptional, the Prince not

being a sovereign. The grenadiers of the imperial
guard and the troops of the line formed a double
row from the Hotel Brighton to the shore.

At eleven o'clock the yacht *Victoria and Albert*,
saluted by twenty-one guns, arrived in port. When
it approached the custom-house, where Napoleon III.
was standing a little in advance of his staff, the
sovereign and the Prince recognized and saluted
each other by removing their hats. Meanwhile the
military bands were playing the two national English airs, *God save the Queen* and *Rule Britannia*.
The yacht landed her passengers at once. A gang-
way covered with carpet having been stretched
across, the Prince ran ashore to meet the Emperor.
Both uncovered and gave each other a cordial shake
of the hand. The Prince bowed several times in
acknowledgment of the friendly remarks addressed
to him by the sovereign, and seemed much affected
by the hearty greeting that he received. Both then
turned towards the open carriage which had brought
the sovereign. His Majesty begged his guest to
enter it first; as the Prince hesitated, the Emperor
insisted, and the Prince finally entered it first,
though he was unwilling to sit on the right side;
again the Emperor insisted and placed the Prince on
his right. Then they drove to the Hotel Brighton
between the double line formed by the imperial
guard and the chasseurs of Vincennes. All along
their route the windows were filled with women in
full dress who waved their handkerchiefs.

The Emperor and his guest, after dining with the English ambassador, Lord Cowley, M. Drouyn de Lhuys, Minister of Foreign Affairs, and the brother-in-law of the Empress, the Duke of Alba, who had arrived that morning, mounted horses and went to visit the camps of Wimereux, Ambleteuse, and Honvault.

Did the inhabitants who gave the husband of the Queen of England so warm a reception think of what had happened in this same city of Boulogne fifty years before? In 1804 Napoleon I. had concentrated on the plateau which overlooks the city on the north an army composed of one hundred and seventy-two thousand infantry and nine thousand cavalry, under command of Marshals Soult, Ney, Davout, and Victor. At the same time he had assembled in the roadstead a flotilla of two thousand four hundred and thirteen vessels manned by sixteen thousand seven hundred and thirty-eight men. These immense preparations were intended for a descent upon England, the motive being the violation of the treaty of Amiens. The plan was to be carried into execution as soon as the fleets of Antwerp, Brest, and Cadiz should be united so as to protect the flotilla of debarkation. The naval defeat of Trafalgar, October 20, 1805, prevented the accomplishment of this scheme, and the third coalition forced the Emperor to raise the camp of Boulogne and set off for the campaign whose final result was the victory of Austerlitz. A monument, the column

of the grand army, surmounted by a bronze statue
of Napoleon I. has been erected on the left side of
the Calais road, at about two and a half kilometres
from the upper town.   Doubtless Napoleon III. had
no idea of pointing it out to the husband of Queen
Victoria.   In visiting the camps of Wimereux, Ambleteuse, and Honvault that evening with his guest,
he could see from the beach the shores of England
which his uncle had vainly intended to invade.   At
night the city was magnificently illuminated, and
fireworks set off on the hills which dominate it.
The next day, September 6, the Emperor and the
Prince reviewed the army corps cantoned on the
plateau of Helfaut.   The four regiments of cuirassiers,
their helmets and cuirasses shining in the sun, were
what chiefly excited the admiration of the Prince.

The influx of foreigners to Boulogne continued.
Among them was noticeable an Indian prince in his
national costume, covered with gold and precious
stones, who had come from London to see the Emperor and be present at the military fêtes.

On the 7th the Emperor and his guest went to
visit the royal yacht, the *Victoria and Albert*, which
was moored at the custom-house dock.   The sailors,
ranged in the forepart of the vessel, gave three
cheers.   The Prince wished to do the honors of the
yacht in person to the Emperor.   He afterwards accompanied him to the plain of Marquise, where an
inspection of the bivouacs of the army took place.
On the 8th, a splendid day, a mock battle was

fought on this plain by two army corps, one commanded by the Emperor and the other by General
Schramm. Noticeable in the staff of Napoleon III.
were General Wedel, sent by the King of Prussia,
and several officers of that nation. Prince Albert
watched the manœuvres of the corps with the
keenest interest. An immense crowd was on the
ground. The Prince's departure occurred the next
day, September 9. He had spent four and a half
days in the closest intimacy with the Emperor, and
they had conversed incessantly on various subjects :
diplomacy, military matters, contemporary history,
political economy. The Prince summed up as follows, in his letters to the Queen and his memorandum of his visit, the impression made upon him by
the sovereign : " The Emperor has been friendly and
cordial. . . . He looks younger than his portraits
and not so pale. . . . He seems to be tranquil, naturally indolent, not easily excited, but cheerful and
good-humored when he is at his ease. He pro-
nounces German better than he does English. I
noticed a certain turn of mind in him which astonished me less when he told me that he had been educated at the college of Augsburg. He recited to me
a poem by Schiller, on the respective advantages of
peace and war, which seems to have had some influence over his destiny. . . . He told me that the
young King of Portugal had quite gained his heart,
and that he is very glad to have made the acquaintance of King Leopold. He added that the Duke

of Brabant had surprised him by the precocity of his judgment and the acuteness of his reflections."

Prince Albert expressed to Napoleon III. the pleasure it would give the Queen to see him in England, and to make the acquaintance of the Empress. The Emperor thanked him, adding that he would be most happy to receive the Queen in Paris the following year, when the Louvre should be finished for the exposition. He also told the Prince that one of the things which had made the pleasantest impression on him was to see Queen Victoria, then eighteen years old, open Parliament for the first time. This was in 1837. Banished to Rio de Janeiro, and then to the United States after the Strasbourg affair, he had returned to Europe on account of his mother's serious illness, and was in London at the time of the death of King William IV.

The conversations of the Emperor and Prince Albert were confidential, friendly, and unreserved. They parted, September 9, very well pleased with each other, the Emperor, followed by a brilliant cortège, accompanying his guest to the royal yacht. The next day the following appeared in the *Moniteur:* "The final adieux were exchanged on board the British vessel. Boulogne and France will retain the memory of this notable interview, in which the close alliance of two great nations seems to be personified."

As soon as he reached England, the Prince wrote to the Emperor : "The souvenir of the days I have passed with you, and of the confiding cordiality with which you have honored me, will never be effaced from my memory. I found the Queen and her children in good health. She desires me to say a thousand pleasant things to you."

On the whole, everything had gone off very well. This was the honeymoon of the English alliance. Waterloo was forgotten.

Napoleon III. remained in Boulogne until September 16, and then returned to Paris, which he quitted the next day but one in order to go to Bordeaux to meet the Empress on her return from Biarritz. Reaching Bordeaux some hours before she did, he went to the cathedral, where he was received by the cardinal-archbishop at the head of all his clergy. Then he went to the railway station to meet the Empress. They departed together and arrived at the palace of the Tuileries at nine o'clock in the evening of September 20. On that day the French and English troops had won the battle of the Alma.

Now let us return to the Crimea.

CHAPTER XXI

THE CRIMEA

THE fixed idea of Marshal de Saint-Arnaud for some months past had been to conquer the Crimea. April 27, he had written from Marseilles: "The Crimea—'tis a jewel! I dream about it, and I hope that prudence will not prevent my stealing it from the Russians." On reaching the Orient, he had not found the thing quite so easy. "The Crimea is my favorite idea," he wrote June 9, "but I have seen the embarkations and the debarkations, and I reflect that to make a descent on the Crimea, long preparations, a whole campaign, perhaps one hundred thousand men, will be needed." But, adventurous though it might be, the project had become the dominant ambition of England. At the thought of destroying Sebastopol and the Russian ships in the Black Sea, the London merchants and the stockholders of the East Indian Company could not contain themselves for joy. The *Times* of June 15 said: "The taking of Sebastopol and the occupation of the Crimea would defray all the costs of the present war"; and on June 29 Prince Albert wrote to the Duke of Newcastle, the Secretary of

174

War: "England's policy should not be to send troops onto the marshy soil of the Danube and the exhausted fields of Wallachia; but its aim should be the destruction of Sebastopol, — the point which really dominates the Black Sea."

The rumor of a descent upon the Crimea had been current in the army of the Orient since August. It was a scheme which was far from gaining the approbation of all the generals. Concerning this, we cite two extracts from letters of General Bosquet, dated from Yéni Kalé : —

"August 18, 1854. It seems they are thinking of seizing the Crimea. That would be doing a good thing for England, but not for ourselves. We are real Don Quixotes, — paying with our blood and money for results useful to others but not to us."

"August 24. We are about to embark for the Crimea — a very serious operation, which would have been less serious and more sure at the end of June. Now it is attempted as if in despair, and as a thing more personal to England than to us. It seems to me that it is throwing down the gauntlet to Russia once for all. If it succeeds, it will be an astonishing feat of arms; if not, it will be a great shame. Who will have any ideas? Who will say, at this serious moment, what is to be done? Curious epoch, singular army : English, Turks, and French without a general commander. It is all haphazard."

Many other officers shared the apprehensions of this valiant soldier. They considered a descent upon a territory unknown except from stories as a more than foolhardy enterprise. They dreaded the dangers of the debarkation, the equinoctial storms on the dangerous waters of the Black Sea, and thought of the fate of the Armada of Philip II. August 25, an order from headquarters officially announced the near departure for the Crimea. There was no more room for criticism. All that any one thought of was how to conduct himself like a hero.

The same day the Marshal wrote to his wife: "I promise thee to conduct things so vigorously in the Crimea that we shall soon finish. We shall have plenty of trouble to extricate ourselves for the first few days, but we shall come out all right. . . . It is thy fête to-day, my Louise, and I not near to congratulate thee. That makes me suffer keenly. Yesterday I sent thee a little souvenir by the *Mouette*, which will reach thee to-day. Perhaps thou hast thought I had forgotten thy fête : it would have been almost pardonable in the midst of so many affairs; but no, thou wilt receive a bouquet of flowers of all sorts, — odoriferous, and not mingled with anxieties; them I keep."

The heroic soul of the Marshal exulted in the approach of danger. He wrote to his brother, August 28 : "When you are reading this letter, I shall be on the sea. The most redoubtable fleet that has been seen for a long time — if ever one saw the like — will be sailing towards the Crimea, there to vomit in the face of the Russians sixty thousand men and one hundred and twenty pieces of cannon. We surpass Agamemnon, and our siege will not last so long as that of Troy. . . . All we ask is a hospitable sea for a fortnight. . . . Ah! brother, how I will rest myself after that! I have spent my night in laying siege to Sebastopol and making proclamations to my soldiers."

In another letter, of August 31 : " We have not come from so far, we have not undergone so many trials, only to be wrecked in the harbor. If I succeed, I will not stay long to enjoy success. I shall have done more than my task, and I will leave the rest to be done by others. My part in this world will be ended. We shall live for ourselves in retreat and repose."

Unhappily, the Marshal's state of health grew still worse. His life had become a torture. What sadness, but what heroism, breathes through his last letters from Varna to his wife who was still at Constantinople !

" August 28. I suffer, but thou knowest that I know how to suffer. Oh! the weather! It is the sixth day of the moon, and it is fine. All the month will be fine, according to the calculation of my venerable master, the Duc d'Isly ; and I believe it, as in everything else that comes from him. I hope that from the heights of heaven he will inspire me when I face the enemy.

"Prince Napoleon has told me that he wished to take thee aboard the *Roland*. Thou wouldst have come, and I should have been very happy, but for some of these brief joys one pays too dear. It is better not to see thee. I should have been very much affected, and that would have done me harm."

"August 30. The acute stage is becoming permanent. I hope that the long-repeated echoes of the cannonading will act on my nerves and my breast. It is to that chance that I cling, like a drowning man to a branch of willow. The branch may break. All that is in the hands of God."

"September 2. Dear Louise, I rise in the saddest possible condition : an atrocious night, weakness, suffering, a stiff gale in the roadstead, — in fine, all imaginable contrarieties, physical and moral. In spite of everything, I am going to embark at two o'clock. . . . Have I drunk deep enough of the chalice of bitterness? There are moments when my whole soul revolts and grows indignant. Prayer has no more effect on me than on a tempest. I love thee with all the strength of my soul, and for that I find plenty."

The troops are at last about to embark. The French, to the number of thirty thousand, have four divisions, commanded by Generals Canrobert, Bosquet, Forey, and Prince Napoleon. On account of the paucity of transports, the cavalry division has had to be left behind, — a grave mishap which will

have disagreeable consequences. The only cavalry-
men embarked are a squadron of chasseurs d'Afrique
and some spahis intended as an escort for the Marshal. An Ottoman division of seven thousand men
is placed under his orders. The commander-in-
chief of the English army, Lord Raglan, takes with
him five divisions of infantry, one of cavalry, nine
field batteries, in all twenty-one thousand men.
They were to have sailed September 2, but on
account of a delay on the part of the English, they
did not do so until the 7th.

Marshal de Saint-Arnaud is on board the flagship, the *Ville-de-Paris*, commanded by Vice-Admiral Hamelin. On the 6th a malignant fever had
come to aggravate his malady of the aorta and his
angina pectoris. During the passage he wrote to
his brother : " On board the *Ville-de-Paris* September 11, 1854. Since the 6th I have not left the bed,
and a bed of anguish. I had brought from Varna
the germs of a malignant fever of the worst kind.
I have gone through the three critical attacks ; the
fourth failed to appear; well for me, I could not
have endured it. But what an assault! what a
struggle! what weakness it has left behind it!
What disorder in the principle of life! Add to
all this my preoccupations, my cares, the thought
of leaving an army on the eve of debarkation without direction and without a leader, and dying myself
of a fever in front of the enemy! By divine grace
I have subdued all that; let us thank God, brother."

The voyage continues in stately fashion. The assembled fleets and convoys occupy a space of more than seven leagues. There are two hundred and eighty sail. The Marshal admires this imposing spectacle. But he knows very well that he will not command much longer. September 12, he dictates the following letter to the Minister of War, Marshal Vaillant: "I have had the pain of recognizing lately, and especially during this voyage in which I have found myself on the point of succumbing, that the moment approaches when I shall not have sufficient courage to bear any longer the heavy burden of a command which requires a vigor that I have lost and scarcely hope to regain. I will hope that Providence will permit me to fulfil to the end the task I have undertaken, and that I may be able to lead to Sebastopol the army with which I shall descend upon the coast of the Crimea; but that, I feel, will be a final effort, and I beg you to ask the Emperor to appoint my successor." Two days later, September 14, at two o'clock in the morning, the weather being magnificent, the sky clear and filled with stars, the signal is given for getting under sail. They are reaching this Crimean ground where so much blood will be spilled. The place of landing is four leagues south of Eupatoria and ten leagues north of Sebastopol. It is a place designated on the maps by the name of Old Fort, recognizable by traces of some old ramparts. Begun on the 14th, the landing of the French is completed the 16th, that of the English the 18th.

On touching the soil of the Crimea, longed for as a promised land, the Marshal has regained surprising strength. The 14th he remained six hours on horseback, visiting the bivouacs. From Old Fort he wrote on the 16th : " Dear brother, September 14, 1812, the grand army entered Moscow. September 14, 1854, the French army landed in the Crimea and trod the soil of Russia. The Russians have not come to oppose our landing, which was effected with admirable order and rapidity."

His letters to his wife are full of enthusiasm : " Old Fort, Crimea, September 16. In the memory of man no finer sight has been seen than this debarkation to cries of Long Live the Emperor ! . . . I have been all through the line on horseback. . . . The troops are superb, full of ardor. We shall beat the Russians. I send thee with a kiss a little flower gathered under my tent."

" Old Fort, September 17. The faster time goes, dearly beloved, the sooner it brings me to thee. It is that which redoubles my courage. I think of nothing but the moment when we shall be very tranquil at home. In the spring we will go travelling in Italy, and come back by way of Switzerland and Germany. We will travel with only two domestics, like respectable citizens. Do not build too many castles in Spain, that brings bad luck."

At this moment the Marshal banishes every

gloomy presentiment. He writes to his brother:
"Old Fort, September 17. A week from to-day I
surely hope that some one will say, to the roll of
cannon, a solemn Mass of thanksgiving under the
walls of Sebastopol. This morning low Mass was
said under my grand tent."

The army is full of ardor and confidence. In his
fine military work, *Souvenirs de la guerre de Crimée*,
General Fay, former aide-de-camp of Marshal Bosquet, says : "The absence of the enemy at the time
of landing assured our success in the first battle,
and after the evening of the 14th no one doubted
it. On the voyage we had learned by a proclamation of the Emperor the news of the taking of
Bomarsund by General Baraguey-d'Hilliers, along
with two thousand prisoners, and this first victory
had seemed to us a good omen."

Marshal de Saint-Arnaud is right when he writes
to the Minister of War: "Our situation is good.
The voyage and the debarkation were two of the
most formidable contingencies presented by an enterprise almost without precedent, regard being had
to distances, to judgment, and to the numberless
uncertainties which surround it. I consider that
the enemy who allows such a storm to pile up at
several leagues' distance from him without doing
anything to dispel it at its source, places himself in
a very unfavorable position."

Up to the last moment the Russians could not
bring themselves to believe in so foolhardy an enter-

prise as a descent on the Crimea in the middle of September. It seemed to them that the season was too far advanced for the allies to dream of making such an attempt, or of entering a country where the rigors of the climate and the lack of resources would render their existence so difficult. Prince Menchikoff, commander-in-chief of the Russian army, thinking that he would arrive too late to oppose a debarkation the locality of which he does not know, has decided not to prevent the invaders from landing, but to await them in front of Sebastopol and bar their way. He is expecting them on the heights dominating the river Alma, with forty thousand men and ninety-six pieces of cannon.

At seven o'clock in the morning of September 19 the allies set off gayly on their first march in the direction of Sebastopol, going southward along the coast in splendid weather. The vessels of the two nations, advancing on the same line and almost touching the shore, afford the extraordinary spectacle of two armies and two fleets going to battle abreast. At three in the afternoon they arrive near the Boulgarak, a stream flowing through a ravine running east and west, and falling, like the Alma, into the sea. They are about to camp on the road, in the vicinity of the wells, when the skirmishers signal the presence of the Russian army on the heights overlooking the Alma and some movements of troops on the right bank of that stream. Thereupon the allies establish themselves in two lines, facing the enemy at two leagues' distance.   Several discharges of cannon are exchanged by the outposts. But it is too late to open the attack.   It is the next day, September 20, that the battle of the Alma will be fought.

CHAPTER XXII

THE BATTLE OF THE ALMA

THE plan of the battle is this : to outflank the two wings of the Russian army, and afterwards crush it by an attack in front. It is determined that : —

1. At the extreme right, the second division, commanded by General Bosquet, will march the first, cross the Alma near its mouth, go up the slopes, and then fall upon the Russian left, to surround and force it back upon the centre.

2. After the movement of the Bosquet division, the first and third divisions, the one commanded by General Canrobert and the other by Prince Napoleon, will cross the Alma, supported by a part of the English army, climb the heights between Almatamak and Bourliouk, and deliver the principal attack.

3. At the left of the French line, the rest of the army will seek to outflank the Russian right.

4. The fourth division, under command of General Forey, will remain in reserve.

On the eve of the battle, Marshal de Saint-Arnaud has assembled the generals to give them his final instructions. "I rely on you, Bosquet," he has said to the commander of the 2d division. "Yes, Marshal," the latter has replied; "I expect to draw down a part of the enemy's centre on me; but do not forget that I cannot be crushed longer than two hours."

September 20. Six o'clock in the morning. The Bosquet division sets out. It is composed of two brigades, — one under the orders of General d'Autemarre, the other under General Bonat. Starting from the shores of the Boulgarak, it is not more than two kilometres from the Alma, when an aide-de-camp of the Marshal brings it to a halt, the English army being not yet ready.

Half-past eleven. The Bosquet division resumes its march. Tambours, clarions, bands, make themselves heard all along the line. The battle will soon begin. The Russians on the heights have forty-three thousand two hundred men to oppose to fifty-six thousand of the allied troops. The course of the river Alma, which the latter are going to cross, is deep and sinuous, and the fords are difficult and infrequent. Into the bottom of the valley, covered with trees, gardens, houses, and into the village of Bourliouk, the Russians have sent a body of very well-sheltered sharpshooters, armed with excellent rifles, who will greet the heads of the advancing column with a sharp and very disagreeable fire.

Half-past twelve. The Bosquet division reaches

the Alma. The Bonat brigade is somewhat delayed by the difficulty of crossing the ford of the Barre. The D'Autemarre brigade, on arriving near Almatamak, being hidden from the enemy by the escarpments of the adjacent shore, find it easier to cross the river. Soon followed by the rest of the brigade and by General Bosquet, the first battalion of the 3d Zouaves crosses the ford, climbs the perpendicular ascents which dominate the shore, and attains the heights with prodigious agility. Achieving what the Russians had thought impossible, they succeed in hauling several pieces of artillery up the cliffs.

The Bonat brigade has rejoined the brigade D'Autemarre. During more than an hour and a half the dozen pieces of artillery, directed by Commandant Barral, reply to the forty cannon opposed to them. But the ammunition is giving out. It is time that the Bosquet division should be supported by the other divisions.

One o'clock. The attack in front begins. The first division, under General Canrobert, and the third, under Prince Napoleon, turn towards the Alma, which the one crosses near Almatamak, the other near Bourliouk. The interest of the struggle will be concentrated around the telegraph station, situated between these two villages. Here the Russians are massing their resistance.

General Bosquet, whose position on the crest of the hill is growing critical, listens joyfully to the trumpets of the Zouaves of the Canrobert division. With an ardor copied from that of its intrepid leader, it is climbing the heights by the most precipitous acclivities. Struck in the breast by the bursting of a shell, Canrobert nevertheless remains on his horse until the close of the action.

Prince Napoleon's division, after seizing the village of Alma, under fire from the Russian batteries, takes a brilliant part in the fighting on the plateaux.

The regiments of Minsk and Moscow begin a heroic contest against the divisions of Bosquet and Canrobert. Listen to General Fay, who, in his admirable account, does justice so loyally to the Russians: "One of our batteries opened fire with grape-shot so violently and at such short range that the ranks of the enemy's column were soon in disorder, in spite of the vigor of its officers. One of these remained in the thick of the danger, calling back his men and shoving them into place with his hand. 'The brave officer!' cried General Bosquet. 'If I were there, I would embrace him.'"

The 1st light infantry, the 1st Zouaves, and the 39th of the line rush forward at the same time. The flag of the latter regiment is floating above the telegraph station. Ensign Poidevin, who had the honor of carrying it, receives his death wound gloriously.

Meanwhile, the English are fighting an almost distinct, but perhaps a still more bloody, battle.

After crossing the Alma, in front of the village of Bourliouk, they moved towards the positions fortified by the Russians, where considerable bodies of troops were massed. Their object was to occupy the heights above and up the river from Bourliouk, which command the road from Eupatoria to Sebastopol. By dint of energy, they accomplish this difficult task.

Half-past four. Supported by the reserves, General Forey's division, the three divisions commanded by General Bosquet, General Canrobert, and Prince Napoleon are victorious at all points. The battle is definitively gained.

Five o'clock. The English rejoin the French, and mingle their shouts with those of the victors who are occupying the conquered positions. The defeat of the Russians would be changed into a rout, if only the allies had cavalry regiments to pursue the vanquished. Unfortunately, the French have no cavalry, but a squadron of chasseurs d'Afrique and a platoon of mounted Turks. The English have a cavalry division, but it arrived too late. The next day General Bosquet will write : " We have no prisoners but several fugitives and the mass of wounded men who cover the battle-field. It was a fine battle, but incomplete, — lacking trophies and prisoners by reason of its lack of cavalry." And Marshal de Saint-Arnaud will say in his report to the Emperor : "I shall regret all my life not having at least my two regiments of chasseurs d'Afrique."

All day long the Marshal has bravely exposed his person, going from one to another of the most perilous positions, and sparing neither his staff nor himself. To-morrow he will write to his wife: "I am satisfied with my staff. Gramont received a splinter from a shell in his cloak. Maurice (M. de Puységur) showed great bravery. Eynard (M. de Clermont-Tonnerre) conducted himself well. I made them all listen to the sound of bullets and balls. Raoul (M. de Lostanges) is very brave. My fanion was shot through by a ball and Raoul's horse touched."

In a picture which is affecting but inexact, the painter Bellangé has represented the Marshal on horseback during the battle, supported by two horsemen, on whom he leans, one on the right and the other on the left. Doctor Cabrol has written: "This poetic action is due to the imagination of the excellent artist. . . . Without any one knowing it, we were putting on the Marshal a strong magnet enveloped in a little flannel bag. For this operation he had halted for a moment, and bent over the pommel of his saddle. He applied the naked magnet over the cardiac and epigastric regions. That relieved him momentarily. He maintained himself perfectly on his horse throughout the battle." The victor of the Alma will be able to write to his wife: "I remained twelve hours in the saddle, always on Nibor, who was magnificent, galloping in the midst of the bullets in the evening as he did in the morning."

It has been a bloody day. According to General Fay the Russians lost eight thousand men and the allies three thousand three hundred and five. The English have three hundred and forty-three dead and sixteen hundred and twenty-two wounded; the French one hundred and forty dead and twelve hundred wounded.

The allies remain master of the battle-field. The Marshal bivouacs on the very spot occupied by the commander-in-chief of the Russian army, Prince Menchikoff. He has seized the carriage and the correspondence of the Prince, but the latter and his whole army have retired in good order to regain Sabastopol. Harassed with fatigue, and for the most part not having eaten since morning, both French and English need repose. Many of them have gone down again to the banks of the Alma for their knapsacks, which they had left there to be more at their ease in climbing the heights. Night approaches. The tents are set up. Officers and soldiers lie down and sleep. The Marshal watches. He is dictating his general order of the day : "Battle-field of the Alma, September 20, 1854. Soldiers, France and the Emperor will be satisfied with you. At Alma you have proved to the Russians that you are the worthy sons of the victors of Eylau and the Moskowa. You have vied in courage with your English allies, and your bayonets have seized the most formidable and well-defended positions. Soldiers, you will meet the Russians again on your route, you will conquer them again as you have to-day to the cry of 'Long Live the Emperor!' and you will not halt except before Sebastopol; there you will enjoy a repose that you have well deserved."

Afterwards the Marshal addresses to Napoleon III. the first victorious bulletin of the second Empire : "Sire, Your Majesty's cannons have spoken ! . . . We have gained a complete victory. . . . Your Majesty may be proud of your soldiers. They have not degenerated; they are the soldiers of Austerlitz and of Jena. Never have I seen such enthusiasm. The shout of 'Long Live the Emperor!' resounded all day long; the wounded raised themselves to repeat it. Lord Raglan's bravery is antique. The calmness which never forsakes him is unaltered amidst balls and bullets. Prince Napoleon, at the head of his division, seized the large village of Alma under fire from the Russian batteries. The Prince has shown himself worthy of the name he bears. . . . General Canrobert, to whom belongs in part the honor of the day, has been slightly wounded. He is doing very well. The Zouaves have gained the admiration of both armies. They are the finest soldiers in the world."

At the same time General Bosquet is writing to his mother : "A battle, and a fine battle, successful and glorious for the 2d division ! I commanded the right, and my orders were to be the first to attack the Russian positions. You ought to have seen my brave soldiers proudly climbing the steep banks of the Alma, followed by the artillery and the rest of their brigade. In the distance the centre of the army and the English were watching and applauding us.

"In an instant I had to support the effort of more than half the Russian army : forty pieces of artillery concentrating their fire on my 1st brigade. I felt proud of having such brave soldiers to present to the enemy. We were one to five or six, and twelve cannon against forty, and we held the positions relinquished by the Russians. 'Twas fine ! But that always lasts a little too long; the centre of the army came up with Canrobert, the Prince and the Marshal. The English did not debouch until very late. As soon as the enemy's attention had been divided, I took the charge with my two brigades and eight Turkish battalions which had been given me, and we forced the Russians to retreat. . . . The Marshal sent an officer to congratulate me and to thank my division.

"I write you my impressions at once. Yes, my heart is at ease, because it has been my fortune to be the first to attack the Russian army and to force it to quintuple its forces in front of me ; I have had the pleasure of seeing the enemy fleeing, and of following him with volleys of cannon ; my heart is at ease, because friendly hands and those of persons whom I greatly esteem have come to press mine and to make much of the 2d division."

Glory to heroes who speak and act like this !

CHAPTER XXIII

THE LAST DAYS OF SAINT-ARNAUD

MARSHAL DE SAINT-ARNAUD has just written to the Emperor: "I shall regret all my life not having had at least my two regiments of chasseurs d'Afrique." All his life! Alas! he will be dead in a week. September 21, the day after the battle, he is still full of confidence, ardor, and enthusiasm. He writes to his wife: "Victory, victory! my beloved Louise. Yesterday I beat the Russians completely; I carried their formidable positions, defended by more than forty thousand men, who have been soundly whipped; but nothing can resist French vehemence and English order and solidity. . . . The moral effect is immense. All the army love me and have great confidence in me. My health keeps up. . . All the disposable forces in the Crimea were before me yesterday. That will not prevent me from taking Sebastopol. Adieu, my Louise. God protects us. Be calm and tranquil. This is a fine page to record in my register of service."

September 22. The Marshal is still on the ground where the battle was fought. Again he writes to his wife: "My health is not worse; it remains still the same. No appetite, no sleep. . . . What a glorious victory, my Louise! Everybody is proud and happy, and burning to meet the Russians again. At present, I could lead the army to the ends of the earth. But my career is accomplished, I will think of nothing more except getting well. How happy all the family will be in Paris. How many things are running in my poor head, which is hardly able to endure them. . . . Heaven is with us, but the English are always delaying me. Adieu, dear love, I will write from Sebastopol."

Again the same day: "The English are not ready yet, and I am kept back as I was at Baltchick and Old Fort. True, they have more wounded men than I, and are farther from the sea." And he adds in his journal: "What sluggishness in our movements! War can't be made in this way. The weather is admirable, and I do not profit by it! This is maddening."

September 23. . Marching is resumed. At four o'clock in the afternoon the outposts catch their first glimpse of Sebastopol and the lighthouse of the Chersonese.

September 24. The epidemic reappears. Several cholera patients are put aboard the fleet, which advances on a line with the army during the day, and anchors opposite the camp during the night.

From the bivouac of Belbek the Marshal writes to his brother: "To-morrow I move towards Balaclava.

I shall sleep on the Tchernaya, and on the 26th I shall be to the south of Sebastopol, master of Bala-clava, having outflanked all the strong batteries and redoubts of the enemy on the north.   It is a splen-did manœuvre.   Sebastopol is in sight, and from the city they can see the bivouac fires, which are spread over nearly three leagues."

On that very day he feels that, notwithstanding all his energy, his physical strength is deserting him.   To Colonel Trochu, urging him to resign his command, he replies: "I thank you for a candor which does you credit; I needed to hear this; I know my condition; my strength is gone; my con-science bids me give up my command, since I do not wish to endanger our success."   He resigns himself to the will of God like a good Christian, but he cannot help exclaiming: "Why am I not spared just long enough to enter Sebastopol?   If I could only go there, I would be content!"

On that day, too, — September 24, — at the bivouac of Belbek, the Marshal, already harassed by so many painful maladies, feels the first attacks of cholera.

September 25.   The sickness increases.

September 26.   There is no more hope.   The victor is obliged to resign the command to General Canrobert.   With a hand already cold he signs this order of the day, an adieu to the army: —

"Headquarters of the bivouac of Monkendié, September 26, 1854.   Soldiers, Providence denies your commander the satisfaction of continuing to lead you in the glorious path opening before you. Vanquished by the cruel malady against which he has struggled in vain, he faces with profound sadness, yet knows how to perform, the imperious duty imposed on him by circumstances: that of resigning a command whose weight his utterly ruined health no longer enables him to bear.

"Soldiers, you will pity me, for the misfortune by which I am stricken is immense, irreparable, and perhaps unexampled. I resign the command to General Canrobert, whom the Emperor, in his farsighted solicitude for this army and the great interests it represents, has invested with the necessary powers in a secret letter now lying before me. It is an alleviation of my grief that I can resign into hands so worthy the flag confided to me by France. You will surround with respect and confidence this general officer, whose brilliant military career and the splendor of the services he has performed have merited the most honorable celebrity in the country and the army. He will continue the victory of the Alma, and have the happiness of leading you to Sebastopol, which I had dreamed of for myself, and which I envy him."

Alas! in spite of their heroism, neither Canrobert nor Saint-Arnaud will enter Sebastopol.

The troops have established their bivouac on the banks of the Tchernaya. The touching farewell of their chief affects them, and their emotion increases when they see him turning towards Balaclava in the

carriage of Prince Menchikoff, taken at the battle of
the Alma. He halts for a moment, and seeing his
former companions in Africa, the Zouaves, who
respectfully draw near, he gives them a kind but
melancholy smile. On reaching Balaclava his only
thought is to embark on the *Berthollet* as soon as
possible, in the hope of again seeing his wife, who
is still in Constantinople. But the vessel will not
be ready until the 29th.

September 28. The progress of the cholera is
momentarily checked. The Marshal has some one
write from Balaclava that he is out of danger, and
that within a fortnight the flag of France will certainly wave above Sebastopol.

September 29. Eight o'clock in the morning.
The *Berthollet* is about to weigh anchor. This is
the ship on which the Marshal arrived in the Orient
from France. Here comes the victor of the Alma
on a litter carried by sailors, a tricolored flag at his
feet, and two companies of Zouaves lining his passage on either side. The English and French salute
him as he passes. He is put aboard the *Berthollet*.
The vessel sets sail.

During the voyage, on that very day, September
29, at four o'clock in the afternoon, without the
final blessing of a priest, the Marshal renders his
soul to God.

M. Benedetti, chargé d'affaires of France at
Constantinople, writes to M. Drouyn de Lhuys:
"Therapia, October 4, 1854. The mortal remains of

Marshal de Saint-Arnaud have been provisionally deposited in the chapel of the embassy, and I have had a funeral service celebrated, to which, in conformity with the wishes of Madame la Maréchale de Saint-Arnaud, I invited nobody but the officers attached to the Marshal's person and the principal functionaries. The English ambassador, accompanied by his secretaries and attachés, wished to join us in doing homage to the illustrious commander of our army, and to be present at this ceremony. The flags of the two embassies were at half-mast and will remain so until after the departure of the *Berthollet*, which sails to-day from the Bay of Therapia to convey the body of the Marshal to Marseilles.

"Wishing to accompany the mortal remains of her husband, Madame la Maréchale takes passage on board this vessel. I learn that the Ottoman government, desiring to express publicly its share in our regrets, has ordered the Seraskier and the Admiral to follow the convoy in two steamships as far as the Sea of Marmora, and has also given orders that all the batteries of the Bosphorus shall salute the *Berthollet*, as it passes, with nineteen volleys of cannon."

The *Moniteur* of October 11 reproduces an article by M. Louis Veuillot from the *Univers*, in which he says: "A profound affliction blends with the joy caused by the glorious news from the Crimea. God has taken a great victim. The hero of this prodigious campaign is dead. The ships which brought us his bulletins, so full of courage and martial ardor, are followed by that which bears his inanimate body. Three nations lower their grateful flags above his tomb. . . . In withdrawing him for a few hours from the anxieties of his command and the din of arms, Providence gave him what he had no doubt entreated of it, — time to humiliate his heart. This great general was a humble and fervent Christian."

France loves heroism. The imperialists will not be alone in celebrating Marshal de Saint-Arnaud. Legitimists, Orleanists, republicans, will forget the minister of the Coup d'Etat of December to remember only the commander-in-chief of the army of the Orient, the victor of the Alma, the man whose shroud was a triumphant flag.

CHAPTER XXIV

SEBASTOPOL! It is the name which for more than a year will resound throughout the world. Sebastopol! It is the city whose siege will be as renowned in modern times as the siege of Troy in those of old. Never at any period of history have such bloody battles been fought before ramparts; never have adversaries displayed such bitter perseverance. Sebastopol! For Russians it is the Holy City, the cradle of their orthodox faith. It is there, in the old city of the Chersonese, reduced by his arms, that the Grand Duke Vladimir professed the Christian faith in the year 988. Sebastopol! It is a religious and a military city. In its streets one sees only soldiers and sailors for fighting, and priests and monks to bless them. Of its forty-two thousand inhabitants, thirty-five thousand belong to the army and the navy. The surplus is composed of artisans and merchants, kept there by their occupation. The five thousand women are all accustomed to the rough life of maritime populations. They are heroic.

As M. Camille Roussot has said so well: "No

idle crowds, no vagabond classes, the usual elements ·
of disorder; no political divisions nor social an-
tagonism; no internal enemy demanding precautions
on the part of the defenders. The discipline of
minds is easy, because it has two principles: patriotism and religious faith. The military leaders can
invoke God and the patron saints of the city without being taxed with weakness or turned into
ridicule. People respect them because they are
great models of patriotic devotion and moral conduct."

The sound of church bells will alternate with the
roar of cannon, the orders of the chiefs with hymns,
the standards with the Cross. From the top of the
ramparts the allies were first seen on September 27.
Long files of priests, preceded by banners and
carrying holy water, went in procession all along
the unfinished wall. Two intrepid sailors, Vice-
Admirals Nakhimoff and Korniloff, the one commanding the active squadron and the other the
general staff of the fleet, inspire the inhabitants
with unbounded confidence. To them has just been
joined an officer of engineers from the army of the
Danube, Lieutenant-Colonel Todleben, who will
construct those formidable earthworks in front of
which such cruel slaughter will take place. "Children," cries Admiral Korniloff, "we must fight to
the very last. Kill any one who dares talk of
retreating. Kill me, if I order you to do so."
Soldiers, sailors, citizens, even women, set to work

at the improvised fortifications which are to render Sebastopol so long impregnable.

Since September 27 the allies have been established on the plateau of the Chersonese, opposite the city. This plateau, about to become so famous, is thirteen kilometres long by fifteen wide. On the north it is bounded by the great roadstead of Sebastopol, on the east by a line of acclivities known as Mount Sapoune, on the south and west by the sea and sundry promontories, of which the foremost is called Cape Chersonese. The landscape is severe and gloomy, the vegetation precarious and sickly; the stony ground, sometimes burnt by fierce sunlight and again drenched by torrents of rain, is furrowed by numerous ravines, one of which runs to the sea, the others towards the roadstead. No streams, only wells and cisterns; no villages, merely several farms. Trees are few, and nearly all are bent by the sea wind. The general impression is profoundly sad.

The victors of the Alma would like to take the town by storm. But that is already impossible. Earthworks have accumulated with prodigious rapidity. September 20, Prince Menchikoff had ordered Admiral Korniloff to destroy five vessels and two frigates, in order to defend the entrance of the road with their submerged wreckage. In despair at such an order, the admiral deferred the execution of it for more than two days. He thought it a sort of suicide. But he had to resign himself to it.

Thenceforward Sebastopol was in no danger of a sudden attack either from land or sea.

Writing before Sebastopol, October 4, 1854, General Bosquet says: "My good mother, we are before Sebastopol, which the Russians have allowed us to invest. . . . The operations of the siege are to begin to-morrow, for to-day we are completing the landing of our artillery and engineering stores. It is devilish hard work for an army without horses and carts. With nothing at all, we shall, I hope, make a *tour de force*, and the soldiers of the old Empire may salute us without regret.

"Marshal de Saint-Arnaud left us in a dying condition. Letters from the Emperor, kept secret until then, gave the command to my old friend Canrobert, who is the most capable and the most worthy of it. My joy on that head you can understand. His wound is improving; still he suffers and is very tired."

The French troops are to be divided into two corps: 1. The army set apart for the operations of the siege, under General Forey, composed of the 3d and 4th divisions; 2. the army intended to confront the relieving troops under Prince Menchikoff. This, which comprises the 1st and 2d divisions, some reserves of mounted artillery, and the cavalry who are landing, is commanded by General Bosquet. The English troops are similarly divided.

In the same letter the general adds: "This is a very great enterprise, and it is not easy to foresee

whether the resistance of Sebastopol will be long
and serious, or whether the place will surrender
after a week of cannonading and assault."

The opening of the trenches is decided on for the
night of October 9. At nine o'clock in the evening,
eight hundred foot soldiers advance in two files,
their muskets thrust through their belts, a shovel
and a pickaxe on their shoulder, as far as the wall
of the Maison Brûlée. At the final signal: *Arms
up!* eight hundred pickaxes rise and fall back upon
the earth. A violent northeast wind favors the
work by preventing the sound of the pickaxes from
reaching the fortified town, but fills the eyes of the
men with an annoying dust. At midnight twelve
hundred fresh workmen come to replace their comrades, who, after taking a short rest, renew their
task at four o'clock in the morning.

The English, on their part, have constructed
during the night a long trench at twelve metres'
distance from the Russian bastion called the Grand
Redan, their work having likewise been concealed
from the vigilance of their enemy.

At dawn of October 10 the Russians perceive all
these operations of the siege. They are surprised,
but not disturbed. They had feared a sudden
attack. The sight of the trenches reassures them.
Every day gained has permitted them to increase
their means of defence. Between September 30 and
October 17, Prince Menchikoff has augmented the
garrison of Sebastopol by thirty battalions. The

English army contains twenty-two thousand men,
the French forty-two thousand, and the Turkish
division five thousand.

By October 17, the day fixed for the bombardment, the allies have greatly advanced their
trenches. The firing begins at half-past six in the
morning. Three bombs, thrown by the 3d French
battery, give the signal by exploding in the Russian
bastion of the Flagstaff. One hundred and twenty-
six howitzers, of which fifty-three are French, simultaneously eject a multitude of projectiles. All the
allied troops, out and under arms, await the result
of this terrible bombardment. The Russians, who
expect the appearance of assaulting columns, respond with extreme energy to the fire of the allies
by that of two hundred and fifty cannon. Towards
ten o'clock two French powder magazines explode
and throw the French batteries into such confusion
that, unable to reply any longer to the deluge of
projectiles showered upon them, they discontinue
firing. But the English keep on with success.

It had been decided that the allied fleets should
combine their action with that of the land forces,
and bring their broadsides to bear on the forts of the
town to bombard it. But a contrary wind forced
them to delay their movement until half-past twelve.
At that hour the line of broadside begins to form
in an arc of more than three kilometres. At about
fourteen hundred metres from the Quarantine Fort
and Fort Alexander, fourteen French vessels form

in two ranks, next come two Turkish vessels; then, in front of Fort Constantine and the coast batteries of the cliffs, eleven English ships. The French flagship, the *Ville de Paris*, opens fire. It is one o'clock. Everything is enveloped in a thick cloud of smoke. The fire of the allied vessels produces little effect on the Russian batteries, which, protected by masonry, inflict more harm than they endure. The *Ville de Paris* is struck by fifty balls, and part of its poop is carried away by a shell.

On land, if the fire of the French batteries is stopped, that of the English continues in the most brilliant fashion and crushes the Russian bastion of the Grand Redan into a mass of ruins, upon which the Russians expect to see the English rush, plant their flag, and precipitate themselves into the suburb of Karabelnaïa. But this will not happen. Prudence will take the upper hand of audacity. An assault is not dreamed of. As the day advances, the firing slackens. By six in the evening the cannons roar but seldom, and the last vessels of the allied fleets quit the line of battle. They had launched more than thirty thousand projectiles. During the bombardment the English have lost forty-four killed and two hundred and sixty wounded; the French, eighty wounded and thirty killed. The Russians have had one hundred and sixty-eight men killed or wounded. Their principal victim is the heroic Admiral Korniloff, whose last words were: "Tell them all that it is sweet to

die when the conscience is pure. My God! bless
the Russians and the Emperor! Save Sebastopol
and the fleet!"

The bombardment is renewed on the 18th and
19th, but no more successfully than on the 17th.
General Bosquet writes on the 20th: "We are
knocking at the doors of Sebastopol, but the Russians defend themselves vigorously, and there will
be glory in getting in. We are not going quite so
fast as those terrible warriors in dressing-gowns
who so finely misled the Emperor by announcing
the taking of the city. Really, we have gained a
very serious battle; but Sebastopol has nearly three
hundred pieces of ordnance in battery and twenty
thousand Finnish sailors to man them. That is
something to think about, and we are making a
regular siege. I am writing you, dear mother, from
my headquarters, to the noise of a furious cannonading."

Again, on November 2: "My good mother, we
are firing harder than ever on the Russian batteries,
and the hundreds of pieces of naval artillery with
which they have surrounded their city; we go on
sapping, compelled to dig a great many of our
trenches and spring our mines in the rock, which is
enormously difficult. Nearly ten thousand Russian
sailors from Finland are allowing themselves to be
crushed by inches in order to defend by land their
fine fleet, which they cannot bring themselves to
abandon; they are fine soldiers, very resolute. This

is the business of General Forey, who commands the besieging troops.

"For my part, with the corps of observation of from sixteen thousand to seventeen thousand men, thirty pieces of artillery, and from twelve hundred to fifteen hundred horses, I hold in awe, thanks to good lines, an army of forty thousand Russians, who lie in wait for me day and night. It is beginning to grow very cold, and it is unpleasant to spend a part of the night out of doors. It is very rough, but we are nearing the end of it, I hope.

"It is a very great affair, very difficult; one of these days it will seem an almost impossible feat. I cannot understand how the notion came to be so easily invented in France that it was a very simple thing to tear away from a warlike nation the stronghold of its power in the south, a vast harbor, an arsenal of cannon. It is enormous, and you may believe that the most hardened of us will be worn out by the end of the campaign. May God give us strength!"

General Bizòt, who commanded the engineer corps of the French army, had written to Marshal Vaillant, Minister of War: "General Canrobert is very anxious to precipitate an attack by main force; so is Lord Raglan. . . . For my part, I fall back as far as I can, thinking that our chances of success will be all the greater the nearer we bring together our point of departure, our base of operations, and of retreat for our columns." Every night at least two thousand, sometimes three thousand, laborers extend the network of the siege. By October 23, the first parallel, some two-fifths of a mile in length, is finished, and the second carries the French attacks to within three hundred and sixty yards of the bastion of the Flagstaff. The first parallel of the English goes to within twelve hundred yards of the Grand Redan; the second is about nine hundred yards from the spur of this bastion. The hour is approaching when the English army, instead of attacking, will have to defend itself.

CHAPTER XXV

BALACLAVA

IN addition to Sebastopol, the Russians continue to occupy a considerable part of the Crimea. Their army of succor, posted in the windings of the Belbek and the woods of the northern plateau, is constantly receiving reinforcements, and they hope to surround the besiegers and beat them back to the sea.

The port of Balaclava, at the southern extremity of the Crimea, is the English base of operations. The port is garrisoned by only a thousand marines. But in front of the place extends an intrenched camp, capable of containing an army three times as large as that of the English. The outposts have been confided to a thousand Turkish soldiers. Four kilometres to the north of the town, on a succession of rounded hillocks, and at wide intervals, are five redoubts, which, from the foot of Mount Sapoune to the village of Kamara, divide on the north the plain of Balaclava from the valley of the Tchernaya.

Prince Menchikoff has observed that the English have not men enough to defend their positions. He brings together a body of twenty-one thousand seven

hundred soldiers, who fall upon the English lines in
the morning of October 25, 1854. The Turks, having been forced to abandon the five redoubts, the
assailants debouch into the plain of Balaclava, and
send a brigade of hussars and Cossacks toward
Kadikoi. The 9th Highlanders are awaiting them.
"Then," writes M. Camille Rousset, "was seen
what a solid infantry can do by the mere firmness
of its attitude. Drawn up in line of battle, arms
down, the Scotch seemed indifferent to the noisy
avalanche rolling towards them, until at thirty
paces' distance the officers ordered them to make
ready arms. At the mere sight of this coolly executed manœuvre, the mere aspect of the raised
muskets, not yet lowered, the horsemen changed
their bearing on the instant. The horses, suddenly
drawn in, began to rear, the ranks fell into confusion." At this moment the English cavalry of
the line, the Scarlett brigade, composed of Scotch
Greys and dragoons, moved forward to assist the
Highlanders. Led to the charge by three intrepid
officers, they plunged like a wedge into the midst
of the Russian cavalry. These whirled around for
an instant, and then, turning their horses, galloped
to the rear of the centre redoubt, to re-form under
cover of their artillery and infantry. This retreat
of the Russian cavalry was a real success for the
English. Unfortunately, their brigade of light cavalry, the Cardigan, placed in echelons too far in
the rear, could not arrive in time to complete this

success ; otherwise, it might perhaps have averted the disaster awaiting it.

The Russians seemed less disposed to resume the offensive since reinforcements had been sent their adversaries, and the battle was apparently ended.

From the summit of a plateau overlooking the plain of Balaclava, Lord Raglan, the English commander-in-chief, had been watching all the vicissitudes of the combat. Towards noon he noted through his spy-glass that the Russians were taking away some guns seized from the Turkish redoubts. Thereupon he summoned an aide-de-camp, Captain Nolan, and commissioned him to carry to Lord Lucan, commander of the English cavalry, this order, which was to be fatal : —

" Lord Raglan desires the cavalry to move rapidly to the front and try to prevent the enemy from carrying off the cannon. A troop of mounted artillery may accompany them. The French cavalry is on your left. At once." Lord Raglan supposed that the Russians were still retreating, and that all that was necessary was to pursue the fugitives. He was completely deceived. At the moment when Captain Nolan was delivering this unlucky order of the English commander-in-chief, the Russians had ceased retreating, and installed themselves in excellent positions. Their infantry and divisional artillery occupied the hillocks and southerly slopes of the Fedioukhine hills. The reserves were at the back of a sort of funnel. In the middle the cavalry and

mounted artillery had resumed their position. How
could a mere brigade of light cavalry be hurled
against such masses of men in such positions? It
seems madness, and yet it must be done. Stupefied,
Lord Lucan read and re-read the order without being
able to comprehend it. Could he in conscience send
men to certain death without the least chance of success? But the order was formal, and Captain Nolan
insisted violently on its immediate execution. Lord
Lucan sent for Lord Cardigan, the commander of the
brigade of light infantry, and ordered him to charge.
Though bravery itself, Lord Cardigan hesitated a
moment, not for himself, but for his soldiers. He
thought it his duty to make the objections indicated
by good sense. But the order was formal. The
trumpets sounded. The heroic leader rode at the
head of his brigade! "Forward!" he cried; "forward the last of the Cardigans!" The bearer of
the order, Captain Nolan, galloped on his right.

Posted on the heights, thousands of Frenchmen
perceived in the distance this foolhardy raid, this
incomprehensible manœuvre: "Halt! it is madness!" they shouted, as if their cries could reach
the ears of Lord Cardigan's riders. These continued intrepidly their terrible and bloody *steeple
chase*, flinging themselves under the cross-fires of
the enemy as into a gulf. But human energy has
its limits. What can a brigade do against an army?
It clashes against the Russian infantry, cavalry, and
artillery. Captain Nolan is one of the first men

killed. To advance further becomes an impossibility. They can only turn and beat a retreat. At this moment two squadrons of African chasseurs, under General d'Allonville, came to the assistance of Lord Cardigan's cavalry. Forcing the line of sharpshooters, they passed behind the Russian battery established on the Fedioukhine hills, and drew upon themselves the fire of the battalions formed in a hollow square. The Scarlett brigade, English cavalry of the line, who had made such a brilliant fight in the morning, and who were held in reserve when the charge of the Cardigan brigade began, now got into motion so as to allow the latter to rally its few remaining men. Of seven hundred horsemen who had begun the charge, five hundred lay dead on the field of battle. By a miracle Lord Cardigan survived.

The charge of Balaclava will remain legendary. It is one of the most useless yet most chivalrous exploits in military history. It will always be incomprehensible, and the heroism with which it was conducted will not excuse it from the military point of view. But in it the English displayed so much audacity and courage that this slaughter will always hold a splendid place in the glories of the Crimean War. In London it was the subject of the most animated discussions in the clubs, the newspapers, and in Parliament. Lord Raglan's order and the haste with which it was executed by Lord Lucan evoked the most contradictory criticisms.

But, after all, England was justly proud of the heroism of her sons.

The partial engagements we have just described have been called the battle of Balaclava. Lord Cardigan's charge, at once glorious and fatal, has remained its most famous episode. On the whole, the battle of October 25 had not been bad for the Russians. Their taking the offensive had produced a good moral effect on their troops, who, on establishing themselves in the valley of the Tchernaya and the plain of Balaclava, made ready for a new attack on the besiegers, fancying that the defeat of the Alma would be speedily avenged.

CHAPTER XXVI

INKERMAN

INKERMAN has been for the second Empire what Eylau was for the first : a sinister victory in foggy and glacial weather under a sombre sky ; a battle in which the sufferings and calamities of war were displayed in all their horror. " Everything combined," says M. Camille Rousset, " to give the battle-field of Inkerman a lamentable aspect : man and nature. Clouds of fog hung low above it, while the smoke of cannon rolled heavily over the damp ground. On the plain of Eylau the fog was equally low, but snow reflected back what little light there was, and the white earth illumined the black sky. On the plateau of Inkerman all was gray, dull, livid, dirty. . . . The men tramped through bloody mire. The drums, slackened by the rain, emitted only a broken, raucous, muffled sound ; beaten like this, the charge was no longer inspiring ; it became dismal."

On the 5th of November, the day of the battle, the allied army in the Crimea amounted to sixty-five thousand men, — forty thousand French, twenty thousand English, and five thousand Turks : the

Russians had one hundred thousand. Relying on their superior numbers and the resources of Sebastopol, the latter had conceived the scheme of falling upon the besiegers and hustling them back to the sea. They knew that the English lines to the right of Sebastopol, from the Voronzoff road to the lower course of the Tchernaya, were not defended by sufficient forces, and that could they make an unexpected attack on the plateau of Inkerman, cut up by ravines, hollowed out by sinuosities, bristling with thickets and lending itself to surprises, they would have great chances of success.

Encouraged by the partial success of Balaclava, the defenders of Sebastopol were filled with hope. On October 30 Prince Menchikoff had written to Prince Paskievitchf : " The future will preserve the memory of the exemplary chastisement inflicted on the presumption of the allies.   Holy Russia is visibly protected by Heaven."   Coming from Saint Petersburg, two sons of the Czar, the Grand Dukes Nicholas and Michael, made their entry into Sebastopol, November 3, surrounded by an enthusiastic crowd. An attack on the English lines had been decided for the 5th, but this was not even suspected by the allies.

The 4th of November had been dull and rainy, and the rain continued to fall in torrents through the night.   At midnight all the church bells of Sebastopol rang the signal for beginning the prayers for the combatants of the next day.   The air resounded with the shouts of the soldiers in response to excited harangues and the benedictions of priests. In their trenches outside the town the allies at three o'clock in the morning heard distant rumors, cries, chants, the grinding of wheels. But they felt no alarm. Were not the Russians in the habit of praying night and day? Did not their steeples and their hymns resound as often as their cannons? Were not the wagons those of the market gardeners who supplied the town?

The English by no means anticipated a surprise. The night was thick with clouds. The earth was soaked with icy dampness. The pools of water will soon be pools of blood. So soon to be the theatre of such horrible slaughter, the plateau of Inkerman is as yet silent. All are sleeping except a few sentinels who are painfully struggling against sleep.

Night has just ended, but without giving place to day, so heavy is the fog. Leaving Sebastopol by the suburb of Karabelnaya, the Russians approach the plateau of Inkerman. At first the English can distinguish nothing but the fire and smoke of cannon and musketry. But it soon becomes evident that under cover of a host of sharpshooters the enemy have carried cannons of large calibre to the high grounds on the left, just opposite the 2d English division, while heavy columns of infantry are attacking the brigade commanded by the Duke of Cambridge. The Russians have placed ninety cannon in position. Sheltered by a terrible firing, the Russian columns are advancing in great force ; it needs great heroism to enable the English troops to continue their resistance.

At the extremity of their lines the English had constructed a work which they called the *Battery of the Earth-sacks*. Here the fight was chiefly concentrated. Never has there been a bloodier mêlée. In the evening General Bosquet, halting at this spot and beholding such a pile of corpses, will exclaim : "What an abattoir !" And the *Battery of the Earth-sacks* will retain the name : *Battery of the Abattoir*.

General Bosquet is the hero of Inkerman. At daybreak, at the first sound of the firing, without even giving his troops time to take any food, he set in motion the French corps of observation who were encamped on the southern plateau of Mount Sapoune. He went himself as far as Moulin, where, meeting the two English generals Brown and Cathcart, he offered them the assistance of his troops. They replied: "Our reserves are sufficient to provide against contingencies; merely be kind enough to cover our right at the back of the English intrenchment." Still, General Bosquet remained convinced that the English were presuming too much on their strength and would soon be forced to call on the French for help. Hence without delay he united the 6th battalion of the line and the 7th of the light troops under the command of General Bourbaki, and put them in position to the right of

Moulin, near a little village known as Canrobert's redoubt, ordering them to be in readiness to march at the first signal.

At this moment a new cannonade is added to that of Inkerman; that of General Gortchakoff, who, with troops debouching from Tchergoun, is making a diversion in the valley of Balaclava. General Bosquet, who has returned to his encampment of the Telegraph, feels that this diversion will be unimportant. " Go to Inkerman," says he to an aide-de-camp of Lord Raglan; "everything will happen there."

With rare comprehension, that admirable soldier, General Bosquet, had divined coming emergencies. The time is at hand for the French troops to take part in the battle. The English are exhausted; they have been heroic, but they are worn out. General Strangways has just been killed at Lord Raglan's side. General Canrobert, who had gone to Inkerman after leaving orders at the siege, has been wounded in the arm by a bursting shell. As at the battle of the Alma, he has had his wound dressed on the spot and rejoined Lord Raglan. The latter writes afterwards in his report of the battle: "I am glad to have occasion to say publicly how highly I appreciate the precious assistance I have received from the commander-in-chief, General Canrobert, who was personally on the ground and in constant communication with me; I cannot give too much praise to his cordial co-operation in all circumstances."

It is almost nine o'clock. Colonel Steel, an aide-de-camp of Lord Raglan, comes at full gallop to the Telegraph, where he finds General Bosquet. "The English are overwhelmed," he cries; "there is not a minute to lose if the day is to be regained." — "Go tell my allies," replies the General, "that the French are coming at breakneck speed."

A few minutes later the English hear the bugles of the French infantry. Here come the 6th of the line and the 7th light with four companies of light infantry and two mounted batteries. General Bosquet rejoins his troops just as they are about to form in line. As soon as the English see the red trousers beginning to stand out on the gray horizon, they applaud, they shout "*Hurrah for the French!*" There are but one thousand six hundred and fifty of the latter, hardly as many as the effective of an English brigade. But their heroic charge produces the greatest impression; presently reinforcements reach them, two battalions of the 3d Zouaves, two of the 50th of the line, one of Algerian sharpshooters, and a mounted battery. The Zouaves, as General Bosquet will say in his report, "manœuvre with that intelligence, that tried bravery, which remains unconcerned even when the enemy surrounds you a moment." The Algerian sharpshooters, led by Colonel de Wimpffen, who has a horse killed under him, "bound into the thickets like panthers." The 6th of the line avenges the heroic death of Colonel de Camers. The Battery

of the Earth-sacks is retaken after ferocious assaults.
A great number of Russian soldiers, driven to the
extremity of the counterfort which ends perpendic-
ularly over the Tchernaya, are flung from the top
of this natural wall, and fall dead or mortally
wounded near the aqueduct and the river. "After
the peace," writes General Fay, "we went through
all these points, which we had known either not at
all or badly, and on descending to the foot of these
heights our hearts were constricted by the sight of the
bones piled up in the crevices of the rocks. Doubtless, all who had not been assisted, and who were
unable to gain the other shore, had dragged themselves thither. On the day of the battle the Russians had four days' provisions; it is not difficult to
imagine the terrible scenes which must have been
enacted in these assemblies of the wounded, where,
as in shipwrecks, the strongest were obliged to prolong their existence with the provisions of the dead,
and perhaps by violence, at the expense of those
who, though still breathing, were no longer able to
defend themselves."

Let us return to the battle. It is eleven o'clock.
The allies have evidently gained the day, even
though there is still a furious cannonading going on.
General Bosquet's horse is shot under him near the
Battery of the Earth-sacks. The diversion effected
by General Timofeief, who made a sortie from
Sebastopol, and fell upon the French troops, has
failed. The general has been recalled to the city.

Unfortunately the French had allowed themselves
to be drawn on too far, and in their compulsory retreat have lost one of their bravest leaders, General
de Lourmel.

At last the terrible day nears its close. " Just as
the Russian fire was dying down," General Bosquet
will say in his report, " I sent a divisional battery
to the high ground, whence they could cover with
shells and balls the Inkerman bridges by which were
escaping the Russian troops which we had had the
pleasure of seeing fly before us in utter rout. However, their flight was protected by the marshes which,
unfortunately, we have been unable to cross; otherwise we should have had a fine close to a victorious
battle. I thank Generals d'Autemarre and Bourbaki, who led their troops so courageously, and Colonel de Cissey for the cordial way in which he
seconded me. I wish I could mention all the heroes
who have fought so well at Inkerman, but that would
be to name everybody."

Evening comes. General Bosquet's soldiers are
going to sit down amidst the dead and dying to the
first meal they have taken that day, around the Battery of the Abattoir, since this is henceforward the
name of the Battery of the Earth-sacks. General
Fay, then General Bosquet's aide-de-camp, thus
describes the scene : —

" From the top of the breastwork of the battery
on which we were sitting, we looked sadly at those
masculine faces surprised by death in the moment

of action ; some of them still biting off the cartridge, others hanging from the embrasures, nearly all without a trace of anger on their countenances, and with features as composed as if in slumber. They at least were dead, but the wounded, what sufferings they endured after the battle ! "

There was no armistice, and as the enemy's sharpshooters fired on those who attempted the work of burial, it was impossible to look for the dead and dying at the further extremity of the positions. " Wounded men were brought in even after eight days," adds General Fay, " and what days they must have been for the poor fellows ! . . . They were crowded under tents, to languish sometimes for a week or ten days before they could be attended to. Those who survived these long hours of suffering were finally taken to the ambulance camp of the second French division, that tent in which the operations were performed, and the very thought of which makes one shudder. . . . And yet, amidst these melancholy scenes, one often found among these brave soldiers the good humor and gaiety which saves our French soldiers from homesickness. ' Ah ! then, Major, so we must wait our turn here as at the Porte Saint Martin,' said a Zouave quietly to a doctor. He was smoking a pipe while awaiting his, and it was a matter of cutting off his leg. One laughed and cried at once, listening to the simple and heroic words of this child of Paris."

Considering the number of the troops engaged,

few battles have been as bloody as that of Inkerman, justly described as a whirlwind of combats. Out of the eighty-two hundred French who had fought on the plateau, seven hundred and ninety-three were killed or wounded. The English, all of whose disposable forces had been engaged, with the exception of one brigade left at the siege, and another at Balaclava, had twenty-eight hundred and sixteen men disabled. As to the Russians, out of the thirty-four thousand men who had taken part in the fight, twenty-nine hundred and eighty-eight were killed and sixty-one hundred and fifty-one wounded. Their funeral statistics added to this list eighteen hundred and ninety men missing. These were neither deserters nor prisoners, but the wretched soldiers flung over the cliffs above the valley of the Tchernaya, whose skeletons, bleached by sun and washed by rain, were recovered after the peace.

We shall terminate this account by two letters from General Bosquet: "November 7, 1854. My health is perfect, good mother; fatigue does not affect it. That is because I have had a little happiness now and then. Day before yesterday, November 5, in a battle near Inkerman, I beat the Russians and drove them across the bridges of the Tchernaya. The next day, the Duke of Cambridge came to my tent to thank me for having saved the remnant of the English guards, who lost heavily that day. Lord Raglan — who has only one arm — said to me to-day, holding out his only hand, that he wished he had several with which to shake mine. We are engaged in one of the most foolhardy enterprises that has been attempted since the Crusades. But it is the right cause; you can all pray for us, and I fully believe that God will assist us."

"December, 1854. My good mother, here is my New Year's gift; this year the Russians and the Emperor have assisted me to prepare it for you; it is the grand officer's cross of the Legion of Honor, which I have just received, and which with Anna's help I am pinning on your big shawl, — as we did one day, if you remember, with my commander's badge. . . . What fine soldiers these brave fellows of the 5th are whom I have led against the Russians! What courage! what intelligence! what address! A sign was enough to make them comprehend and strike."

CHAPTER XXVII

NOVEMBER 21, 1854, the Emperor wrote from the palace of Saint-Cloud to General Canrobert : "General, I have been profoundly affected by your report on the victory of Inkerman. Tell the army for me how entirely satisfied I am with the courage it has displayed, the energy with which it has endured fatigues and privations, and its ardent cordiality towards its allies. Thank the generals, officers, and soldiers for their valiant behavior. Say that I sympathize keenly with their sufferings and their cruel losses, and that it will be my most constant care to alleviate their bitterness."

The letter of Napoleon III. ended in this way : "If Europe has not been alarmed at the sight of our long-banished eagles spreading their wings with so much splendor, it is because it knows well that we are fighting only for its independence. If France has resumed the rank which is her due, and if victory has once more made our flags illustrious, I declare proudly that it is to the patriotism and the indomitable bravery of the army that I owe it."

November 22, cannon were fired at the Invalides to announce the victory of Inkerman.

At this time, only the splendid aspects of the war were regarded in Paris; its horrors were passed over in silence, its torrents of blood forgotten. Of the terrible sufferings endured by the troops, only vague notions were formed. In writing to their families, officers and soldiers alike made light of these in order not to enhance their grief. The tendency of people's minds was to optimism. The army was glad of a chance of advancement. The diplomatists were elated with the part played by France. The army contractors made great fortunes. Commerce and industry profited by the war. In the conscription of 1854, all young men of means who drew a bad number and felt no inclination for war, procured substitutes; and no one dreamed of blaming them for it. The democratic sentiment was not then so fully developed that this privilege of wealth to exempt itself from the blood tax could arouse objections. As the Crimean War made only a minority suffer, and was carried on in a distant region, selfishness was not immediately affected. The splendid setting of the second Empire was in no wise disturbed by it. It may even be said that it gave it added brilliancy.

Nowadays the human conscience revolts against war. In 1854 people were ready to believe it a necessity for nations. To-day they comprehend the saying of that pre-eminent scientist, Pasteur, who has described himself as "a man who has an invincible belief that Science and Peace will conquer Ignorance and War ; that the peoples will agree not to destroy, but to enlighten each other." In 1854 such ideas appeared fantastic.

Nowadays France would be content with the second place in Europe if Russia occupied the first. But in 1854 her views were far more ambitious. She did not admit the supremacy of any power. Hence the Crimean War seemed legitimate, because its object was to take away the Czar's predominance in Europe and give the leading part to France. Had its delays and cruel vicissitudes occurred towards the close of the second Empire, the newspapers and the opposition would have used them skilfully against the government and would doubtless have succeeded in weakening and discouraging public opinion. But in 1854 Napoleon III. had crushed all opposition, and his foreign policy had no adverse critics; even the hostile parties approved the Crimean War.

From his prison on Belle-Isle, the famous revolutionist, Barbès, had written to a friend, September 18, 1854: "If you are touched with chauvinism because you put up no prayers for the Russians, I am still more fanatical than you, for I long for victories for our Frenchmen. Yes! yes! may they thrash the Russians well over yonder; it will be all the more gained for the cause of civilization

and the world. . . . Since Waterloo we are the conquered people of Europe, and to do any good, even
at home, I think it is useful to show foreigners
that we know how to eat powder."

Becoming acquainted with this letter, Napoleon
III. had it published in the *Moniteur*, which simultaneously published another letter addressed by the
sovereign to the Minister of the Interior, October 3,
1854, in which he said: "A prisoner who retains
such patriotic sentiments in spite of long sufferings
cannot remain in prison under my reign. Therefore have him set immediately at liberty, and without conditions."

Barbès had almost to be forced to accept his freedom. When free he would not remain in France,
but went to Holland. From The Hague he wrote
to George Sand, October 22, 1854: "I was a patriot
in my cradle. As a child it made me ill to learn the
defeat of Waterloo, and so long as it is not demon-
strated to me that there is a country more advanced
than France, a country with a better heart and
greater devotion, in spite of all the faults of which
she may be accused, I shall desire that her flag may
triumph, no matter what hand carries it."

In 1854 Russia was not in vogue either with the
partisans or the adversaries of Napoleon III. Republican and Orleanist sympathies were entirely on
the side of Poland, and possibly it did not displease
the Orleans princes to see .the autocrat who had
been ill disposed toward their father in difficulties.

They followed with eager interest all the phases of a war in which their former brethren in arms were distinguishing themselves, and whose dangers and glories they bitterly regretted that they could not share. The Duchesse d'Orléans, as French at heart as her brothers-in-law, was then at Eisenach with her two sons. Each of them made lint for the wounded around her tea-table. It was touching to hear the exiles say: "Our army; our brave troops." The young Comte de Paris knew the towers and forts of Sebastopol as if he had seen them with his own eyes.

As to the legitimists, although an alliance with Russia would have been popular among them, their attitude was irreproachable and they were grateful to the government for having defended the rights of Catholics in the Holy Places. In fine, it may be said that the Bourbons of both branches manifested sentiments inspired by the purest patriotism. The exiles remembered but one thing: their character as Frenchmen.

Seeing that even his adversaries did not blame him for a war which existing public opinion considered essential to the equilibrium of Europe, Napoleon III. was convinced that his troops were contending for the cause of law, justice, and civilization. He was incessantly told so. He believed it with the utmost sincerity. He delighted in the martial ardor which was displayed in France. "The Emperor Napoleon III.," writes General du

Barail, "had the soldier's passion, and neglected no
occasion of being amongst the troops. . . . Of all
the institutions of the first Empire the most tempt-
ing to him was naturally the imperial guard, that
beautiful legendary guard the appearance of which
on the field of battle was enough to secure victory."
He revived it at the close of 1854, at first in very
modest proportions from the numerical point of
view : a regiment of guides, a regiment of cuirassiers, four batteries of artillery, a platoon and two
battalions of gendarmery, two regiments of grenadiers, two of light cavalry, a battalion of foot-sol-
diers, and a company of engineers.

November 27, 1854, the Emperor held the first
review of the newly reconstructed imperial guard.
The infantry was drawn up on either side of the
grand alley of the Tuileries garden, from the palace
as far as the Place de la Concorde. The cavalry
occupied the grand avenue of the Champs Elysées.
The troops were under the orders of general of
division Regnault de Saint-Jean d'Angély, commanding the guard, and Generals Mellinet and
Urich. The weather was superb. People admired
the Guides with their plumes, the grenadiers with
their French coats, white breast-plates, cross-belts,
and tall hair caps, the light cavalry with their
tasselled shakos, which reminded one of the young
guard of Napoleon I., the cuirassiers with long
heavy boots, white leather breeches, and helmets
with two manes. After walking his horse along the

front of the lines, the Emperor placed himself in
front of the Horloge pavilion to see the march.
The Empress was on the balcony. Lord and Lady
Palmerston, Lord and Lady Cowley, and several
ladies invited by the Empress were present at this
review. The troops cheered heartily in passing in
front of Their Majesties. "It would be difficult,"
said the *Moniteur*, "to describe the effect produced
by these fine regiments whose martial bearing not
less than their uniform recalled the imperial guard
of glorious memory."

While Paris was taking pleasure in the sight of
new, brilliant, magnificent uniforms, there were
some on the plateau of the Chersonese which victory
indeed had worn threadbare, but which had also
suffered from rain, snow, and mishaps of every kind.
The Crimean nights were long and cold. The days
seemed as dismal as the nights. Every sort of
calamity fell at the same time upon the army. On
November 14 there was a frightful cyclone. Never
in the memory of man had this region, subject as it
was to violent winds, known such a tempest. Never
had the elements been unchained with such fury.
All the tents were blown down, all the soldiers' huts
broken like glass. The wind panted with rage.
The thunder never ceased to rumble. Some of the
ambulances, partially sheltered in the ravines, could
be saved from destruction; but there were others
whose huts were carried off by the wind, leaving the
sick and wounded exposed to torrents of rain and all

the shocks of the tempest. These unfortunates uttered horrible cries. But for the devotion of their comrades, who carried them to the few buildings saved, all would have perished. The water gushed into the trenches as from a spring. At sea the devastation was still greater than on land. Never had the Euxine better deserved its evil repute. Through the roaring of the waves and the whistling of the wind the alarm guns could be heard, and the repeated cries from a multitude of vessels in distress. The French merchant marine lost several ships. Two war-vessels, the *Henri IV.* and the *Pluton*, went ashore near Eupatoria. Several English vessels lost both crew and cargo. The cyclone was followed by frost, snow, and thaw. No provision had been made for such a winter campaign, and the sufferings of the troops outstripped all imagination.

The echo of the cry of anguish did not reach so far as Paris. The commander-in-chief continued to represent matters under the most favorable aspect. The *Moniteur* of December 12 published a report addressed by him to Marshal Vaillant, Minister of War. In it he said : "Our situation is improving in every respect. We are receiving reinforcements, and our regiments of Zouaves, like all those born in Africa, especially present a most satisfactory ensemble. Our victualling has assumed grand proportions, and from to-day I shall be able to distribute a daily ration of wine or brandy to the soldiers.

This is a very important point, which will avert
many maladies and enable us to safeguard our effective forces.   On the other hand, our winter clothing
is arriving, and already the hooded cloaks and
sheepskin overcoats are in the majority in our
camps.   The soldier will nobly and courageously
endure the trial of bad weather, seeing that he is the
object of cares hitherto unknown to him, and which
show so much solicitude for his situation on the part
of the Emperor and his ministry."

General Canrobert concluded his report in this
way: "I can assure you, M. le Maréchal, that the
army is acquiring a rare solidity, and you could not
imagine to what degree our young fellows, suddenly
matured by the greatness of the struggle, quickly
become old soldiers.   You could not have beheld
without keen satisfaction the deployed lines remaining calm and motionless under a cannonading which
Lord Raglan has told me was superior to that which
he heard at Waterloo."

Such reports inflamed the national imagination.
The military and the diplomatic situation were
viewed with satisfaction.   The treaty signed December 2, at Vienna, between Austria, France, and
Great Britain was considered the first step towards
a speedy peace.   By its first article the three powers
bound themselves not to enter into any treaty with
Russia without previously deliberating together.
By the second the Austrian Emperor promised to
defend the frontier of the Danubian Principalities

against any return of the Russian forces. The third stipulated that if hostilities should break out between Austria and Russia, the Emperor Francis Joseph and the Emperor Napoleon III. and Queen Victoria promised their mutual offensive and defensive alliance.

What dominated in Paris was a sentiment of optimism. Not a diversion, not a pleasure, had been abandoned. All the salons were open. The fashionable season promised to be very brilliant. At the Opéra the reigning diva, Mademoiselle Sophie Cruvelli, was triumphant. December 21, to celebrate the birthday of Racine, Mademoiselle Rachel played *Phèdre.* The next night, Verdi's *Trovatore* was produced for the first time, at the Italian Theatre. It had a tremendous success, and the touching and poetic Mademoiselle Frezzolini was greatly applauded.

December 26, Napoleon III. opened the legislative session at the Tuileries, in the hall of the Marshals, and his speech produced a great impression. He said : " A great empire, renewing its youth by the chivalrous sentiments of its sovereign, has detached itself from the power which has threatened the independence of Europe for perhaps the last forty years. The Emperor has to-day concluded a defensive treaty, soon perhaps to become offensive, which unites his cause with those of France and England." After celebrating the English alliance Napoleon III. added : " Unite with me on this solemn occasion in

thanking Parliament, in the name of France, for its
warm and cordial demonstration, and the English
army and its worthy commander for their valiant
co-operation.   Next year, if peace is not sooner proclaimed, I hope to offer the same thanks to Austria
and to that Germany whose union and prosperity
we so much desire." Alas! the union of Germany,
in what conditions was it one day to be realized!

The troops in the Crimea next received this well-
deserved eulogy: "Up to this day the army of the
Orient has suffered and overcome all things : epi-
demics, conflagrations, tempests, privations, a fortified town incessantly revictualled, defended by land
and sea by formidable artillery, two hostile armies
superior in numbers ; yet nothing has diminished its
courage or lessened its enthusiasm.   Each has nobly
done his duty, from the marshal who seemed to force
death to wait until he had conquered, to the soldier
and sailor whose dying cry was a prayer for France
and an acclamation of the elected of the people.
Let us then affirm together that the army and the
fleet have deserved well of the Fatherland."

Napoleon III. thus ended his speech : "The
struggle which is going on, circumscribed by
moderation and justice, alarms private interests so
little that we shall soon bring together here from
the different parts of the world all the products of
peace.   Foreigners cannot fail to be struck with the
impressive spectacle of a country which, relying upon
divine protection, energetically maintains a war six

hundred leagues from its frontiers, and which with equal energy develops its internal wealth ; a country where war does not prevent agriculture and industry from prospering, the arts from flourishing, and where the genius of the nation reveals itself in all that can conduce to the glory of France."

December 30, the Emperor reviewed in the court of the Tuileries all the troops comprising the army of Paris under command of Marshal Magnan. The Empress saw the review from the balcony of the hall of the Marshals. The next day, December 31, there was a grand review in the Crimea. The 1st and 2d corps and the corps of observation of the army received on this occasion the recompenses so nobly deserved by courage, labor, and discipline. General de Montebello, aide-de-camp to the Emperor, had brought a decree to the commander-in-chief which authorized him to fill vacancies up to the rank of chief of battalion or squadron, to make nominations and promotions in the Legion of Honor, and to confer the military medal. More than once the music of the bands was drowned by the roar of Russian cannon. "This review held in presence of the enemy," writes General Fay, an eye-witness, " these rewards distributed to heroes on the ground where, alas ! so many of them were to die, these acclamations of our troops mingling with the heavy rumbling of the cannon in the city, all gave to this distribution of recompenses a character of grandeur which deeply impressed our allies and caused a very noble emotion

in those of them who participated in it." Generals
Forey and Bosquet distributed the crosses each to
his own army corps, in the name of the commander-in-
chief.   General Bosquet himself attached the cross
to the breast of the Abbé Stalter, military chaplain.
So the year 1854 ended with reviews and the blare
of trumpets in Paris and before Sebastopol.

CHAPTER XXVIII

THE DEATH OF THE EMPEROR NICHOLAS

EVERY patriotic and religious anguish of Russia was concentrated in its Emperor's soul. Like the entire Russian people, he considered the war against the Turks and their allies as a sacred duty, as the conflict of the Cross against the Crescent. The sufferings undergone by Holy Russia struck him to the heart. In him the man, the sovereign, the Christian, suffered equally. A reign of thirty years, which had been an unbroken succession of splendid triumphs, was ending in catastrophes.

All the previsions of the Emperor Nicholas, whether diplomatic or military, had just been baffled by events. The Czar regarded Europe with astonishment and did not recognize it. He had believed that the reign of Napoleon III. would be only an ephemeral dictatorship, received coldly by the powers, and Napoleon III. was directing the European concert against Russia. He had been convinced that an alliance between the victors and the vanquished of Waterloo was impossible, and he beheld a cordial understanding established between England and France. He had believed that the

Emperor of Austria, whom he had saved in 1849, would be always loyal to him, and the Emperor of Austria, the diplomatic ally of the two western powers, had forced him to evacuate the Danubian Principalities, once placed under his protection. He had counted on the absolute devotion of his brother-in-law, the King of Prussia, and the little German powers whom he regarded as his vassals, and their neutrality was more favorable to France and England than to Russia. He had believed that the Turkish troops would not hold out against his own, and the Turkish troops had everywhere opposed to them the most energetic resistance. He had been convinced that a landing in the Crimea in the second fortnight of September was an impossibility, and the landing had been accomplished without resistance.

Surprise following surprise and disappointment, the Czar became profoundly sad, but there was neither weakness, discouragement, nor remorse in his sadness. Everybody felt that even if Sebastopol fell, the sovereign would not give way. *Impavidum ferient ruinæ.* Fortune was adverse to him. He stiffened himself against its blows with indomitable tenacity. Convinced in mind and conscience that he was defending Christian civilization against Turkish barbarism, he repented of nothing, he accused himself of nothing. Believing that Austria, in amazing the world by its ingratitude, was committing a fault and a crime, he was more incensed with Francis Joseph than with Napoleon III. The neutrality of the petty German states, formerly his dependants, seemed to him a sort of rebellion. In his eyes the sovereigns had become revolutionists, renegades, and he was profoundly convinced that his anger was righteous indignation.

While Paris, more animated, more brilliant than ever, interrupted none of its usual diversions and was dreaming of the coming splendors of its Universal Exposition, the city of Saint Petersburg, gloomy and sombre, was plunged in manly sorrow. The Czar would have been ashamed to give entertainments while his people were suffering so bitterly. Day and night Sebastopol was the one thought of the inflexible sovereign. He had sent two of his sons there, the Grand Dukes Nicholas and Michael, and they were behaving like heroes. In spite of the severity of the winter, he sent thither all the reinforcements at his disposal. "I see with pleasure," he writes to Prince Menchikoff, November 23, 1854, "that you have not lost hope of saving Sebastopol, and that the heroism and audacity which animate our soldiers only increase with the intensity of the danger. It would be criminal to doubt it, and yet on reading these accounts my heart beats very hard. How I long to fly to you and share your fate, rather than torment myself here by incessant fears! I could not keep back my tears while reading what my children have written me and what Stürler tells me of the sailors. They are heroes."

Again, on November 27: "I thank you, my dear Menchikoff, for the haste you have made to tranquillize me: the lack of powder gave me great anxiety. According to what you tell me, our fire can keep up with that of the enemy, even if it is resumed with the same vigor, which is what I am expecting."

Stronger than men, winter, almost forcing the weapons from their hands, had somewhat allayed hostilities. But they were soon to be renewed more terribly than before. The Emperor Nicholas believed less than ever in a speedy end to the war. "I do not expect peace," he wrote to Prince Menchikoff, February 7, 1855. "It is indispensable to unite all our efforts to dismay the enemy in the Crimea. Every reinforcement that can be sent you is already on the way. When they are all united, you will have troops enough to make head against the enemy. I am sure of the bravery of the men and their commanders. Everything in the past witnesses that my expectation is not vain. May God do the rest!"

It is evident that the Emperor Nicholas was neither cast down nor discouraged. To fortify himself he incessantly thought of his brother, the Emperor Alexander of glorious memory, and of the army of 1812. But he followed the different vicissitudes of the war with emotions whose poignancy ruined his health. There was no telegraphic communication between Sebastopol and Saint Petersburg. News arrived but slowly, often confused, often contradictory, and gainsaid by information coming from different capitals. The Czar suffered alternations of hope and fear, enthusiasm and doubt, which would have broken a heart less well-tempered than his own. In spite of his extreme energy and robust constitution, he could not defend himself, in what concerned him personally, from gloomy forebodings. Although not yet sixty (he was born July 6, 1796), he thought his death was imminent. "I have reached and gone beyond," said he, "the number of years which God accords to those of my race." And yet, in spite of the chagrins which sapped his strength, he fulfilled all his duties as sovereign with superfluous solicitude and zeal.

He had announced that on February 21, 1855, he would review the troops about to start for the Crimea. On that day he was attacked by a feverish cold, and the weather was worse and the cold more severe than usual. The doctor entreated the Czar not to leave the palace, if he did not wish his condition to become desperate. "Doctor," replied the sovereign with a kindly smile, but in an absolutely imperative tone, "you have done your duty, allow me to do mine." He went out, mounted a horse, and held the review as calmly and with as much majesty as ever. On re-entering the Winter Palace he had an attack of chills, the malady having increased in a frightful manner.

It has been said that the Emperor Nicholas,

despairing of the state of things in the Crimea, voluntarily sought death in order to be done with a life that had become a torture to him. We do not believe it. If he persisted in reviewing the troops in spite of his sufferings, it was because, having often been severe both to himself and others, he wished to give the example. He knew all that his soldiers had to endure. He was not ignorant of the long marches from north to south, wherein so many badly fed victims, exhausted by fatigue and frozen by cold, would die on the road. He knew the formidable vicissitudes of the contest at Sebastopol. It distressed him sorely that the government of his immense empire obliged him to remain in his capital. But if he could not share the sufferings and dangers of his troops in the Crimea, at least he would not spare himself in Saint Petersburg; he would prove to his subjects that the idea of taking care of his health, impaired as it was, did not even occur to him.

The Czar's illness became still more alarming when he learned that the imprudent ardor of General Khronlef had provoked another defeat before the ramparts improvised by the allies at Eupatoria. This new repulse caused the Emperor a chagrin from which he could not rally. February 28, the danger became imminent. March 1, paralysis of the lungs set in, and all hope was lost. In the fulfilment of his duty, the physician informed his master that he had nothing further to expect on earth. For an instant the autocrat attempted to resist destiny and govern death. But after this final effort, the once powerful sovereign was nothing but a tranquil and resigned Christian. Unwilling to deceive either his people or himself, he sent to Moscow, Kiev, and Warsaw a despatch containing only the words: "The Emperor is dying." He summoned his principal counsellors, Count Orloff, Prince Dolgorouki, Count Adelsberg, and recommended them to his dearly loved son the Czarevitch, who was to become Alexander II. To him he said: "I wished to leave you an empire in good order and at peace. Providence has otherwise determined. I can do nothing more but pray for Russia." Then he requested that his generals, his guard, his army, all the defenders of Sebastopol, should be thanked. After receiving the last sacraments, he begged the Empress to recite the Lord's Prayer with him. When she repeated the words: "Thy will be done on earth as it is in heaven," he exclaimed: "Always! Always! . . . And now I hope that God will open His arms to me." He ordered the members of his household and the servants to be brought in, that he might bid them farewell. They were all dissolved in tears. It was Friday, March 2, 1855. In the morning the Emperor of all the Russias rendered his soul to the Supreme Judge.

In Paris no one had suspected that the Czar was ill when, on opening the *Moniteur* of March 3, they read the following telegrams: "Königsberg,

March 2. The Emperor Nicholas is very ill, he has received the sacraments and bidden farewell to the royal family."

"The Hague, March 2. The Emperor Nicholas died this morning of paralysis of the lungs. The news was received by the Queen at one o'clock. A telegraphic despatch from Berlin confirms the news of the death of the Emperor Nicholas."

On this unexpected news French stocks had a rise of five francs on the Paris Bourse. The rise was not an insult, but a homage to the memory of the Czar. It showed how much he had been feared. After his death peace became possible if not certain. People knew that while he lived Russia would never have given way, and that had she even been invaded by all the powers of Europe, she would have remembered 1812 and stood her ground.

The news of the Czar's death reached General Canrobert and Lord Raglan the evening of March 6. The defenders of Sebastopol were still unaware of it. The next day a messenger with a flag of truce conveyed it to the commander of the Russian army, who kept it secret until the tidings had been confirmed from Russia. Then he put in the order of the day the following rescript from the new Czar, Alexander II.: "In the profound and general grief caused by the death of our benefactor, may the truly Russian courage with which the troops under your command have confronted the enemy and withstood his undertakings be our consolation! Thank in my name all the heroic defenders of Sebastopol for the glorious exploits with which they have illustrated our military annals. Passed into the everlasting life, the supreme chieftain of the orthodox warriors blesses from on high their unequalled firmness and intrepidity."

France, which knows how to render justice to its adversaries, had none but respectful words for the sovereign whom Europe for so many years had regarded as its arbitrator, and who, the worthy heir of Peter the Great, had been the continuer of his ideas and his work in spite of his recent reverses.

CHAPTER XXIX

NAPOLEON III. AND THE CRIMEA

LIKE the Emperor Nicholas in the closing months of his life, Napoleon III. had a fixed idea: the Crimea. His disappointments had not been so bitter as the Czar's, but they had been equally great. Marshal de Saint-Arnaud's letters show what were the contemporary illusions. The victor of the Alma thought that Sebastopol would fall within a few days. Like everybody else, Napoleon III. had erroneous notions about the character and duration of the Crimean War. No one could have believed that the siege of Sebastopol would last a whole year, and that the allies would never be able to seize the entire city. Public opinion in France, mistaken from the start, was nervous and impatient. People did not consider the enormous difficulties presented by such an enterprise. The generals were criticised with a levity but too characteristic of the French disposition. The drawing-room soldiers, as General Bosquet called them, read their newspapers and amused themselves with devising preposterous plans of siege and battle.

The Emperor followed the military operations

with the keenest interest and most anxious attention. His military studies had been made in
Switzerland under General Dufour, and he had a
special knowledge of artillery and engineering.
Weary of the vain effort to judge matters from a
distance, and impressed by the wide differences
existing in the estimates of his generals, he conceived the scheme of going to the Crimea in person
and putting into practice what he knew of the art
of laying sieges. The idea of wearing the uniform
of a French general without ever having fought
under the banners of France offended his chivalrous
sentiments. He did not forget that the Orleans
princes had distinguished themselves at Antwerp
and in Algeria, and he was unwilling to seem less
valiant than they. Courageous, fond of adventures,
accustomed to astonish the French as well as other
peoples, he dreamed of making his appearance in
the ancient Chersonese like a *Deus ex machina* and
cutting with his imperial sword the Gordian knot
which his generals could not untie. Marshal de
Saint-Arnaud having taken his wife with him to the
Orient, he would take the Empress, who would
remain at Constantinople while he should be fighting
in the Crimea and examining the trenches at Sebastopol, as the Duc d'Orléans and the Duc de Nemours
had inspected that of Antwerp. He was not averse
to the notion of leaving the regency to the brother
of Napoleon I., being convinced that the former
King of Westphalia would perform its duties well.

Hence he resolved to sail for the Crimea with the Empress, and seemed determined to pay no attention to the objections of his advisers.

The Minister of Foreign Affairs, M. Drouyn de Lhuys, wrote to M. Benedetti, chargé d'affaires at Constantinople, February 20, 1855: "The rumor is current, and will doubtless reach Constantinople, that the Emperor will soon start for the Crimea. It is true that His Majesty, whose magnanimous heart identifies itself with all that constitutes our national life, and is incessantly preoccupied with all that affects its interests, whether abroad or at home, cannot contemplate the severe fatigues of our army in the Orient without conceiving the idea of going in person to share the glorious deeds and sufferings of his soldiers. At the same time, this thought is not a definitive resolution. Therefore you must neither deny nor confirm the news of the Emperor's project, His Majesty intending to reserve entire liberty of action in the matter."

By the 23d of February the rumor of the approaching departure of the Emperor began to be widely credited. On that day Marshal de Castellane wrote in his journal, always so curious: "Things will drag along diplomatically until May, at which period, if peace is not made, the war may become general. The expedition to the Crimea, where we have our best troops, is considered to weaken our position on the Continent. The departure of the Emperor causes great anxiety. England makes the strongest possible objections to it. Lord John Russell should have said to him: 'Sire, if you go to the Crimea, it means war to the knife, and it is useless for me to go to Vienna.'

"The Emperor is growing more and more unapproachable. When he takes a resolution, nothing can turn him from it. They say that the Empress, who is to accompany him, will remain at Constantinople.

"General Canrobert is very unjustly attacked, firstly, because he has inherited the conduct of an expedition to which he was opposed; he has been able to maintain an excellent spirit in his army and to keep up its courage."

Marshal de Castellane, a man essentially loyal and devoted to duty, was one of the few who, in 1855, had the courage to tell Napoleon III. the truth. February 24, he had a conversation with him at the Tuileries, which is thus related in his journal: —

"*The Marshal.* Your Majesty's departure is disquieting. The Crimean expedition was begun too late or too early. It is lucky that General Canrobert has been able to keep up the courage and spirits of his army as he has done.

"*The Emperor.* Between ourselves, I expect a response from Prussia. I will not go to the Crimea unless she gives way; I have organized three army corps, the North, Paris, and Lyons, so that in case of necessity you can march with the others. I think of going to the Crimea because certain information makes it credible that the Russian army can be annihilated. With the fifteen thousand Pied-montese, the English, and the Turks, there will be more than one hundred and fifty thousand men in the Crimea. The Russian army once crushed, I shall re-embark with the army, leaving the Turks to guard the Crimea.

"*The Marshal.* Sire, when the Emperor Napoleon I. was in Egypt he was not a sovereign. If we were going to the Crimea, we should have gone sooner. The Russians were not ready. There are chances of defeat also in the Crimea, and consider what that would be if it happened to the sovereign."

Discerning men like the Marshal well knew that a new dynasty needs to be successful, and that, firm and solid as he seemed, the Emperor would find it very hard to withstand such a catastrophe as a personal defeat before Sebastopol. The old parties bowed their heads in presence of a victorious empire. They would rise up again before a conquered one. After the disasters of 1870 Napoleon III. sorrowfully said, at Wilhelmshöhe: "It does not do to be unfortunate in France." Nothing is sadder or more true than this remark.

February 27, Marshal de Castellane had another conversation with the Emperor at the Tuileries, which he thus relates: "After dinner the Emperor went with me into the adjoining salon to talk. I said: —

"Sire, your voyage to the Crimea is causing great anxiety. I think it will be an unfortunate thing both abroad and at home. We should have gone into the Crimea on arriving in the Orient, not at the beginning of winter, or else we should have waited until spring. And then we should have marched the day after the battle of the Alma.

"*The Emperor.* Saint-Arnaud wanted to, but Raglan was unwilling; it is always difficult to act with allies, which is another reason why I think it would be well for me to be in the Crimea. . . . I ought to beat the Russians, if only by the number of battalions. You say yourself that the Crimea is a blind alley. We must get out of it with honor.

"*The Marshal.* But, Sire, a defeat is always possible. People are justly alarmed by Your Majesty's departure. One good thing about the rumor is that it proves they feel their need of the Emperor.

"*The Emperor.* When I am gone all they will think about is my return."

The Empress, who was not alarmed by bold and adventurous resolutions, found a certain pleasure in the prospect of a journey to that Orient which was attracting the attention of all the world. She did not urge her husband to go, but she did not advise him to remain. In any case she was determined to follow him, if not to the Crimea, at least as far as Constantinople.

Colonel de Béville had just arrived in the Turkish capital in the capacity of imperial quartermaster.

M. Benedetti replied as follows to the despatch of
M. Drouyn de Lhuys which we have already cited: —
"Pera, March 5, 1855. I have received Your
Excellency's despatch of February 20. A rumor of
the speedy arrival of the Emperor has, in fact,
reached Constantinople, and I have frequently been
asked about its origin and authenticity. I had
abstained from replying before receiving your direc-
tions, and I have complied with them strictly.
Without contradicting the rumor, I have avoided
confirming it. Still I cannot leave Your Excellency
in ignorance that all the correspondents, not excepting those of the Ottoman ambassador (Vely-Pasha),
agree in representing His Majesty's departure as
imminent. The Sultan and his government regard
the appearance of the Emperor in the midst of his
army as a pledge of our success, and a precious
guaranty for the interests of Turkey. Hence the
news has been received by the Sublime Porte and at
the Palace with lively marks of satisfaction. At
all events preparations are being made as fast as
possible for such a contingency."

In an article published in the *Revue de Paris*,
June 15, 1896, M. Louis Thouvenel gave some
curious details drawn from letters addressed to
his father by M. Benedetti, concerning the impression produced at Constantinople by the project of
the Emperor's journey. The Sultan expressed to
Colonel de Béville the greatest desire to receive
Napoleon III. in his own palace, to share his apart-

ments with him, and treat him like a brother. For
the accommodation of the Empress, should she
arrive, Colonel de Béville gave the preference to the
Balta-Liman palace, the summer residence of the
Princess Fatmé, daughter of the Sultan and wife of
Ali Ghalib Pasha, son of the Grand Vizier Rechid
Pasha. Abdul Medjid himself gave orders for the
building of stables for the horses of the hundred
guards, had boards provided for two neighboring
kiosks for the suite of Their Majesties, and assigned
his farmhouse of Ayaz Pasha as lodgings for the
guard intended for the interior service of the palace.
Moreover, he announced to Colonel de Béville his
intention of going in person to meet the Emperor
and Empress in the Sea of Marmora, where he would
go aboard of the imperial vessel to conduct them
himself to the Balta-Liman palace. He added that
Their Majesties would be greeted with salvoes of
artillery and volleys of musketry from the Turkish
army drawn up on the shores of the Bosphorus, and
that in the evening daylight would be replaced by
the splendor of a general illumination. The bedroom of the Empress Eugénie was covered with
tapestry ornamented by a multitude of real pearls.
The largest diamonds were brought forth from the
treasury. The finest specimens of Turkish art,
going back to the time of the Sultan Murad, were
brought together. M. Benedetti wrote to M. Thouvenel: "We shall have a veritable page from the
Thousand and One Nights." A thing unprecedented

was that the Commander of the Faithful had decided to give his arm to a woman, the Empress, to lead her to his palace and to a state dinner he intended offering to the Emperor.   But the fairy scene imagined by Abdul Medjid was not to be realized, at least in 1855.   Before long there was no further question of the departure of Their Majesties for the Orient.   Napoleon III. was to be deterred from his design by the exhortations of his ministers, the advice of Queen Victoria and the English government during his stay in England, and finally by the assault to which he nearly fell a victim after his return to Paris.

CHAPTER XXX

WE have said that on September 7, 1854, at Boulogne, Prince Albert had expressed to Napoleon III. the desire of Queen Victoria to receive the Emperor in England and to make the acquaintance of the Empress Eugénie. This plan was realized in April, 1855. On the 15th of that month, at half-past eleven in the morning, the Corps législatif, with its president, Comte de Morny, went to the Tuileries to present the recently enacted laws to the sovereign. He said to them : " I wished to thank you before departing. I think I shall correctly interpret your wishes in assuring the government of Her Majesty the Queen of Great Britain that you share in my appreciation of the advantages of the alliance with England. We all desire peace, but only on condition that it shall be an honorable one ; if we must go on with the war, I count upon your loyal support."

The Emperor and Empress left Paris for Calais, with their suite, at half-past one that afternoon, reaching their destination towards nine in the evening. They took boat for Dover, Monday morning,

259

April 16, landing there at half-past eleven, and being met by Prince Albert, who accompanied them
to Windsor Palace. At five in the evening they
made a ceremonious entry into London, through
which they passed to the Paddington station. More
than a million persons thronged the streets through
which they drove, most of them wearing the French
colors and shouting lustily. Never was a foreign
sovereign given a more cordial or splendid reception
in London. Two hours later Their Majesties arrived at Windsor Castle, where the Queen was awaiting them. Windsor had erected triumphal arches in
its streets, and the crenelles of the castle were illuminated. The military bands played Queen Hortense's hymn, *Partant pour la Syrie*, the drums
beat a salute. Napoleon III. and the Empress
Eugénie alighted from the carriage. The Queen
shall describe what followed : " I cannot express," ·
she writes in her journal, "the emotions which I
felt. I went forward. The Emperor kissed my
hand. Then I kissed him twice, on each cheek.
Then I embraced the sweet and graceful Empress."
The presentations took place in the throne room.
Then the Queen and Prince Albert led their guests
to the apartments prepared for them. These were
a suite of magnificent rooms among which were the
Rubens salon, decorated with twelve paintings by
that master, and the Van Dyck room, which contains
the portraits of Charles I. and his family. The
chamber intended for Napoleon III. was the one

which had been occupied by the Emperor Nicholas and by Louis Philippe.

The Queen describes in her journal the conversation she held after dinner with the Emperor. She says she was charmed by his exquisite manners and perfect tact. "He is really calm," she adds; "he speaks in a low tone and gently; he makes no set speeches." Napoleon III. spoke of the great anxiety caused him by the siege of Sebastopol. "I confess," said he, "that I fear a great disaster, and that is why I wish to go there. Our generals are afraid of assuming any responsibility." The Queen insisted upon the dangers and the distance. "Yes," replied the Emperor, "I know the distance is great. As to the dangers, they are everywhere."

Tuesday, April 17. After breakfast a walk in the park of Windsor. Again the war is spoken of. The Emperor still insists on his desire to go to the Crimea. The Empress is even more eager than her husband to see this wish realized. "There would be no more danger in the Crimea," said she, "than there is anywhere else. I am seldom uneasy about him in Paris, except when he goes out all alone in the mornings." The Queen, whom the Empress was pleasing more and more, wrote in her journal: "She is full of courage and spirit, and yet so gentle, with such innocence and playfulness, that the ensemble is charming. With her great liveliness, she has the prettiest and most modest manners."

During breakfast Napoleon asked where Queen Marie Amélie was. Queen Victoria replied that she was in England. She might have added that the widow of King Louis Philippe had paid her a call at Windsor, four days before, in a carriage whose simplicity contrasted strangely with her former splendors. The Emperor said that when Queen Marie Amélie was in Spain the previous year, he had proposed to her, through King Leopold, to pass through France on her return to England. "If," he added, "Your Majesty will have the kindness to repeat this to Queen Marie Amélie, I shall be much pleased."

Four o'clock in the afternoon. Grand review in the park of Windsor. The Queen and the Empress sit in the same carriage. The Emperor, Prince Albert, and the Duke of Cambridge are on horseback. An immense crowd of sightseers is present. They admire the Life Guards, the carbineers, the artillery. Lord Cardigan, riding the same horse on which he made the famous charge of Balaclava, attracts general attention. The Queen thinks that the Emperor is an excellent rider and looks very grand on horseback.

In the evening there is a ball in the Waterloo salon, decorated by Lawrence with portraits of the notable personages of 1814–15, — Wellington, Blücher. Castlereagh, Metternich, Alexander I., Canning, Humboldt. The Queen opens the ball with the Emperor, "who," says she, "dances with dignity and animation." And she adds : "How strange it is to think that I, the granddaughter of George III., should be dancing in the Waterloo salon with the nephew of the great enemy of England, with the Emperor Napoleon, who is now my closest ally, and who was living in this country six years ago, poor, unknown, and in exile ! "

Wednesday, April 18. The Emperor receives a telegram, announcing the sad news of the death of one of his best advisers, M. Ducos, Minister of the Navy. At eleven o'clock he is present at a council held in his own apartments, in which Prince Albert, Lords Palmerston, Panmure, Hardinge, Cowley, Sir Charles Wood, Sir John Burgoyne, Count Walewski, and Marshal Vaillant take part. Although all of them are opposed to the Emperor's departure for the Crimea, they do not succeed in convincing him. At three o'clock a chapter of the Order of the Garter is convoked in that beautiful chapel of Saint George which was rebuilt during the reigns of Edward IV. and Henry VIII. The stalls of the knights of the order are in the splendidly decorated choir, in the middle of which are the tombs of Henry VIII. and his third wife, Jane Seymour, and that of Charles I. A subterranean gallery leads from the altar to the royal vault, where lie the bodies of George III., George IV., and William IV. The banners and escutcheons of the knights of the order hang on the wall above their stalls. On this occasion the knights wear their purple velvet mantles with ornaments of crimson velvet. The majority of them, lord lieutenants of counties, have rich uniforms under their mantles. Preceded by Prince Albert, the Duke of Cambridge, the king-at-arms of the Garter, bearing the insignia of the order on a cushion of crimson velvet, and an usher with a black mace, the Emperor, on his entry into the chapter hall, is received by Queen Victoria and the knights standing. At the close of the ceremony, the Queen, wearing the mantle of the order and a bracelet with the famous inscription, "*Honi soit qui mal y pense*," "Evil to him who evil thinks," takes Napoleon's arm and conducts him to his apartments. "I thank Your Majesty very much," says the Emperor. "It is an additional tie. I have taken an oath to Your Majesty, and I will scrupulously observe it. To me, this is a great event, and I hope to prove my gratitude to Your Majesty and to your country."

Napoleon III. was radiant. Saint George's chapel had left a dazzling impression on him. But could he have forgotten that Louis Philippe had received the Order of the Garter in the same chapel, October 11, 1844, and that his career had nevertheless closed in the bitterness of exile? . . . How sad the Emperor would have been could he have foreseen that, like Louis Philippe, he also was destined to return, exiled and conquered, to this England, where he was then a conqueror! At this moment he ardently desired a son. It was his dearest wish, and Providence was soon to realize it. Alas! could one have suspected that this longed-for son was to die at twenty-three in a distant land, wearing an English uniform, and that in this very chapel of Saint George, where Napoleon III. had just been received as a knight of the Order of the Garter, Queen Victoria would erect a monument to the victim of Zululand, the heroic and unfortunate Prince Imperial!

During the dinner the conversation happened to turn on the French refugees in London. The Queen wrote in her journal: "The Emperor said that when men openly commend assassination, they ought not to enjoy the benefits of hospitality. . . . We were speaking of the attempts made against me, although attempts against a woman are still more atrocious. For his part, he agreed with his uncle in thinking that there is no danger from a conspiracy which is known in advance, but that no precautions can be taken against a fanatic who is willing to risk his life in attacking you. We afterwards spoke of the lack of freedom from which people in our position suffer. The Emperor said that the Empress was greatly affected by this, and that she called the Tuileries a beautiful prison. He shared the same impression. He added: 'I wept hot tears when I quitted England.'"

After dinner the Queen talked with Marshal Vaillant, who was always much opposed to the Emperor's going to the Crimea. The Queen said: "I have dared to make some remarks." "Dared!

Dared! Madame," replied the Marshal. "You are in the same boat. You must talk plainly."

It is plain, therefore, that England and the French ministry agreed in attempting to prevent the Emperor's departure for the Crimea. The latter thought that the Empire was not sufficiently consolidated to permit the sovereign to expose himself to such a remote adventure. Meanwhile, England was reflecting that if the Emperor appeared in person before the troops, his rank would give him an indisputable supremacy, — a prospect not at all flattering to British self-esteem.

Thursday, April 19. Their Imperial Majesties had but a few hours more to remain at Windsor. Two days before the lord mayor and the aldermen had come to present them with the address of the city of London, and to invite them to a banquet offered by the city for the 19th. On the morning of this day the Emperor said to the Queen : "If Your Majesty will permit, I am going to read you my reply to the address from the city, so that I may know if you have any remarks to make. I must deliver it in English, and I beg Your Majesty to point out to me any mistakes in pronunciation." The Queen found the speech admirable and the pronunciation excellent.

At eleven in the morning Their Imperial Majesties quitted Windsor with the Queen and Prince Albert. This departure left the Queen somewhat sad. The guards in full uniform were standing on the steps of the stairway. The military band played *Partant pour la Syrie.* "I was melancholy," the Queen has said, "and I wondered what the future would be. I knew that the Empress also was sad on leaving Windsor." And not being jealous like other women, the Queen added : "I was delighted to see how much Albert admired her."

CHAPTER XXXI

LONDON

THE reception offered him by the city of London caused the Emperor great joy. He had a real predilection for England and its capital city. On his way from New York to Switzerland to visit his dying mother in 1837, he spent several days in London. When exiled from Switzerland, he returned to England, where he resided from October 26, 1838, to August 4, 1840, the day on which he embarked for his disastrous expedition to Boulogne. And lastly, after escaping from the fortress of Ham, he arrived in London May 25, 1846, remaining there until September 23, 1848, on which day he set off for Paris, where he was to take his seat as a deputy at the Palais Bourbon before installing himself at the Elysée as President of the Republic. Thus he had been the guest of the English during four years. He had familiarized himself with their manners and their language, which he spoke almost without an accent. At that time he was not received at court, and had never spoken with either the Queen or Prince Albert. But he had established pleasant relations with many notable personages of English society. He was grateful to the English for an asylum which had permitted him to attain to supreme power, and his fondness for the country is witnessed by the fact that he preferred it to all others as a permanent residence after losing his crown.

The 19th of April, 1855, was certainly one of the most brilliant days of the Emperor's life. When he arrived at noon in London with the Empress, the Queen and Prince Albert, he was greeted by transports of enthusiasm and frenzied applause. An innumerable crowd thronged about the procession as it moved towards Buckingham Palace. Here the Emperor and Empress remained but a short time, afterwards going alone to the city. The lord mayor, the aldermen, and the highest notabilities of England were awaiting them at Guild Hall.

Guild Hall, at the end of King street in the city, is the *Hôtel de Ville*, the City Hall of London, the meeting-place of the guilds and corporations. The fine façade on King street was built in 1789. Above the entrance are the arms of the city and the motto : " *Domine, dirige nos,*" " Lord, direct us." In its great hall is given yearly on November 9 the banquet offered by the new lord mayor to the authorities to celebrate his entrance on his official functions, and to which about one thousand guests are always invited. It is also in this hall that the ministers deliver important addresses.

Queen Victoria and Prince Albert, who had

remained at Buckingham Palace, were somewhat
anxious about the safety of their guests while on
the way to Guild Hall. What occurred in Paris
nine days later, shows that this anxiety was not
groundless. But nothing unpleasant happened in
London. The political refugees were closely
watched and made no hostile manifestation. Their
leaders had left the city, either for prudential reasons
or because they were unwilling to look on at a spectacle which displeased them. As soon as it was understood that France was fighting merely for ideas,
and did not dream of enlarging her territory, her
successes did not revive hereditary jealousies.ⁱ All
fears concerning a revenge for Waterloo were dispelled. The spectre of a Franco-Russian alliance,
which had so greatly alarmed England under the
reign of Napoleon I., at the time of the interview at
Tilsit, and under the Restoration at the end of the
reign of Charles X., was now laid. In applauding
and dining Napoleon III., the English abandoned
themselves to unalloyed pleasure.

On arriving at Guild Hall the Emperor and Empress were conducted to the great hall where the
banquet was to take place. The lord mayor having
delivered a little speech of welcome, the Emperor, in
the midst of solemn silence, replied as follows in
English : " My lord, after the cordial welcome which
I have received from the Queen, nothing could affect
me more than the sentiments you have just expressed
to the Empress and me in the name of the city of

London ; for the city of London represents all possible resources, whether for civilization or for war in a commerce which embraces the universe. However flattering your praises, I accept them because they are intended for France much more than for myself. As for me, I have preserved on the throne the sentiments of esteem and sympathy for the English people which I professed in exile, when I enjoyed here the hospitality of the Queen, and if I have conformed my conduct to my conviction, it is because this was made a duty by the interests of the nation which elected me, as well as by those of general civilization. . . . Our two nations are still stronger by virtue of the ideas they represent than by the battalions and ships they have at their disposal."

The Emperor closed his speech, which was loudly applauded, as follows : " I am very grateful to the Queen for having provided me with this formal occasion of expressing to you my sentiments and those of France, of which I am the interpreter. I thank you in my own name and that of the Empress for the frank and hearty cordiality with which you have welcomed us. We shall take back with us to France the profound impression left upon souls capable of comprehending it by the imposing spectacle afforded by England, where virtue on the throne directs the destinies of the country, under the empire of a liberty which does not endanger its greatness."

The Emperor wore the uniform of a general, with the grand cross of the Legion of Honor and the ribbon and star of the Order of the Garter. His speech was delivered in a clear and strong voice, and was received with immense enthusiasm. The beauty of the Empress, who was in green satin trimmed with white lace, and a white crêpe bonnet with marabout feathers, excited lively admiration. Their Majesties visited Guild Hall, one room of which had been hung with portraits of the Bonaparte family. On recognizing that of his mother, Napoleon III. exclaimed: " What a pleasing attention ! "

From Guild Hall Their Imperial Majesties went to the French embassy, where the diplomatic corps was presented to them, and returned to Buckingham Palace at half-past six o'clock. The day had been a series of ovations. In the evening a full-dress representation of *Fidelio* was given at the Covent Garden theatre in honor of the Emperor and Empress. The next day, April 20, was the Emperor's forty-seventh birthday. The Queen congratulated him and presented him with a little gold pencil-case. Afterwards they visited the Crystal Palace at Sydenham, which was all the more interesting to the Emperor because he was making ready for an international exposition at Paris. Saturday, April 21, was the day set for the departure of Their Imperial Majesties. The Emperor wrote in the Queen's album: " I feel for Your Majesty the sentiments one experiences for a queen and a sister, — respectful devotion and tender affection." Then, after having inscribed this sentence : " I have tried," said he, " to write what I feel."

The farewells were most cordial. After expressing very warmly his gratitude for the reception given him, the Emperor said to the Queen : " You will come to Paris if you can, will you not?" The Queen replied : " Certainly, unless my public duties prevent me." To which the Emperor returned : " I thank you again for the little pencil-case you gave me for my birthday. To have spent that near you will bring me good luck." They parted with tears in their eyes. It was half-past ten o'clock in the morning. And again the band played *Partant pour la Syrie.*

Accompanied by Prince Albert and the Duke of Cambridge as far as Dover, Their Imperial Majesties were saluted by all the cannon of the English fleet, and embarked in splendid weather. They arrived at Boulogne at half-past three, and at Paris at six in the evening. The next day, April 23, the *Moniteur* announced their return and published this despatch from General Canrobert : " Before Sebastopol. We continue to maintain the superiority of our fire without wasting our ammunition. Up to now the attack has been made chiefly by the artillery ; but the engineers are combining their efforts, and opening roads which bring us nearer to the town. These works make regular progress, in spite of the difficulties of the ground."

So it was during the whole of the Crimean War that music and dancing alternated at Paris and London with the frightful noises of the siege of Sebastopol. The aspect of things was at once lugubrious and joyful. The medley of slaughters and festivals afforded a truly Shakespearian contrast. At the very moment when the Emperor was returning in great happiness from his journey to England, a fanatic was planning to assassinate him in the midst of his triumph.   •

CHAPTER XXXII

THE ATTEMPT OF PIANORI

ONE fine spring day, Saturday, April 28, 1855, the Emperor mounted his horse to go from the Tuileries to the Bois de Boulogne by way of the Champs Elysées. With his aide-de-camp, Colonel Edgard Ney, on his right, and Colonel de Valabrègue, chief equerry, on his left, he had already passed the meeting of the roads and was on a level with the Château des Fleurs, when a well-dressed person ran suddenly from the pavement on the right and advanced along the causeway towards the sovereign, who supposed that he was about to be presented with a petition. But it was not a petition which this man had in his hand, but a pistol, with which he intended to kill the Emperor. The presence of Colonel Edgard Ney forced him to move almost directly opposite the sovereign, in which position he fired his first shot, but with no result. The rapid advance upon him of Colonel Ney changed the direction of his second shot, which was a failure like the first. The assassin was immediately arrested by the police. It was half-past five in the afternoon.

275

With his usual impassibility, the Emperor betrayed no emotion. With the greatest calmness, he reassured the crowd pressing around him; and, without changing his horse's pace, quietly resumed his ride as far as the Bois de Boulogne, where he rejoined the Empress, who had started in a carriage a quarter of an hour before him. A great throng of society men and women who were riding in the Bois spontaneously escorted the Emperor back to the Tuileries. I was in the Champs Elysées at the time, and I remember having seen him pass by in the midst of acclamations. The Empress followed him in a carriage; she was pale and deeply affected, frequently carrying her handkerchief to her eyes.

On reaching the Tuileries, Their Majesties found King Jerome, Prince Napoleon, the other members of the family; and the great officers, the chief officials of their households of both sexes, who had been notified of the attempt, had also hastened to congratulate the Emperor. "You see clearly," said he, smiling, "that it is not so easy to kill me." In the evening he went to the theatre with the Empress.

An eye-witness, Count Horace de Vieil-Castel, has written in his memoirs : "At nine o'clock in the evening I saw the imperial carriages arrive at the Opéra-Comique, and I must say that if I had read what I saw I would not believe it; I would accuse the journals of flattery. The cries

of 'Long live the Emperor!' thundered like continuous discharges of artillery in the distance ; the
emotion was general. I saw people weeping at the
Opéra-Comique. The Empress was pale and preoccupied, in spite of her efforts to appear calm.
On their return Their Majesties were welcomed
with the same ovations, and houses were splendidly
illuminated all along their route."

The next day, Sunday, April 29, the Emperor
received the Nuncio and the diplomatic corps at the
Tuileries, coming in the name of their sovereigns to
express the indignation caused them by this attempt
on his life, and to felicitate him upon his providential preservation. The senators were afterwards
received. The president of the Senate said : " Sire,
we bless the admirable logic which presides over the
decrees of Providence. It has willed that your
throne should rise like a rampart between France
and revolutions. Consequently, it wills that factions
shall not prevent you from fulfilling the great mission on which depend the destinies of Europe and
the future of civilization. We unite our sentiments
to those of the Empress. There is no French heart
that does not palpitate like hers."

Napoleon III. replied : " I thank the Senate for
the sentiments it has just expressed. I do not fear
the attempts of assassins. There are existences
which are the instruments of the decrees of Providence. So long as I have not accomplished my mission, I incur no danger."

Their Majesties then went to the chapel of the château, where they heard Mass, at which King Jerome was also present. A *Te Deum* was chanted after Vespers in every parish church in Paris. Thoroughly convinced of the feelings entertained for him personally by the French people, the Emperor expressed the desire that no addresses should be presented by the municipal bodies or the authorities. He thought that the general indignation rendered all official manifestations useless. Every church in France was crowded by people, coming to thank God for having saved the Emperor. In foreign countries there was also much emotion, especially in London where he had been so magnificently received a few days before. Count Walewski, French ambassador at London, wrote to M. Drouyn de Lhuys, April 30: " Words fail me to give a faithful description of the impression produced here by the abominable attempt against His Majesty's precious life. Day before yesterday the Queen and H. R. H. Prince Albert made haste to telegraph Lord Cowley, to express to the Emperor what they feel so deeply. As soon as he received the news, Lord Clarendon wrote me that he could not help shuddering at the thought of the dangers to which all Europe had just been exposed. The entire diplomatic corps came to inscribe their names at the embassy yesterday. Journals of every shade are striving to outdo each other in adapting themselves to the pitch of public feeling. Cardinal Wiseman has asked me to forward the enclosed letter

to His Majesty, and while telling me how greatly
he had been horrified by the attempted assassination,
he announced that an official *Te Deum*, at which he
would himself officiate, would be celebrated at the
French chapel. On this occasion the *Domine salvum
fac Imperatorem* would be sung. I call Your Excellency's attention to the fact that this will be the
first time that the *Domine salvum* will have been
sung in the chapel since it ceased to belong to the
embassy, that is, since 1830."

The true name of the assassin was not ascertained
at first. A false passport induced the belief that he
was called Antonio Laverani. But it was soon
known that he was Giovanni Pianori, a native of the
Roman States, twenty-eight years of age, and by
trade a shoemaker. A second pistol and a poniard
were found in his clothes. Questioned as to the
motive of his crime, he replied : " I acted that way
because the Emperor made the Roman campaign and
ruined my country." Pianori was a member of one
of those sects who did not forgive Napoleon III.
for the expedition of 1849, though perhaps it was
rather the work of his ministry and the National
Assembly than his own. The murderer claimed to
have had no instigators but himself. It was nevertheless ascertained, that he came from England, and
the gunsmith who sold him his pistols was discovered
in London. London was, in fact, the centre of all
the conspiracies against the Emperor. The capital
of England was at that time the headquarters for the

Italian refugees, whose chief was Mazzini, and whose programme the assassination of the French sovereign. To overthrow the Emperor in order to overthrow the Papacy was an idea which incessantly haunted the brains of these fanatics, all of whom then considered the Napoleonic dynasty as the natural guardian of the pontifical sovereignty. Concerning this, M. A. Granier de Cassagnac has said : " The event certainly proves that this theory of the solidarity of the Pope and the Emperor was not absolutely groundless, for the fall of the one delivered the other to the machinations of 'his enemies."

The culprit having been taken in the very act, and having nothing to deny, the trial could take place May 7, eight days after the crime. Arraigned before the court of assizes, Pianori was condemned to death and executed. His crime was the signal for other attempts, several of which, discovered in time, did not even begin to be put into execution, while others came within an ace of destroying the Emperor. Every one of them was organized in England, and had Mazzini for its instigator. This man believed that conspirators should be few in number in order to have any chance of success. Hence he did not usually send more than one, two, or at most four assassins to France at a time. The French police, always on the alert, displayed great vigilance. Without the Emperor's suspecting it, he was himself watched day and night

by faithful agents who were charged to follow him
step by step, so as to turn aside the blows which
threatened him.

A fatalist and inaccessible to fear, Napoleon III.,
with the imperturbable calm from which he was
never seen to depart, never gave a thought to the
attempts, and braved them with the carelessness of
an intrepid soldier on the battle-field.   But the Empress felt anxieties for her husband's life which
overshadowed her happiest days.

CHAPTER XXXIII

M. DROUYN DE LHUYS

WHILE Napoleon III. was making his triumphant journey in England, and when he escaped in a providential manner from the attempt of the Italian sectary after his return, his Minister of Foreign Affairs, M. Drouyn de Lhuys, was at Vienna, where, in a conference which brought together the representatives of Austria, England, France, Russia, and Turkey, he made praiseworthy efforts for the restoration of peace.

Born in 1805, this statesman was then in his fiftieth year, and enjoyed a great reputation as a diplomatist. Attached to the French embassy to Madrid in 1830, he had passed through all grades of the service before attaining its highest rank. He had simultaneously distinguished himself in the parliamentary and the diplomatic career. Appointed director of commercial affairs in the Ministry of Foreign Affairs in 1840, he had been elected deputy from Melun in 1842. Three years later he was deprived of office by M. Guizot for having voted against the ministry. Being now a simple deputy, he took an active part on the side of the opposition, and signed a request

for the impeachment of M. Guizot and the members
of the Cabinet several days before the revolution of
February 24. On becoming President of the Republic, Louis Napoleon entrusted to him the direction
of French diplomacy.

M. Drouyn de Lhuys was Minister of Foreign
Affairs four times : 1. From December 19, 1848,
to June 2, 1849 ; 2. from January 9 to January
24, 1851 ; 3. from July 28, 1852, to May 8, 1855 ;
4. from October 15, 1862, to September 1, 1866. One
of his most brilliant subordinates, Count Bernard
d'Harcourt, former ambassador, has said of him :
" During thirty years his house was the rendezvous
of all persons who, directly or indirectly, have
touched on foreign questions. He was surrounded
and consulted with the same deference by men of
every shade of opinion. The portfolio of Foreign
Affairs, placed in his hands four times, seemed never
to be withdrawn for more than a moment. When
the agents of the Ministry of Foreign Affairs were
no longer obliged to go to him for orders, they came
to ask his advice or his impressions."

I had the honor of serving under the orders of
M. Drouyn de Lhuys, as clerk in the political department, throughout the term of his fourth and last
ministry. At that time I saw him constantly. He
encouraged my modest productions and my diplomatic beginnings with extreme kindness, and I am
happy to have the occasion to pay homage to his
memory.

M. Drouyn de Lhuys was a man of talent and a good man. His ideas were lofty and liberal, his private life irreproachable, his character and manners most dignified, his mind broad and independent. Very learned and very literary, he wrote remarkably well, expressed himself with as much clearness as elegance, gave his instructions with rare lucidity, and preserved absolute calmness in the most difficult situations. He imposed respect on all who approached him. He was a typical minister, and held in as much consideration abroad as at home.

Such was the man who bore to Vienna a message of pacification. Baron de Bourqueney, Minister of France in Austria, wrote to M. Thouvenel, in charge of the home department of the Ministry of Foreign Affairs : "Vienna, April 7, 1855. M. Drouyn de Lhuys arrived last evening. This morning he called on Count Buol, who has informed him that the Emperor will give him a private audience to-morrow. Count Buol said to him : 'We know that you are bringing us directly and confidentially the secret mind of the Emperor Napoleon, and we cannot sufficiently congratulate ourselves on being thus placed in contact with him by you. We have already managed affairs very well from a distance. Permit me to hope that we shall conduct them still better at shorter range.' "

After having been received by the Emperor Francis Joseph, M. Drouyn de Lhuys wrote to Napoleon III. : "The young sovereign is tall, slender, well made ; his countenance, ordinarily serious and even a trifle severe, becomes benevolent when he smiles. Evidently the premature responsibilities of empire have hindered the development of the graces of adolescence on this face, and in looking at the Emperor one recalls involuntarily the touching expression which escaped him when he received the crown : 'Adieu, my youth !' If the whole countenance is studied attentively, one finds beneath a thin veil of timidity a will capable of obstinacy. His Majesty received me with affectionate kindness."

A convinced partisan of the Austrian alliance, M. Drouyn de Lhuys said to the Emperor Francis Joseph : " The great problem is to master the revolution without the help of Russia, and to curb Russia without the help of the revolution. For the last thirty years this problem has been insoluble, and that is why Russia and the revolution have been simultaneously triumphant during that time. Now the solution is found in the alliance of France with Austria. What has brought me to Vienna is far less the desire to make peace with Russia than to consolidate and make fruitful the alliance with Austria."

A conference, containing representatives of Austria, England, France, Russia, and Turkey, had been in session at Vienna since March 15. They were discussing what were called the four points, or the four guarantees. These four points on which Aus-

tria was of one mind with the cabinets of Paris and
London in signing the treaty of December 2, 1854,
were the following: 1. It is important that the
Russian protectorate over the Danubian provinces
should be replaced by a collective protectorate of
the powers.   2. The navigation of the Danube
ought to be entirely freed from restrictions.   3. The
independence of the Ottoman Empire ought to be
assured.   4. Russia should renounce all exclusive
patronage over the Christian subjects of the Porte.

Dreading to see Austria declare war upon her,
Russia had accepted the four points in principle ;
but when it became a question of putting them in
practice, the disputes had begun.   The Russian
ambassador at Vienna, Prince Gortchakoff, was a
consummate diplomatist, who at first used every
artifice to delay the assembling of the conference,
and afterwards to paralyze its labors.   There was
an agreement on the first two points, but the third
raised inextricable difficulties.   Austria, France,
England, and Turkey maintained that the independence of the Ottoman Empire demanded the
suppression of the Russian naval forces in the
Black Sea.   Russia, on the contrary, refused any
limitation of her forces.   They turned in a vicious
circle.

Things were at this point when M. Drouyn de
Lhuys arrived at Vienna.   There he met one of
the principal statesmen of England, Lord John
Russell, Colonial Minister, who had come to take

part in the work of the conference, and there he was rejoined by Ali Pasha, Turkish Minister of Foreign Affairs. The conference, which assumed the character of a congress from the presence of these notable personages, assembled April 7, 1855. After several sessions and long deliberations, M. Drouyn de Lhuys and Lord John Russell elaborated, subject to the approbation of their governments, a scheme of compromise which Austria sanctioned, and which contained the following articles :

1. European guaranty of the independence and territorial integrity of the Ottoman Empire. 2. Absolute closing of the straits for the Russians, saving exceptions for the allies. 3. Each of the allies may have two frigates in the Black Sea. 4. If Russia increases her existing naval forces in the Euxine, each ally may send thither a number of vessels equal to half the Russian vessels. 5. In case of danger, the whole of the allied naval forces enter. 6. France, England, and Austria will sign at once a treaty, naming as a cause of war the augmentation of the Russian fleet above the effective force of ·1853.

Baron de Bourqueney wrote to M. Thouvenel, April 23 : "The conference has adjourned without date. Austria reserves to herself its reunion when she shall learn the decision of the French and English governments on the plan elaborated during the last days. I can only join with M. Drouyn de

Lhuys in hoping that the government of the Emperor may adhere to it. This project not merely confirms the alliance of December 2, but renders it indissoluble, whether the existing crisis finds its solution in peace or war. Lord John Russell, who is imperatively recalled by his ministerial duties, leaves for England this evening filled with the idea I have just expressed. Having come to Vienna much prejudiced against the alliance, he has been convinced of the honesty of Austria, and reproaches only her prudence. From that day his choice was made. He has preferred a less brilliant peace to the continuation of the war without Austria: this is what he will maintain among his colleagues, and, if necessary, against them before Parliament."

M. Drouyn de Lhuys had believed his views to be in conformity with those of his sovereign. Napoleon III. had, in fact, telegraphed him as follows, April 15: " I have received your courier; all you have said and done is so good that I have no new instructions to give you ; I am starting for London."

In England the Emperor had changed his mind. He was persuaded by the English ministers, who wanted the war to go on at any cost, that the projected treaty was insufficient and inefficacious. On the other hand, he believed that the taking of Sebastopol was necessary to the prestige of the French army. On returning to Paris he sent M. Drouyn de Lhuys a telegram, April 23, containing these words: " I returned yesterday from my visit to

England, which was admirable in every way. . . .
Nothing in the world would induce me to accept
anything which should maintain the condition before
the war."

Feeling that he was disavowed, the French Minister of Foreign Affairs had nothing further to do
in Vienna. The day before he left, April 24, he
wrote to Napoleon III. : "I have just come from
the farewell audience granted me by the Emperor
Francis Joseph. Here is a summary of his remarks:
'I regret sincerely that it may be impossible for me
to go further than the plan you have had to send
to Paris. But when the Emperor knows it as it
was finally formulated, I hope that he will agree
with me in thinking that a perpetual alliance between us to defend the Ottoman Empire against
Russia by land and sea is better than a higher or
lower figure. This ultimatum means war, but a
war in which I shall have on my side the approval
of my conscience, the assent of my people, and the
support of Germany.'" The Austrian government,
having resolved to propose the plan of treaty to
Russia under the form of an ultimatum, still hoped
that M. Drouyn de Lhuys and Lord John Russell
could succeed in getting their views adopted by the
Cabinets of Paris and London. After the return of
the former to Paris, the following telegrams were
exchanged between him and Baron de Bourqueney,
Minister of France at Vienna :

"Vienna, May 3, 2 P.M. Here is the identical

declaration of Count Buol: The non-acceptance of
Austria's ultimatum constitutes the *casus belli* and
entails the immediate. signature of the military convention, which fixes the measure of co-operation of
each of the powers and "the date of entry on the
campaign."

"Vienna, May 3. The Emperor has ratified completely the declaration of his minister. Let us urge
on the solution. Do not compromise an excellent
situation for the sake of secondary details. Count
Buol requests you, in the Emperor's name, to send
instructions without delay to your military plenipotentiaries to proceed to the signature of the military convention the very moment when the Russian
plenipotentiaries shall declare themselves unable to
accept without reserve the ultimatum of England."

M. Drouyn de Lhuys to Baron de Bourqueney. —
May 5, 1855. "The Emperor and the British Cabinet reject the proposition of Vienna. I have given
in my resignation this morning. Keep these pieces
of information secret."

Count Bernard d'Harcourt has written in his
remarkable work: *Les quatre ministères des Affaires
étrangères de M. Drouyn de Lhuys:* "Although the
retirement of M. Drouyn de Lhuys in May, 1855,
did not seem to modify very sensibly the general
aspect of affairs, the acceptance of his resignation
was an indication of a profound change in the
foreign policy of the Empire. M. Drouyn de Lhuys
thought that the Austrian alliance would be at once

a lever and a curb for Napoleon III. When the minister whose views this alliance seconded withdrew from power, other ideas prevailed, and the doctrines which acted so powerfully on the court of the Tuileries, later on, made their first appearance."

When Count Walewski took possession of the portfolio of Foreign Affairs, May 8, 1855, the watchword was to say that no change had been made in the great lines of imperial policy. The public, knowing little of diplomacy, paid small attention to an incident whose importance it was incapable of appreciating. Parisians talk of a good many things, but they seldom talk of two things at once. At this moment they thought of nothing but the great ceremony they were about to witness: the opening of the Universal Exposition. This diversion made them forget, for several days, all the preoccupations of home or foreign politics.

CHAPTER XXXIV

THE UNIVERSAL EXPOSITION

AT the very moment when the last hopes of peace had vanished and new slaughters were preparing in the Crimea, Paris, by a strange contrast, beheld a ceremony which seemed like the symbol and glorification of peace. The opening of the Universal Exposition took place at the Champs Elysées, in the Palais de l'Industrie, Tuesday, May 15, 1855. The external façade was decorated with trophies, escutcheons of the imperial arms, flags of all nations. Followed by a numerous procession, which included the entire diplomatic corps, the Emperor and Empress made their entry as an orchestra of one hundred and fifty musicians struck up the air of *La Reine Hortense*. A platform had been raised in the middle of the nave, opposite the principal doorway, and upon this, under a canopy of crimson velvet surmounted by the imperial crown, was a throne on which the sovereign took his seat, with the Empress at his side.

Prince Napoleon, who had exchanged the command of a division in the Crimea for the duties of president of the Commission appointed to organize the Exposition, made a speech beginning thus: "Sire, a

Universal Exposition would have been a considerable event at any time, but this one becomes unique in history through the circumstances under which it takes place. For more than a year France has been engaged in a serious war, eight hundred leagues away from her frontiers, and is struggling gloriously against her enemies. It was reserved for the reign of Your Majesty to show that France is worthy of her past in war, and greater than she has ever been in the arts of peace. The French people are making it plain to the world that whenever their genius is understood, and they are well guided, they will always be the great nation." Prince Napoleon announced that there were twenty thousand exhibiters, nine thousand five hundred of whom were French and ten thousand five hundred foreigners. Even Russia had been invited, but had not responded to an appeal which circumstances rendered peculiar. On this head the Prince remarked: "Even the power with which we are fighting has not been excluded. If Russian manufacturers had presented themselves under the rules established by all the nations, we would have admitted them, in order to firmly establish the demarkation between the Slav peoples, who are not our enemies, and this government, whose preponderance civilized nations must contest."

The Emperor replied in a few words to Prince Napoleon's long discourse. He said: "My dear cousin, in placing you at the head of a commission

called on to overcome so many difficulties, I wished
to give you a special proof of my confidence. I am
glad to see that you have justified it so well. I beg
you to thank the Commission in my name for the
intelligent care and indefatigable zeal which they
have manifested. I open with joy this temple of
peace, which invites all peoples to concord."

Thus, in the midst of one of the most ruthless and
sanguinary wars known to history, was inaugurated
the edifice called a temple of peace by the chief of
one of the belligerent powers. The opening ceremony was splendid. The success of the Exposition
was immense. The Palais de l'Industrie, expressly
built for its purposes on Marigny square, between the
Champs Elysées and the Seine, appeared magnificent
at the time. Its principal hall, with its immense
proportions and Maréchal's gigantic glass windows,
had a suggestion of Babylon. The Exposition was
like a Tower of Babel, with order in place of confusion. All nations of the earth seemed to have made
it their trysting place. One heard all languages
spoken. Paris began to assume that cosmopolitan
character, so much developed since, which has made
it a city apart, the capital of capitals. The Exposition was more than an immense bazaar intended to
delight the eyes. It was like the synthesis of the
industrial and economic transformation going on in
the world. It was not merely an incomparable entertainment for the crowd, but an element of salutary reflections for the thinker and the workingman.

Never had human activity better displayed its energy and power. In passing through its numberless galleries, one observed Boileau's precept, and went

" From grave to gay, from lively to severe."

The most futile things figured beside the most serious : precious stones, ball dresses, children's toys, beside agricultural implements and all the machines which have modified industry from top to bottom. The gallery of *Domestic Economy* attracted the special attention of those who are chiefly concerned with improved conditions for the greater number. Beside the industries of luxury, of the decorative and the industrial arts, appeared those which might be called the humanitarian arts. One was struck by the prodigious progress of science, and by those as yet timid and unknown discoveries destined to take a rapid flight so soon. Thus one admired the beginnings of photography, that future great rival of the pencil and the brush, and noted the first applications of electricity, — of electricity, which must change the face of the globe.

As an antithesis to the marvels of peace, there was a gallery which evoked all the horrors and sufferings of war. Here had been placed ambulance wagons, surgical instruments, instruments for the wounded. Many a face grew dark in presence of such a spectacle. Thought flew towards the Crimean ambulances, towards the dying. There were mothers who wept there. *Bella matribus detestata.* But the dismal

impression lasted but a moment. The joyous orchestras went on playing. Crowds are so indifferent. Paris forgets so quickly.

The number of exhibiters was so much greater than
had been anticipated that, in addition to the Palais
de l'Industrie, a long supplementary gallery had to
be constructed. At the end of this gallery, on the
Avenue Montaigne, was the vast building intended
to receive the statues, paintings, and drawings sent
by the nations to this general competition opened by
France. No such liberal provision had been made
for art at any time or under any reign. "This is
the first time," wrote Théophile Gautier, "that the
fine arts of all peoples meet on the pacific battle-field
of the Universal Exposition. Grand idea, which
only our century could realize with its prodigious
means of communication in presence of which neither
seas nor mountains, neither distances nor obstacles,
exist! *There are no more Pyrenees* is a saying which
is now applicable to all frontiers, and across the
fictitious blue, green, and red lines on the geographic
maps the countries chat familiarly with each other
from one end of the world to the other."

To resume: arts and sciences, commerce and industry, expanded magnificently in the pacific assizes
where their most brilliant manifestations had been
assembled. There resulted from this grand spectacle
a lesson of progress, of pacification, of international
solidarity, which peoples and sovereigns have not
sufficiently conned. The whirl of fashion, the con-

tinual series of amusements and pleasures, forced into oblivion the philosophic side of this Exposition in which thinkers were alone in beholding an eloquent protest against the frightful struggle which was reddening the plateau of Chersonese. People should have reflected that every war between Christian nations is a fratricidal war. The marvels of commerce and industry should have made them comprehend what the nations might do if, instead of exhausting themselves in such sterile expenses as those entailed by armaments, they made only the fruitful and productive expenses of peace. It is in the Gospel, the book of true progress, the book of the future, that should have been sought the moral of the Universal Exposition. What this great pacific fête should have recalled is the saying of Christ : " They that take the sword shall perish by the sword." Because it has forgotten this saying the last half of the nineteenth century will see again the hecatombs of its early years, and groan under the weight of calamities, which will obstruct the march of civilization, and compromise the future of the human race.

Napoleon III. had opened the Exposition, May 15, 1855. The next day, May 16, he received a telegram by which General Canrobert gave his resignation as commander-in-chief of the army of the Orient. Let us see what had taken place in the Crimea since the beginning of the year, and what inextricable difficulties had induced the valiant general to abdicate his command.

CHAPTER XXXV

GENERAL CANROBERT

THE winter had been as dismal and doleful in the Crimea as it had been brilliant and joyous at Paris. To the torrents of rain which had signalized the last days of 1854 had succceded, since the beginning of January, 1855, snow, hail, the icy blasts, the hurricanes of the north. Men who had spent twenty-four hours in the deep and frozen mud of the trenches, found not even a poor fire by which to warm themselves on returning to the tents. Hence frozen limbs requiring operations almost always fatal. The plateau of the Chersonese was like a circle of Dante's Inferno.

General Canrobert wrote : " The army will long remember the 16th of January. During twenty-four hours night did not cease to reign over our bivouacs. Heavy clouds, inundating the atmosphere with a powder of snow chased by an icy wind from the northeast, hung down to the ground. No more intolerable situation could be imagined, yet neither discouragement nor disorder was anywhere produced." The commander-in-chief possessed in the highest degree the talent of maintaining the morale of the troops amidst the most deplorable sufferings. No one could apply to this essentially good and humane soldier that saying of Bossuet : " Away with heroes who lack humanity ! They may force respect and ravish admiration, as extraordinary objects do, but they will not gain hearts." Canrobert won hearts, because he loved his soldiers as a good father loves his children. His speech, somewhat emphatic, but always vibrant, plausible, generous, produced a great impression upon the troops. A model of abnegation, disinterestedness, and bravery, prodigal of his own blood and miserly with that of others, he encouraged, consoled, strengthened, his soldiers by his example. I knew him very well. He said to me one day, in telling the story of his first campaigns : " I loved war as a lover does his sweetheart." Yet while loving it passionately, he deplored its miseries more than any one. In the soul of this modern Bayard there was an incomparable depth of kindness and pity.

M. Charles Bocher, aide-de-camp of the commander-in-chief, wrote, April 21, 1855 : " The bravery of our soldiers is brought into prominence by the small combats that take place nightly. The Russians are always laying ambuscades within range of our works, both to stop them and to cover the approaches to their city. It is necessary to get rid of them, a delicate and dangerous operation which can only be performed at night. We lose a good many men there ; General Canrobert's heart bleeds

whenever he has to sign an order for this sort of
fighting. To give an idea of his humane sentiments,
he lately reviewed a detachment got together in the
evening for one of these night affairs. Foreseeing
that it would be bloody, he spoke to the troops in
language calculated to inflame their courage, and
ended by saying that if any of these brave fellows
felt himself weakening before the thought of danger,
he might go quietly back to his tent and nothing
would be done about it. The general would have
kept his word, but he could not have used language
more capable of touching his audience and inspiring
them with the loftiest sentiments."

Canrobert went to the trenches every day, and
showed himself in the most exposed places. He
was heard to exclaim after a dangerous tour of inspection, and one that had been profuse in tragic
incidents : " See how thickly strewn the road of
glory is with anguish and ruins ! " He ended his
day among the ambulances. " It is the reverse of
the medal," said he. He consoled the wounded by
kind words, promised them rewards, and distributed
his pay among them, being unwilling to keep any of
it for himself. His headquarters, so well described
in the work of M. Charles Bocher, *Lettres et récits
militaires*, was like the cell of an anchorite. Situated on bare ground, where in bad weather one sank
either into mud or snow, it was composed of some
old tents ruined by the rains. As severe to himself
as he was gentle to others, he slept and worked under

a simple soldier's tent. His table was as frugal as that of a monk. After the evening meal he made his guests forget the bad cooking by telling them some good military story.

Born in 1809, General Canrobert was at this time forty-five years old. From childhood he had had the qualities of a true soldier. He told one day how, at the age of ten, having to be sent to the institution of Senlis, where the sons of poor chevaliers of Saint Louis were educated, his father had taken him behind him on a farm-horse and carried him in that way as far as Brives-la-Gaillarde. There the child was confided to the driver of the mail-coach to be taken to Paris, to the house of his uncle, General Marbot, the celebrated military historian, who conducted him to Senlis. When young Canrobert left the military school of Saint-Cyr, his mother, whom it inconvenienced a good deal, sent him fifteen louis in gold, which seemed to him a fortune. This was the only money he received from his parents throughout his career. In Africa he was one of the most popular officers in the army. He distinguished himself in the storming of Constantine, where he was wounded at the side of Colonel Combes, who, before expiring, recommended him to Marshal Valée in these words : "There is a future in that officer." He was one of the first to begin the assault on Zaatcha, and was appointed commander of the Legion of Honor. A brigadier general at the time of the Coup d'Etat, he was unwilling to receive the three

stars for a feat of civil war, and did not become
general of division until January 14, 1853.

A model of military virtues, Canrobert spoke like
a Christian of war and glory. On the very day
before the young General de Lavarande was killed,
he said to him : " I have never forgotten the inscription on the door of the cemetery of Senlis : ' *Hic
arguantur vanitatis præterita*,' ' Here all the vanities
of this world will have to render their accounts.' "
The religious sentiment is always found in the heroes
of the Crimea, in Saint-Arnaud and Canrobert as in
Bosquet. In March, 1855, after a terrible fight,
which took place in darkness, the latter wrote :
" What a night! There was the place for a man to
learn how to turn his eyes to heaven and his soul to
God, keeping and using his heart and his sword for
his country. God is on our side, for we are winning
great and very risky games; and every one of us
sees in it the effect of our mothers' prayers and those
of all the good souls of France."

Indeed, divine force was not too much to sustain
souls amid such trials. Never had war worn a more
horrible aspect. One might have thought he was
fighting in hell. Listen to General Fay: " The daylight fighting seemed nothing but sport in compari-
son with the work in the bowels of the earth and
its accompanying dangers; there, the miner, hearing
all around him the blows of his enemy's picks, sought
how to surprise him when he was not surprised himself. He was incessantly exposed to a loss of air, to

asphyxia from the gas of the enemy's mines. . . .
Men often seized smoking shells and bombs in the
trenches and threw them over the parapet at the risk
of their own lives, thus saving many of their comrades by their presence of mind and courage."

On Sunday, April 8, 1855, the bells rang a full
peal in all the churches of Sebastopol. The Russians were giving each other the kiss of peace. It
was Easter Sunday. Alas! the next day the horrors of war went on with increasing fury. The
allies began an infernal bombardment against the
city. On that day a terrific tempest succeeded
the twenty days of fine weather which had just
preceded it. Rain and wind never ceased. A thick
fog made firing difficult, and prevented the works of
the enemy from being seen. The trenches were
deluged. The bombardment went on for ten suc-
cessive days without other result than disabling six
thousand one hundred and twenty-one Russians, one
thousand five hundred and eighty-seven French, and
two hundred and sixty-three English. Among the
victims was General Bizot, who commanded the engineers so admirably. He was mortally wounded,
April 11. Omar Pasha and his Mussulman officers
were seen sprinkling holy water on the corpse of a
Christian. General Canrobert made some remarks,
which brought tears to the eyes of all who heard
them. He wrote to General Bosquet : " The death
of General Bizot is one of the bitterest griefs I ever
experienced," and to Marshal Vaillant : " This death

is a real public misfortune ; it is a grief to the whole
army.   General Bizot had a most worthily acquired
popularity among the men. . . . Our soldiers all
knew him, they admired his ardor, his bravery, like
that of an ensign, and every day were astonished
at seeing him come back alive from the trenches,
after perils braved with a carelessness and gaiety
that gave a peculiar quality to his courage."

Cruel anxieties and perplexities were at this time
disturbing the mind of General Canrobert.   Torn
by contradictory influences, and unable to satisfy
both the Emperor and the allies, he recoiled above
all from the final slaughter without which the taking
of Sebastopol would be impossible.   On April 17
General Niel, who replaced General Bizot at the head
of the engineers, wrote to Napoleon III. : "The
assault is so difficult, so perilous for the army, that,
when the moment comes, one recoils before it.   The
truth is that in this pretended siege we are pursuing
an end which we dare not attain when we approach
it, and which has no solution but the investment of
the city."   Such was also the sentiment of the commander-in-chief, but the English would not hear of
anything but the continuation of the siege, and refused participation in any other military operation.
A generalissimo was needed to import unity into the
command, and there was none.   Napoleon III. in his
cabinet in the Tuileries, whence he continually sent.
if not orders, at least counsels to the army, insisted
in vain upon a campaign at long distance, in the

interior of the Crimea, for the purpose of arriving at the investment of Sebastopol. Lord Raglan obstinately opposed the execution of this plan.

Despairing of his ability to remedy so disturbed a situation, General Canrobert addressed the following telegram in cipher to the Emperor : "Crimea, May 16, 10 A.M. My health and my mind, fatigued by constant tension, no longer permit me to bear the burden of an immense responsibility. My duty towards my sovereign and my country obliges me to ask you to allow me to remit to General Pélissier, an able leader and one of large experience, the letter of commandment which I have for him. The army which I shall leave to him is intact, inured to service, ardent and confident. I entreat the Emperor to leave me the place of a combatant at the head of a simple division."

Great was the surprise of the army when it learned, May 19, that General Canrobert had resigned the chief command to General Pélissier and was henceforth merely in charge of his former division (1st of the 2d corps). The chagrin was universal. If the man who had given with so much simplicity such an example of self-abnegation had been killed, he would not have been more regretted.

Once more a simple general of division, the former commander-in-chief was a model of devotion and discipline. He exposed himself more than ever. His aide-de-camp wrote, July 14: "It is seldom that on the day after being on guard I do not attend the

burial of some officer of my acquaintance. Life slips
on here in the midst of deaths ; at the entrance of
the trenches there are large graves all ready for the
dead. New ones are dug every day ; close by, on
the way to the trenches, the ambulances are established. It is scarcely a promenade calculated to
enliven one, and yet it affects nobody; one grows
accustomed to everything. Moreover, Providence
gives to souls a moral force equal to the greatest
extremities to which it destines them. This must
be so, because none of us seem to weaken."

General Canrobert was scrupulously careful to
assist his soldiers in bearing their miseries patiently.
Seeing him so resigned and firm, no one else vent-
ured to complain. Nevertheless his health gave
way. Marshal Vaillant wrote to General Niel:
"Tell General Canrobert that he must absolutely
return here, even if it is only for a time. The
Emperor desires it. He has heard from several
quarters that Canrobert is suffering, that his eyes
trouble him, that his pains are so great that he can
hardly remain in the saddle. The Emperor wishes
this worthy general to rest; he will return to his
division later on. Insist strongly on his coming
home." Pélissier advised his friend to take a short
furlough in conformity with the sovereign's wish.
Canrobert replied : "In accepting my return to
France, on account of my health, I should be giving
the army a bad example, and I pique myself on
never having given and never intending to give any

but good ones." Possibly it was thought that the former commander-in-chief retained a moral authority and prestige which ought to belong only to his successor. However that may be, it was necessary for the Emperor to give a formal command. He ordered Canrobert, who was his aide-de-camp, to resume his duties near him, and the general was obliged to obey. He had behaved like one of Plutarch's heroes. The two and a half months he had just spent in the Crimea as a simple general of division, did more for his popularity and his fame than all his other exploits. Nothing gives a better idea of the sentiments which Canrobert inspired in his military comrades than the following letter from General Bosquet, whose chief and whose subordinate he had been by turns :

"August 11, 1855. When you receive this letter, my good mother, you will know already that my brother-in-arms, Canrobert, has left the Crimea in compliance with a formal command of the Emperor, who wishes to have him near him. We did not separate without emotion ; he knows that you pray for him as you do for me, and that in your holy prayers we are doubly brothers. He will probably be obliged to try the waters of Barèges for a knee which fatigue and cold have rendered somewhat stiff. To console me, he said he would certainly make a short visit at Pau. Seated beside you, your hands in his, he will tell you all you would like to know, answering all questions and being able to answer them, because for eighteen months we have been living not far from each other and meeting nearly every day. You will be happy to have him near you for a moment; his countenance is so gentle, and expresses so well the benevolence and generosity that are in his heart. Here it is seven days since we parted; I count them almost as separated lovers do; but no jealousy mingles with this sentiment, for I am sure that he thinks of me as I think of him." Happy the brave soldiers who render such justice to each other! The paladins of the Middle Ages, the heroes of the crusades, had not been more chivalrous.

CHAPTER XXXVI

BORN November 6, 1794, General Pélissier was fifteen years older than General Canrobert. His age, his character, and his services gave him great prestige. He had entered the Royal Guard as an ensign, March 18, 1815, two days before Napoleon returned to the Tuileries. He had distinguished himself in the war with Spain in 1823, and in the expedition of Morea in 1828. He commanded the left wing at the battle of Isly in 1844. He took a brilliant part in the campaign of Kabylia in 1852, and contributed much to the taking of Laghouat. At the commencement of the Crimean War he was at the head of the division of Oran. He was heard at that time to make this prophetic remark : " There is but one man who can take possession of Sebastopol ; and I am that man." His military reputation caused him to be summoned to the war in the Orient. Arriving in the Crimea February 11, 1855, he took command of the 1st corps the same day. On the 16th of the following May he replaced General Canrobert as commander-in-chief.

General Pélissier's dominant quality was his strength of will. Tenacious, absolute, inflexible,

hard to others as he was to himself, he went straight
as a cannon ball to his object. He was a man of
iron, inexorable as destiny. He thought that nothing was more natural in war than bloodshed, and
that nothing ought to move one less. Those who
knew him best say that he was kind, but endeavored
to hide this kindness. The soldiers, who feared,
respected, and admired him far more than they loved
him, nicknamed him "*Tête de fer blanc*," Tin
Head, as much to characterize his obstinate and
immovable will as in allusion to his white hair,
standing up like a brush, and contrasting oddly
with his brown face.

Captain Charles Bocher wrote from before Sebastopol June 1, 1855 : "The new commander-in-chief
is not the same man as he whom he replaces; he is
an altogether different character, but he is a character. . . . Fierce, energetic, decided, he is capable of sacrificing everything to success, — his own
life as well as those of his soldiers. A man of
great probity, he makes no compromises either with
his opinions or his conscience; he always goes
straight to the mark without concerning himself
about others. . . . Despising by instinct those
whom he does not esteem, he likes to surround himself with distinguished men, as do all choice spirits.
He has a great deal of wit, and of the most biting
sort; he has sometimes abused it towards his infe-
riors and his equals, but never through spite. He is
something of a churl, but a beneficent churl."

If General Pélissier's table was very much more carefully served than that of his predecessor, the conversation around it was not so easy and familiar; his guests felt themselves under the eye of a chief who forgave nothing. M. de La Gorce has said: " Such a one who might freely have advised the kind and loyal Canrobert could not enter the new commander's tent without fear. Orderly officers, aides-de-camp, messengers coming from Paris, advisers of all sorts, not one escaped this salutary apprehension, and most of them, when in presence of so severe a commander, hardly dared to stammer out what they had meant to say. That this silence betokened fear rather than sympathy was a thing which did not trouble the commander-in-chief; it was enough for him that tongues were bridled, discipline preserved, and his plans not thwarted." Such was the man who, by dint of energy, was to bring to an end the most difficult, most perilous of enterprises, and to impose his own will not merely on his subordinates, but even on his sovereign.

Like his representative, General Niel, the Emperor wished that in addition to the siege there should be a development of operations at a distance, leading up to the investment of Sebastopol. Pélissier's plan, on the contrary, was summed up in a single phrase, — the siege and nothing but the siege. This plan permitted neither profound combinations nor great strategic efforts. It required nothing but perseverance and obstinacy, but it required a good deal of

these.   The general knew what enormous sacrifices,
what slaughter his system would entail; but the
bloodshed which had brought Canrobert to a halt,
did not intimidate or disturb his successor in the
least.

June 7, Pélissier opened with a brilliant success.
The Green Mamelon and the White Works were
taken.   The Russians were thus deprived of their
exterior positions, and the defence had no longer an
aggressive character.   This victory, which cost the
French fifty-four hundred and forty-three men killed
or wounded, and the English between six hundred and
seven hundred, emboldened the allies to the point of
attempting an assault which was a great imprudence,
seeing that the French trenches were still more than
four hundred metres distant from the Malakoff, and
the English two hundred and fifty metres from the
Grand Redan.   General Pélissier fixed on June 18
for the assault, hoping that a victory on that date
would palliate the dolorous memory of Waterloo.
But alas! after a lapse of forty years, the 18th of
June was still a fatal day.   In spite of their heroism
the allies failed under the terrible cross-firing of the
Malakoff and the Grand Redan.   For an instant the
light infantry of the 5th battalion got a foothold in
the first of these works, but, overwhelmed by the
Russian artillery, they were driven out again.   The
French had uselessly lost thirty-three hundred and
twenty-one killed or wounded, the English between
fifteen hundred and sixteen hundred.

General Pélissier did not attempt to conceal the extent of this disaster. He sent the Minister of War the following despatch, published in the *Moniteur* of June 22: "The attack of June 18 did not succeed, although our troops, who displayed great enthusiasm, forced a partial entrance into the Malakoff. I was obliged to order a retreat into the parallel. This was effected in an orderly manner. It is impossible for me to state our losses exactly." This laconic bulletin made the deepest and most painful impression in France. Almost at the same time it was learned that cholera, which had ceased during the winter in the Crimea, had reappeared in a frightful manner. The fifteen thousand Piedmontese who had just been sent to reinforce the allies by the government of King Victor Emmanuel, suffered particularly from this plague. One of the victims was the English commander-in-chief, who died June 28, of the same disease as Marshal de Saint-Arnaud. His coffin, covered with the English flag, was placed on a cannon drawn by eight artillery horses and taken on aboard the *Canada*, which carried him to England. Men honored this military nobleman, so polished, so correct and brave, who had lost an arm at Waterloo, and made himself famous by numerous feats of arms.

Such a multitude of deaths and calamities, such painful uncertainty as to the issue of the fight, saddened even the loftiest souls. The brave Colonel Cler wrote: " We are beginning to get tired of this

stupid war they are making us fight, and every one
of us, generals, officers, and soldiers, would like our
health and our blood, which we always sacrifice will-
ingly, to be of some use to our country. . . . God
alone knows how this war will end." It could never
end, according to a remark of General Bosquet
(letter of June 1, 1855), save "in a *day of general
rage*, when men would break the very walls, using
their heads as battering rams."

Even among the heroes of this truly epic struggle
there was a presentiment that the results could never
in any case be proportionate to the sacrifices. In a
letter of July 10 General Bosquet regrets that the
success of June 7 had not been utilized by making
overtures of peace. " I think," he writes, " that
after this success and the resultant dangers for the
besieged, Russia would have made acceptable propositions. . . . It was a good situation. . . . As-
suredly there was a chance for concluding this war,
from which France will gain nothing but a little
glory, and in which she may lose her best soldiers,
and with them her chance to resist some day a
Russo-German invasion, when she will be left alone,
deserted by England whose interests are already
different from ours, in spite of the alliance. Poor
France ! always sword in hand, fighting for God
and the right, and always alone at the end of the
struggles, paying for the progress of the civilized
world with the purest of her blood and the last
penny of her savings."

The torrents of blood spilled disturbed Napoleon III. The fatal results of June 18 seemed to him to justify his own ideas and condemn those of General Pélissier. July 3, he resolved to supersede the latter by General Niel. But the despatch removing him was sent by post, and not by telegraph. Marshal Vaillant and General Fleury succeeded in inducing the Emperor to change his resolution. The despatch was stopped at Marseilles, and General Pélissier retained his command without suspecting how near he had come to losing it.

The die was cast. Abandoning himself to fatality, the Emperor renounced giving either orders or advice to General Pélissier, and allowed him to play as he pleased one of the most terrible and hazardous games known to military annals. What rendered this formidable contest still more bitterly painful was that there did not exist the slightest trace of antipathy between the combatants, especially the French and Russians. War is explicable when hate puts arms into the hands of the belligerents, or when they are moved either by passions or positive interests. If they are fighting to keep or to gain their independence, or if their object is merely to gratify national greed or enlarge their territory, hostilities are comprehensible. But there was nothing of the sort in the strife between the Russians and the allies. The latter knew very well that even if they were the victors, they would not keep either the Malakoff tower or the other works they were

trying so desperately to seize, and that they would
take Sebastopol only to restore it to the Russians.
At bottom nothing was at stake, if not for the
Turks at least for the French, the English and the
Sardinians, but diplomatic combinations, questions
of European influence and equilibrium, whose very
existence was not suspected by the majority of the
combatants.

Curiously enough, the French felt much more
sympathy with their Russian enemies than with
their English allies.   General Fay shall describe for
us an armistice concluded for the purpose of bury-
ing the dead : " The Russian and the French officers
went to meet each other midway between the works
while the soldiers were picking up the dead and
wounded.   During this dismal operation the officers
of the two nations were chatting amicably ; one of
ours, a gay and friendly cavalryman, appointed by
his own wish adjutant of the trench, complimented
a Russian prince on the freshness of his gloves, and
asked with a laugh if the shop girls of Sebastopol
were pretty.   Others talked of Paris and the pleasure they would have in meeting again when peace
was made, and meanwhile in exchanging cigars.   The
burials finished, they shook hands before becoming
enemies once more.   The signal given, each hastily
regained his own lines. . . .   Hardly had the flags
of truce disappeared when the men were in their
ambuscades, gun in hand, and watching for the first
head to show itself above the parapet ; they take

aim at the possible risk of killing him whose hand they have just taken, and whom they quitted with the smile of adieu upon their lips."

Another combatant, M. Charles Bocher, in a letter dated June 18, 1855, gives equally significant details concerning the mutual sympathies between the French and Russians, even in the midst of such frightful carnage : "I happened," he says, "to be present while the bodies were being removed on the second day after the affair of the Green Mamelon. The Russian officers were full attention and courtesy. Among them I noticed an aide-de-camp of General Luders, one of Galiffet's acquaintances, who told us that he wished to see the war ended so as not to be obliged to treat us any longer as enemies. We made appointments with each other for the winter in Paris. While this was going on some English officers came up out of curiosity, for they had no business there. The Russian officers stopped talking. One Englishman spoke of the speedy taking of the Malakoff. A Russian officer, turning round, said : 'The French may possibly make themselves masters of it, but you never will !' It is to be remarked that there is not the least animosity between us and the Russians, and that we have more sympathy with our enemies than with our allies. That arises from many causes, but it always happens when a common enterprise is not successful : one takes a grudge against his best friends." M. Bocher adds that the Russian officers taken prisoners after

the affair of the·Green Mamelon were invited to the
tables of different French officers, and to see the
cordiality prevailing at these reunions, and the desire
to be agreeable to these foreigners, no one would
have suspected that they were at war with each
other. He ends with this prophetic reflection :
" Nothing proves better the sentiments of sympathy
which reign between the two peoples. To-day they
are learning mutual esteem in order to agree and
come to an understanding on the matters which the
future is reserving for us."

In the Crimea, near Balaclava, on the seashore, is
the venerated monastery of Saint George. As soon
as they arrived on the plateau of the Chersonese, the
French sent a squadron of spahis to protect this
sanctuary. Later on, from the day when the provisions of the monks were exhausted, they sent them
regular rations of food. One day General Canrobert
and Omar Pasha went there unexpectedly to breakfast. Before the repast they were present in the
chapel at the prayers chanted by the archimandrite
and the monks for the glory of the Czar and the
success of his armies, the cannons of the allies meanwhile thundering against Sebastopol. This was on
a Sunday. In the morning the French had been
present at the Mass said in the camps. Alas ! why
did not the Lord of Hosts, invoked by either side,
put an end to this fratricidal war between Christian
nations, which ought always to be united by respect
for the Cross ?

Paris, intoxicated by festivities and pleasures, thought little of the Crimea and the poor fellows who were fighting and dying with such heroism and resignation. Amidst the bitterest trials the latter retained their enthusiasm and even their gaiety. The soldiers of the 2d Zouaves had constructed a little theatre in their camp, where they played comic pieces, in which the beardless or the least bearded took the female parts in dresses borrowed from the canteen women. General Fay shall describe the spectacle : " There was to be a rehearsal on Sunday, June 10. The programmes had been lithographed on the 6th, and were to have been distributed among the different corps, when the great plans for the next day became known in the camps. Of course there could be no rehearsal, and the actors had to change their costumes and their parts. The soubrettes of the theatre of Moulin had to take off their borrowed petticoats to seize the musket, and the firing spared neither the artists nor their admirers. Two days afterwards, the programme, which there had been no time to begin over again, was going the round of the camps; I have it before me, and I own that I never look at it unmoved, for behind these comedies there is always a drama. This programme, erased in several places because some of the pieces had to be changed, begins thus : '*Monday, June 11, 1855. — For the benefit of the wounded of June 8. — Extraordinary representation.*' Then follow these simple and very

touching lines :"'Two amateurs having been killed
and several wounded, it has been necessary to
change the play intended to be given.'"

The disaster of June 18 and the ravages of the
cholera threw a cloud for some days over the allied
camps. But it soon passed over. The almost complete disappearance of the disease, the beautiful
weather, and the continual arrival of reinforcements
restored the spirits of the troops. August 16, the
Russians attempted a diversion which did not succeed. They came down into the valley of the
Tchernaya, where they were repulsed by the Camou,
Faucheux, and Herbillon divisions, losing eight
thousand men in the fray, which took the name of
the battle of Traktir. In it the Sardinians received
nobly the baptism of fire beside the French. They
had been fighting for the future Italy.

It was felt on both sides that a frightful carnage
was near at hand. Prince Michael Gortchakoff, who
had replaced Prince Menchikoff since March, was
making ready to defend Sebastopol with supreme
energy. The parallels of the allies were so close to
the city that the besiegers and the besieged almost
touched. They might have questioned each other.
The noise of their picks and shovels blended. Even
the most intrepid of the French were wondering
whether, notwithstanding prodigies of heroism, they
could succeed in the formidable assault so soon to
begin. In spite of their admirable tenacity, the
English were asking themselves the same question.

MARSHAL PÉLISSIER

It was rumored in the camps that the Russians had mined all the works, and that if they were obliged to evacuate them they would blow them up with the enemy's troops inside, so that they should possess them only for a moment. Victory might become as lugubrious as a defeat. Such were the reflections the combatants in the Crimea were making at the very moment when the Queen of England arrived in Paris and was received with magnificent festivities.

CHAPTER XXXVII

THE ARRIVAL OF QUEEN VICTORIA

ON Friday, August 17, 1855, Napoleon III. left Paris for Boulogne-sur-Mer to receive Queen Victoria, who was expected on the following day. The Emperor slept there the 17th. Early the next morning he went to the camp occupied by the troops under the command of the victor of Bomarsund, Marshal Baraguey d'Hilliers. An eye-witness, author of a book entitled, *An Englishman in Paris*, has made the following reflections: " On that morning the sovereign's face was more than usually impassive and gloomy. And yet, even to such a fatalist as he, must not that day have seemed prodigious? The blind goddess of fortune, the lucky star in which he had such faith, had she ever favored a mortal as she was then favoring him? How the contrasts in his destiny must have forced themselves upon his mind that autumn morning at Boulogne, while his legions were taking position from Wimereux on the right as far as Portel on the left, to pay homage to the queen of a country which had been the most irreconcilable enemy of his family, on these heights at the foot of which, fifteen years before, August 6, 1840, he had been powerless to rouse the enthusiasm of France, at the very spot where he had made himself the laughing-stock of the world by the comedy of the tame eagle ! And yet not a glimmer of joy or pride illuminated his sphinx-like mask. He remained impassive amidst the most signal honors that the world could bestow."

From the landing-place to the station (at that period the trains did not go to meet the vessels) two regiments of lancers and dragoons formed a double row all along the route, while on the bridge crossing the Liane three hundred bearded sappers with white leather aprons, and hatchets across their shoulders, were massed in three lines. On reaching the landing the Emperor, who had spent the morning on horseback, alighted and remained standing while awaiting the Queen.

At a quarter past two the royal yacht, *Victoria and Albert*, entered the roadstead of Boulogne. The Emperor crossed the footbridge, which was draped with purple velvet and carpeted. The Queen embraced him twice and took his arm to go ashore. Her Britannic Majesty, born May 24, 1819, still retained the brightness of youth. She was accompanied by two of her children, the Prince of Wales, born November 9, 1841, and the Princess Victoria, born November 21, 1840, at present the widow of Frederic III., Emperor of Germany.

We will leave the task of description to an eye-witness whom we have already cited, the anonymous

author of *An Englishman in Paris.* "A spacious
and magnificent carriage, lined with white satin and
capable of containing six persons, awaited the royal
family; it was drawn by two horses only; but what
admirable beasts! Napoleon III. knew how to select
them, and in that respect had not wasted the time
he spent in England. He remounted his own horse
and rode on the right side of the carriage, while
Marshal Baraguey d'Hilliers rode on the left. The
procession moved on amidst the frenzied acclamations of the crowd. But for all that a trooper said :
'It is droll that we should have fought each other
like dogs to come to this. If the old man should
come back he would be very mad.' And I may say
that in spite of the sympathetic attitude of the population, this was at bottom the prevailing sentiment. A
Parisian said: 'Waterloo is arranged, not avenged.'"
The Queen, however, could hear the enthusiastic
shouts of an army of forty thousand men massed on
the cliffs. They drove directly to the station and
immediately took the train to Paris.

The great capital had been in commotion since
morning. Myriads of foreigners, mingling with the
Parisians, invaded the boulevards and installed themselves in the best places, which they had taken care
to secure several days beforehand. The liveliest animation prevailed especially at the approaches to the
new Boulevard Strasbourg, and the station of the
Eastern Railway, by which the Queen was to arrive.
At seven in the evening the station was illuminated.

sky. Prince Monchikoff had just arrived at Constantinople as extraordinary ambassador from the Czar, and his mission had a character which boded ill for the peace of Europe.

CHAPTER XIII

CONSTANTINOPLE is in an uproar on February 28, 1853. Prince Menchikoff is landing. Never had such a scene been prepared for the entry of an ambassador. One would think it the triumphal return of a victorious general. The Christians are thronging to salute the avenger of the orthodox faith. Greeks and Armenians vie with each other in enthusiasm. As soon as the vessel bearing the envoy of the Emperor Nicholas appears in the Bosphorus, the air resounds with frenzied acclamations. The Prince is surrounded by a whole staff of generals, officers, and Russian functionaries: Prince Galitzin, Vice-Admiral Khorniloff, aide-de-camp to the Czar, General Nikapotchinski, Count Dimitri Nesselrode, son of the chancellor. He is himself one of the greatest personages of the Empire. Admiral, Minister of the Navy, Governor of Finland, he has been loaded with honors by his sovereign, whose trusted agent, confidant, and friend he is. Before coming to Constantinople he has just been reviewing, near Odessa, the troops which are going to swell the army already collected in Bes-

Gilded chandeliers and lamps were lighted. At twenty minutes past seven twenty-one volleys of cannon were discharged. The royal and imperial train was arriving. General de Löwestein offered the Queen a magnificent bouquet in the name of the 9th battalion of the National Guard, on duty at the station. The military bands played *God save the Queen.* The Queen took her seat in an uncovered carriage drawn by four horses; the Princess Victoria was beside her, and on the front seat were the Emperor, in the uniform of a general of division, and Prince Albert as a field-marshal. A second carriage was occupied by the Prince of Wales and Prince Napoleon; in the remaining carriages were the Marchioness of Ely and Lady Churchill, ladies of honor, Lord Clarendon, Minister of Foreign Affairs, Lord Breadalbane, Grand Chamberlain, and Lord Cowley, the English Ambassador. At the exit of the station was a deputation of pupils from the Polytechnic School, who, having lost relatives under the walls of Sebastopol, wore crape on their arms. The Emperor drew the Queen's attention to them, and she regarded them with interest. All along the route resounded shouts of "Long live the Queen of England!" "Long live the Emperor!" "Long live Prince Albert!" It was the Queen's first visit to Paris, and she was in constant admiration of the magic spectacle afforded by the incomparable capital. Just at twilight the lamps of the carriages were lighted. A sudden illumination radiated the whole length of the road and preceded the cortège as if by a line of flames. The boulevards, the Rue Royale, the Place de la Concorde, the Avenue des Champs-Elysées, and the Arc de Triomphe de l'Etoile, were resplendent. They entered the Bois de Boulogne. Illuminated by thousands of lights, it was like the gardens of Armida. Never was there a more radiant evening. At a quarter of nine they reached the château of Saint-Cloud. The drums beat the general; the trumpets blew, shouts blended with salvos of artillery. The Empress, the Princesse Mathilde, the officers and ladies on duty, were awaiting the august travellers at the foot of the grand staircase with columns of marble. The cortège entered the palace. They went up the steps on which stood the hundred guards like caryatides, their superb aspect reminding the Queen of her own favorite regiment, the Life Guards. On reaching the grand apartments, the Emperor presented to Her Britannic Majesty the ministers, the grand officers, and the functionaries of his household. After dinner, served with marvellous luxury in the salon of Diana, they returned to the state apartments, where Their Majesties remained until eleven o'clock. Marshal Magnan told the Queen that the Parisian population had never displayed similar enthusiasm, even at the time of the triumphs of Napoleon I. From the windows could be seen a magnificent spectacle. Saint-Cloud and Boulogne were illuminated, Paris appeared on the horizon like a giant stretched out in the light.

CHAPTER XXXVIII

THE QUEEN AT SAINT-CLOUD AND PARIS

Sunday, August 19, 1855. The weather is radiant ; not a cloud, magnificent sunshine. On awaking the Queen is amazed by the beauty of the château of Saint-Cloud, by the double perspective presented, — one on the side of the court of honor, the other on that of the park, — by the avenues, the ponds, the fountains, the great trees, the clumps of flowers. As soon as she had risen she walked in the park with the Emperor. After breakfast a Protestant service took place in one of the rooms of the château. The Queen and Prince went afterwards for a drive in the Bois de Boulogne. Her Majesty expressed a desire to see the remains of the château of Neuilly, delivered to the flames at the time of the revolution of February 24. She sadly contemplated the two small pavilions, strewn with ruins, without dreaming that the palaces of Saint-Cloud and the Tuileries would have the same fate as the favorite residence of King Louis Philippe. In the evening they dined in the salon of Diana. General Canrobert, who had arrived in Paris August 14, was one of the guests. He had received from the Emperor

the welcome deserved by his qualities and his services.
" Fifteen days ago," said he, " I was in the trenches."
The Queen conversed with him for a long time,
speaking of Crimean affairs as well as a soldier could
have done.   Recollecting that the London fishmon-
gers had made him an honorary member of their
corporation, he said : " I am almost one of Your Majesty's subjects." He eulogized Lord Raglan highly,
saying : " He was a noble gentleman, whom we
greatly regretted," and he added, alluding to the
repulse of June 18 : " That killed the poor milord."
After his conversation with the Queen he said to
Lord Clarendon: "I do not know anybody who is
more conversant with the Crimean War than your
sovereign."

Monday, August 20. The Emperor and Prince Albert went to visit the Fine Arts section at the Exposition.   Among other pictures the Prince especially
remarked *La Rixe* by Meissonier, which the Emperor afterwards bought for twenty-five thousand
francs and offered to him.   Thence they went to the
Elysée, where, after lunch, took place the reception of
the diplomatic corps.   Afterwards the Emperor and
his guests went in an open carriage to the Sainte
Chapelle and the Palais de Justice.   While crossing
the Pont au Change Napoleon III. pointed to the
Conciergerie, saying : " That is where I was imprisoned." Next they visited Notre-Dame, whence
they returned to Saint-Cloud by the boulevards,
the Champs-Elysées, and the Bois de Boulogne.

The decorations of Saturday were still intact. The crowds were as great as ever and the applause unanimous. In the evening at Saint-Cloud, the Emperor's comedians in ordinary, as the actors of the *Comedie Française* were called, played Dumas' *Demoiselles de Saint-Cyr*, the principal rôles being very well taken by Augustine Brohan and Regnier. The Queen seemed enchanted.

Tuesday, August 21. The party started in post-chaises for Versailles with an escort of carbineers. A triumphal arch had been erected at the entry of the avenue Saint-Cloud, hung with the united flags of France and England. On the front, facing the avenue Picardy, had been inscribed the names : Victoria and Prince Albert ; on the city side, Napoleon and Eugénie. The Emperor and Empress did the honors of the château of Louis XIV. to their guests. Afterwards they went to the Grand Trianon, where the Queen asked to see the little chapel, built during the July Monarchy, in which was celebrated in 1838 the marriage of "poor Marie," as the Queen designated the daughter of Louis Philippe. Next they visited the Little Trianon and the gardens so full of souvenirs of Marie Antoinette. Here they walked among the trees and entered the cottages of the martyr-queen's hamlet, the band of the regiment of Guides playing excellent music meanwhile.

Wednesday was occupied by a visit to the industrial section of the Exposition, where the Emperor presented Prince Albert with a fine Sèvres vase, representing the Exposition of 1851, organized in London by the Prince ; and another to the Tuileries, where the Queen was much interested in examining the imperial apartments. She and her family afterwards drove through Paris incognito, in a hired carriage. Thursday, August 23, by a visit to the Louvre, and in the evening a ball at the Hôtel de Ville, where Baron Haussman, prefect of the Seine, had achieved marvels of decoration.

On Friday there was a grand review on the Champ-de-Mars in honor of the Queen. Leaving the Tuileries at half-past four in the afternoon, the royal and imperial party crossed the Place de la Concorde, the quay, the Pont de Jena in the carriages, arriving at the Champ-de-Mars, where forty thousand soldiers were assembled under command of Marshal Magnan. Their Majesties watched the review from the balcony of the Military School. When it ended, at seven o'clock, the Queen said to her host : " I am enchanted to see your magnificent soldiers, comrades of the brave troops who are fighting with mine in the Crimea." The Emperor replied : " I hope that this alliance will continue, and that you may always consider my troops as yours."

After the review Their Majesties went directly to the Invalides. General d'Arnano, its governor, had not been apprised of this visit until the last moment, but, nevertheless, all the old soldiers were under arms. Nothing was more imposing than this visit which, according to the Queen, was possibly the most important act of her journey, for it was symbolic, in a way, of the reconciliation between the two peoples who were hereditary enemies. The old soldiers had lighted torches. At the very moment a thunder storm came on. The Queen of England stood up before the tomb of Napoleon. It is amazing that no great painter has chosen this scene for a picture. The Queen herself shall describe it: "I," says she, "the granddaughter of the king who hated Napoleon so much, and made such ruthless war against him, I am there before the tomb of the Emperor at the side of his nephew, who has become my closest and dearest ally. The church organ plays *God save the Queen*. Torches are lighted, and at the same time there is a storm. Strange and wonderful sight! It seems as if this tribute of respect rendered to a dead enemy banished all enmities, all rivalries, and that the celestial seal is placed upon the happy alliance formed between two great and powerful nations. May Heaven bless and prosper it!"

Saturday morning the Emperor conducted his guests to Saint-Germain to show them the château offered as a residence by Louis XIV. to James II. of England after his dethronement. After walking in the forest they rested for a moment at the Château de la Muette, where they saw the imperial kennels with the huntsmen and whippers-in. On their return they stopped at Malmaison and the fortress of Mont-Valérien. In the evening there was a

grand ball at the palace of Versailles, which Their
Majesties opened at half-past ten in the Gallery of
Mirrors.   The Queen danced two quadrilles, — one
with the Emperor, the other with Prince Napoleon.
She waltzed also with the Emperor.   Several for-
eigners of distinction were present, among others
Count Bismarck, Prussian Minister at Frankfort.
Supper was served in the theatre of the château, on
small tables seating ten persons, each presided over
by a lady.   The imperial and royal table, in the mid-
dle of the hall, was somewhat higher than the
others.   Nine guests sat down at it : the Queen, the
Emperor, the Empress, Prince Albert, the Prince of
Wales, Princess Victòria, Prince Napoleon, Princesse
Mathilde, Prince Adalbert of Bavaria.

After supper they returned to the Gallery of
Mirrors.   The Emperor waltzed again with Princess
Victoria.   Could he have dreamed that this charming young girl of fourteen whom he was so pleased
to dance with, would one day be the wife of the
chief author of the catastrophe of Sedan?   Would
it not be a curious subject for a *genre* picture :
Napoleon III. waltzing with the young Princess
Victoria in the Gallery of Mirrors before Bismarck,
mingling with the throng of courtiers?   Ah, how
fortunate it is that mortals cannot divine the future !
What a shudder would have chilled the Emperor's
veins could he have foreseen that this grandiose gallery would be a hospital for the wounded and dying
during the fatal year, and that in the succeeding

year the conquerors of France would select it for the formal proclamation of the Empire of Germany!

But there is no room for gloomy presentiments in the midst of a superb entertainment. Napoleon III., delighted with his destiny, was animated by all the joy of receiving the Queen of England. At the close of the ball he said to her: "It is terrible that this should be the last evening but one. But you will come back, will you not? As we know each other now, can't we exchange visits between Windsor and Fontainebleau without much ceremony?"

Sunday, August 26. The great fêtes are over. The last day at Saint-Cloud will be spent in family privacy. It is Prince Albert's thirty-sixth birthday. The Queen, who has a sort of adoration for her husband, congratulates him most affectionately. In the morning, during a drive in a phaeton with the Emperor, she said to him: "There is one thing I have at heart and which I wish you thoroughly to understand, and that is the friendship I still retain for the Orleans princes." Napoleon III. replied: "I understand very well that you could not forsake them in misfortune. I have no animosity against them myself. I have not turned any of their partisans out of place. I hope you have told Queen Marie Amélie that I should be glad to have her pass through France on her way to Spain." Queen Victoria went on to praise the widow of Louis Philippe and his sons. She commended their tact and discretion. "Yes," returned the Emperor, "but it is

regrettable that their agents should be in constant
relations with my worst enemies." " What could
you expect?" asked the Queen; "is it not natural
that exiles should be tempted to conspire? Did you
not conspire yourself?" The Emperor put an end
to the conversation by proposing to take her during
the day to the chapel of Saint Ferdinand. This is
the sanctuary erected at Neuilly, on the right of the
Révolte road, on the site of the grocer's shop where
the Duc d'Orléans, eldest son of Louis Philippe,
breathed his last in consequence of an accident to
his carriage, July 13, 1842. The Queen gratefully
accepted the offer.

After breakfast the Emperor and the Empress
made their birthday presents to Prince Albert. The
Empress gave him a beautifully mounted ivory cup,
and the Emperor Meissonnier's *La Rixe*, which the
Prince had admired at the Exposition. Then they
repaired to the chapel of Saint Ferdinand. Napoleon
bought there a medal commemorative of the Duc
d'Orléans, which he gave to the Queen, saying:
" Keep it as a souvenir." In the evening the family
dinner was followed by a concert of the classic music
of which Prince Albert was so fond.

CHAPTER XXXIX

Monday, August 27, 1855. This was the day of departure. In the morning Queen Victoria wrote: "To-day in my beautifully decorated room in this fine palace of Saint-Cloud, to the sound of the fresh fountains which reaches my ears, I wish to write a few words of farewell. I am profoundly grateful for the eight happy days I have spent here. May God bless England and France! May He especially protect the precious life of the Emperor!" The weather was warm, but radiant. The Empress offered the Queen a handsome fan, with a rose and a heliotrope from the garden, and the Princess Victoria a bracelet adorned with rubies and diamonds, surrounding a small medallion containing some of the giver's hair. At half-past ten the Queen and her family left the château with regret. The Emperor and Empress accompanied them. On the road they saw several wounded soldiers from the Crimea, among them some Zouaves, "my favorites, the Zouaves," as the Queen called them. On arriving at the Tuileries, the Empress bade farewell to the royal family, who went on to the Eastern Station with the

Emperor and Prince Napoleon, who were to escort
them as far as Boulogne-sur-Mer, where they arrived
at five o'clock in the evening.

Almost immediately after their arrival, Their
Majesties reviewed the troops of the camp assembled on the beach. The Queen chatted for a few
moments with a canteen woman, whose uniform and
whose good figure attracted her attention. " I wish
there were some like her in my army," said she.
They dined afterwards at the Imperial Pavilion.
The illuminations of the city and the harbor vied
with the moon and stars of a radiant night. The
Emperor attended his guests to the jetty where the
royal yacht awaited them. The Emperor and the
Queen, both of them deeply affected, exchanged
the following words at the moment of departure,
after embracing each other twice : " You will return,
will you not? " " Once more, adieu, Sire." "Adieu,
Madame, until we meet again." " I surely hope so."
It was eleven o'clock. The yacht weighed anchor
to the sound of volleys of musketry and the acclamations of the crowd covering the quays on the jetty.
It reached Osborne at eight o'clock the next morning.

The Queen's visit and her relations with her hosts
had impressed her with a sentiment of real gratitude.
She had been dazzled, charmed, fascinated by all that
she had seen and heard. An exchange of friendly
letters between the Emperor and his guests took
place immediately after their return to England.

Prince Albert to the Emperor of the French. — "Osborne, August 29, 1855. Sire and dear brother, I cannot allow another day to pass without renewing to you in writing the expression of gratitude for the many marks of kindness and friendship which Your Imperial Majesty has bestowed on me. . . . These are of that sort of impressions which are never effaced, and which serve to compensate us in the many moments of difficulty and vexations which life brings with it. Our children have been much affected by their reception in France, and cannot tell their brothers and sisters enough about it. The hope you have held out of seeing us again from time to time is very sweet. May God protect you, Sire, as well as the Empress, and bring to her the happy accomplishment of her desires!"

The Queen to the Emperor. — " Osborne, August 29, 1855. Sire and my dear brother, one of my first occupations on arriving here is to write to Your Majesty and express from the bottom of my heart how deeply we are penetrated and affected by the reception given us in France by Your Majesty and the Empress, as well as by all the nation. The souvenir will never be effaced from our memory, and I love to see in it a precious pledge for the future of the cordiality which unites our two governments as well as our two peoples. May this happy union, which we owe chiefly to the personal qualities of Your Majesty, be consolidated still more firmly for the welfare of our two nations as well as of all Europe.

"My heart was very full when I took leave of you, Sire, after the beautiful and happy days we spent with you, and which you knew how to render so agreeable.   Alas ! like all things here below, they are past, and these ten holidays seem like a lovely dream. . . .

"I cannot sufficiently express, Sire, how much I am touched by all your kindness and your friendship for the Prince, and also the affection and good nature you have shown to our children.   Their visit in France has been the happiest time of their life, and they are never done talking about it.   We found all the other children in good health, and little Arthur (the Duke of Connaught, born May 1, 1850) trots about with his policeman's cap, which is all his joy, and from which he will not be separated.

"May God watch over Your Majesty and the dear Empress, for whom I form so many wishes.   You said to me once more on the boat : ' *Au revoir,*' and I repeat it with all my heart.

"Permit me to express here all the sentiments of tender friendship and affection with which I call myself, Sire and dear brother, your very dear and affectionate sister and friend.

" VICTORIA, R."

The Emperor to Prince Albert. — "Saint-Cloud, September 1, 1855.   Sir, my brother, need I tell you that the more I know you the more esteem I experience for your character and friendship for your person? You must be convinced of it, for we divine those who love us. I greatly regretted the brevity of your stay, because when people have an equal love of what is good, the more they see of each other the greater is their mutual comprehension. I thank Your Royal Highness for your amiable letter, and have been much affected by this appreciation of your sojourn in France, since you consider it as a compensation for the vexations inseparably connected with exalted functions. I take the same view of it, and your visit will always remain a very sweet memory to me and to the Empress.

"I beg of you to remember me to the Prince of Wales and the Princess Royal, as well as to the other princes and princesses; I never separate them from the friendship I bear towards you. The Empress is very grateful for your good wishes, and desires me to assure you of her affectionate sentiments."

The Emperor to the Queen. — "Saint-Cloud, September 1, 1855. Madame and my dear sister, after my happiness in offering Your Majesty a cordial and eager welcome, I have experienced another not less great in knowing that you have been satisfied with your journey in France. Certainly I appreciate, like Your Majesty, the capital importance for our two countries of a sincere union between the two governments; but I appreciate above all these intimate relations now established between us and founded upon true and sincere friendship, for the satisfaction

of the heart will always rank in my view far above
the satisfactions of ambition ; and, although I experienced a just sentiment of pride in being for a moment the host of the Queen of so powerful an empire,
I am still better pleased with the memory of the
amiable and gracious woman, the distinguished man,
the charming children, with whom I have spent days
of a sweet intimacy, the souvenir of which will never
be effaced from my memory.   Hence I need not say
how greatly I desire that it may be speedily renewed.   I thank Your Majesty for the good wishes
you form for the Empress ; you touch me profoundly
by the interest you take in what is dearest to me.

"I have received good news from the Crimea.
Pélissier says that all is going well and that he has
good hopes. . . .

"I beg Your Majesty to allow me to express the
real attachment and sincere affection with which I
am, Madame and dear sister, Your Majesty's most
devoted brother and friend.

"NAPOLEON."

How many changes had taken place since the
Coup d'Etat !   At that time the Duke of Wellington daily predicted an imminent catastrophe to his
country if it did not take up arms.   The English
militia was called upon as if the naval fleet of Boulogne had already made its appearance in the Chan-
nel.   Mr. Cobden was the only one willing to wager
against his compatriots.   And now not only were

all fears dispelled, but a cordial alliance united two
nations accustomed to hate each other. This reconciliation was the personal achievement of Napoleon
III. and Queen Victoria. Seven centuries of rivalries and wars seemed to be forgotten.

The evidences of friendship lavished by the Queen
of England on the Emperor of the French were not
merely perfunctory and official protestations. They
came from her heart. One should read in the
Queen's journal the portrait she drew of Napoleon
III. at the close of her visit. " One cannot imagine,"
she writes, " how attached one becomes to the Emperor on seeing him in private life as we have just
done, spending ten or twelve hours with him daily,
and on the last day, fourteen. He is so calm, so
simple, often even naïve, delighting to learn what he
does not know! And so gracious, so full of tact and
dignity, of modesty and respect, so attentive to us !
I know few persons with whom I have been so confidential. There is nothing I could not tell him.
His society is particularly agreeable. There is
something fascinating, melancholy, attractive about
him which wins one in spite of every prejudice.
The children liked him very much. His kindness
towards them was very great, but at the same time
very judicious. I consider the time I spent with
him as one of the most agreeable and most interesting periods of my life. The Empress has a great
charm also. We were all enraptured with her."

And now let us return to the Crimea. While the

Queen was at Saint-Cloud, the *Moniteur* had published a letter from the Emperor to General Pélissier,
dated August 20, in which he felicitated the troops
on the victory of Traktir.   In it he said : " The
glory acquired in the Orient has moved your companions in arms in France ; they are all burning
to share your dangers.   Desiring not only to respond
to their wishes, but to procure repose for those who
have already done so much, I have given orders to
the Minister of War that all the regiments remaining in France shall go as soon as possible to replace
those now in the Orient.   You know, general, how
I have groaned at being detained so far from that
army which is adding new glory to our eagles ; but
now my regrets are diminishing, since you show me
the near and decisive success which must crown such
heroic efforts."

The dénouement was approaching.

CHAPTER XL

THE approaches of the French had arrived to within forty metres of the Central bastion, within thirty of the bastion of the Flagstaff, twenty-five of the enceinte surrounding the Malakoff tower, and those of the English to within two hundred metres of the Grand Redan. Generals Pélissier and Simpson decided that the time had come for making the assault. It was to take place on Saturday, September 8, 1855, at noon.

On the right the troops of the 2d French army corps, commanded by General Bosquet, were to attack the Malakoff, the Curtain, and the Little Redan (also called the redan of the Carénage). In the centre the English were to attack the Grand Redan. On the left the attack on the Central bastion and the bastion of the Flagstaff was reserved to the 1st French army corps, commanded by General de Tolles and to a Sardinian division. The most important point to seize was the Malakoff. Successful there, it is all up with Sebastopol, even though failure is the result everywhere else.

The front of the Malakoff was some three hundred

343

and fifty yards long by one hundred and fifty
in width.   Its parapets projected more than six
yards above the ground, and in front of them was a
ditch more than six yards deep and seven wide.
This immense citadel of earth called Malakoff was
armed with sixty-two cannon of varying calibre.   In
the front of it, enclosed by the parapet, was the
Malakoff tower, of which the Russians have preserved only the ground story, which is crenellated.
The work is united by the Curtain to the Little
Redan.

The Malakoff is the key of Sebastopol.   Should it
be taken, the Russians could no longer defend the
suburb of Karabelnaya, communication between the
city and the northern part of the roadstead would
be cut off, and resistance would become impossible.
The honor of attacking it is reserved to the 1st
division of the 2d army corps, led by General
MacMahon, lately arrived in the Crimea, where he
had taken General Canrobert's place at the head of
this division.   It is to be supported by the Zouaves
of the Imperial Guard.   The Dulac division and the
La Motterouge division, both of them belonging to
the 2d corps, are to attack the Little Redan and
the Curtain, respectively.   They are to be supported
by the light infantry and the grenadiers of the
guard.

On Friday, September 7, in a little hut built
on a tumulus adjoining the headquarters of the 2d
corps, General Bosquet assembled all the generals

placed under his command, as well as those of the artillery and engineers, and explained to them with great clearness the plans for the next day. " As first reserves," said he to General MacMahon, " I shall give you the vigorous Wimpffen brigade, composed of soldiers seasoned in the trenches; then to parry at the last hour the offensive returns of the enemy, I have selected for you the Zouaves of the Guard, those veterans of the army of Africa who would let themselves be killed to the last man rather than abandon to the enemy this conquest of the 1st division." (The next day the Zouaves of the Guard had three hundred and eleven killed and wounded men out of six hundred and twenty-seven.) Bosquet's words are warmly applauded. From all sides comes the cry : " Count on us, general."

Saturday, September 8, 1855. The weather is bad, the sea rough. A violent northwest wind prevents the English and French vessels from leaving their anchorages and taking part in the operations.

At eight o'clock the engineers throw into the Malakoff, where they explode, two barrels of powder of one hundred kilogrammes each (about two hundred and twenty pounds); moreover, they explode three charges of five hundred kilogrammes, in order to destroy the galleries of the Russian miners and to reassure the French soldiers who knew the soil was mined.

The 2d corps gets under arms at the same hour. General Bosquet's order of the day, announcing the assault, concluded as follows: "It is a general assault, army against army; it is a question of crowning the young eagles of France with an immense and memorable victory. Forward then, children! Malakoff and Sebastopol to us! and long live the Emperor!"

This is General MacMahon's order of the day: "Soldiers of the 1st division and Zouaves of the Guard, at last you are to quit your parallels and attack the enemy corps to corps. In this decisive battle the most important point has been confided to you by the commander-in-chief: the seizing of the Redan of Malakoff, key of Sebastopol. Soldiers, the entire army has its eyes upon you, and your flags, planted on the ramparts of that citadel, must respond to the signal given for the general assault; twenty thousand English and twenty thousand French will support you on the left by precipitating themselves on that side of the fortress. Zouaves, foot soldiers, men of the 7th, 20th, and 27th of the line, your bravery answers for the success which must immortalize the members of those regiments. Within a few hours the Emperor will know in France what the soldiers of the Alma and of Inkerman can do. I give you *Long live the Emperor!* as our signal. Our countersign will be *Honor and Country!*"

All the watches have been regulated. The assault is to begin at noon precisely. In a glass case, containing what might be called the military relics of

General MacMahon, his widow has placed a repeater, on the inside of which is the inscription : " I sounded the assault on Sebastopol."

General Bosquet is in his tent in the centre of the 6th parallel, his fanion lowered. It is noon. The eight hundred cannon which have been firing on Sebastopol are silent. Drums beat, trumpets blare. " Forward! " cries General Bosquet, and his fanion is at once raised by Quartermaster Rigodit. The three divisions, MacMahon, Dulac, and La Motterouge, come out of the trenches to cries of " Long live the Emperor ! " General Pélissier has said : " The moment is solemn."

This is the 1st brigade of the MacMahon division which rushes on the Malakoff, the 1st Zouaves at its head, followed by the 7th of the line, with the 4th battalion of light infantry on its left. The breadth and depth of the ditch, the height and steepness of the talus, render the ascent extremely difficult. Yet, without waiting for ladders, the intrepid Frenchmen climb the sides ; some jump over the parapet, others pass underneath the rope doorways, under the embrasures. Then begins a terrible hand-to-hand fight. In default of guns, the surprised Russians had armed themselves with picks, stones, artillery sponges, anything on which they could lay their hands. After a ruthless struggle the 1st Zouaves, Colonel Collineau, and the 7th of the line, Colonel Decaen, surround the tower and penetrate as far as the first trenches of the work. The 1st Zouaves plants its eagle on

the rampart.   At this moment occurs a providential
event for the French.   A hundred Russians, sheltered in the casemates of the Malakoff tower, have
opened a murderous fire.   On their refusal to surrender, some fascines are set afire to smoke them out
and thus oblige them to lay down their arms ; but
some one remembers just then that the spies had
said that all the bastions were mined.   The barely
kindled fascines are extinguished, trenches being
hastily dug beside the tower and earth thrown upon
the flames.   It is while doing this that the electric
wires are discovered which the Russians had prepared in order to blow up the work should the
French get inside of it.   This discovery saves General MacMahon and his troops.

The General is in the Malakoff.   But what efforts
he must make to remain there !   The 2d brigade of
his division comes to his aid.   It is composed of the
20th and 27th of the line, under General Vinoy.

At the moment when MacMahon's troops rush
upon the Malakoff, the Dulac division attacks the
Curtain, and the La Motterouge the Little Redan.
But their success is only temporary, in spite of their
heroic bravery.

Meanwhile General Pélissier is established with
his staff on the Green Mamelon, called also by the
French the Brancion redoubt, because General de
Brancion had been killed there, June 7.   Seeing
that the eagle of the 1st Zouaves is planted on the
rampart of the Malakoff, he has the Queen's flag

hoisted beside the French colors on the Green
Mamelon. This is the signal agreed upon between
him and General Simpson for beginning the English attack upon the Grand Redan. To reach it, the
English have to cross a space of more than two hundred yards under a rain of grape-shot. This space
is speedily strewn with dead men. The attacking
column goes down into the ditch, almost five yards
deep. It climbs the overhanging rampart and takes
the salient of the Grand Redan. After sustaining
an unequal combat for two hours, it decides to evacuate it, but does so with such a firm bearing that the
enemy is afraid to pursue it.

The attack on the Grand Redan was still in progress when, a little before two o'clock, a bouquet of
fireworks set off from the French observatory sig-
nalled the commander of the 1st corps of the French
army to assail the Central bastion. Notwithstanding the extreme energy of the troops, this attack succeeded no better than that on the Grand Redan.

Half-past two. The attack will miscarry at all
points except the Malakoff, where the MacMahon
division is only sustaining itself by prodigies of
energy and at the cost of the most bloody sacrifices.

At this moment a great misfortune befalls the
army, — General Bosquet, who, in front of the Malakoff, is surveying all the operations of the 2d corps,
is grievously wounded by the explosion of a shell.
One of Yvon's pictures in the gallery of Versailles
represents Bosquet at the moment he was struck.

Of all the officers who figure in this picture, — General Mellinet, commanding the division of the imperial guard, General de Cissey, Commandant de Rumford, Captain de Dampierre, etc., — but one survives, namely, Captain Fay, General Bosquet's aide-de-camp, since become a general of division and the head of an army corps. I have the honor to be a friend of this brave soldier, a military author of the first rank. His writings and conversations have supplied me with most valuable observations.

And now let us give place to another of our friends, whom Yvon has not represented in his picture, and yet who had every right to be there : Captain Bocher, orderly officer of the illustrious wounded man. "General Bosquet," he says, "is struck on the right side and totters. Being close beside him, I receive him in my arms. By the suffering expressed on his countenance, his pallor, his heart-rending groans, I think all is over with him. What a painful impression around us ! The loss of such a leader at such a moment might endanger success. The courageous wounded man was still strong enough to be aware of everything and to send word to General Pélissier, who was at the Green Mamelon, to fill his place. It was not until later, when his strength was completely gone, that he consented to be carried from the field of carnage. What a time it took us to get out of the trenches ! They were encumbered with defenders, with the dead and wounded. We had to take a thousand precautions, and halt at every step, in obedience to the general, who was suffering cruelly. After quitting the trenches we often picked our way under a rain of fire. It was night when we reached our headquarters and deposited our chief in his wooden hut. There only could he find a little relief from his excessive sufferings."

Before his banishment from the action that had been so well prepared, Bosquet had had the joy of following the progress of MacMahon's troops, who, being reinforced by the Wimpffen brigade and the Zouaves of the Guard, victoriously maintained themselves in the Malakoff, in spite of the Russian attempts to drive them out.

The French troops triumphed in the Malakoff, but the Russians were succeeding in the Curtain and at the Little Redan. In the Curtain the explosion of a covered powder magazine made great ravages. The standard of the 91st, buried under the débris, was not found until the next morning, in the scorched hands of the officer who had kept it even in death. General de La Motterouge had been wounded by a bursting shell. At the Little Redan General de Marolles and General de Saint-Pol had been killed, Generals Bourbaki, Bisson, Mellinet de Pontevès wounded, the latter mortally. The Dulac division, which had carried the work in the first place, had in the end been obliged to evacuate it.

In the attack on the Central bastion, which had likewise failed, Generals Rivet and Breton had been killed and General Trochu wounded. The ever ardent troops of the 1st corps were making ready to renew the attack when the commander-in-chief sent an order to General de Salles not to keep it up any longer.

Thereupon the siege batteries, silent since noon, again opened fire. The bombardment was renewed before the city, as well as in front of the Great and Little Redans.

All efforts are now concentrated on the Malakoff, which is to be retained at any cost. Important reinforcements reach it : 3d Zouaves, 50th of the line, light infantry of the guard, Algerian sharpshooters. The Russians are about to make a final, desperate attempt. Formed in three deep columns, they thrice attack the entrance of the bastion. Three times they are obliged to fall back before the solidity of the French troops. After this last struggle, which is not over until near five o'clock, they seem decided on abandoning the game.

General Pélissier, who has just seen his aide-de-camp, Colonel Cassaigne, fall mortally wounded at his side, is still posted on the Green Mamelon. From there, towards the close of the day, he observes a great movement on the bridge of boats uniting the northern and southern shores of the roadstead of Sebastopol. Groups of men, files of vehicles, constantly succeed each other, constantly moving towards the north. Are they convoys of wounded ? Are they wagons going after munitions ?

No, it is the mass of Russians who are evacuating the city to take shelter on the north side of the roadstead.

Night has come. The allies do not yet know whether the fight will be resumed next day. At midnight many explosions in Sebastopol are heard. All the batteries of the Point, the Maison-en-Croix, the Little Redan, the Grand Redan, the bastion of the Flagstaff, the Central bastion, every bastion, in fact, except the Malakoff, where the French had providentially discovered the electric wire and cut it in time, explode one after another. The check sustained at the Little Redan, the Curtain, the Grand Redan, and the Central bastion was all that prevented the troops from falling victims to the explosion. The Russians have decided to leave nothing but ruins to the victors. The powder magazines, the forts, all explode with terrific noise. It is a gigantic conflagration, like that of Moscow in 1812. The sun, rising on September 9, lights up this work of destruction. The bridge of boats has bent back upon itself. The Russians have sunk what remained of their Black Sea fleet, not even sparing the *Imperatrice-Marie*, that beautiful vessel which carried Admiral Nakhimoff to the battle of Sinope. They have kept only the steamers which take away the last fugitives and some fanatics still trying to spread the conflagration in the city. But soon these few men, as well as the steamers, are, obliged to withdraw and seek shelter in the creeks and coves of the north shore of the roadstead. Sebastopol was taken, all but this shore, which still belonged to the Russians.

"September 10," writes General Fay, "General Bazaine was given the chief command of the fortress, with a brigade of infantry, and it was agreed that the French should occupy the city and the English the suburb; a pontoon bridge was to unite these two parts of Sebastopol. But this occupation soon became difficult on account of the numerous batteries immediately established all along the north shore of the roadstead; in order to answer these and to destroy them, we were ourselves obliged to set up batteries all along the south shore and provide ways of reaching them under cover; so the second winter passed in a continual exchange of bombs and bullets which fortunately did not effect much."

And now we leave the tale to the commander-in-chief. In his report of September 14, 1855, he says: "Thus has been terminated this memorable siege, during which the relieving army has twice fought in pitched battle, and in which the means of defence and attack have attained colossal proportions. The besieging army had in battery, in the different attacks, about 800 pieces of ordnance, discharged more than 1,600,000 times, and our parallels, dug during 336 days of covered trench work in rocky ground, and nearly five miles long, were executed under constant fire from the fortifications and incessant combats by day and night. The battle of

September 8, in which the allies got the better of an army of almost equal size, not invested, intrenched behind formidable defences provided with 1100 pieces of ordnance, protected by the cannon of the fleet and the batteries on the north of the roadstead, disposing altogether of immense resources, will remain an example of what may be expected from a brave, disciplined, and well-seasoned army."

The Russian losses on the 8th had amounted to 12,913 men, 2972 of whom were dead. The French army counted 145 officers killed, 254 wounded; 1489 inferior officers and soldiers killed, 4259 wounded, 1400 missing; total, 7567 men disabled. The English army, 385 killed, 1886 wounded, 176 missing; the Sardinian brigade, 4 killed and 36 wounded.

Now that France and Russia are closely allied, and the latter have resumed their former position at Sebastopol and in the Black Sea, may not one inquire what end was served by such heroic efforts, such sublime sacrifices, such cruel slaughter? Alas! how heavy a price is paid for glory, and often to what good?

CHAPTER XLI

PARIS at first understood but imperfectly what had just taken place in the Crimea. The *Moniteur* of September 10, 1855, published the following despatch dated from Varna, and received by the Minister of War at eleven o'clock the previous evening : "September 9, 3.35 A.M. The Malakoff was assaulted at noon. Its redoubts and the redan of the Carénage (the Little Redan) were taken by our brave soldiers with admirable spirit to cries of 'Long live the Emperor!' We immediately proceeded to establish ourselves in them, one after another, and at Malakoff we have succeeded. It was impossible to keep possession of the Carénage under the heavy artillery fire that poured in upon the first occupants of this work, which our solid installation at Malakoff will soon reduce, as well as the Grand Redan, whose salient our brave allies carried with their usual vigor. But, as it was at the Carénage, they were obliged to recoil before the enemy's artillery and powerful reserves. On seeing our eagles floating above the Malakoff, General de Salles made two attacks on the Central bastion. They were unsuccessful ; our

356

troops returned to the trenches. Our losses are serious, and I cannot specify them. They are amply compensated, for the taking of the Malakoff is a success which will have immense consequences." Notwithstanding this last sentence, public satisfaction was very moderate. People had been so often the sport of false news and vain joys that they had become incredulous ; moreover, the despatch did not say that Sebastopol was taken.

The next day, September 11, the *Moniteur* published two despatches which were more explicit. One from General Pélissier, dated from the Brancion redoubt at three in the morning of September 9, announced that the faubourg of Karabelnaya and the southern portion of Sebastopol no longer existed, and that the Russians had decided to evacuate the town after having blown up nearly all the defences. The other telegram, addressed by Admiral Bruat to the Minister of the Navy, September 9, 10.15 A.M., announced that the Russian vessels had slipped away, and that the French soldiers were scattered about in isolated groups on the ramparts of Sebastopol, which seemed to be entirely deserted.

September 12, the news of the taking of Sebastopol being completely confirmed, Napoleon III. signed at the château of Saint-Cloud the decree which raised General Pélissier to the rank of Marshal of France. It was decided that on the next day, September 13, a *Te Deum* should be chanted at Notre-Dame, and that all the Parisian theatres should give

free entertainments. The Emperor was present at
the *Te Deum* of Notre-Dame, which was celebrated
with great pomp. He said to the Archbishop of
Paris : " I come here, Monseigneur, to thank Heaven
for the triumph it has granted to our arms, for I
rejoice to recognize that in spite of the ability of the
generals and the courage of the soldiers, nothing can
succeed without the protection of Providence." On
Sunday, September 16, a *Te Deum* was chanted in
every church in France, and there were public
rejoicings everywhere.

September 21, the Emperor wrote to Bosquet :
" My dear general, the taking of Sebastopol is
largely due to you ; Marshal Pélissier proclaims this
and it does not surprise me. This final and decisive
co-operation on your part is in keeping with previous
feats of arms since the opening of the campaign.
There you were skilful and intrepid as you have
been on all occasions. I love to recognize it openly
and to congratulate you upon it. I am assured that
your wound will not have serious consequences ; I
hope so and am sincerely glad of it."

The Russians, as well as the French, rendered homage to General Bosquet. This is what he wrote to
his mother, September 25 : " A score of Russian officers, prisoners, brought to my headquarters on the
8th, just as I reached it on an ambulance litter, made
inquiries about my wound with great interest, saying
that without me we should not have succeeded, and
that if the assault had been conducted by Pélissier, it

would have failed like that on the 18th of June. And as one of my officers said to them: 'Since the battles where General Bosquet made the charge against you have all been fatal to the Russians, how is it that you speak of him so kindly?' They replied: 'We have been conquered, but we cannot withhold our esteem from your general, and if he is sent to Russia when peace is proclaimed, he will be received in triumph. We know that he has appreciated our troops and our officers.'"

During the Crimean war all hearts in France beat in unison. Imperialists, legitimists, Orleanists, republicans, were all animated by the purest patriotism. Party rancors had vanished before the national sentiment. Witness the beautiful letter which a personal adversary of Napoleon III., General de Lamoricière, wrote to General Bosquet from Brussels, September 20, 1855: " My dear general, so long as it was only a question of applauding your successes, I abstained, as you could not doubt my sentiments, from sending you any commonplace felicitations which might have the inconvenient result of interfering with your career. Among the necessities imposed on us by the ostracism to which we are subjected, one of the hardest is that which very often obliges us to refrain from expressing the sympathies which we must retain within our hearts. But now you are wounded, even severely, it is said, I cannot resist the impulse to send you these few lines, the writing of which you will recognize. May the cordial souvenir and the old friendship of him who traces them assuage for a moment your glorious sufferings ! "

Bosquet had a profound gratitude and admiration for Lamoricière. He replied : " My general, my very dear general, a common friend will hand you this letter and tell you, better perhaps than it can do, all the warmth of my affection and gratitude towards you, my general, who put my foot in the stirrup and the reins in my hand. You will easily believe, and your kind heart will comprehend, that the thought of you has never left me during this severe campaign ; in solemn moments I have always invoked it, and it seems to me that the good inspiration came to me from you. Since fate kept you away from us, your mind at least was present with all its resources of devotion and firmness. We have made war as we learned it under your command, and our soldiers, whom you would have recognized, were inspired by that sentiment of duty which you taught them in Africa. We have beaten the Russians with the soldiers and the methods which you created, and for my part, if fortune has favored me in several rencounters, you will believe, my general, that it was to you, as my master, that I gave the credit of it at the close of the battle. Why can I not, while holding your two hands, describe to you these combats where you would praise your pupils, your children ! The few lines you sent me to the Crimea have been like balm to my wounds, and have brought sweet tears to my eyes. For me it was the completest of rewards."

The attitude of the Orleans princes was both noble and generous throughout the war. Following the military operations with the most ardent, impassioned, and patriotic interest, they felt profound grief at being unable to share the dangers of their former brethren in arms. The Duc d'Aumale, that great soldier, great citizen, that "admirable and symbolic representative of old France," as François Coppée has called him, the Duc d'Aumale, to whom all parties have rendered homage, and whose recent death has grieved the whole country, wrote from Twickenham, August 2, 1855, to Captain Bocher those lines truly worthy of his great heart : "I am very sad, and my old fund of natural gaiety is beginning to be exhausted. I cannot reconcile myself to the idea that my comrades are fighting and dying and I not in the midst of them. A war without us is what I have always dreaded most since the revolution of February ; I was almost accustomed to the rest, but I cannot become so to that." Alas ! why were men such as the Duc d'Aumale, Generals Changarnier, Bedeau, Lamoricière, condemned to an inaction so painful to them? Why was not the Crimea a ground of general reconciliation for all Frenchmen?

CHAPTER XLII

THE CLOSE OF 1855

A S yet no one could say whether the war was
at last to end. At the close of October the
assembled contingents of the allies in the Crimea
amounted to almost two hundred thousand men, and
there was no talk of reducing them. But on both
sides there was a general weariness of slaughter, and
the situation somewhat resembled a truce. September 20, at the village of Koughil, near Eupatoria,
General d'Allonville conducted a brilliant cavalry
combat, and on October 17 a Franco-English expeditionary corps, embarked at Kamiesch and Balaclava, seized the Russian fortress of Kimburn, at the
extremity of the gulf of the Dnieper ; but the end
of the year was not signalized by any other military
incident. The troops went into winter quarters
and enjoyed a relative calm, without knowing
whether the war would begin in the spring with
renewed fury or not.

The dénouement depended chiefly upon the Emperor Alexander II. In November, while the ruins
of Sebastopol were still smoking, he went to the
Crimea to thank its brave defenders ; he addressed

a rescript to the commander-in-chief, Prince Michael
Gortchakoff, in which he said : " The excellent
condition of the army placed under your command
evinces the solicitude and the persevering efforts,
thanks to which you have been able to attain this
end. This does you the more honor because all
your intelligence and activity were simultaneously
concentrated on the task of combating a redoubtable and courageous enemy who shrank from no
sacrifices." This courteous phrase of the Czar,
concerning his enemies, could be construed as a
symptom of conciliation.

Napoleon III. hesitated somewhat, but he was not
long in discovering that while England would be
pleased to have hostilities continue, public opinion
in France was unanimously in favor of peace.
Thenceforward the aspect of French policy ceased
to be bellicose. His particularly cordial welcome of
the Duke of Brabant (now King of the Belgians
under the name of Leopold II.), and to his wife
(Marie Henriette, Archduchess of Austria), proved
that the Emperor did not dream of annexing any
territory. The Duke and Duchess of Brabant were
his guests at Saint-Cloud from October 12 till October 27, 1855. He overwhelmed them with attentions. On the 26th a review of forty squadrons of
cavalry was held in their honor at Versailles.
After their departure the *Moniteur* of October 29
said : " The reception given by the Emperor and
the Empress to the Duke and the Duchess of Bra-

bant, the evidences of sympathy exchanged between Their Imperial and Their Royal Highnesses during their stay in France, have faithfully reflected the sentiments which animate the two countries. France and Belgium are sisters by origin, language, manners, and interests. The two nations comprehend this at present as their sovereigns do. But nothing could contribute more to strengthen the union between the two peoples and facilitate their relations than these cordial relations between the reigning families."

November 15, 1855, a grandiose ceremony, wholly pacific in its character, took place in Paris at the Palais de l'Industrie. Napoleon III. presided at the distribution of the awards of the Universal Exposition. More than forty thousand persons were assembled in the nave. An immense orchestra, directed by Berlioz, executed compositions of Beethoven, Gluck, Mozart, Rossini, and Meyerbeer. A colossal amphitheatre, constructed against the three sides of the transept, rose to the height of the galleries and faced a platform supporting the throne. On the innumerable benches of this amphitheatre was unrolled, as some one has said, a map of the living and breathing world. In the galleries, hung with red velvet trimmed with gold bullion, was a crowd of women in the most elegant toilettes. A frieze of crimson cloth embroidered in gold and surmounted with the coats of arms and the flags of all nations which had taken part in the Exposition extended all along the galleries. The throne was surmounted by a dais sown with golden bees.

The Emperor and Empress, followed by a very numerous cortège, made a splendid entry to the noise of fanfares and acclamations. Napoleon III., who had a very powerful voice, made a speech which was heard by all the audience, in spite of the immensity of the hall. The following passage produced a great effect : "The first impression produced by the sight of so many marvels spread before our eyes is a desire for peace. Peace alone can still further develop these remarkable products of human intelligence. You ought all to join with me, then, in wishing that this peace may come promptly and be durable."

The Emperor thus ended his remarks : "In our present epoch of civilization, it is public opinion, after all, which always gains the final victory. Let all of you then, on returning to your countries, tell your fellow-citizens that France has no hatred against any people, that she sympathizes with all who desire, as she does, the triumph of justice. Tell them that if they desire peace, they should at least pray for or against us, for in the midst of a grave European conflict indifference is a bad mistake and silence an error. As for us, peoples allied for the triumph of a great cause, let us forge weapons without slackening work in our manufactories, without interfering with our trades ; let us be as great in the arts of peace, as in those of war ;

let us be strong in unity ; let us place our confidence in God that He may cause us to triumph over
the difficulties of the present and the chances of the
future."

The conclusion of this speech was greeted by
several rounds of applause. Then followed the distribution of the awards. As each class arrived in
front of the sovereign, an usher carrying a banner
indicating the number of this class, halted at the
foot of the throne. Prince Napoleon presented the
medals and crosses to the Emperor who gave them
to the exhibitors with his own hand. The master-
pieces of painting and sculpture, as well as the discoveries and marvels of industry which had merited
the highest awards, were grouped in an ensemble,
forming the most superb of pacific trophies.

On the whole the Universal Exposition had succeeded beyond all expectations. Visitors had come
there from all parts of the world. The number of
entrances had risen to 5,162,530 a figure which
seems insignificant enough to-day, but which appeared enormous in 1855. The success of this Exposition, coincident with one of the most bloody
wars remembered by Europe, formed an exceedingly
strange contrast.

Not many days after the formal conferring of the
awards, Napoleon III. received a royal visit which
seemed wholly pacific, but in which certain shrewd
observers caught a fleeting glimpse of future war.
Even before the arrival at the Tuileries of the King

of Sardinia, Victor Emmanuel, the *Moniteur* of November 23 published this significant article : " The King of Sardinia will receive the most enthusiastic and hearty welcome from the population of Paris. This august sovereign is not merely the descendant of one of the most glorious reigning families of Europe, the head of a nation whose destinies have been linked with those of the French nation from time immemorial ; his eminent personal qualities, his tried loyalty and courage, the alacrity with which he sent his brave troops to fight beside ours for the same cause, have entitled King Victor Emmanuel in a special way to the sympathies of France."

The King landed at Marseilles, November 22, 1855, at nine o'clock in the morning. The troops were drawn up in battle array on the wharf. The Bishop of the city accompanied the sovereign as far as the prefecture. Leaving at eleven o'clock, he was greeted at Avignon by the Archbishop, and arrived at Lyons at six in the evening. Marshal de Castellane said to him : " Sire, the Emperor my master is happy to receive you in his dominions. The army of Lyons is proud to be seen by a military sovereign whose valor on the battle-field is proverbial. The Piedmontese soldiers in the Crimea have rivalled their king ; the French soldiers were delighted to fight beside them." Victor Emmanuel rested for some hours at the Hôtel de l'Europe, where he seated Cardinal Bonald, Archbishop of Lyons, at his right hand at the dinner table. At four in the morning he left for Paris, where he arrived at one in the afternoon, November 23. He was accompanied by Count Cavour, Massimo d'Azeglio, and Chevalier Nigra.

The station was splendidly decorated with the flags of the four allied powers and the armorial bearings of the King. Salvoes of artillery greeted him as he entered in the uniform of a colonel of hussars. The band of the Guides played the fanfare of the House of Savoy and the national air of Piedmont. On leaving the car Victor Emmanuel was received by Prince Napoleon, and went to the Tuileries in a carriage escorted by a squadron of guides, the hundred guards, and a squadron of cuirassiers of the imperial guard. After passing the arch of the Carrousel, he reached the château, where the Emperor, with the great officers of the crown and the officials of his household, was awaiting him at the foot of the grand staircase. Napoleon III. embraced his ally with much effusion, and after conducting him to the Empress, who had remained with her ladies at the head of the stairs, he took him to the apartments reserved for him in the Marsan pavilion.

November 24, Victor Emmanuel paid a visit to King Jerome and the Princesse Mathilde. The ministers, the presidents of the Senate, the Legislative Body, and the Council of State were presented to him by the Duc de Cambacérès, grand master of ceremonies. In the evening the Emperor and the

King went to the Gymnase. The next day they heard Mass together in the chapel of the Tuileries. The 26th, they were shooting in the forest of Saint-Germain, and in the evening witnessed the ballet of *Jovita* at the Opéra. The 27th, they reviewed the troops of the 1st military division at the Champ de Mars. The 28th, they attended a grand ball at the Hôtel de Ville, the Emperor dancing with the Duchess of Hamilton in the quadrille of honor, the King with the Princesse Mathilde, and Prince Napoleon with the Marchioness of Villamarina, wife of the Sardinian minister. The next day the King started for London. On his way back to his dominions he passed through France and met the Emperor again at Compiègne, December 6. Napoleon III. and his guest returned to Paris, December 8, and on the 9th the King left for Turin, taking a most affectionate leave of the Emperor. Possibly the days which the two sovereigns had just spent together already presaged those of Magenta and Solferino. But in 1855 the friend of the Italian cause absolutely needed the assistance of Austria in order to manage Crimean affairs, and at this time he took care not to betray his ulterior dispositions.

December 10, an imposing ceremony took place at the Invalides: the funeral solemnities of Admiral Bruat, who had died in the Crimea of cholera, like Marshal de Saint-Arnaud and Lord Raglan. The brave sailor had been made an admiral of France less than three months previous, September 15, in

acknowledgment of his eminent services as commander of the French fleet in the Black Sea.   Rear-
admiral Jurien de la Gravière made an eloquent
speech above his tomb.

On Saturday, December 29, Paris celebrated the
triumphant return of a division of infantry of the
line and some regiments of the imperial guard on
their return from the Crimea.   The capital looked
splendid.   All the population turned out to see the
victorious troops.   The streets were hung with the
national colors blended with the flags of England,
Turkey, and Sardinia.   Triumphal arches had been
erected all along the boulevards.   Another gigantic
one rose over the Place de la Bastille, at the entrance
of the Boulevard Beaumarchais.   It was surmounted
by two colossal eagles, with outspread wings, and a
laurel crown, bearing this inscription in gilt letters :
"To the glory of the army of the Orient : Sebastopol, Alma, Inkerman, Traktir, Malakoff, Silistria,
Eupatoria."   A double row of soldiers lined the
entire route from the Tuileries to the Bastille, the
National Guard on the right, and on the left the infantry, the guard of Paris, and the firemen.

At half-past eleven in the morning the troops
returning from the Crimea were drawn up in line
of battle in the Place de la Bastille.   At the same
hour the Emperor, in the uniform of a general of
division, attended by a brilliant escort, set out from
the Tuileries on horseback to rejoin them.   On
reaching the Place, where stands the column of

July, he passed slowly through the ranks, and then, still on horseback, he stopped in the middle of the troops, drawn up in a semicircle, and harangued them as follows : " Soldiers, I come to meet you as of old the Roman Senate went to the gates of Rome to meet its victorious legions. I come to tell you that you have merited well of the country. I am greatly moved, because the happiness of meeting you is blended with painful regrets for those who are no more, and with a profound chagrin at having been unable to lead you to combat in person. Soldiers of the guard as well as soldiers of the line, you are welcome. . . . The country, attentive to all that is being done in the Orient, welcomes you all the more proudly because it measures your efforts by the stubborn resistance of the enemy.

" I have recalled you, although the war is not over, because it is just to send substitutes for the regiments which have suffered most. Each can in this way go to take his part in glory, and the country, which maintains six hundred thousand soldiers, is interested in having a sufficiently numerous and well-trained army in France at present, ready to go wherever necessity requires.

" Be careful, then, to preserve the habits of war, strengthen yourselves in the experience you have acquired, hold yourselves ready to respond, if need be, to my appeal ; but, on this day, forget the trials of a soldier's life, thank God for having spared you, and march proudly amidst your brethren in arms

and your fellow-citizens whose applause awaits you."
The troops, who had not lost a word of this discourse, delivered in a very powerful and sonorous
voice, shouted three times: "Long live the Emperor!"

Followed by his cortège, the sovereign then returned by way of the boulevards and the Rue de la
Paix, and, still on his horse, took his place with his
staff opposite the Vendôme column, in front of the
Ministry of Justice.   I was there, and I still seem to
see that magnificent winter day.   The Empress,
King Jerome, the Princesse Mathilde, the Murat family, the great dignitaries, the English ambassador and
Lady Cowley, the Turkish ambassador, the Minister
of Sardinia and the Marchioness of Villamarina,
were at the windows of the ministry.   What animation in the crowd!   What joy and pride on the
faces!   What frank, what sincere enthusiasm!   At
the foot of the column were assembled some of the
remaining soldiers of the first Napoleon.   How
imposing was the meeting between the veterans of
the first Empire and the soldiers of the second!

The troops posted in the Place de la Bastille
begin to move.   After passing through the boulevards and the Rue de la Paix, amidst acclamations
and under a reign of flowers and crowns, they reach
the Place Vendôme.   Who is it comes first, at the
head of the division of the line, and is greeted with
frenzied acclamations?   It is the former commander-
in-chief of the army of the Orient, the hero of the

Crimea, Canrobert. He went to the Place of the Bastille in the suite of the Emperor, whose aide-de-camp he is. It was the sovereign who had ordered him to march at the head of the troops. The valiant general has the gift of affecting, of electrifying, the crowd. They know him to be so brave, so humane, so devoted to the soldiers! His abnegation, his modesty, his disinterestedness, have won for him so pure a popularity! The pupils of the Polytechnic School and the battalion of the Saint-Cyr, led by General de Monet, wounded in the Orient, have preceded the troops and come to range themselves to right and left of the Emperor in the Place Vendôme. The march by begins. Here in the first place, with Generals Canrobert, Forcy, and Blanchard, come the three regiments of infantry of the line, the 20th, the 50th, and the 97th. What a success for these foot soldiers! What a grand effect they produce with their bronzed faces, their martial bearing, their fighting uniform, their gray cloaks, worn threadbare by victory! And now the imperial guard, with Generals Regnaud de Saint-Jean-d'Angély, Mellinet, and Manèque, who march in the following order: the battalion of foot soldiers, the regiment of Zouaves, the two regiments of light infantry, of artillery and engineers, the two regiments of grenadiers, the regiments of gendarmerie.

Each regiment is preceded by its band and a troop of unarmed soldiers covered with glorious wounds. The wounded men shout, " Long live the Emperor ! "

with even greater energy than the able-bodied soldiers. A sentiment of gratitude appears on the
countenance of Napoleon III. His face, ordinarily
impassive, lights up. It is long since the people of
Paris have witnessed so beautiful and so touching a
solemnity.

CHAPTER XLIII

THE COMMENCEMENT OF 1856

ON January 1, 1856, no one could say as yet whether the year was to be warlike or peaceful. On the 15th there was a great military ceremony at Paris: the distribution by the Duke of Cambridge of the so-called Crimean medal, just instituted by Queen Victoria. On this occasion Napoleon III. reviewed in the Place du Carrousel and in the court of the Tuileries the troops coming from the Crimea. They formed two fine divisions: one of the guard, under General Mellinet; the other of the line, under General Forey. General Regnaud de Saint-Jean-d'Angély commanded the entire body.

On either side of the Emperor were the Duke of Cambridge and Prince Napoleon. A large number of English generals and several French heroes from the Crimea were noticeable in his staff: Generals Canrobert, Bosquet, Niel, Espinasse. The Emperor was in the balcony of the hall of the Marshals. After passing in front of the troops, the staff halted under this balcony. The Duke of Cambridge moved forward several paces to meet the officers and soldiers designated to receive the medal, and delivered in French the following speech: " Her Majesty the

Queen of England has deigned to charge me with
the presentation to the generals, officers, and soldiers
of the French army, our brave and worthy comrades,
of these medals, as emblems of the esteem and friendship existing between the two nations, and of the
admiration experienced by Her Majesty and the English nation in beholding the glorious military feats of
the army of the Orient.   In the grand combats of the
Alma, Inkerman, and Sebastopol the alliance has been
consecrated by the two armies.   God grant that this
great alliance may ever continue to the advantage
and the glory of both nations !   For my own part, I
esteem the honor accorded me all the more highly
because I have served with you and have seen with
my own eyes your bravery and the loyalty with
which you have supported such dangers and fatigues.
I am sincerely grateful to the Emperor for his kindness in conferring on me the honor of distributing
these medals in his presence."

The discourse of Queen Victoria's relative was
greeted by unanimous cries of : " Long live the
Queen ! "   " Long live the Duke of Cambridge ! "
Descending from his horse, and surrounded by his
aides-de-camp, the Duke distributed with his own
hands to each of the generals, officers, and wounded
soldiers of the army of the Orient the silver medals
bearing on one side an effigy of the Queen, and on
the other the figure of the god of war crowned by
Victoria with the word " Crimea."

Constantly reinforced by new troops, the French

army in the Crimea numbered at this time one
hundred and forty-three thousand men and thirty-
seven thousand horses, sixty-five hundred of which
were cavalry horses. Peace was being negotiated,
but preparations for continuing the war were going
on none the less actively. Public joy at Paris was
very great when this brief paragraph made its
appearance in the *Moniteur*, January 18 : " Paris,
January 17. The Minister of Foreign Affairs received this morning from the Minister of France
at Vienna the following despatch : ' Vienna, January 16. Count Esterhazy wrote to-day from Saint
Petersburg that M. de Nesselrode had just notified
him of the acceptance, pure and simple, of the propositions contained in the ultimatum, these propositions to serve as preliminaries of peace.' "

Napoleon III., whose sentiments at this time were
very pacific, was deeply moved by this good news.
Comte Horace de Viel-Castel has written in his
Memoirs : " On receiving the despatch containing
Russia's acceptance of the propositions, the Emperor
was unable to control his emotion. Dr. Reyer was
present ; he saw the Emperor turn pale ; then His
Majesty said to him : ' I must sit down, doctor ;
read that and you will not be surprised.' In the
evening (January 17) I saw the Emperor and the
Empress at a ball at the house of the Princesse
Mathilde. Yesterday (18) there was a small party
given by the Empress; we wore dress coats, knee-
breeches or tights."

The *Moniteur* of February 2 gave some details concerning the paths of peace just entered upon. Russia might still have resisted had she only France, England, Turkey, and Sardinia to contend against. But from the moment that the government of the Emperor Francis Joseph sent its ultimatum, it was understood at Saint Petersburg that a struggle against five powers would be too unequal. To what are called the *Four Points*, that is to say : 1. Substitution of a collective protectorate of the powers for the Russian protectorate over the Danubian Principalities ; 2. free navigation of the Danube ; 3. guaranty of the independence of the Ottoman Empire ; 4. renunciation by Russia of any exclusive rights over the Christian subjects of the Sultan, Austria had added a fifth point, the neutralization of the Black Sea, and she had notified the cabinet of Saint Petersburg that if it did not accept these five propositions as preliminaries of peace, she would discontinue diplomatic relations with Russia. It must be admitted that it was this ultimatum which put an end to hostilities. A protocol signed at Vienna, February 1, established the agreement of the parties and stipulated that the plenipotentiaries should meet within three weeks at furthest to proceed to the signature of the preliminaries, the conclusion of an armistice, and the opening of general negotiations.

Napoleon III., as a pledge of his moderation, had proposed Brussels as the place of reunion. The Russian Emperor had proposed Frankfort, then the seat of the German Diet. At the last moment Paris was chosen unanimously. It was pleasant for the plenipotentiaries to repair to so brilliant and fashionable a capital.

The first session of the Congress took place on Monday, February 25, 1856. The chief plenipotentiaries of France were Count Walewski, Minister of Foreign Affairs, and Baron de Bourqueney, Minister of France at Vienna. The other plenipotentiaries were for England, Lord Clarendon and Lord Cowley; for Austria, Count de Buol and Baron von Hübner; for Russia, Count Orloff and Baron du Brunnow; for Turkey, Ali Pasha and Djemil Bey; for Sardinia, Count Cavour and the Marquis of Villamarina. Prussia was not yet represented at the Congress. Count Walewski was unanimously appointed president. The duties of secretary were confided to M. Benedetti. The first act of the Congress was the conclusion of an armistice which was to last until the end of March.

The Minister of Foreign Affairs in France enjoyed at this time a veritable prestige, and diplomacy benefited by the success of the army. The ministry, or better, the palace on the quai d'Orsay, had been opened but a few months. The first time that the Emperor visited it, he exclaimed : " My dear minister, you are better housed than I am." It was a magnificent frame for the reunion of a congress. There was a concert in the evening at the ministry, at which all the plenipotentiaries were present. I had been appointed attaché to the political division of the ministry, September 1, 1855, and I recollect how happy I was, in my neophyte's ardor, to be invited to such a fête. With their new furniture and their splendid gildings, the salons were radiant. The beautiful and gracious Countess Walewski did the honors admirably. Mario, the tenor, who was also a noble, and the inspired diva Madame Frezzolini were greatly applauded. Mario breathed forth delightfully, in Italian, the romance from *La Favorita*, "Angel so pure," *Spirito gentile*. The duet from the *Elisir d'Amore*, sung by him and Frezzolini, was marvellously effective. "We hope," said the dilettanti, "that the European concert will be as harmonious as this concert." People did not pay much attention to the secondary plenipotentiaries, because they knew them already, but Count Orloff, Lord Clarendon, Count de Buol, Ali Pasha, and Count Cavour, all first plenipotentiaries, excited general attention. He who produced the greatest effect was undeniably Count (since Prince) Orloff. His fine bearing, his tall figure, his grand air, drew all eyes. A septuagenarian, one would have thought him scarcely fifty. This superb old man, with manners so noble and dignified, was a finished type of the soldier, the diplomat, and the courtier. His personal success was so great that, thanks to him, one might have fancied Russia the victorious power. Already French sympathies were inclining towards Russia and foreboded a future agreement. Even in

Paris people were asking whether the Crimean war had really been necessary, whether it was not, after all, a heroic but fatal misunderstanding. The partisans as well as the unfavorable critics of this bloody struggle were all delighted to see its end approaching. All were glad to learn that the armistice had been decided on. France had become the most peaceful of nations.

March 3, the opening of the session took place at the Tuileries in the hall of the Marshals. The speech from the throne was pacific, even while admitting the possibility of a continuation of the war. It concluded as follows: "To-day the plenipotentiaries of the belligerent powers are assembled in Paris to settle the conditions of peace. The spirit of moderation, which animates them all, should make us hope for a favorable result; nevertheless, let us await with dignity the end of the conferences, and be equally prepared to draw the sword again should that be necessary, or to extend a hand to those with whom we have fought so loyally. Whatever may happen, let us employ every means calculated to augment the strength and riches of France. Let us draw still closer, if possible, the alliance formed by a community of glory and of sacrifices, the mutual advantages of which will be made still more evident by peace. Let us, in fine, at this solemn moment place our confidence in God, that He may direct our efforts in the way most conformable to the interests of humanity and civilization."

. Everything pointed to the conclusion that conciliatory ideas would in the end prevail, and that
the labors of the Congress would terminate favorably. Napoleon III. displayed especial courtesy
towards the representatives of the Czar. It was
plain that Russia bore a grudge, not against France,
but England, and above all against Austria. In
speaking of the plenipotentiaries of the latter power,
Count Orloff said : " They talk as if they had conquered Sebastopol." The sessions took place every
other day, and alternated with brilliant entertainments. March 16, public attention was diverted
from the Congress by an event which seemed to
fill up the measure of the favors bestowed by Providence on the former prisoner of Ham. The Empress presented him with a son.

CHAPTER XLIV

MARCH 12, 1856, the Archbishop of Paris had issued a charge to the clergy and the faithful of his diocese which commenced as follows : "Dearly beloved brethren, everything announces that the time is not distant when the vows and prayers we have been offering to Heaven for several months, according to the pious intentions of the Emperor, are to receive their fulfilment. The august companion whom he has seated beside him on the throne, after receiving her from the hands of God and the Church, is about to present him with the first-fruit of their union and the celestial benedictions. God, who is the author of all paternity, is preparing to crown with His most precious gifts this house founded by Himself in the midst of tempests, and whose crest is now illuminated by the sunlight of the most dazzling prosperity."

The charge concluded with these sentences : "The house of the Prince is also ours ; he is the father of the nation ; nothing which goes on there can be foreign to us. . . . When in him the father and the sovereign are equally moved, we should

383

share in this emotion ; and when our eyes turn to
Heaven, we should beg for him the graces by which
we shall be the first to profit.

" When the cannon announce the happy delivery
of the Empress, the great bell of Notre-Dame will
ring for an hour, as likewise the bells of all the
churches.   On the Sunday following the birth, there
will be chanted after the High Mass in the metro-
politan church and in all other churches of our
diocese the *Te Deum* with the prayer *Pro gratiarum
actione* and the *Post mulieris partum.*"

On Saturday, March 15, towards five o'clock in
the morning, the grand mistress of the Empress's
household sent word to the princes and princesses of
the imperial family, the members of the Emperor's
family holding rank at court, the great officers of
the crown, the ministers and the president of the
Council of State, the marshals, admirals, the grand
chancellor of the Legion of Honor, the governor of
the Invalides, the superior commandant of the national guards of the Seine, the adjutant general of
the palace, the officers and ladies of the households
of Their Majesties.   All these personages repaired
to the château of the Tuileries in great haste, there
to remain until after the delivery of the Empress.
The Senate, the Legislature, and the Municipal
Council of Paris met in permanent session to await
a communication from the Emperor.

All day long and throughout the evening numerous
groups collected in the Tuileries garden and on the

Place du Carrousel. I mingled with these groups and I recollect their sympathetic attitude.

Surrounding the Empress were her husband, her mother, the Princesse d'Essling, grand mistress of her household, the wife of Admiral Bruat, governess of the children of France, and the Duchesse de Bassano, lady of honor. As her hour approached, Prince Napoleon, Prince Lucien Murat, the Minister of State, and the Keeper of the Seals were brought into the room as witnesses. On Palm Sunday, March 16, at 3.15 A.M., the Empress brought the Prince Imperial into the world. The governess of the children of France presented the newly born to the Emperor and the four witnesses. An official report of his birth was then entered upon the civil register of the imperial family by the Minister of State, assisted by the Keeper of the Seals. The child, who had the Pope for godfather and the Queen of Sweden, granddaughter of Prince Eugène, for godmother, received the names of Napoleon-Eugène-Louis-Jean-Joseph.

At six in the morning the cannon of the Invalides announced by a salvo of a hundred and one guns the birth of the Prince Imperial, and the bells of all the churches rang a full peal.

The private baptism of the Prince was administered after Mass in the chapel of the Tuileries. Close to the steps of the altar had been placed, on a carpet of white velvet, a table covered with the same stuff; on this had been set a silver-gilt vase,

intended to be used as a baptismal font. In the
middle of the choir were an armchair and a prie-dieu
for the Emperor. On the left were chairs for the
cardinals, and on the right benches for the arch-
bishops and bishops. The Abbé de Place, who had
been preaching the Lenten sermons, invoked the
blessings of Heaven on the newly born : " My God,"
he exclaimed, "watch over this cradle, the deposi-
tory of so many hopes. Form Thyself, for the welfare of a great people, the son of the Emperor.
Give him the magnanimity of his father, the kindness and inexhaustible beneficence of his mother.
To sum up all in one word, give him, my God, a
heart worthy of his destiny and his name." After
the Mass said by the Bishop of Adras, the governess
of the children of France was introduced, bearing in
her arms the Prince Imperial, to whom private baptism was given by Monseigneur Menjaud, Bishop
of Nancy, first almoner of the Emperor. Palms
were distributed to all who were present at the
Tuileries.

In the evening Paris was illuminated. The Comtesse de Damrémont wrote to M. Thouvenel, then
Ambassador of France at Constantinople : " In all
quarters of the city, in spite of wind and rain, lamps
and paper lanterns attested an overwhelming majority of favorable wishes. Besides, it is chiefly in the
popular quarters that this demonstration has been
most widespread, a favorable circumstance, because
it proves that the revolutionary spirit has been well

and duly mastered on its own ground. The Faubourg Saint-Germain has been less expansive."

The Emperor was overjoyed. He resolved that he would be the godfather and the Empress the godmother of all legitimate children born on March 16, 1856. He ordered that a sum of one hundred thousand francs should be deducted from his civil list and distributed between the relief offices of the principal cities and communes where the estates of the crown were situated. He also deducted from his civil list sixty thousand francs to be divided between the benefit funds of the society of dramatic authors and composers, that of men of letters, dramatic artists, musicians, painters, engravers, designers, inventors, and industrial artists.

Pardons were joined to these acts of munificence. After the events of June, 1848, eleven thousand persons had been condemned, under the Republic, to transportation to Algeria; but thanks to the clemency of the Prince-President, not more than thirty-six of these now remained in Africa. In December, 1851, eleven thousand two hundred and one persons had been transported or expelled; the pardons already granted by the Emperor had reduced the number to ten hundred and fifty-eight. On the birth of the Prince Imperial he determined that there should be no more proscripts, and that all who would declare that they submitted loyally to the established government should be authorized to return to France.

March 18, Napoleon III. received official homage and congratulations at the Tuileries. The plenipotentiaries of the Congress of Paris were the first to make their appearance. Count Walewski was their appointed spokesman. "The plenipotentiaries of the Congress," said he, "have desired me to be their mouthpiece to Your Majesty. I am proud and happy, Sire, at finding myself called upon to express to Your Majesty, in the name of Europe, the universal joy experienced on account of the happy event with which Providence has deigned to crown you, and which, by assuring and consolidating the Napoleonic dynasty, is a new pledge of security and confidence for the whole world."

The Emperor replied : "I thank the Congress for the good wishes and felicitations it addresses to me through you. I am happy that Providence should have sent me a son at the moment when an era of general reconciliation approaches for Europe. I shall bring him up to feel that peoples should not be selfish, and that the repose of Europe depends on the prosperity of each nation."

Then came the diplomatic corps, for whom the nuncio was the spokesman, and next the great bodies of the State. "Already," said the president of the Senate, " France feels that she lives more freely by the life of this child. When he comes to rule over this empire which Grotius called the most beautiful of all, next to the kingdom of heaven, the nineteenth century, arrived at its close, will reap the fruits

whose fertile germs our generation is depositing in
the bosom of the present. Africa, brought to the
front by your powerful hand, will be one of the
most beautiful ornaments of his crown. The Orient
and the Occident, which have been seeking each
other since the crusades, and are beginning to meet,
will have married their seas and shores for the beneficent flood of the ideas and wealth of civilization.
Then may this sovereign of our children follow in the
footsteps of his august father ; may he recall a reign
in which the helm of government is guided by
moderation, justice, and equity ; and in that march
of humanity France will still be, as now, a regulator
for Europe, a lever for progress, a torch for intelligence."

The Emperor replied to the president of the
Senate : " You have saluted as an auspicious event
the coming into the world of a child of France.
This, gentlemen, is because he is born an heir destined to perpetuate a national system ; this child is
not merely the scion of a family, but veritably the
son of the entire country, and the name indicates his
duties. If this were true under the old monarchy,
which represented more exclusively the privileged
classes, how much truer is it now that the sovereign
is the elected of the nation, the first citizen of the
country, and the representative of all."

The Emperor triumphed, but with modesty. In
his response to the Comte de Morny, president
of the Corps Législatif, there was evident a name-

less anxiety and melancholy. One would have said that the sovereign, arriving after so many trials at the summit of his power, was seeking to reassure himself against the caprices of fate, and to banish gloomy presentiments. He thought of the King of Rome, of the Duc de Bordeaux, of the Comte de Paris, and wondered if his own son would be more favored. "The unanimous acclamations which surround his cradle," said he, "do not prevent me from reflecting on the destiny of those who were born in the same place and in similar circumstances. If I hope that his fate will be happier, it is because, confiding in Providence in the first place, I cannot doubt of its protection when I see it raising up by a concurrence of extraordinary circumstances all that for forty years it had been battering down, as if it had designed to mature by martyrdom and misfortune a new dynasty arising from the ranks of the people. History, then, has instructions which I shall not forget. It tells me on the one hand that we must never abuse the favors of fortune, on the other that a dynasty has no chance of success but in remaining faithful to its origin, and occupying itself solely with those popular interests for which it has been created. This child, consecrated in his cradle by approaching peace and the benediction of the Holy Father, brought by electricity an hour after his birth, and finally by the acclamations of this French people *whom the Emperor loved so much*, this child, I say, will, I hope, be worthy of the destiny which awaits him."

And now see how Napoleon III. spent the evening of March 18. One of the heroes of the Crimea, Bosquet, shall inform us. He wrote on the 19th: " My good mother, there was a family fête last evening at the Tuileries, and you were missing. The Emperor sent me at half-past five an order to dine with him that very night. . . . I found Canrobert there and nobody else except the officers on duty. The Emperor came into the waiting-room as simply as possible, and led us in to dinner. Canrobert was on the right and I on the left of His Majesty. During dinner the Emperor talked a good deal about acoustics and the phenomena pertaining to that branch of physics. And then he said : ' Gentlemen, have your glasses filled with champagne, I am going to propose a toast to two good friends of mine whom I have near me : to *Marshal* Canrobert; to *Marshal* Bosquet.' And there we were, almost speechless, seeking the hand of His Majesty, who held it out to us with the most gracious simplicity of manner. On leaving the table the Emperor went into the apartments of the Empress, and we went down into the cabinet of the aides-de-camp on duty, where I sent you two words by telegraph. I would have liked to follow the wire as well as the fluid; I would have liked to press you in my arms, my good mother, and wished you a good sleep and the sweetest dreams.

" Every one here talks to me about you, every one salutes the mother of a marshal of France, and knows very well that the credit of it belongs to her. God be blessed, since He permits the son to honor his mother and to render her the object of the felicitations of all the mothers in France! To you, good mother, one of those moments when we do not speak, but when your head is on my shoulder." Napoleon III. could not more worthily celebrate the birth of his son than by giving the Marshal's baton to the two brave warriors who had so eminently deserved it.

CHAPTER XLV

IN 1856 Napoleon III. seemed a monarch strong enough to be clement, powerful enough to be moderate. Fortune, so severe towards him at first, now crowned and overwhelmed him with favors. The private man was not less happy than the sovereign. He had every success and every joy. People were forever telling him that his throne was immovable, his dynasty consolidated once for all. In the midst of his triumph this arbiter of Europe, as his courtiers then called him, remained always calm and modest. Lord Clarendon said of him during the Congress: "The more I know him, the better I like him." The second Empire will have its age of iron. 1856 was its age of gold.

In recurring to the dazzling period of which I was a witness, I cannot resist a sentiment of melancholy, of sadness. Men and things alike suggest painful reflections. I wonder what end was served by such efforts, agitations, sacrifices? What is left of the personages and events of which I have been speaking? The eight Ministers of Foreign Affairs who were my chiefs under the Empire, the fourteen pleni-

potentiaries of the Congress of Paris, all these
men, whose faces and voices I seem still to see
and hear, are dead. What sudden transformations on the stage of the world! What changes
in aspect! It is like the whistle of an invisible
scene-shifter. I recall a saying from the *Imitation
of Jesus Christ:* " Oh, how quickly passes the glory
of the world ! "

Where, now, are the results of that stubborn, that
heroic, Crimean war? The Malakoff, the Little
Redan, the Green Mamelon, the Central bastion, the
Grand Redan, the bastion of the Flagstaff, — all those
works attacked and defended with such bitterness, —
what has become of them? Not a trace remains.
Of the theatre of such hecatombs nothing exists but
the cemeteries where the combatants sleep in death.
In meditating on these gigantic struggles, one asks
nowadays whether peoples have the right to kill each
other when no hatred is lurking in their hearts, and
mere questions of equilibrium or diplomacy are all
that puts arms in their hands. A few years are all
that is needed to change all the pieces on the European chessboard. All is uncertainty, contradiction,
and instability in the alliances. Men desire what
they dread, dread what they desire. France made
war to destroy Russia's situation in the Black Sea.
At present Russia has regained this situation, and,
instead of grieving over it, France rejoices. Men
think themselves the masters of events when in reality they are their slaves. The history of France in

the nineteenth century is nothing but a perpetual disillusion.

At the moment of the Prince Imperial's birth Napoleon III. had good reason to recur philosophically to the past. Forty years before almost to a day, March 20, 1811, a child was born, whose coming into the world had excited still greater transports of enthusiasm. The president of the Senate said at that time to the great Emperor: "Your peoples salute with unanimous acclamations this new star which has just arisen on the horizon of France, and whose first beams dispel the last vestiges of the darkness of the future." The future! it was that this so lauded child would be another Astyanax; that, deprived not merely of his titles of King of Rome and Prince Imperial, but of his baptismal name Napoleon and his family name Bonaparte, he would be called nothing but Francis, Duke of Reichstadt, and would die young, in exile, having never worn any uniform but the Austrian.

Nine years and a half after the birth of the King of Rome — September 20, feast of Saint Michael the Archangel, one of the protectors of France, — was born another child whom the Papal Nuncio, in congratulating Louis XVIII., called *the child of Europe.* What did *the child of Europe, the child of miracle,* become? A proscript. Eighteen years after the birth of the Duc de Bordeaux, August 24, 1838, the Comte de Paris was also born in the château of the Tuileries. Less than ten years later the Comte de

Paris went into exile; he and the Duc de Bordeaux were in their tenth year when their proscription began.

Napoleon III. remembered all the lessons of history, when on the day after his son's birth he reflected in the palace of the Tuileries "on the destiny of those who were born in the same place and in similar circumstances." Like the King of Rome, the Duc de Bordeaux, the Comte de Paris, the Prince Imperial had been sung by the poets, Théophile Gautier and Camille Doucet, who predicted for him the most marvellous destiny. These poets were not prophets. But on the other hand a strain had been addressed by Victor Hugo to Napoleon III., which might have been dedicated to Napoleon IV. This one contained strophes truly prophetic, an exact prediction of September 4, of the siege of Paris, of the disasters of the great capital:

> "Oh! to-morrow is the great thing.
> Of what will to-morrow be made?
> Man sows the cause to-day;
> To-morrow God ripens the effect.
> To-morrow 'tis the lightning on the sail,
> 'Tis the cloud above the star,
> 'Tis a traitor who unveils,
> 'Tis the ram which batters towers,
> 'Tis the star which changes zone,
> 'Tis Paris following Babylon,
> To-morrow 'tis the wood of the throne.
> To-day it is the velvet."

Napoleon II. died under the Austrian uniform. Napoleon IV. will die under that of England. Providence reserved the same fate, proscription, for all the four princes born in the palace of calamities. Exiled even in death, the King of Rome is buried in the vault of the church of the Capuchins in Vienna ; the Duc de Bordeaux at Goritz, in that of the church of the Franciscans ; the Prince Imperial and the Comte de Paris in England, one in the chapel of Farnborough, and the other in that of Weybridge.

In France it is not enough that dynasties succumb. There fatality must pursue things as well as persons. In other countries monuments at least are respected. Among us an iconoclastic rage urges their destruction. One could make a long list of palaces which have been razed to the ground. One might think that our people take pleasure in realizing that saying of Châteaubriand : " The destructions of men are more violent than those of ages. The latter mine ; the former overthrow : *Tempus edax, homo edacior.*"

It was not enough for the second Empire to disappear. Its winter palace and its summer palace, the Tuileries and Saint-Cloud, have also been annihilated. What has become of that superb palace which held its own so well in that grandiose quadrilateral : the Arch of Triumph, the Madeleine, the Corps Législatif, the Tuileries, glory, religion, law, authority? It would have been as easy to repair the legendary palace as to restore the Vendôme column. People were unwilling. They were con-

tent with restoring the pavilions of Marsan and
Flora, which at least remain as souvenirs of the
demolished palace.   At Saint-Cloud they were still
more pitiless for the ruins.   They were so embit-
tered against their last vestiges, they have been so
completely destroyed, that the stranger who strolls
in the park is obliged to ask where the palace stood.
Et campos ubi Troja fuit.   "Tear down" seems to be
in our days the motto of architects.

While I am writing these lines the Palais de l'Industrie is falling in the Champs-Elysées under the
hammers of the demolishers.   Every morning I see
the work of destruction advancing with terrifying
rapidity, and I evoke the spectacles of glory and
prosperity of which this palace, so quickly condemned, was the theatre.   I recall the triumphant
days of November 15, 1855, June 17, 1867, when
Napoleon formally distributed the awards to the
pacific victors of the two Universal Expositions.
The ceremony of 1867 was especially magnificent.
The Emperor left the Tuileries at two o'clock, in
a splendid carriage, drawn by eight horses, to go to
the Palais de l'Industrie.   At the same hour Sultan
Abdul Aziz started in the same manner from the
Elysée for the same destination.   At the Palace the
conqueror of Magenta and Solferino was seated on a
platform with the Sultan on his right, and around
him the Prince of Wales, the Prince of Orange, the
Prince of Saxony, the Grand Duchess Marie of Russia, the Prince of Prussia (the future Emperor Fred-

erick III.), Prince Humbert (future King of Italy), and the Duke of Aosta. He celebrated in a fine discourse "the new era of harmony and progress." The Empress was there in all the splendor of her beauty, and when the Prince Imperial handed to his father the prize awarded by the international jury to the all-powerful sovereign for farm models and the habitations of workingmen, a triple salvo of applause resounded.

Since that day, how many ceremonies, how many exhibitions of every kind, how many horse shows, have taken place under the roof of that palace which is falling, after having rendered so many services to Paris ! Alas ! the final one will have been to give asylum to the corpses of the victims of the Charity Bazaar. By the light of torches unfortunate parents sought, often in vain, to distinguish in the pell-mell of the dead, the pulverized, carbonized bodies, —

"Which even the eye of their own father would not recognize!"

What a dismal end for this palace, razed from the earth after forty-two years of existence ! Forty-two years ! for a monument, that is to die very young ! Could one have believed that this temple of industry and the arts, where civilization and progress had held their assizes with such éclat, could disappear so soon ?

An anniversary recurs to my mind in closing this book. To-day it is the 14th of June, forty-one years since the baptism of the Prince Imperial was solemnized at Notre-Dame. On that day I donned for the first time my uniform as a diplomatist. Since then, at how many metamorphoses, how many cataclysms, have I not been present? What mourning, what ruins! In our profoundly troubled epoch we need a Bossuet to make the funeral oration, not of such or such a personage, but of whole dynasties, a Massillon to exclaim, not before the coffin of a single monarch, but before the remains of royalties and empires: "God alone is great, my brethren." In thinking of so many vanished hopes, so many fruitless agitations, so many bitter disillusions, I am reminded of the verses of Persius :

"Oh, the cares of men! oh, what great inanity in things!"
O curas hominum, o quantum est in rebus inane.

INDEX

www.ingramcontent.com/pod-product-compliance
Lightning Source LLC
Chambersburg PA
CBHW021342110726
47900CB00005B/1579

* 9 7 8 3 3 3 7 3 5 0 1 6 1 *